KU-386-236

ACCIDENTAL AMNESIA

TYLER ANNE SNELL

STALKING COLTON'S FAMILY

GERI KROTOW

MILLS & BOON

All rights reserved including the right of reproduction in whole or in part in any form. This edition is published by arrangement with Harlequin Enterprises ULC.

This is a work of fiction. Names, characters, places, locations and incidents are purely fictional and bear no relationship to any real life individuals, living or dead, or to any actual places, business establishments, locations, events or incidents. Any resemblance is entirely coincidental.

This book is sold subject to the condition that it shall not, by way of trade or otherwise, be lent, resold, hired out or otherwise circulated without the prior consent of the publisher in any form of binding or cover other than that in which it is published and without a similar condition including this condition being imposed on the subsequent purchaser.

® and ™ are trademarks owned and used by the trademark owner and/or its licensee. Trademarks marked with ® are registered with the United Kingdom Patent Office and/or the Office for Harmonisation in the Internal Market and in other countries.

First Published in Great Britain 2022
by Mills & Boon, an imprint of HarperCollins*Publishers* Ltd
1 London Bridge Street, London, SE1 9GF

www.harpercollins.co.uk

HarperCollins*Publishers*
1st Floor, Watermarque Building,
Ringsend Road, Dublin 4, Ireland

Accidental Amnesia © 2022 Tyler Anne Snell
Stalking Colton's Family © 2022 Harlequin Enterprises ULC

Special thanks and acknowledgement are given to Geri Krotow for her contribution to *The Coltons of Colorado* series.

ISBN: 978-0-263-30339-1

0422

MIX
Paper from
responsible sources
FSC™ C007454

This book is produced from independently certified FSC™ paper to ensure responsible forest management.

For more information visit: www.harpercollins.co.uk/green

Printed and Bound in Spain using 100% Renewable electricity at CPI Black Print, Barcelona

ACCIDENTAL AMNESIA

TYLER ANNE SNELL

DUDLEY LIBRARIES

000003122915

Askews & Holts	08-Apr-2022
AF ROM	£6.99
2WG	

This book is for Kiddo. We met you for the first time while writing this book and we hope you're officially adopted by the time it releases. But, you know, don't actually read this book until you're older. Much older.

Prologue

The members of the Dawn County Sheriff's Department in attendance were all wearing suits and dresses and had glasses of champagne, bottles of beer and small glasses filled with alcohol that burned when going down. Sheriff Chamblin was in the middle of the semicircle they'd made in the room and had his own whiskey neat lifted high.

"And this is to a lifetime of happiness with two of the best sleuths I know," he roared, cheeks red and a smile that covered his whole body staying strong. "Here's to our boy, Kenneth, and one of our favorite ladies, Willa!"

Everyone around them cheered, glasses clinking and laughter erupting when someone dropped their drink and someone else yelled, "Party foul."

It was an interesting sight, mostly because when Sterling Costner had left the department and his job, the people who had stayed felt the same as he had when he left town.

Betrayed. Angry. Broken.

Now here they were, celebrating the wedding of one of their detectives.

And doing so with a whole lot of noise and love.

He gave the sheriff an uncertain look when the older man's gaze swung to him as the crowd started to join the rest of the reception.

Brutus Chamblin, someone Sterling hadn't seen in a

long while, was all gray now. Though Brutus had mostly been gray before he'd come out of retirement, maybe now there was a weight there that Sterling hadn't seen previously and it was throwing him off.

Brutus looked tired. Tired all the way down to his bones. Even through the smile he greeted Sterling with.

"Sterling Costner, as I live and breathe."

They clasped hands before Sterling pulled the man in for a hug. He'd always been a fan of Brutus's.

"I didn't know you were back in town," Brutus said, pulling his cowboy hat off and pressing it against his chest. Out of all the employees of the sheriff's department that Sterling had known before he'd left town, only Brutus had liked wearing a cowboy hat.

Other than Sterling, of course.

He pulled his own down, too, and thumped it against his thigh as they talked.

"I came in last week to get settled and hang out with my brother," Sterling started. "I was hoping to catch up with you next week, but then Carlos caught wind of me. He dragged me here as his plus-one. Though, between you and me, I'm pretty sure I stopped existing the moment he saw Dr. Alvarez in that frilly dress." They both grinned at that. Carlos Park was a longtime sheriff's department deputy, which was a rare thing given what had happened five years prior. Not many people had stuck around. Sterling was ashamed to say he was one of those who had hightailed it away.

Though his reasons had been a little more personal.

"I have to say I'm glad he wanted to bring me along," Sterling added. "I wouldn't have believed the warm fuzzies coming from the department that I just witnessed had I not seen it with my own eyes."

At that, Brutus seemed to become younger in spirit. He was beaming.

"I hate to say anything against the men and women from when I was sheriff the first time around, but I don't think I've ever been prouder of a group of people than I am with this lot. They've done some amazing things for the department and the town against some stacked odds."

Sterling nodded. The shame of leaving buried deeper, but he refocused on why he was here.

Brutus stayed quiet, most likely knowing he was at the waiting end of the conversation. For a moment they watched as the last wedding guests left the room.

Then it was just the two of them and their future.

"I'm back, Brutus," Sterling said. "For good."

Brutus looked him up and down and then nodded.

He put on his cowboy hat, a worn brown leather Stetson.

"Things have changed around here," he warned. "Not all for the good, sad to say. We might have won back some trust from the town, but there's still a lot of unsettled things. It won't be easy. The fix won't be quick, either. Might be years before any real progress is made."

"No way to know until we do it."

Sterling put emphasis on the *we* part.

That seemed to be enough.

"Come in tomorrow for an official interview," Brutus said. "After that I'll introduce you to the people who have moved in since you left. Maybe even take you out for a drink later so you can see some of the things in town that look a whole lot different, too."

Sterling couldn't help but grin.

"I can swing that."

"Good."

Brutus gave him another widening smile and clapped him on the back.

"Welcome back to Kelby Creek, Sterling Costner."

Sterling put his cowboy hat back on.

"It's good to be back."

He said the words, but Sterling hoped he wasn't lying.

Chapter One

Three months later and Deputy Sterling Costner had fire in his eyes and anger on his tongue.

Anyone in Kelby Creek, Alabama, could see it if they were so inclined. Sterling was an open book in a cowboy hat. An open book in a cowboy hat with a flashlight on it and narration available. He didn't keep things close to the vest, unlike some of his Dawn County Sheriff's Department colleagues.

Nope. He was what his brother, Sam, called an expresser. A bullhorn with the button stuck to *on*. He didn't brood—he projected.

He was also a man who wasn't about to let someone who called themselves Top Tier give him any more lip than he'd already given him during the house call.

"Listen, I'm not standing here on your doorstep, wearing this uniform despite the heat, humidity and the fact that I had to skip lunch to be here, because I'm a glutton for punishment," Sterling said, looking down his nose at the young man. "I came because two neighbors complained that your music was so loud it was making their windows vibrate. That needs to stop."

For some people, Top Tier might have been a nickname that painted a picture of a towering, muscled person, but the twenty-two-year-old standing in front of Sterling fell woefully short of that image. He was small, thin and had a little squeak to his voice despite his immediate and continued defiance against Sterling from the get-go.

Though his size and name wouldn't have mattered at all had he not spoken ill of Sterling's partner. Once he'd called Marigold a nosy you-know-what, all civility had frolicked off into the South Alabama heat. Which was why Sterling wasn't in the mood to listen to any more of the man's ranting.

So he underlined his point.

"You need to turn the music down or else there are going to be some real consequences for you, no matter what name you give me." Another reason Sterling had been called a bullhorn was due to how deep his voice was. Never mind when he was trying to make sure he got a point across. Top Tier seemed to consider it more than he had when they'd first met. "But that's only if you apologize to my partner for being indecent. Do you understand or do we need to escalate this situation?"

Top Tier wavered, but only for a moment.

He took a small step to the side and nodded to Marigold, who was farther back on the sidewalk, looking two kinds of angry and one kind of bored.

"I'm—I'm sorry," Top Tier called out. "I think I drank too many 5-hour Energy drinks today."

Sterling wasn't about to ask what that had to do with being decent, but he let it slide. They were only there for a noise complaint, after all.

"I accept," Marigold responded.

Sterling looked back to Top Tier.

"All right, now what happens next for you?"

Top Tier thumbed back to the house behind him.

"I turn my video game down to an acceptable volume,"

he answered, repeating Marigold's original request before the young man had started calling her names. "Right?"

"Right," Sterling confirmed. "And no time like the present."

Sterling waited as Top Tier hustled inside. Marigold joined him on the porch.

"His real name is Anthony, you know?" she muttered. "My sister babysat him a few times when she was in high school. He was a twerp then, and he's a twerp now. 'Top Tier.'" She snorted. Sterling kept a straight face until the music had gone silent. When that held, they went back to their SUV.

"Hey, reinvention isn't always a clean process," he said. "Some people just miss the mark. We shouldn't judge the attempt."

Marigold crossed her arms but laughed.

"I mean he did call me the B-word, so I'm going to judge a little."

He joined in and pulled out onto the street.

"Fair enough."

Apart from the noise complaint, Kelby Creek, Alabama, was mostly quiet on that Monday. The weather was playing nice, too, or at least nicer than it had been the week before. Hot and humid but with a breeze. Best you could ask for, considering.

Sterling pointed his cruiser in the direction of the north side of Kelby Creek.

Marigold seemed to pick up on his thoughts.

"We're grabbing lunch from that new food truck? The one with the tacos that Rossi hasn't stopped talking about?"

"Unless you want to hit the lunch crowd at Crisp's."

Marigold mock shuddered. Her former mother-in-law owned every local's favorite restaurant in town. While Marigold had been justified in ending her marriage, her ex's mother had never been quiet about her displeasure that it happened.

And that displeasure from a Southern woman translated into passive-aggressive comments and actions.

Which made everyone around uncomfortable.

"Tacos, it is."

They fell into a conversation about Top Tier, another about a cold case that the task force was working at the moment and then about when they thought Kelby Creek would see its first tornado of the year.

It was only when he realized he'd taken the long way round to the food truck stop that Sterling fell quiet.

Marigold noticed. She was good with body language and sensing shifting moods. It was one of the reasons she'd been hired the year before and why Sterling had been glad to be partnered with her. She was good at her job, but she was also good at people.

She nodded out the window.

They were passing a small neighborhood situated around two streets that ended in cul-de-sacs.

"Did you mean to take us this way or was it a subconscious thing?"

Sterling, the human bullhorn, didn't lie.

"I wasn't thinking about it, so I'm guessing it was a subconscious thing." He sighed and kept his eyes firmly on the street ahead. Marigold tried to be sympathetic.

"Hey, sometimes it doesn't matter how much time has passed. Some things just stick."

She meant "some people," and by that she meant "a particular woman," but Marigold kept it vague for his sake.

Normally, he would have admitted that they were both talking about someone who had once lived in that neighborhood, but nothing in Kelby Creek was that normal anymore.

Instead Sterling turned down the volume on his bullhorn

thoughts and switched gears to what he was thinking about ordering for lunch. Marigold threw in her two cents, and soon that neighborhood was in his rearview. Along with the house Sterling had once lived in.

And the woman who had lived there with him.

Before she'd destroyed everything.

Before she'd destroyed him.

Sterling didn't even glance back once as they drove away.

Because, as much as he'd tried to forget her, Melanie Blankenship never stayed in his rearview for long.

MEL KNEW SHE was in trouble. There were just no two ways about it.

She opened her eyes and tried to answer several questions all at once.

Why was she lying down?

Why was she wet?

Why was it so hot?

What was that noise?

Where was she?

She groaned, unable to answer any of them.

Movement entered the list of things sending her into sensory overload.

Mel finally opened her eyes to find a woman hovering over her, concern clear in her drawn brow.

"Hey, can you hear me? My name is Anna." Mel tried to sit up, as if the new position could help her process the information faster. Instead all it did was make her wince as pain shot up her side. The woman named Anna gently pushed her back down. "Take it easy. You were in an accident. We're in an ambulance on the way to the hospital to make sure you're okay. Do you understand?"

Mel didn't.

Her head hurt as much as it was confused.

Though that confusion started lifting when she heard someone over a radio chirp out the name of said hospital.

Mel struggled to sit up again.

"Wait. Where am I?" Mel asked.

The gentle pressure of Anna's hands managed to push her back down.

"In the back of an ambulance, on the way to the—"

"No, *where* are we? What town?" Mel interrupted.

Anna's look of concern seemed to double down on itself.

Mel didn't care.

She *did* care about what was said next.

Anna had the audacity to make the answer sound casual.

"We're heading into Kelby Creek."

This time Mel didn't need help staying down.

Instead she closed her eyes tight and swore.

"You should have left me where you found me."

THE NEXT TIME Melanie Blankenship opened her eyes, the world had once again seemingly changed all at once.

This time, at least, she could remember the point B that had led to this point C. But how she'd gotten from point A to that point B?

Foggy.

Blank.

She'd been in the ambulance.

She was at the hospital now.

Everything else?

Might as well have been cotton candy beneath running water.

"I have amnesia?"

Mel's doctor, a graying man who must have been a hoot for children based on how many times he'd used the word *noggin* and how often he chuckled at the sight of blood, laughed lightly.

"Temporary memory loss due to a traumatic event," he said, not for the first time. He pointed to the bandage on Mel's hairline. "Thanks to the impact of being in a car accident."

Mel went to touch the bandage again, but the doctor was quick. He gently took her hand and steered it away from the wound.

"Like you said, it appears to be short-term loss only, and, as frustrating as that can be, let's count our blessings that it isn't worse." The childish grin he'd been wearing since he'd come in to see her became more serious. "Rest, give it time and the memories should come back. Your body just needs time to heal."

"Should? Not will?"

The doctor had the good sense to look apologetic.

"Everyone's different. There's a chance you might not get every detail back but, hey, thankfully you only seem to have lost less than a day. Luckily, not too much time in the grand scheme of things."

Considering Mel had woken up in an ambulance in Kelby Creek, she very much disagreed. Her fewer than twenty-four hours had packed a punch.

She just didn't know where that punch had come from or why she'd been punched at all.

Mel had about 2.3 billion questions left to ask, but the headache that the meds hadn't dismantled kept all of them behind her lips.

"Now, I'll ask again," started the doctor. "Are you sure there isn't anyone you want us to call? The nurse said you were insistent against your current emergency contact, but now that you've had time to settle?"

Mel shook her head too quickly. She winced, then tried to play through the show of pain.

"I'm good, thanks."

The doctor hesitated a moment but then let it lie. He was back to a big smile. Then he was gone.

Mel took the moment after to try to dig deep again.

What had happened in the last day?

Sunday she had been at her apartment in Birmingham, finishing an article when…

She was packing a bag and getting into her car…

Then it was Monday afternoon and she was in a hospital hours away.

Mel groaned.

It was like trying to recall a dream. The attempt itself was making the memory harder to grasp.

She kicked her legs over the edge of the hospital bed and hit the ground running, so to speak. Mel shimmied back into her jeans beneath the hospital gown. Her bra and blouse weren't going to go through the same motions. Since the ambulance had picked her up and the paramedics had been unable to wake her right away, they'd cut her shirt and bra wide-open. Now both were in the garbage bin.

At the very least, the first responders had grabbed her purse.

Mel, not for the first time, went to it and through it quickly.

Nothing seemed out of place. At least not what she'd considered normal before her memory had decided to fragment.

Her cell phone was even resting inside—no missed or outgoing calls during her memory lapse. No texts, either.

For some people the lack of communication from friends or family would have been concerning. For Mel it was oddly comforting.

Whatever had happened between Sunday and that Monday had at least not concerned anyone else.

Well, that she remembered.

Mel straightened and slowly looked around the hospital room.

There had to be a reason she'd pointed her car toward Kelby Creek.

The one place she'd sworn to never visit again.

"Why now?"

The hospital room didn't answer her, and she decided staying wouldn't get her any answers, either. Mel had spent too much of her life being in the dark. Being oblivious. That wasn't her anymore.

She needed to figure out what was going on.

Resolved to calling a coworker from their home decor magazine *P's & Q's* to see if anything had happened there, Mel readied to leave.

A knock on the door, however, stopped her in her tracks.

Her heartbeat sped up.

There were many reasons why Mel didn't want to be back in Kelby Creek.

When the door opened to show a man staring at her, she felt a pit of nerves bunch in her stomach.

He definitely was one of the reasons why she'd never wanted to cross the town limits again.

"Jonathan."

Jonathan Partridge was exactly three things: a true platinum blond, a lover of freshly pressed suits and a terrifying lawyer. The fact that he was only a few years younger than Mel somehow made him more menacing than if he'd been more seasoned.

It didn't help that he was her former brother-in-law and, unless something had changed since she'd been gone, not at all a fan of hers.

"What are you doing here?" she asked before he could start in.

Mel smoothed down her hospital gown as Jonathan smiled.

Shark's teeth.

And he looked like he'd already smelled blood in the water.

"Small town, fast news." He shrugged and sauntered over. If someone wasn't sure of the man's worth, he made sure to act like he was top-shelf quality at all times. Everyone else? Expired off-brand. "It didn't take long to hear about a nasty wreck out at the town limits and a woman being taken to the hospital. It certainly didn't take long for the name of that woman to travel faster than the rest of the details."

He stopped at the foot of the hospital bed. Even though Mel was standing on the opposite side of it, she felt vulnerable with him there.

She didn't like it.

Jonathan shook his head a little. He chuckled.

"Mel Blankenship. I have to say, I'm surprised on many fronts," he continued. "You being back in town was enough, but then to hear you'd been at the receiving end of a nasty hit-and-run with nothing more than a packed suitcase in the trunk? And now, to top it all off, you're allegedly having memory problems? Wow. Color me— Well, color me surprised. I guess there isn't another word for it."

Mel felt the heat in her face. She knew she was turning a nasty shade of red.

Just as she knew that letting her rising anger out at Jonathan was a dangerous game that she didn't want to play.

It was true, he wasn't as cunning as his brother, but underestimating how crafty the youngest Partridge was would be a mistake she wasn't going to add to her life's list of regrets.

"Surprised or not, me being back is none of your business." She kept her voice even. It was a difficult move.

Jonathan shrugged again.

This time he put his hands into the motion, turning his palms up to the ceiling. Whether or not he did so to showcase the burn scars on his skin, she didn't know.

"It might not be my business, but it is my concern." His cheeky smile deepened into a frown. He dropped his hands at this side. "The last time you were in Kelby Creek, you almost cost me everything. I don't want a repeat performance."

Mel didn't know why she'd come back to Kelby Creek, but in that moment she wished she could remind herself how bad an idea it had been.

There was "disliked by the general public" and then there was "hated by enough individuals that crossing the town limits wasn't just dumb, it was a gamble."

Why had she made it?

What had she hoped to gain?

"I don't want any trouble," she decided on when it was clear that Jonathan was remaining rooted to the spot. "After I get my things and a ride, I'm leaving."

Jonathan gave her a long, cool stare.

It made her skin crawl.

Yet, for all the things she didn't like about Jonathan, one thing she was grateful for about him was that he looked nothing like his brother.

Small blessings and all that.

"And what about the house?"

She felt her body stiffen in defense.

Mel didn't want to talk with him or anyone about the house.

Jonathan's gaze scanned her up and down quickly.

In turn he tensed.

Mel wanted to avoid a fight, but she wasn't about to be corralled into a trap.

"We're no longer family, and we were certainly never friends," she started. "There's no reason for you to be here, especially now that you've said your bitter little piece. And that's exactly what I'll say to the authorities if you don't leave now." Mel took a small step forward and crossed her arms over her chest. "And before you remind me of why that would be a bad idea, since the sheriff's department and the town aren't crazy about me, let me remind *you*. I may be Rider Partridge's ex-wife, but you're his brother, and around these parts blood is thicker than water."

Mel imagined she was a tree that had been growing roots all the years she'd been gone. Roots that were worn and weathered but tough.

Stronger than any Partridge man's.

She didn't move an inch while Jonathan went through his emotions in silence.

There was anger. There was regret. There was more anger.

Then there was blazing blame written clearly across his scowl.

But she wasn't wrong.

"Kelby Creek isn't the same as it was when you left," he said, already angling toward the door. "There are a lot scarier things lurking in the shadows now. I suggest you don't go looking for any of them."

Mel watched as Jonathan and his fancy suit slithered back out in the hallway.

Instead of taking the moment after to breathe, she doubled down on her plan of leaving the hospital.

And then Kelby Creek. This time for good.

Chapter Two

The sunset was probably nice, but Sterling wasn't paying it any attention. He'd seen Southern sunsets before, knew they had a look to them that made you want to paint them. Just as he knew that today's sunset was probably particularly nice. No clouds in the sky and a nice breeze across the ground. In fact, he wouldn't be surprised at all if his brother, Sam, didn't send him a picture of it from his back porch with a caption of a smiley-face emoji with hearts around it.

But Sterling wasn't looking at the sky when he got out of his truck.

He wasn't looking at the oranges and purples and pinks hanging above him as he patted down his shirt or straightened his cowboy hat.

He surely wasn't trying to see the stars peeking out, ready to shine for the night.

Instead, his focus and thoughts had all but narrowed on a woman.

Sterling had practiced during the ride over to the hospital what he'd say and do when he first saw Melanie after all these years—something he'd actually practiced before throughout those same years—but he couldn't seem to find anything that felt right.

That made what she'd done, how he'd felt about it and the last five years feel better.

"You sure you should be going there at all?" Marigold had asked when the call had come through from the sheriff. "Like the sheriff said, it can be one of us that goes. You don't owe her anything."

"Melanie isn't just my ex," he'd responded, trying to be delicate. "Her history with this town is complicated. Better me go than someone who hasn't had the time to deal with their feelings about her. It's simpler if I go."

Marigold hadn't been satisfied with the answer.

"I'd say what happened between you two is nothing but complicated."

Sterling didn't dispute that, but he had left, focus narrowing.

All he had to do was ask Melanie a few questions and give her the suitcase she'd left in the trunk of her car.

Then he could leave and go back to not seeing her again.

Nothing complicated with that.

A simple plan.

One as easy as not looking up at the sunset.

And one that didn't last past the sidewalk.

"Oh, excuse me."

A woman wearing a hospital gown hurried out of the hospital's front doors and ran smack-dab into Sterling's shoulder. It took him half a second to realize she had the gown tucked into jeans like it was a shirt. It took him the other half of that second to realize that gown was a cool ways south from a pair of truer than true ice-blue eyes.

Ones that made you forget about the world.

"Mel?"

The woman's eyes widened, but he didn't need any confirmation from her.

Sometimes a minute felt like a lifetime, and then sometimes five years felt like no time had passed at all.

Melanie Blankenship looked like she did the day she'd left.

Beautiful from head to toe.

Coal-black hair always wrapped up into something messy, a button nose that scrunched when she was being mischievous or when she thought something was particularly great, and a dimple in her chin that made her acts of defiance that much more defiant. The freckles that had been a complement to her tanned-skin growing up were maybe a bit more pronounced, but she probably hadn't been sunbathing like she used to since she'd left Kelby Creek.

Then again, time *had* passed between them. Even when it felt like it hadn't.

Sterling was reminded of that fact when Mel took a quick step back from him, mouth dropping open.

"Sterling."

Two syllables jam-packed with the sound of regret.

And it wasn't regret at their past but at seeing him now.

That much he could pick up on quicker than a sunset could be beautiful.

"I— Sorry," she hurriedly tacked on. "I just didn't expect to see you. Here. I told the nurse I didn't want them to call anyone."

Sterling tilted his head a little.

"The nurses didn't call me. I'm here for the department." He tapped his badge. "You were in a pretty serious accident where the other party left the scene. I'm here to take a statement."

Mel's face darkened a shade.

"Oh. Yeah, okay."

She touched the bunched-up fabric of her gown.

Sterling looked around at the parking lot behind them.

"Is someone here to pick you up?"

Mel shook her head. It was hard not to look at the bandage on it. When the news had come in about the accident and the victim having issues with her memory, it had been interesting enough. When the sheriff heard that it was Mel, everything had changed.

Sterling felt the familiar pull of anger toward someone who had dared to hurt the woman in front of him.

He tried to keep things professional.

"Then why are you running away?"

So much for professional. At his own question, he felt another familiar pull. This time toward his own anger. His own confusion and resentment.

One minute into seeing Mel and he was back to waiting on that front porch for a woman who wasn't coming.

"From the hospital," Sterling added. "I heard about your head, and I can't imagine they'd just let you leave."

At that, Mel snorted.

It was unlike her.

"All they're giving me in there is ibuprofen and making sure I don't have any reactions to anything. I can do that where I don't have to worry about unwanted visitors."

"Unwanted visitors? Someone already giving you trouble?"

There again was that anger toward someone else for her sake.

Sometimes those five years really did feel like nothing.

Mel shook out her shoulders a little. She cast her gaze out to the parking lot as she answered.

"Jonathan just came by and was his usual charming self."

Sterling grumbled on reflex. He'd never been a fan of Jonathan Partridge.

"Did he threaten you?"

At that Mel met his eye. She looked more annoyed than scared. Still, he thought he heard some hesitance.

"He was being Jonathan and talking out of his suit. I told him to beat it or I'd call in the department myself, and he scurried out fast. You know me—I don't suffer Jonathan Partridge long if I can help it."

Sterling had thought he'd known everything there was to know about Melanie Blankenship at one point in their lives. From her favorites to her dislikes to the subtle things she did that she did subconsciously.

He thought he'd known her, full body and soul.

Then she'd gone, a simple text in her wake that read, I'm sorry, Sterling. I hope you have a good life.

How had he not seen that coming?

And did that mean he hadn't known her at all?

Keep it simple, he told himself with force. *This doesn't have to be anything complicated.*

Sterling cleared his throat.

"Well, if you're on your way out, then why don't you come by the department tomorrow for your statement? That is, assuming you're staying in town." He pointed back to his truck. "I have your packed suitcase they found in the trunk of your car, so I was guessing you might be."

At this Mel's entire demeanor changed. Though for the life of him he couldn't figure out what emotion was making that change.

"I'm staying the night," she said. "Just need to call a cab and get a ride since, apparently, my car has seen much better days."

Sterling shouldn't have said it.

But he did.

"I can give you a ride. I know the town, and it'll be a lot faster than waiting for Grant to drive over here."

Mel's eyebrow rose. She didn't turn him down, though. "That would actually be a big help. Thanks."

FIVE YEARS OF memories didn't compare an ounce to the man they'd been made about. Not when he seemingly materialized out of midair wrapped in a uniform that fit nicely, topped with a cowboy hat his daddy had given him and carrying some emotions behind clear blue eyes.

Eyes that, once they found Mel during her attempt to flee the hospital, never strayed.

Not that she'd expected anything but full attention when Sterling Costner found out she was back in town.

Though, silly ol' Mel had been hoping that she'd have more time before she had *this* face-to-face.

Because, as much as she was hoping no one else would catch wind of her arrival, she knew the gossip mill around town was probably already aflame. Not just Jonathan and his sketchy connections.

"I'm glad this wasn't destroyed," Mel said lamely once she slid into the passenger seat, picking up her suitcase in the process. She placed it on her lap.

She remembered leaving her apartment with it but not what she'd packed inside. At least now she could change out of her hospital gown.

Sterling slid into his truck like a knife through butter.

The man could make anything look good.

"I didn't see your car, but Deputy Rossi said it looked like someone hit your back end," he said once the door was shut. "Then you most likely spun out and hit the ditch, causing you to flip. Whoever hit you probably got spooked and took off. We're looking for them, though, so don't worry."

Mel's stomach moved a little at that last part.

"Don't worry" in Sterling's voice used to be the soundtrack

to her life. A comforting repetition that felt like it could fix everything.

But there was no time for that now.

She played with the zipper on her suitcase.

"I guess I'll deal with the technical stuff tomorrow. Not sure what my insurance is going to say about the whole situation. I suppose it depends on how many cases of *amnesia* they get."

Sterling shrugged. He was such a big man that even the most subtle movements drew attention.

"I'm sure you'll do fine with them," he said. "You've always been a grade-A talker."

Mel snorted at that.

"Out of everyone in my life, I've been the least charming of them all. It took me almost a year to convince my neighbor to call me Mel. If I can't get someone to call me by my preferred name, then I don't think I can be counted as a grade-A anything."

Like his shrug, Mel noticed Sterling straighten.

She decided talking about her past was as bad as talking about theirs, so she looked out the window and tried to pretend for a moment that nothing had changed.

That she hadn't married Rider Partridge.

That she hadn't waited so long to divorce him.

That she hadn't fallen in love with Sterling.

That she hadn't—

Mel sat up straighter.

She glanced at Sterling and found him already looking at her.

She smiled.

It wasn't returned.

They both went to looking back out of the windshield.

"Where are we headed?" he asked.

Another simple thing that felt unbelievably weighted.

The answer would feel that much more uncomfortable because, while going to a motel made sense, the moment Jonathan had asked her about her old home had been the moment Mel had decided it was time to go back.

Even if it was the last place she wanted to go.

THE HOUSE COULD have been a home. If only Rider Partridge hadn't made it to out be a castle for his throne instead.

In retrospect, Mel saw it for what it was. She understood now that Rider hadn't wanted a family, a place to belong, like her back then. He'd wanted a kingdom for the townspeople to wish was theirs. He wanted power in every way. Visible like his castle, but subtle, too. So subtle that no one realized it until it was too late.

Mel looked at the two-story almost-mansion and took a small amount of pleasure at seeing the weeds that had popped up along the sprawling lawn, the gutters that needed cleaning and the various spots of mold across the custom shutters. There were a few missing shingles, too, no doubt from a rough storm, and one of the windows from the second floor had lost its screen.

Not a derelict building, but certainly not the pearl in the oyster Rider had paid so much to build.

That small satisfaction at something he'd loved so much wilting just a smidge lasted as long as a breath.

But, for Mel, it was a good breath.

"You can call down to the auto shop tomorrow to see if Frank can give you a better idea of your car situation." Sterling appeared at her side, eyes on her and not the house. "Not too sure how that will shake out. Frank isn't as fast as he used to be when you were here last. Since his hip replacement, he's let his nephew do more and more, but, well, you know Frank. He's a helicopter boss. He'll tell you to go at something and then come back and just do it himself in the end."

Mel nodded, because she did know how Frank was. He'd been that way since they were teens, riding around with their busted cars and not a care in the world.

Now it was different. They were different, so the nod was enough.

Sterling pulled her suitcase up and started to walk it to the front door. The last time they'd done the same song and dance, it had been in the opposite direction.

Five years ago.

A lifetime ago.

Sterling stopped at the top step of the porch. Mel passed by him, key out.

"There's an alarm that I have to go in and type a code into," she warned. "If not, all the bells and whistles will start going off and the department will be called. I…would like to avoid that."

Sterling nodded this time. He was tracing the porch with his eyes. Mel couldn't read anything on him other than mild disinterest.

Which meant his poker face must have gotten a whole lot better in the last few years, or else he was really over what had happened.

Rider. The house. Her.

Which would be a good thing, Mel reminded herself. *No reason for him to still be on about you. Just like you're not on about him. Get it together. Bigger fish.*

The door unlocked with ease. As soon as it swung open, a beeping started. Mel hustled in and hurried straight through the grand foyer to the kitchen at the back of the house. The keypad lit up under her fingers as she typed in the code.

The beeping stopped when she hit Enter, but she took a moment to hover.

It had been a long time since she'd been in this kitchen. Like the rest of the house, it was grand and upscale. Brand-new, barely used appliances, top-notch countertops and fixtures, and a pantry that was half the size of her apartment in Birmingham now. It also was the one room in the house that had more doors than the rest.

One led outside to the covered brick patio, one led into the office, the one she'd come through went back to the foyer and then the last one, tucked next to the pantry, led downstairs to the basement.

Mel's gaze stuck to that door now.

She knew nothing that had or would ever happen was because of that door, yet every time she saw it she felt nothing but anger, resentment and guilt.

If it would have done any good, she would have punched it. Taken an ax to it. Thrown it into the wood chipper and had a glass of wine as she watched it disintegrate.

But she wouldn't do any of that.

It was just a door, after all.

It hadn't kidnapped a young girl, taken her to the basement below and held her there for two days.

It hadn't been oblivious upstairs, unaware that her husband was an actual monster, letting it happen, either.

So Mel let that anger, that hurt and shame, simmer and went back through to the foyer and to the only man who had never blamed her for what had happened in that basement.

Sterling whistled low and motioned to the staircase. It curved up and around to the second-floor landing.

"I forgot how fancy this place is," he said. "It looks like it belongs in a magazine."

Mel snorted.

"It belongs somewhere, but definitely not a magazine."

The way she said it must have keyed him into some of what she was feeling. He set her suitcase down. By the scrunch of his brow, she knew what was coming next.

"Why don't you sell it? Surely the upkeep isn't worth it at the very least."

Mel sighed.

"I have enough from the settlement that the upkeep doesn't bother me a bit."

Sterling took a small step forward and motioned around them.

"But the house does."

It wasn't a question. So she didn't give him an answer. Instead Mel smiled and ignored.

Two things she'd proven to be too good at in the past.

"Thank you for the ride, Sterling. I mean it. I'll come to the department tomorrow to give my statement."

She didn't move an inch. Sterling's eyes—had they been that blue before?—settled on hers.

He opened his mouth but didn't say anything right away.

For a moment they were just two people standing in a room with a slight echo, the only thing between them a past too complicated to talk about. At least, for her.

"Okay," he finally said. Sterling gave the room one last look around. Then a small nod before meeting her eye again. "I hope this all works out for you. Whatever it is you're doing, Mel."

Mel went with polite but to the point, the only response she could at the moment.

"Thank you. I shouldn't be here long."

Then the cowboy deputy left without another look or word.

Mel's stomach dropped a little, but she shut the door behind him and threw the dead bolt.

She might not remember why she was back in town, but she knew enough to avoid bringing Sterling into her problems again.

Chapter Three

Marigold was abuzz when Sterling got back to the sheriff's department.

"You gotta give me a minute before I talk," he was quick to say. "I'm boiling beneath my collar, and I need to cool down before I say something I'll regret."

They were in the break room, both already having ended their shifts. Marigold had coffee in her hand. The other coffee had been handed to Sterling upon his arrival. It wasn't something they often did—drink the stuff—but he couldn't deny it might help with the headache clustering behind his eyes.

Sterling would always give it to Marigold—she was good at reading people.

He drank a few long pulls and then put his cowboy hat down on one of the tabletops. His father, Callahan, had gifted it to him on his eighteenth birthday. It gave him some comfort. Enough so that he was ready to talk.

He still couldn't believe that no more than twenty minutes ago he'd been staring at Mel. A ghost from his past come back to haunt him. A ghost who had grabbed all of his attention, only to tell him she wouldn't be wailing through town for long. Not that he could believe her on that one, either. Mel couldn't remember why she was in town so how would she know how long she was staying?

Sterling clenched his jaw, frustrated for every reason in the book.

Then he let out a long, loud breath.

Marigold watched, quiet, but he could see some questions behind her eyes.

"All right," he decided. "Ask whatever it is you want to know, because I know you're not here just to give my sorry self some caffeine."

Marigold straightened but didn't defend herself.

"I'd be offended at the implication that I hung around just to get information out of you. If it wasn't true... Now, I know the bare bones of your past with Ms. Blankenship and her connection to what happened in town, *but* I think I'm missing some more nuanced details. At least based on how Deputy Juliet acted when she heard that Melanie was back in town. And I'll be honest, she wasn't the first person around here who I saw tense at the gossip."

Sterling dropped his head a little and swore.

He hadn't thought about how others close to him might react to Mel's sudden reappearance.

"Juliet's brother left town after what happened to try and get a more respectable job," Sterling explained. "He was killed in a car accident shortly after. He was all Juliet had in the way of family."

"But how exactly is that Melanie Blankenship's fault?"

It was a simple question, but there was never a simple answer when it came to what had happened almost six years ago to Kelby Creek during what the locals still referred to as The Flood.

"It's easier to blame Mel for what Rider Partridge did, since he's in prison." Sterling looked around and lowered his voice, not wanting to trigger anyone else. "Tell me everything you know about the story of Annie McHale and I'll tell you something you don't know."

Marigold raised her eyebrow but was game.

"Beloved daughter of the even more beloved McHale family goes missing six years ago and the entire town pulls together to find her," she recited. "A few days later, kidnappers send a hefty ransom demand, and the sheriff convinces the McHales to use it as a way to ambush them and get Annie back. But instead several people were killed and injured in a shoot-out where the kidnappers got away. Then the case caught national attention when the kidnappers hacked the town's website and posted a video of Annie tied up and bloody, where they demanded more money or else. That's also when the FBI became serious about it."

He nodded as she continued.

"Two agents came to town to investigate. One agent said she found a lead before that agent disappeared. When her partner went looking for her, he got caught during a flash flood, where he happened upon the mayor, who had crashed into a ditch. While the agent tried to help him, he stumbled upon Annie McHale's necklace in the back seat. The agent decided to dig deeper into the mayor after that and found out he *and* the sheriff were behind Annie's kidnapping. But that's not where the corruption stopped. Or started."

People said misery loved company, but corruption was the real people person. After a new FBI task force had come specifically for the town, Kelby Creek had been forever changed. Cases of corruption surfaced that had come way before Annie's kidnapping and spread a lot further than anyone had imagined. It turned the town against local law enforcement and government officials. Anyone with authority, really. The guilty were arrested, killed in attempted apprehension or, for a few, fled. Those who weren't guilty transferred, quit or stayed with new chips on their shoulders.

It was why Brutus was the sheriff now and why he'd

spent every day since his appointment trying to find good men and women to redeem the tarnished name of the department.

It was also why Marigold had, in part, applied to become a deputy after a few years in the business world. She'd told Sterling she wanted to do something good but only do it around other people trying to do the same thing.

Sterling wasn't about to tell her he wasn't exactly sure if he qualified as one of those people. He had left after the investigations had ended and the department was crippled and in the most need, after all.

"So everyone knows the main players of The Flood," he said. "The sheriff, the mayor, hell, even the coroner got the spotlight for a good while. But you know the saying 'behind every successful man, there's a strong woman'? Well, behind every corrupt man, there's an even more corrupt one holding it together."

Marigold picked up on what he was saying.

"Rider Partridge, Mel's ex-husband," she guessed.

Sterling nodded.

"The sheriff and mayor were all flashy and shiny so everyone looked at them at first, but then the FBI started to realize that they would have needed serious help with Annie, not to mention their less-than-legal adventures before her kidnapping. That's when loyalties were really tested, and eventually some people caved and gave up Rider's name as not only an accomplice, but a man who'd been running the 'behind the scenes' for a lot of people for a long time." Sterling remembered the day Rider's name was announced on the news. Though he remembered Mel's horrified face as a reporter tried to get her to open up about her husband after a media ambush more. Now he fisted his hand against the thigh of his jeans.

"It might not have been such bad news had his bad deeds

stopped there," Sterling continued. "But then it leaked that Rider had held Annie McHale in his basement for two days of her captivity, including the day the ransom video was recorded."

Marigold sucked in a breath.

"And I'm assuming Mel had no idea about it."

"None," he was quick to answer. "Though, since Annie and the missing FBI agent were never found, not everyone in town believes Mel. And of those who do believe that she had no idea, they blame her for having no idea about any of it. Annie, the corruption, everything wrong that Rider Partridge ever did during their one year of marriage. She was damned if she did, damned if she didn't."

Marigold took a moment to process that. Then, slowly, Sterling saw it.

Saw the question. If anyone else had asked him, he would have done what he always had before and become defensive, angry even.

But Marigold wasn't quick to blame, just curious.

"And you believed her? When she said she had no idea about what Rider was up to?"

Sterling picked up his hat and placed it on his head.

He was done with his coffee but stayed sitting long enough to answer.

"I've known Mel since we were teens. The only wrong thing she's ever done, in my opinion, was marry the wrong man."

That was all Marigold needed. He was glad to not have to spell out how Mel had become his closest friend after they'd met and kept the title long after they'd graduated. That he'd still been by her side when she'd started dating Rider and had been there for the marriage, too. Just as he had been at her side when he thought she needed him the most. Just as he had been with her up until the day she left him behind without a word.

Instead, Marigold let the conversation end and gave Sterling his space. It should have been time to go home, but he couldn't. Not yet. Not when he was still itching beneath the skin.

Sterling's feet instead led him to the sheriff's office.

Brutus Chamblin wasn't as jovial as he had been at Kenneth and Willa's wedding. In fact, he looked more than worn down.

"Before I tell you what's stuck in my craw, why don't you tell me what's stuck in yours?" Sterling used as a greeting.

Brutus had been at the department before Sterling had left it the first time around, but he hadn't been sheriff then. Maybe that's why he wasn't as formal as the title of sheriff deserved. Brutus didn't seem to mind. He waved a hand over some papers on his desk. One was the local paper, folded so Sterling couldn't see the main headline.

"The anniversary of Annie McHale's disappearance is coming up," Brutus started. "I've been told by the news editor that they plan to do an edition of the paper dedicated to everything that happened before, during and after The Flood. A 'very involved' piece."

Sterling whistled low.

"That's going to stir up some strong feelings," he decided on. "I just gave Marigold some bonus facts about The Flood, and it stirred up some feelings in *me*."

Brutus rubbed his chin.

"It surely will." He sighed. "This job as sheriff was supposed to be temporary, you know? I stepped in as interim sheriff because there was no one else. But can you even call me interim anything if I've been here for five years now?"

Sterling took a seat across from the older man. He rested his cowboy hat on his lap. Brutus's was on his desk already.

"You ever think about leaving? That'll force someone to step up. Or do you already have someone in mind for the job here?"

Brutus ran his thumb along his jaw.

"I've had a list for a while now but, as much as this department is changing, there's still a stench on the sheriff's office that everyone seems to smell. Can't blame good men and women for wanting a different path." He shrugged. "I almost didn't take the job myself, even when it was pitched to me as temporary."

He leaned back so far in his chair that Sterling thought he'd fall over. The older man cracked a smile. It wasn't amused, just something nice to do.

"There a reason you're here talking to my old bag of bones instead of doing something more fun?"

Sterling laughed.

"Well, I was going to come complain about how Kelby Creek doesn't let the past go, but, seems to me, we both might have had enough talk about that for today."

He stood and flipped his hat back onto his head. Brutus placed his hand on his own hat but didn't put it on.

Sterling didn't like how old he looked in the moment. He looked too worn.

"Maybe we both should go home and take a rest," Brutus finally said. "Would be nice to get some sleep finally."

He flashed a tired but genuine smile.

Sterling returned it.

"Might be nice," he agreed.

Brutus returned the sentiment.

"Might be nice."

MEL FELL ASLEEP in the guest room down the hall from the master bedroom. The cleaning crew had done a great job of keeping the interior of the house clean and dust-free. Mel even found that the sheets and linens smelled fresh, and she slept surprisingly well on them. Waking up, however, was a bumpier process.

Mel opened her eyes and knew she was drenched with sweat. She'd had a nightmare. It wasn't uncommon, but it wasn't exactly comfortable, either. She got out of bed and took her suitcase straight to the attached bathroom.

Mel cringed when she caught sight of her reflection in the mirror over the sink. The bandage had come off her forehead in her sleep and now she saw a nasty scab where she'd hit, she assumed, some part of her car. Along with her matted hair, thanks to the sweat, she looked worse for wear. Almost like she'd gotten drunk at a bar, tried to fight someone—and lost—and then had woken up with a hangover.

And that's how it felt, she decided as she got into the shower.

She felt just like she had a hangover. A nasty one at that. Her head hurt, with a tinge of fuzziness around it.

Was that how car accidents felt?

She hadn't been in one before.

"Rest, take it easy."

The doctor's voice echoed in her head. Mel resented that she could remember him clear as day but not why she'd been headed to Kelby Creek, of all places.

It was a dark, empty spot as if someone had holepunched out her reason for wanting to be back and the actual drive in. Everything else was intact.

That frustration, plus her reflection when she got out of the shower put her already foul mood into another gear. She dressed quickly and started to snoop through the house slowly.

Surely there had to be a clue as to why she was there. Why she'd brought the house key with her, too.

Mel started with the second floor and went through the

two guest bedrooms with precision. They, and the bathrooms, were stocked with typical guest bedroom things, just like the bathrooms. When she was done with them, she stopped at the door to the master suite.

She'd never understood why Rider had given the house to her in the divorce. His castle. His pride and joy. It had been just another reason why the town had suspected Mel of being involved in all the bad he'd done. It was also another reason why his brother, Jonathan, had been angry at her. He'd wanted the money that the sale could have gotten him had Rider decided to keep the house in his family.

Not let her have it.

Yet Mel hadn't sold the house. She hadn't lived in it after Rider had gone to prison, either.

It felt tainted.

It felt wrong.

It also was a reminder to everyone in Kelby Creek that with power came temptation and not everyone, when tempted, would resist.

It was also a reminder to Mel.

Ignorance was only bliss until that ignorance hurt someone else.

She turned the doorknob fast and walked inside the room with purpose.

The scream that came out of her mouth at what she saw echoed throughout the house.

Chapter Four

Sterling was rebellious.

He called Carlos, offered him a six-pack and asked if they could switch shifts. All before the sun had risen. Deputy Park was game, mostly because that's just who he was, but partially because Mel was coming in that morning for her statement and Carlos knew about their history.

That same history had kept Sterling up half the night.

"Switching shifts is no sweat off my back," Carlos had assured him. "I've been wanting to get Marigold's opinion on women anyways, so this is almost like a favor for me."

Sterling had thanked the man with a chuckle and then doubted his decision to let Carlos take Mel's statement and not him as soon as the phone call ended.

After that, he felt sure in his decision.

Then again, not so much.

That cycle continued on repeat before he forced his thoughts to turn to what he'd do instead of go into work.

Gym? Go for a run? Try to get a few hours of decent sleep?

Eventually Sterling decided to split the difference between all options.

He dressed in his gym clothes after the sun had risen and went to mow his lawn.

South Alabama had a habit of being a downright pain

in the backside when it came to yard maintenance. You couldn't wait until the humidity or heat broke or else you'd be waiting on the porch watching your weeds grow and your grass turn brown. The only thing you could try to plan around was the rain. Sterling had one eye on the sky as he started his push mower at the curb.

The heat felt good and sweating felt better. Sterling's muscles got a workout, the grass got shorter and, dang sure enough, he was thinking about the first time he'd met Melanie Blankenship.

Sterling had been thirteen and as carefree as a kid could be. His brother, Sam, though, had been having issues. Other thirteen-year-olds had decided that, since Sam was a year younger, he needed picking on, something Sterling wouldn't have stood for, carefree or not. The bullies knew that and so they'd waited for Sam to be alone before picking on him. One day, they'd really been feeling themselves and let their words turn physical. They'd made Sam stand against the gym wall and pelted him with basketballs after practice.

Sterling had gotten the news through the grapevine and had run out of football practice and all the way to the gym, seeing red.

Yet the only person he'd seen getting beat up when he got there was Dan Leben.

The person throwing the punches was none other than a girl half his size. Wearing braided pigtails and a sundress.

"You keep acting like a fool, Dan Leben, and I'll tell everyone that black eye you're going to have tomorrow came from a girl that's not even over five foot!"

Sterling had had a lot of memorable things happen to him in his life, but he'd never forget hearing Mel's little voice echo around the court.

He definitely wouldn't forget Dan listening to her, his cronies following him out, cussing like they were bad.

"Your brother's fine," Mel had assured Sterling when he'd run over. "He probably needs a bodyguard until he learns how to punch or run, though. Do you ride the bus or walk home?"

Sterling had been flustered at how she'd taken charge, but told her they rode their bikes. He'd told her where they'd lived, too, to which she'd shrugged.

"I live a few roads over, but I don't have a bike." She'd turned to Sam, who as a kid had already been quiet when attention wasn't directed at him. "I can walk you home, but you'll have to walk your bike. I have short legs."

To his surprise, Sam had agreed.

For the next three years, Mel had walked Sam home every day after school. The only reason she'd stopped was because she'd gotten her license. Then she drove him.

And when Sam had other plans or Mel's car broke down, Sterling was the one who did the driving.

Sterling finished mowing the lawn with a lot of guilt on his shoulders. This time not for the girl who stood up to bullies but for the kid being bullied.

He should have already told his brother that Mel was back in town. He had been, at one time, the only other person Sterling knew who had cared about Mel with all that he had.

Sterling cut the ignition on the mower and wiped his arm along his brow. He didn't make it a step farther before someone was yelling at him.

"Hey there, cowboy!"

Sterling turned to see his neighbor, Ms. Martha, standing in his drive, her cordless phone waving in her hand. She had curlers tucked tight in her silver hair and was sporting a floral nightgown that was brighter than the sun. When she saw she had his attention, she added on to her greeting.

"Teddy Baker said there's a commotion going on at the sheriff's department," she called out. "I figured he might be lying, but if he wasn't then you might not know about it since you've been out here mowin'."

Sterling dropped his hands to his shorts and cussed low.

"I left my phone in the house," he realized.

Ms. Martha nodded.

"I thought you might've. Better go see if Teddy is a liar or just really good at gossipin'."

Sterling pulled his mower along to the garage while thanking the woman and was searching out his phone, all in under a minute flat.

He found the slick thing buried in his bed.

He had ten missed calls from several different numbers.

All had left messages. He clicked on the earliest one.

It was from an unknown number, but the voice was unmistakable.

"Sterling, it's Mel. I—I need you to come over to the house as soon as possible." Her voice was shaking, but she didn't mince her next words. "I just found a woman in the bedroom—and, Sterling, someone killed her."

THE LAST TIME people in uniforms had swarmed the house, Rider Partridge had left in handcuffs. Behind him, a dazed and shaken Mel with tearstains on her cheeks and the guilt that she'd been nothing but blind. She'd watched him being escorted away by the FBI and the Dawn County Sheriff's Department. Those who were left, at least.

Sterling hadn't been there. Her world had decided to turn upside down while he'd been away with Sam and his father visiting his uncle.

Jonathan had been there, though. The fire hadn't happened yet, but he'd still been angry.

"Say something," he'd yelled at her. "Tell them they have it wrong. Tell them that your husband is innocent!"

But Mel's voice had already tried to convince the agents, and herself, that it was all a misunderstanding.

Then she'd finally gone into the basement. Then she'd seen the chair and rope.

On that front porch, she couldn't tell Jonathan anything. Definitely not that Rider was innocent.

Now it was the second time her house was swarming with uniforms. This time they were all from the sheriff's department.

And there was a body.

Mel was tucked away on the front porch. She was careful not to get into foot traffic. She had her phone in her hand but had only made two calls.

"So you have no idea who the woman is." Detective Foster Lovett was smartly dressed and his badge professionally presented around his neck on a chain. His hair was long but groomed, and his wedding band glinted in the sun.

Mel shook her head. Again.

"Like I told Dispatch and Deputy Park, I didn't get the best look at her," she said. "As soon as I saw the blood and the—the—" She motioned to her chest and felt sick.

"—the gunshot wounds," he supplied.

"Yeah. After that I stopped looking altogether and called y'all."

Detective Lovett was taking notes.

"But you called Sterling Costner first, correct?"

His tone wasn't accusatory or judgmental. Just a man getting facts. Still, she smarted from the remark.

"To be honest, I don't have the best track record with people at the department," she responded. "I figured Deputy Costner wouldn't immediately point fingers at me, at the very least."

Mel wasn't sure if that was only reason she'd called him first, but she wasn't going to admit that.

"When he didn't answer, I called y'all. You can check my phone just like the last guy did."

Detective Lovett waved her off.

"I'm just getting a timeline here the best I can. If I were in your shoes, I might call a friend in the department first, too."

Mel nodded. The county CSI photographer walked out behind them. He'd been one of the first people to go in after Deputy Park had confirmed the body and secured Mel outside.

"I don't know how helpful I can be with all of this," she admitted before he could ask anything else. "Like I told Deputy Park, I'm not even sure why I'm in Kelby Creek."

Detective Lovett flipped his notebook closed. He put it in his back pocket.

"Head trauma is no joke. As for not remembering why you came here, you do know one thing even without having your memory."

Mel felt her eyebrow raise at that.

"And that is?"

"You made the decision within the last day and a half. So whatever prompted that decision now has a time frame. And it's a short one." He looked out at the street. Mel didn't follow his gaze. His demeanor changed ever so slightly from professional to tense. Then he sighed. "Regardless, once we've identified the body, we're going to have more questions for you. Excuse me a moment."

Mel didn't feel any comfort in his words but stepped aside and let him pass.

Had she recognized the woman lying across the bed that Mel had once called her own? No.

Had she looked hard?

No.

She'd seen the woman, the blood and the stillness, and she'd shut down.

Had the woman been there when Mel had come home the night before?

Just another question she didn't know the answer to, but that thought certainly sent a shiver down her spine.

Never mind the million-dollar one.

Who killed her?

Mel wrapped her arms around herself despite the heat. She finally turned to the growing crowd at the road. There she saw Detective Lovett talking to a newcomer.

Sterling's cowboy hat wasn't on, but he sure was sporting an official scowl. His brows were knitted together as he talked to the detective with fast words. He must have gotten her voice mail.

Mel expected those fast words to turn into fast walking toward her, yet the only direction Sterling walked was away. She lost sight of him a moment before he walked back up again. This time with the sheriff at his side.

Mel had known of Brutus Chamblin as a teen, but only because Sterling had been a fan of him.

"Dad said he's a good man and good people are hard to find," Sterling had told her the night he'd admitted he wanted to be a deputy. Sterling had been seventeen, but now Mel could see in the way he looked at the sheriff that that respect still burned just as bright.

They walked alongside each other and stopped at the top of the porch stairs.

"Ms. Blankenship." Sheriff Chamblin made it to her first. He stuck out his hand. Mel shook.

Sterling cut off any more introductions. His cool blue eyes were piercing as they met hers.

"Are you okay?" he asked.

"Yeah. Just a bit, well, shaken, I guess."

The sheriff nodded to that. He tapped Sterling's elbow.

"Understandable. How about you take a seat in one of these patio chairs and we'll be back down in a bit?"

Sterling's attention stuck to her only long enough for her to agree. Then both men disappeared into the house.

What felt like an hour went by, but Mel knew that logically it was more like twenty minutes before Sterling came back out. The sheriff had stayed behind, Detective Lovett and the coroner having been the only others to go into the house since then.

Sterling looked like he'd seen a ghost.

It gave her a deepening sense of dread.

"Other than the obvious, what's wrong?" Mel asked. "Wait. Did you recognize her? Do you know who the woman is?"

Sterling replied with a nod.

It was slow and ominous.

Mel hung on his every word as he answered.

"It's Rose Simon. She had her ID in her pocket."

"Rose Simon."

Mel chewed on the name for a second.

Then she understood Sterling's lead-in-the-belly look.

"Rose Simon, as in the reporter?" Sterling nodded. "As in the same woman who wrote the scathing investigative piece on Rider, which eventually helped lead to his conviction?"

Mel's mouth went dry.

Sterling's voice rumbled like thunder.

"The very same."

Chapter Five

He should have known the moment Cole Reiner came into the meeting room that everything private in his life was about to come to light.

"Hey there, Sterling. First time I've seen you in a while, huh?" Cole had become detective a year before and, as far as Sterling could guess, had been on several assignments that involved undercover work in and out of the county. Given his past—he'd once gone off everyone's radar to solve a mystery no one even knew existed—many people in the department called him an unofficial expert in that area of law enforcement work. Just as he was proving to be a skilled detective.

One who had come into the room with a notepad and pen to see Sterling.

Which couldn't be good.

"Can't say I'm excited to see you looking like you're about to read me my rights."

Cole waved him off and took a seat.

"If we were doing any of that, it wouldn't be me coming. Probably have Foster or Kenneth in here, all suits and stress lines turning into wrinkles. The only reason I'm really here is because there's some kind of kerfuffle at the hospital and everyone else is tied up at the crime scene." Sterling doubted that but didn't say as much. Cole smiled and motioned to himself. "So all you have is this pretty face to look at while I get some things straight."

He pressed the back of his pen and hovered it over his pad.

"Since I was out of pocket for a while, I'm going to need clarification on some things so we're all on the same page."

"And by *things* you mean me and Mel."

Cole nodded.

"If you listen to the gossip mill, it sounds like a simple scandal—Rider Partridge gets caught, arrested, convicted and goes to prison, then you and Mel shack up, become a thing, and then she skips town for 'insert an even more scandalous reason here.'" Cole raised his hand in defense quickly. "Let it be noted that while I listen to the gossip mill, I don't trust it. Once upon a time it said I was dead, so, for right now I'd rather you tell me the truth."

Sterling caught his bullhorn thoughts before they escaped his mouth. Then he settled.

He had known that there was a good chance someone would ask about him and Mel the moment a body had been found in her house.

A body connected to their pasts.

Sterling leaned back in his chair and felt naked without his hat.

"I grew up around Mel. Me, her and my brother, Sam, were close," he started. "When Sam went to college, we became closer."

"Romantic?"

Sterling tensed at the feeling of someone prying but tried to calm himself again. Cole was a good guy and a better detective. Withholding any information from him, for whatever reason, wasn't a good idea.

Sterling shook his head.

"Not romantic, but there was something there that I was

too stupid to see." Cole's eyebrow rose. Sterling simplified. "When Rider Partridge first asked Mel on a date, she came to me and asked if she should go. I encouraged her when I should have admitted I wanted to be with her. But, you know, young and dumb." Cole nodded in commiseration.

"Been there," he commented.

Sterling continued.

"I beat myself up for not doing anything for a while, but she seemed happy, and when they got married, I was already trying to move on." He sighed. "Then Rider was arrested and then convicted, and just like that, everyone turned on Mel like she was the monster in the suit."

"Not you."

Sterling shook his head.

"I went to visit her and found someone the world had worn down for no reason. When Rider was sent to prison and their divorce was final, I did the only thing that seemed right—I offered her a safe place to get her feet back under her. And that was it. I didn't want or expect anything more than that. Just a safe place with an old friend."

Cole put down his pen and nodded.

"But then something happened," he guessed.

Sterling nodded.

"One day she came out of her room and started talking, and it was like no time had passed from when we were kids to then. We got close and I finally told her what I should have when we were younger."

Sterling remembered the moment down to the smell of coffee and the sound of rain against the tin roof of his old house.

"I told her I loved her, and she said it back."

Cole took a moment. Smiled half that time before letting it slip.

"But then she left town."

Sterling felt himself tense. He nodded.

"No warning," he said. "A text that said to have a good life. The next time I saw her was at the hospital yesterday. I gave her a ride to the house."

There it was. The clarification of Sterling and Mel and what had happened five years ago.

It should have felt good to get it off his chest—to some-one other than his brother and father—but it didn't. Ster-ling watched as Cole clicked his pen shut.

"That's rough. Any idea why she left?"

"None. And before you ask, no, I didn't ask yesterday. As far as I'm concerned, it doesn't matter."

That didn't feel entirely true, but Sterling stuck to his metaphorical guns.

"That's why you switched with Deputy Park today? So you wouldn't have to deal with all of that, I'm guessing."

"That's correct."

Cole nodded again, seemingly taking it all in. When he didn't try to get up and wave him on to leave, Sterling became suspicious.

"Am I a suspect in Rose's murder?" he asked.

Cole was quick to say no.

"Is Mel?"

It was something he knew would be questioned—Mel's innocence—but it hadn't occurred to him until then just how bad it probably looked.

Cole helped him see the big picture.

"Even if you take out her involvement with Rider, some-thing is going on with her, Sterling." He leaned forward. "She comes back after five years, loses her memory of the last twenty-four hours or so and wakes up in a house she still owns for whatever reason that just so happens to have a dead body in it. The dead body of woman who, most could argue, put the final nail in the coffin of her husband's—and her—very posh life."

"Mel did not kill Rose." Of that Sterling was certain.

Cole surprised him by nodding.

"That's true. She didn't. But that doesn't mean she didn't have something to do with it." Cole lowered his voice. "Sterling, Dr. Alvarez put Rose's time of death at almost a day ago. During the same time frame of Mel's missing memory. That could very well be a coincidence, but it could just as easily mean something."

Sterling didn't like where this was going.

"So what are you saying? Is Mel under arrest?"

Cole straightened. He closed his notepad.

"No, but she's an extreme person of interest. And, Sterling, past or no past, I'd keep your distance until we get to the bottom of this." He stood but stayed severe. "Melanie Blankenship already broke your heart. Don't let her break the rest of your life, too."

THE ROOM SHE'D been questioned in was cold. The parking lot Mel walked out into afterward was hot. The difference made goose bumps erupt along her arm.

She looked for her car on reflex. It wasn't there, but Sterling was.

"Let's take a ride."

He was long-legged and handsome, leaning against his truck. Mel's stomach did a flip. She let out a breath. It shook a little.

"I don't think there's any place for me to go at the moment."

Sterling pushed off of the truck and opened the passenger's side door.

"I think I can help with that."

Sterling had them cruising away from the Dawn County

Sheriff's Department without another word. He shut off the air-conditioning, rolled down the windows and slung one hand lazily on the steering wheel while the other rested outside the driver's side window.

Mel could almost forget she'd just been questioned about a murder.

Almost.

"Apparently if I hadn't had my accident, I'd be looking for a lawyer right now," she said after a moment. Mel turned her attention out her window. She didn't know where they were going, but at least the sun was out. "They said Rose was killed sometime between me being taken to the hospital and before I left. 'An airtight alibi.'"

She couldn't help but put some spice in her words at the last part. The sheriff had been the one to talk to her and, even though he'd been polite and professional, that phrasing had made her feel…guilty.

And she definitely hadn't killed Rose Simon. Memory or no memory.

By the sound of movement, Mel felt like Sterling nodded deep.

But "I heard" was all he said.

Mel glanced over at the man. He was still driving like they were back to being teens without much care in the world.

"He also asked about us," she said. "The sheriff, that is." Mel felt a warmth in her stomach turn to heat up her neck.

"He asked if we spent any time together last night after you gave me a ride."

Sterling shrugged.

"We didn't."

Mel felt her brow scrunch.

"Well, yeah, I know that. That's what I said."

Sterling nodded again.

The man who had once been fast to tell her exactly what was on his mind was giving her nods now.

Mel didn't like it. She tried again to get a reaction.

"I also had to explain, step by step, what I did when I got into the house," she said. "Including the fact that I slept in the guest bedroom and didn't even go toward the master until I found her. I told him they can search and go through the house as much as they need. It definitely doesn't bother me."

There went the nod again, in sync with him turning them down a new street.

"Makes sense."

Mel couldn't take it anymore. She turned in her seat to face his profile.

"What's going on?" she asked, voice pitching a little high. "I mean, is this not talking to me because of what I did or is this not talking to me because you think I'm—what?—guilty of something? Because, even without my memory, I can assure you I haven't thought about Rose Simon or even known where she was in years and—"

They slowed down.

Mel cut herself off, recognizing the place they were approaching.

She stayed quiet as Sterling pulled in and put his truck in Park.

He had his door open and was out before Mel could say a word.

Then she watched him go into the gas station that had been around since before they were born. A few minutes later he was back, two familiar cups in his hand.

He handed her one through her window before going back to the driver's seat and settling in.

Mel looked down at the slushy in her hand. It was Coke flavored. Her favorite. She didn't need to look over at Sterling's to know his was blue raspberry. It helped that the gas station had only ever had the two flavors.

Sterling wordlessly drove them out of the parking lot and pointed them in a new direction.

Mel held her cup but didn't take a sip. Instead she waited as he turned off the paved street onto a dirt road. They bumped along it, the woods on one side and a field on the other.

The wind was warm against Mel's face. She also smelled rain, despite the clear sky. That and her cold hands around a slushy and Sterling at her side?

She was young and free.

No regrets, no broken heart, no decisions that altered anyone's lives.

She was just a girl sitting next to a boy, ready to waste some time doing nothing.

And that must have been the point.

Sterling turned onto a narrow dirt road that cut into the field before stopping at a section that had been turned into a patch where no grass or crops grew. A spot, they'd found, that had been long forgotten by Kelby Creek.

Sterling cut the engine and got out. Mel took a moment, then followed.

He was already sitting on his tailgate, sipping his slushy and looking out at the tall grass around them.

Mel followed suit.

Then they were both just sitting and sipping.

Just like they used to.

Sterling finally spoke after another few moments.

"Gayle Beecham and Brian Kingsley divorced a few months ago."

Mel turned her head so quickly she could have sworn she heard a snap.

"What? Really?"

He moved his straw around in his drink.

"Yep. And you'll never guess why."

Mel leaned in. Sterling smirked.

"Don't tell me it's because of her sister."

He nodded.

"Yes, ma'am. Turns out we were right. Brian was head over heels for Lydia Beecham this whole time."

That was some gossip Mel hadn't heard. Not that she'd heard any from Kelby Creek since she'd left.

"Ask me who Brian is married to now," Sterling added.

Mel hit his shoulder, mouth agape.

"No way," she squealed. "Don't tell me Brian and Lydia already took that step!"

Sterling laughed.

"They did a courthouse thing, and ten guesses as to who their witness was."

Mel was absolutely stunned.

"If you say Gayle, I will lose it."

Sterling held his hands up in defense and shrugged.

"Then I won't say it."

Mel laughed and slapped at his shoulder again.

"That's either very understanding of her or one heck of a power move," he said. "But, as far as I know, no one has had the courage to ask."

He joined in with his own laughter when Mel couldn't help but keep it up.

It felt nice. Not only to laugh and really mean it, but to do it with him again.

Just catching up.

Because she'd been gone for five years with no contact with anyone, especially him.

Mel let her amusement die down.

The condensation on the side of her cup wet her hands.

She kept her eyes on the distance.

A breeze pressed against them before going on its way.

They could only pretend for so long that everyone was okay.

Mel let out a long, low breath.

"Kelby Creek has a wound." Her voice was quiet, but she knew Sterling could hear her perfectly. "The Flood opened it, and I'm not sure if it can ever really close. Not completely and not without leaving a nasty scar if it did. When you have a wound like that, a scar like that, you become more aware of what made it." She put her cup down and grabbed onto the tailgate, palms down to give her more stability as she leaned forward to talk into the heat. "I'm a reminder. A walking, talking reminder that not all wounds are made by weapons and bad people. Sometimes they're made by people trying to pretend that everything is okay."

She looked at Sterling. He was already staring. There was no trace of humor in his expression, either.

Mel laid out her point.

"I never knew to stop Rider, but I do know how to stop being a constant reminder of him. Sterling, I never planned on coming back to Kelby Creek. Never."

Sterling's jaw set.

Birds chirped in the distance. That smell of rain seemed to become stronger.

When Sterling responded, his voice was hard.

"Then let's figure out why you're back and how Rose Simon is connected," he said, resolute. "After that, you can go again and never look back."

It was what Mel wanted, yet, she felt hesitation at the words.

Sterling's cool blue eyes bit into her.

She almost told him then—the real reason why she'd left town the way she had—but instead she nodded.

If Sterling knew Rider's last words to her before he'd gone to prison, he'd do something heroic.

And one thing Rider had proven to be very skilled at?

Destroying heroes.

So Mel kept her mouth shut and they finished their drinks in silence.

THEY DIDN'T SEE the big picture yet. Or, if Melanie Blankenship was telling the truth, at least one of them didn't remember it.

She straightened her ball cap and looked at the dirt road Melanie and Sterling had driven across minutes ago.

She was waiting, but she didn't know for what yet. Whatever it was, it wasn't going to be good.

Not after the car accident with Melanie.

Definitely not after Rose's murder.

She cussed low and kicked a stick out of the tree line.

Her phone rang shortly after.

She ignored the call.

If Melanie truly didn't remember why she'd come back to town, she definitely didn't remember that it was her who was supposed to be dead in that bedroom.

Not Rose.

She waited a few seconds more, then went back into the woods.

Chapter Six

They went to the accident site first. Sterling watched as Mel gingerly picked through the dirt on the shoulder of the road before combing the area for a fifth time.

He was right there with her.

Neither found anything useful, and no memories surfaced.

Then the rain came and with it a new sense of urgency. It didn't help that they were back at the house they'd been so quick to leave that morning.

"And you're sure there's nothing in there that we will mess up?" Mel peered through the windshield at the front porch. To prove his earlier point of telling her that they could go inside, he pulled away from the curb and drove up to park in the drive.

"Foster said they just all cleared out. We're good to go in."

Mel didn't seem so sure, but the rain had followed them and it was enough to get her moving. They were soon in the grand, slightly ridiculous foyer.

It echoed.

Sterling hated it.

He also wasn't a fan of his phone at the moment. It vibrated with anger.

"And now it looks like we're under a tornado watch." He snorted. "The cherry on top of the day, huh?"

Mel was barely listening. Her eyes were trained on the stairs. Sterling softened.

"We don't have to be here right now," he reminded her. "This place has been checked from top to bottom and nothing came of it."

Mel was insistent. She waved off his concern.

"This is technically my house, so this is my responsibility. At the very least I can not be a coward and pay it the same attention as where I had the accident."

She moved fast up the stairs. Sterling used his long legs to outwalk her. While he'd stood by as the house was being searched and secured several times over that morning, nothing changed the fact that a woman had been murdered there.

So he led the way to the open door of the master bedroom. The bed was bare, linens stripped, but there was a spot on the mattress.

A dark, angry one.

Mel made a noise when she saw it. Out of reflex he reached out and touched her back to steady her.

"That—that's blood," she realized.

"That's something I can take care of when the rain stops," he said. "That's also something you don't need to look at now."

Mel shook her head and stepped into the room. Sterling watched as her face hardened. She didn't say anything as she started to move around the room, searching for something that might help her make sense of everything.

He wished it could be that simple.

After a few minutes, they both admitted defeat.

Mel next showed him to the guest bedroom where she'd

spent the night. Her bag was open, but her things weren't thrown around.

"That's nice at least," she mused. "They were gentle with my unmentionables."

Sterling walked over to the suitcase and knocked on the hard top.

"What *did* you pack for your trip here? Any clue in that?"

"Nope. Just clothes, basic toiletries and a phone charger. My emergency makeup made the trip, but that's because I always have it packed."

Sterling motioned to the case.

"Can I look?"

Mel nodded.

"I don't know what you think you'll find. Me and the detectives went through it already."

Sterling wasn't put off by her skepticism.

"Well, what about your actual clothes?"

"What?"

Sterling pulled out a pair of shorts, jeans and a blouse. He didn't take any of her underthings out, but he did note them.

"Unless something has changed, I'm assuming you weren't coming to town for a romantic tryst." Mel's eyes widened. Her cheeks tinted to a rosy shade. "If you had, I think you would have packed some frilly numbers instead of your sensible ones."

"My sensible ones?" She laughed despite her face becoming the color of a cherry. "Sterling. Are you talking about my underwear?"

He shrugged.

"You wear the frilly, lacy things in the beginning of a relationship but the sensible, comfortable ones when *you're* comfortable." He waved his hand over her suitcase. "I only saw the comfortable ones. Though, to be honest, I always liked those better."

Sterling hadn't meant to say the last part, but it was true. Remembering her walking around the house in his T-shirt and her black cotton panties had been a sight worth seeing.

"So unless you were meeting someone here who you've already been dating awhile, I'm going to go out on a limb and say that your reasons for being here in Kelby Creek are not romantic in nature."

Mel looked like she might disagree with his guess but surprised him with another laugh. This one had some bitterness to it.

"The only long-term relationship I'm in at the moment is with an amazing boss who was kind enough not to fire me when I called her claiming amnesia and asked for a few days."

Sterling felt some relief at her answer, even though he shouldn't have.

"That's the first I've heard you talk about work," he said, spreading out the rest of her clothes on the bed. He recognized every piece but one. "What did you end up doing?"

At this, Mel seemed to tuck in on herself. Like she was timid.

Sterling felt his eyebrow raise.

"Don't tell me you went into some big corporate job or something stock-related." It was something Rider had pushed on her when they'd been dating. A directive that he had probably been hoping would lead to Mel being his accomplice.

Now she shook her head.

"I—uh—write for a home decor magazine."

Sterling felt his brow rise as high as it could but not because he was surprised at the choice. But because it had been a dream of hers since they were kids…and she seemed ashamed of it.

"Mel, that's great. Isn't it?"

She shrugged.

"It's not like I work for the great *Southern Living* magazine."

"But there can be more than one great thing out there. Do you like the work?"

This time there was no shame. Mel nodded.

"I do. It's an up-and-coming magazine, too, so I've been able to see it grow from the ground up."

There it was.

A genuine Melanie Blankenship smile.

Normally, it would have made him happy to see her truly care about something.

But, in that moment, it was a reminder.

A reminder that he'd missed out on the last five years of her life.

Or, more aptly, he'd been left out of those five years on purpose.

It sobered Sterling.

He cleared his throat and put his attention back on the clothing lined up across the bed.

"It looks like you packed for comfort and functionality instead of flashy or official. For the most part." He pointed to the dress. It was slate gray with black trim and a belt. It gave the impression of being severe among the other laidback outfits.

In other words, it didn't fit.

Mel took a step closer. Her shoulder brushed his arm. He kept his attention, however, on her expression.

It, coupled with a slight head tilt to the side, let Sterling know he was onto something before she even said a word.

"It's my interview dress," she stated simply. Mel picked it up, looking at it like it was brand-new.

"Your interview dress?"

"Yeah. I wanted to get an interview outfit that would help people take me more seriously since, well, since sometimes my height makes me look like a child." She shook the dress a little. "I put this puppy on and got my current job. My boss even told me after that I had looked almost intimidating—like I meant business and that she needed to listen to *me*. I'm pretty sure she was just joking, but that always stuck with me. It also has pockets, which is a bonus."

As she spoke, Mel slid her hands into said pockets. At the second one she made a noise.

Then she pulled out a piece of paper.

It was small and folded tight.

Sterling moved closer. He bent over a little while she opened it.

Mel smelled like lavender.

He recognized her handwriting, scrawled across the paper when it was laid flat.

"It's an address. One twenty-four Locklear Lane. I—I don't know where that is off the top of my head."

Sterling felt the tension line his shoulders. Mel looked up at him. He knew he had blue eyes, but hers were on another planet. They pierced right through him every time.

"Do you know it?"

Sterling nodded.

"It's in Kelby Creek."

Excitement filled those nearly gray eyes.

"This could be why I came back, then!"

Sterling didn't share in her joy at having a potential answer.

Especially since he knew exactly where that was.

He took the paper from her hands to make sure he was reading it right.

He was.

"I really hope it isn't."

ONE TWENTY-FOUR Locklear Lane had seen much better days. One of three houses along the street, it was on the far side of town, a cool five-minute walk from the county line. An empty lot stretched behind 124 and had weeds so grown-up that no mower would be able to deal with them without help.

Mel got out of Sterling's truck and did something really unladylike.

She swore low and plenty.

"I never knew the actual address," she said after. "I only came here once with the FBI."

Sterling walked up, a flashlight in his hand.

The rain had let up, but the sky was still dark.

It made the house in the distance feel even more ominous.

Mel glanced up at him, trying to read his face.

He had it closed down, but his words carried enough weight.

"Mark Raynard's house. Aka where our corrupt sheriff met with our corrupt mayor to hash out the details on how they'd go about kidnapping and ransoming Annie McHale."

"The very same house they believe Annie McHale was taken to after being tied up in mine."

Thunder rumbled in the distance.

It fit the mood.

"I haven't thought about this place in years. Why would I have written the address down? Why would I have wanted to come here?"

Sterling clicked on the flashlight.

"The only way to get answers is to go forward. But if we see anything suspicious, we're calling someone."

Mel nodded and followed as Sterling led them up a cracked and crumbling sidewalk. The porch wasn't in better shape.

"The bank took possession of this place a few years back," Sterling said, picking up on her thoughts. "They were supposed to renovate it and try to sell it but, for whatever reason, no one has touched it. Rumor is Annie McHale's parents actually bought it on the down low, though, since it was such a big part of the investigation. Regardless, no one has lived here since The Flood."

The front door was locked and so was the back door. The window at the back that led into the kitchen, however, was unlocked. Sterling slid it open with ease. What he couldn't do with ease was climb inside.

"Sometimes being as big as a mountain has its drawbacks," he joked.

Mel rolled her eyes and took the flashlight.

"And sometimes being as small as a preteen has its advantages."

Sterling hesitated.

Mel put her hands on her hips.

"We need some answers. If this house has to do with why I came to Kelby Creek, then I need to see inside it. Plus, it's clearly not in use. What's the worst that can happen?" Sterling gave her a long look. "Okay, not the smartest thing to say, considering," she admitted. "But I'm going inside the house whether you like it or not. So please, Mountain Man, give me a boost so we can get this over with faster."

It was Sterling's turn to roll his eyes.

"I feel like we're back at Tina Lowell's eighteenth birthday party again."

That made Mel chuckle.

"Except this time we're not trying to escape a weird, rave-like party through a bathroom window because we're too chicken to tell Tina that her college friends are freaking us out."

"I wasn't chicken," he pointed out, turning her around with his hand. Mel felt rosier for it. "I just didn't want to have to deal with watching Sam trying to be overly polite about it. He sure takes care not to hurt anyone's feelings."

Mel felt a stab to her chest at the mention of Sterling's brother. While they hadn't talked much about their time apart, or her leaving the way she did, they certainly hadn't touched once on Sam. Because, as much as she'd hated it, she hadn't just cut off Sterling. She hadn't spoken to Sam since the day she left. It hurt. That pain, that action, hadn't been brought up yet by Sterling, though, surprising her. She wondered if he'd been skirting it on purpose.

"Just unlock the door when you get in," Sterling continued, voice changing to nothing but focus. "Don't go looking around first. Okay?"

"Aye-aye, Deputy."

Sterling hoisted her up and through the opening like she was a feather. If she wasn't doing her own mental focusing, she might have taken a moment to marvel at how, after all these years, it felt good to have his hands on her.

How easy it felt to be together.

But now wasn't the time.

Mel climbed down from the countertop beneath the window and scanned her new surroundings. Unlike her house, abandoned yet still kept, this one looked like a haunted house that hadn't seen a human since the '80s.

It smelled stale and of mold, and dust coated every available surface left behind in the kitchen. When Mel was upright, she wiped the dust from the counter from her hands onto her jeans. On cue, she sneezed.

She never saw the man coming.

Chapter Seven

The baseball bat made a crack against the floor. Mel fell back with a scream. Her elbows hit the counter right before her back collided with the wood.

The man, wrapped in a dark gray hoodie that helped block his face from view, didn't bring the bat back up. Instead he took the stance of a golfer and swung it across the floor.

Right at Mel.

She scrambled to the side but felt the wind from the swing. The bat hit the cabinet next to her. It was so fast and loud Mel didn't have the time to figure out how to avoid the next hit.

The man lifted the bat high.

He never brought it back down.

The back door was off its hinges in an explosion of force and wood.

Sterling was a man enraged.

The man in the hoodie tried to redirect his swing, but Sterling wasn't having it. He caught the bat by its end, halting the swing. He refused to give it up.

Something the man must have felt in the power of the hold. He must have also decided then that a hand-to-hand with Sterling wasn't in his best interest.

The man let go of his weapon and ran deeper into the house within a second flat. Sterling gave her a quick look.

She was fine, scared but unhurt.

He didn't need to protect her now.

He needed to stop the man who'd tried to hurt her instead.

The bat hit the floor as he took off to the next room.

Mel scuttled toward the bat and scooped it up without getting to her feet. Adrenaline made her hands shake; confusion and shock kept her quiet.

That didn't last long, though. The sound of an impact came from the front of the house, followed by glass shattering.

Mel got to her feet, bat clutched in her hands. She moved to the adjoining room, heart in her throat.

The former dining room was small and empty. It gave her an easy view of the living room that came next. There she saw Sterling struggling to his feet in front of a large broken window.

She hurried forward.

"Oh my God, Sterling, are you—"

Mel saw the blood across his lip, but she didn't see the bullet that broke the last living room window next to her.

She certainly heard it, though.

Chaos, loud and violent, broke out. Sterling was yelling right along with it. He threw his weight against her. Another bullet hit somewhere above them.

They met the ground so quickly that the air pushed out of Mel's lungs. She convulsed into a coughing fit as Sterling's body became a cage around her.

The two shots turned into several more. Mel would have screamed if she could have. Instead she held on to the bat and closed her eyes tight.

When the world quieted down, her ears still rang.

"Come on!"

Two large hands wrapped around her side. Sterling moved Mel as effortlessly as he had boosted her into and through the window. One second she was on the living room floor; the next Sterling was pressing her against the hardwood of the old dining room.

"Stay down," he growled at her.

She wasn't about to do anything else.

Gunfire erupted behind them again. At least now there were two walls between them and the outside.

"How is he doing this?"

The words left Mel's mouth in a jumble of sound and fear. She meant to ask how one man was causing so much damage, but all her thoughts got tangled up together.

It didn't help when the second break of gunfire happened and Sterling pushed her across the floor, closer to the wall, his own gun now in hand.

"Stay down," he said, voice so low it seemed to thrum against her hammering heart.

"You can't—" she started, but Sterling was already out of the room.

Mel waited to hear more shots, but nothing happened.

The silence felt infinite. She was too afraid to move—to make a sound. All she had was questions and fear.

Who was the man?

Why was he here?

And why wouldn't he just leave?

Glass crunched in the living room. Mel tensed, worried their unknown gunman had come back, but it was Sterling who appeared through the doorway.

His look of determination and focus had transformed.

He looked nervous.

Which definitely wasn't good news for them.

"We need to move. Now."

His words were rushed. He hooked a hand under her elbow and lifted her up in one fell swoop.

"Did he leave?" Mel asked, stumbling against him. She kept the bat clutched against her chest.

Instead of going out through the now-broken back door, Sterling turned them to a small hallway connecting to the other side of the house. He hesitated between two open doors before shutting the one on the left.

He pushed her through the door on the right.

"The attic access is in here." He opened the bedroom's closet door, and sure enough, the access door was in the ceiling. It was one panel and a small opening.

"Why do we need the attic access?"

"Because I'm pretty sure our gunman brought friends."

The ceiling was low enough that Sterling was able to use his height to split the difference. His fingertips touched the panel, and he jumped. It moved and slid to the side.

Then he turned to Mel.

"I need you to hide."

He didn't leave room for discussion. Sterling hoisted her up and lifted her until her hands found the edge of the access. She didn't need to struggle to get herself all the way up. Sterling used his strength, and her backside, to make the trip an easy one.

The attic was dark—horror-movie dark. When Sterling passed her the baseball bat, she held on to it for dear life.

"Call the department." Sterling was still talking low. He was fast when he tossed her his phone. Thankfully, she caught it one-handed.

Even if that hand was shaking.

"Two cars pulled up. One confirmed shooter."

Mel shook her head.

"Get up here with me." But she knew already that he wasn't going to.

No.

Sterling was going to fight back to keep her safe.

Just like he always had.

Something crashed on the other side of the house.

"Close the door," he repeated.

Mel watched helplessly as he drew his gun.

She hesitated.

Then she closed the door.

The darkness consumed her.

IF HE COULD HAVE, Sterling would have made a series of different choices leading up to his current predicament.

The first decision Sterling would have corrected would have been coming to 124 Locklear Lane with Mel in tow. He simply wouldn't have.

Aside from that blaring fact, he should have called in Foster or the sheriff from the get-go. Hell, he should have called in Cole Reiner since Mel had already landed on his, and everyone else's, radar.

But Sterling hadn't.

Mainly because of what Cole had said about Mel breaking his life.

Sterling had felt defensive of the woman. And the implication that Mel might be malicious.

Even if the first part had been right on the money.

Mel *had* broken his heart. He wasn't above admitting that to himself, even if it took some nudging to admit it out loud.

But Mel breaking his life?

Well, he didn't like anyone thinking she could or would do that to someone.

Not again.

Not because of him.

So, maybe a part of Sterling had kept from telling anyone about their plans because he had wanted to prove that Mel had found herself in someone else's trouble, not her own.

Then there was also the fact that he hadn't actually thought they'd find anything.

What *could* they find there after all these years?

Regardless of any answer, it was a bad call on his part.

Another choice he would have liked to change, had he had the power, was where he'd parked his truck.

It was at the curb. Not in the drive. Had he parked it at the end of the concrete pad, running to it from the back door might not have been that far-fetched a plan.

But now it was an impossibility.

After he'd gone to the window to get a bead on the gunman, he'd seen something no one needed during a fight.

More numbers for the opposing side.

Two cars pulled up, and the gunman ran right up to one without hesitation.

Now, assuming the two new arrivals were associated with their unknown attacker, running out to the road *behind* their vehicles was an absolute no.

The last regret Sterling would have loved to correct?

He wished he'd worn his uniform, not his street clothes, and therefore had all the bells and whistles that came with it. Not just his service weapon and his badge in his back pocket.

Sterling hung inside the bedroom long enough to hear Mel slide the attic access panel door over. Whatever noise had sounded from the front of the house had turned to footsteps.

Sterling took a deep breath and steadied the weight of the gun in his hand.

One twenty-four Locklear Lane was known to most locals of Kelby Creek as the Meeting House. It had garnered the nickname thanks to the corrupt mayor and sheriff holding their clandestine dealings there. But only after The Flood had almost drowned the whole town. The homeowner eventually was suspected when the testimony of a sheriff's deputy in exchange for a lighter sentence led the FBI back to him and the house.

From there the FBI had pulled on that thread until it had connected to Rider Partridge. That was why Sterling didn't know as much about the layout of the actual house as what had happened inside its walls.

Now it was just another regret.

Especially when a man appeared at the opposite end of the hallway that Sterling didn't know even connected to the front of the house.

He was tall and looked like he was built tough. The man was in a T-shirt and jeans. His belt buckle was thick and had a shining Harley-Davidson logo on it. There was an empty holster next to it.

He wasn't the man in the hoodie but seemed as ready to rumble as their first attacker.

He had a gun in his hand.

Sterling opened his mouth to identify himself, but the man pulled his weapon up.

So Sterling shot.

Several things happened at once after that.

The man took the bullet to the shoulder, a sickening sound of impact and pain, just as he let off a round. It burrowed into the wall right next to Sterling's head. His eardrums rang, but he didn't stumble.

Sterling was ready to take a second shot, disabling the man so he could take his gun, when another absolute shock of the day did him in.

Another fighter entered the metaphorical ring through the doorway that led into the kitchen.

This time, it was a woman with blond hair, wearing a ball cap and large sunglasses, and decked out in all black. She wasn't that tall, but what she had, other than the element of surprise, was enough.

She rammed into Sterling, hands out. It caught him off guard, and he went back. He connected with the hallway wall. The woman grabbed at his arm holding the gun. The man at the other end of the walkway could have used the moment as an opening to shoot Sterling.

But he didn't.

He clutched at his wound and ran.

The woman did not.

She was fast and nimble, grabbing at his wrist while throwing a knee to his groin.

Sterling couldn't help the noise he made at the new burst of pain. He also couldn't let go of the gun.

It was Sterling's turn to check the woman. He created space between them with a hard hit of his shoulder against her arm. When that space was enough for him to bring his gun around, Sterling heard something he definitely didn't want to hear.

A man, he wasn't sure which one, yelled out.

"Where is she?"

It pulled both his attention away, as well as that of the woman he was fighting.

"Check the bedrooms," yelled another man.

Footsteps came closer to the other end of the hallway.

The woman didn't blink at the new directives being given. Instead she tried another groin kick. Sterling moved just in time to block. Then he had the room to bring his gun up.

The woman froze.

Just as the man who'd been shot came back into view.

"I'll shoot," Sterling growled, warning the man.

While also hoping they were together. If not, the only leverage Sterling had would be gone and there would be nothing stopping the other man from shooting him right then and there.

Luckily, it seemed they were together.

The man kept his gun aimed but didn't shoot.

"Dawn County Sheriff's Department," Sterling finally was able to say. "Lower your weapon."

Movement behind the woman let Sterling know that his decision to step into the small hallway was another thing to add to his regrets list.

The man in the hoodie appeared over the woman's shoulder.

He had his gun raised, too.

Sterling had no place to go.

"You lower your weapon," Hoodie demanded.

Sterling glanced at the man to his left. He wasn't moving, and without the woman, Sterling was as good as shot.

"Tell your man down there to lower his," he replied.

Hoodie shook his head.

"We both know he's keeping you in check. He stays. But she leaves."

He nodded to the woman.

Sterling could see his reflection in her too-big sunglasses.

"You can get out of this, Deputy," Hoodie added. "Let her go, drop your gun and then we go. Simple."

"Considering both of you have already shot at me, I'm not inclined—"

Sterling stopped talking the moment he heard something new.

Sirens.

Unmistakable and close.

Cruiser sirens.

Hoodie's eyes widened. His entire demeanor changed.

Sterling knew then what would happen next.

Hoodie had made a decision. One that involved blood.

Hoodie's finger moved in sync with Sterling's aim.

Neither had the time to worry about the man at the end of the hallway.

Not when they were about to shoot each other.

Those sirens got louder. Sterling braced for the impact of the other shooter. The woman tensed.

Then the ceiling exploded in a series of bangs. Like someone was hitting it with something hard.

Three people in that hallway and doorway looked up, surprised.

Sterling didn't.

Instead, he pulled the trigger.

Mac Anne Snell

Chapter Eight

Mel lifted the bat as soon as the shooting started. She stumbled back into the darkness of the attic. Her foot missed the wooden beam. She tripped trying to catch herself and landed hard on the plywood that made up the ceiling.

Had it been a newer house she might have crashed through the ceiling to the hallway below, but this house was older and built like a beast. All she did was make an awful thud noise, mixed in with her small yell of surprise.

It must have been louder than she'd thought.

A man's voice boomed beneath her.

Then a shot came through the floor.

Mel screamed, getting to her feet as light came through a hole near her.

She didn't wait to assess the damage.

Mel did her best to run back in the direction of the bedroom she'd been above.

She went the wrong way.

Her foot found air instead of wood. She nose-dived forward from her momentum.

Mel must have found the one part of the Meeting House that wasn't built to last. Whether it was water damage, the ravages of neglect or some small crack she hit just right, Mel went from falling to the floor to crashing through it.

Like a scared animal, she scrambled to grab on to something. All she managed in the end was to shield her face with one of her forearms.

Pain and several other sensations she couldn't grab on to followed her from the darkness to the light of the room below.

The leg of her jeans snagged on something just as a scream tore out of her mouth. It was enough to jolt new pain through her. It also kept her from crashing face-first into the wooden floor below. Debris from the ceiling hit the ground while she stopped and swung a few feet off the floor.

Mel's hair reached downward; her blouse went over to expose her stomach.

Through it all, Mel realized she still had the bat in one hand.

Which was good, since the person who was gawking at her from the doorway wasn't a handsome deputy she knew.

A man she hadn't seen before was clutching his shoulder with one hand and pressing into his stomach with the other. Blood had thoroughly stained his T-shirt.

Mel wasn't about to ask questions.

She tried to swing out, making a strangled sound in the process. All the motion did was start to dislodge her. Her jeans ripped. Finally she dropped the bat. The man ran. Mel tried to focus on minimizing her fall by putting her arms out, but there was no time.

Her jeans were done holding her weight. The tension keeping her in the air broke, and Mel fell straight down.

It was a good thing Sterling was faster. His arms were around her waist, stopping the fall inches from her head meeting the floor.

"I got you," he grunted.

"The man—" Mel started, but Sterling twirled her around like she was a rag doll, shaking his head.

"Trust me. He's not getting far."

Mel let herself be righted by the cowboy deputy.

"What about the other man?"

Sterling studied her. His eyes were narrowed, focused. There was blood on his lip. He was sweating and breathing hard.

The sounds of sirens and squealing tires outside filled the house.

Sterling tucked her into his side, arm around her hip and hand fastened tight.

He didn't move.

"I'm only worrying about you right now."

Mel could have gone the rest of her life without seeing the inside of the Dawn County Sheriff's Department again and been happier for it. Yet, there she was staring at its beige walls and scuffed tile floors for a second time that day.

At least now she was in an open room with windows and a coffee in hand instead of one with only a metal table and the distinct feeling of being judged.

She also wasn't waiting alone.

Sterling was in a mood, rightfully so.

He'd somehow acquired a cowboy hat she didn't recognize and a scowl she did.

He was angry and trying his damnedest to keep it from spilling out. It made the man uncharacteristically quiet. He hadn't even said much on the ride over, though that might have been because he was in some pain.

Under the fluorescent lights of the sheriff's department's meeting room, his wounds looked worse than they had fresh. His lip was busted, and there was a decent bruise ringing his left eye. Mel also suspected there was some bruising beneath his clothes, but he wasn't going to admit that to her. Not when he was like this.

Not when he thought they'd lost.

And that's what had happened, in so many ways.

They'd walked into something and had barely walked out of it.

Mel drank a long pull of her coffee.

"It would be nice if my memory would come back. Even just a little."

Sterling moved his gaze from the whiteboard at the end of the room to Mel.

A thousand-mile stare had his blue eyes trapped somewhere else.

Mel put down her cup and tried to think of something to say to get her past the feeling of discomfort and lingering fear. Something he would respond to—something that would break the barrier that had shot up around him since the attack.

That something never came to mind.

Cole Reiner, however, bustled into the room with a folder beneath his arm, papers in his hand and a pen held between his teeth.

"Sorry," he said around it. "A lot going on."

Detective Reiner dropped down into the seat at the head of the table. The papers and folder hit the table; the pen went on top.

He was red in the face, but she couldn't tell if that was from frustration or sunburn. Mel might have been a local, and she might have had a more intimate knowledge of the inner workings of what had taken place during The Flood, but Cole was largely a stranger to her. The only reason she trusted him was because Sterling did.

Sterling turned in his chair, opening his body language to the man. His voice came out gruff.

"Please tell me you got them."

Detective Reiner shook his head. Sterling cussed low.

"Our mystery blonde and the hooded gunman are in the proverbial wind," Reiner said with notable frustration. "But everyone in Dawn County, the neighboring county and the city police department are looking. We've even activated our reserve deputies. They're limited in number but highly motivated in their work." Reiner clasped his hands together and leaned over onto the table. His expression went from focused to determined, tinged with anger. "They attacked one of our own, and that's not something we take lightly. We'll find them."

Sterling nodded and rolled back his shoulders.

Mel wished she could help. Wished she had the magic answer to whom the people at that house had been, but she didn't. She didn't even know why the paper with the address had been in her dress pocket.

"What about the other man?" she piped in. "The one who was shot."

Reiner glanced at Sterling. Neither was quick to answer.

Which meant it wasn't good.

"He's in surgery," Reiner supplied after a moment. "We're still trying to identify him, since the doctors aren't confident he'll survive the night."

That should have given her some kind of relief—the man who had attacked and shot at Sterling wouldn't be able to do it again—but Mel just felt frustration.

"I still don't understand why they were even there." She balled her fist on top of the table. It was cool against her skin. "I don't understand why *we* were there. Why did I write the address down?"

It was a repeating rhetorical question that Mel didn't expect anyone to answer.

Yet Reiner perked up.

Though it didn't seem like he was waiting to tell them good news.

"That's something I wanted to talk to you about." Reiner looked directly at her. Sterling tensed in his chair. Mel's stomach joined in. Reiner produced a picture from the stack of papers beneath his hands. He didn't slide it over right away.

"Rose Simon's murder was placed at around one thirty yesterday," Reiner continued. "And it occurred somewhere other than your residence. We're still looking for the where, but now we have the how." He looked at Sterling for this answer. "The gun you got away from your attacker had bullets that matched the ones recovered from Rose. Same make and caliber. Even matching marks on the bullet left by the scraping of the old gun."

Sterling took off his cowboy hat and rubbed a hand along his jaw.

He didn't say anything. Maybe because he knew that wasn't all.

Reiner's gaze swung back to her. This time he did slide something over.

It was a picture of a car that had seen better days. The bumper was crunched, and the windshield had a crack running through it. One headlight was broken.

Mel didn't recognize it.

She said as much.

"Whose is it?"

Reiner searched her face. He must have decided what he saw was what he needed. His voice was low.

"Rose Simon's." Sterling took the picture. He shared a questioning look with Reiner before the detective nodded.

"What?" Mel asked. "What is it?"

Sterling sighed.

"This is the other car from your accident yesterday," he answered. "This is the car that hit you and ran. We found it parked outside the Kintucket Woods. Consistent damage with your vehicle."

Mel stood and reached way over to grab the picture back.

"Rose hit me?" She searched the picture with new understanding.

It did no good.

"I just don't get it," she continued. "I come back to Kelby Creek with the Meeting House address in my pocket, am run off the road by Rose Simon, who is then killed by a man I don't know before being placed in my old bedroom? Then we run into that same man at the Meeting House, plus two other people I don't know?"

Mel sat heavily back into her chair.

Tears of frustration started to prick the corners of her eyes.

"It all sounds like some kind of a bad dream," she added. "Sunday morning I was drinking coffee in my apartment, happy to finish an article about high-end patio furniture, and two days later I'm in the middle of *this*. I don't understand."

Mel fisted her hands on top of the table again.

Sterling was the first to speak, but only after he shared one more look with the detective.

Mel realized then that she was missing a piece of the story.

And she probably wasn't going to like that piece.

"I'm not so sure you're in the middle of it," Sterling started. "I actually think you're the point of it."

"What do you mean?"

Mel felt her eyebrow raise just as her stomach dropped. Sterling now looked mad.

"At the Meeting House, before you put up one hell of a distraction, the two men were looking for a woman. And it wasn't the mystery blonde." He turned in his chair so all of him was facing all of her. "I think they wanted you, and, considering how they met us with bats and gunfire, I'm pretty sure you don't want them to find you."

NIGHT CAME TO find them all exhausted. Mel chief among them, even though she wouldn't admit it.

"I'm fine," she said, unprompted, one more time.

Sterling wasn't convinced.

Even more so when they pulled up to her old house and went through the process of grabbing her things.

When they were back in his truck, she let out a breath so deep that every part of her shrank.

He hated seeing it.

"I can stay at the hotel," she said after he started the truck again. "Is it even still open? I could—"

"You can stay at my place," Sterling interrupted.

Mel turned to give him a look that he knew to be stuck between stubbornness and defiance. He shook his head at it.

"If we're right and all of these roads lead back to you, there's no way I'm letting you out of my sight until we have more answers," he said. "If you'd rather we go to a hotel or motel or just spend the night in the truck, that's fine by me. Personally, I'd rather go somewhere I know has a fridge filled with leftovers and that also happens to have great water pressure for a much-needed shower."

Mel's blue eyes searched him for a moment.

Then he knew she'd given in.

"Okay."

Sterling was glad to leave Rider Partridge's mansion and head off across Kelby Creek into the darkness if it meant he was finally going home. Though, when he turned on the street that led up to the house, Mel didn't seem to feel the same.

"Wait."

She sat straighter in her seat as Sterling pulled into the driveway.

"Listen, I have a guest bedroom, and even though it's small it'll work just fine," he defended. "I won't even bother you once we get in. Just give you a quick tour and you can have the run of the house."

Mel shook her head.

"No. That's not what I meant." She went back to looking at the house. The garage light was on, and he could see the light over the sink in the kitchen he always left on. "I— This is where you live."

It wasn't a question, but she was surprised.

"Yeah. For a few months now."

Something was still stumping her.

"You moved. I mean, from the house on Tally Street. I—I didn't know that."

Sterling felt the constant motion of the last day and a half finally slow. Then the weight of the time spent away from each other settle.

Not only had Mel left him in the dust, she hadn't even bothered to look back to see how it had settled.

"Yeah. I moved five years ago."

He could see it in her face despite the low light.

She'd really had no idea.

Sterling tried to keep his emotions in check, but he heard the hardness in his voice when he added on one last bit before getting out of the truck.

"You weren't the only one who left Kelby Creek behind. The only difference is, I chose to come back."

Chapter Nine

The shower was great.

Still, Mel felt like sobbing into the hot water. The only reason she didn't had to do with the man walking around the kitchen, cooking for them.

For her.

Despite everything.

Despite her leaving.

Mel felt guilt unlike any other pulse around her heart. In all this time, she'd never checked up on Sterling—she hadn't wanted to risk it. She'd just pictured him doing what he always had.

Waking up in his bedroom on Tally Street, making coffee in his flannel pajama pants by a sink with a chip in it, getting ready and heading out to the department for another day on the job. Then, maybe after, going to the gym or a bar or his father's or Sam's house.

Just living his life. Happy and healthy and in no way altered by her.

Mel let the hot water beat against her back.

He'd moved. Sterling had left Kelby Creek, and she hadn't known.

And when *he* had realized that?

Mel couldn't shake the way his face had shut down.

There wasn't a whole lot in the world Mel felt she was

good at, but of the few, hurting Sterling Costner was up there in the top five.

Mel finished the shower while trying to keep her thoughts on neutral ground. She wrapped her hair up in a wet, messy bun. Her tired legs slid through the only sleep shorts she'd brought and she settled into an old high school T-shirt that, miraculously, still fit.

The house smelled like bacon, and Mel followed the scent all the way to the kitchen. A man stood in front of the stove.

But it wasn't Sterling.

Adrenaline shot through Mel's body with such ferocity that she froze in place.

Then, within the next breath, the details started to filter in.

Not as tall as Sterling, but with the same dark hair. A smaller frame and slimmer build, with more freckles across his skin and a small scar on his forearm where he'd crashed his bike one day when they were riding across the bridge out near the creek.

The man turned, spatula in hand, and Mel saw the face of the only other man she'd loved in Kelby Creek smiling at her.

"Sam!"

Mel melted as Sam Costner closed the space between them and wrapped her in a hug. All the guilt of her leaving and cutting off all contact with everyone hit her like a brick again. That brick was added to the one she'd already had thrown at her because of Sterling and was topped by the trauma of the last two days.

It was too much for Mel.

So she cried into Sam's shoulder like she had the day Rod Johnson stood her up for prom and the day she'd found out her mother was moving away.

Sam let her, because Sam had always been one of the best people she knew.

And Sterling understood all that.

Mel could hear him moving around the kitchen behind them. When she finally pulled away, wiping at her face, she saw three plates of breakfast food on the table.

"Sam, want a beer?" Sterling asked, as if everything was normal.

Sam was game.

"Only if it's the good kind. Last time you tried to cheat me with the cheap stuff."

He smiled down at Mel and gave her a little nod.

She returned it, sniffling.

"Mel?" Sterling turned to her. Eyes as blue as they had been the first day they'd met. He didn't smile, but he wasn't looking at her like she'd just broken him. "The *good* beer, OJ or some water?"

Mel's smile grew. It was genuine.

"Who am I to turn down some good beer?"

THE FOOD WAS GOOD. The company was better.

Mel finally took it easy on herself and let the guilt and shame take a break while she enjoyed being with the Costner boys. Even though the years had stretched between them, Sam was still more or less the same. Though he did look more tired than usual. Something he explained by way of pulling out his phone to show her a picture.

"And *this* is my daughter, Linney."

Mel scooped up the phone and absolutely cooed at the adorable red-haired baby covered in freckles on the screen.

"You have a *daughter*?" she repeated with a squeal attached. "Oh, Sam! She's so precious!"

Sam laughed.

"If you ask Robbie his feelings on her now that she's

going through sleep regression, he'll tell you she's pre-
ciously the worst."

Mel scoffed.

"One thing I remember clearly about Robbie was his
undying desire to have a bunch of kids. I'm sure he does
almost nothing but dote on her. You, too."

Sterling pointed his beer bottle at her.

"You got that right. Don't let Sam *or* Robbie fool you.
That is exactly how they both are," he said. "Doting and
overprotective. Dad's been trying to take Linney for one
night a week to give them a break, and the best he's been
able to do was convince them to let him come over and
watch her every Wednesday. Even then I'm pretty sure they
watch him on the baby monitor."

Mel felt her heart squeeze at that. Callahan Costner was
a good, wholesome man who loved his family completely.
He'd never once wavered in understanding, support and
compassion for them or for the people they cared about.
Which, at one point, had included her.

Sam shrugged.

"Okay, listen. Linney might be a poop monster sometimes, but she's our poop monster, and that means a whole
lot. Complaining and loving all mixed together."

They all laughed.

Mel wished they could stay in this feel-good bubble all
night. She knew they couldn't. The conversation finally
took a turn for the dark. She was glad she at least had a
good beer for it.

Sam looked at his brother.

"Speaking of Dad, he heard about Rose through the
grapevine, which I think is probably the main reason he
called."

"Let me guess—he wouldn't say who was at the head
of that grapevine?"

Sam shook his head.

"Mr. Kessler isn't one to gossip much, but he's a part of the rotary club, and they gab more than most if given the right piece of news. Rose Simon was the talk of the town back in the day, and her being back and being killed... Well, not many are going to pass up talking about that."

"What exactly did he tell Dad?"

Sterling's brow lined with tension. Mel's stomach tightened.

"Just that he'd heard she was killed...at Rider Partridge's old house." Sterling took a quick pull of his beer. Sam shifted his gaze to Mel. "From what I was able to gather, no one knows you were in the house, though."

Mel wasn't surprised that Sam was already caught up on what had really happened. Once again, the Costner boys had always been close. She *was* surprised that it hadn't leaked out that Mel had been on scene with Rose's body. The sheriff's department had become a lot better at keeping things under wraps since the last time she'd been in Kelby Creek.

"But people do know I'm in town," Mel said. "Jonathan let me know that much when he came to see me in the hospital."

Mel could tell Sam didn't want to nod, but he did.

"Your name was already popping up before the news about Rose broke."

Sterling set his bottle down a little too hard on the table. It made both of their heads snap to attention. He didn't apologize.

"Rose wasn't killed at that house," he almost growled. "She was moved after the fact. If people stopped long enough to get their facts straight, this whole town would be better off. And don't get me started on Jonathan Partridge. He had no right to show up at the hospital and try to intimidate you to leave town. If anyone should be intimidated to leave anyplace, it's him."

Sam agreed with a hearty nod.

Mel opened her mouth to third the notion when a thought popped into her head and she paused.

Sterling's brow scrunched at the sight.

"What is it?"

"The house," Mel said simply.

"What about it?" asked Sam.

Mel's heartbeat started to speed up a little. She put her napkin down and went to the guest bedroom to get her phone off the charger. She hurried back. Sterling had his chair pushed out, waiting.

"It has a security system where you can't open any of the doors or main-floor windows without tripping the alarm. Once you do that, you have thirty seconds to put in a code before the sirens start going off and the police get dispatched."

"You disarmed it when I dropped you off after the hospital on Monday night," Sterling added.

Mel nodded.

"And now we know that poor Rose was already in the bedroom. Which means—"

She opened the security company's app on her phone and logged in. Sterling was already on the same wavelength.

"Which means someone had to turn it off *and* set it before then."

Mel searched for the records of use.

Sam wasn't convinced.

"Isn't this something you already told the detectives about? Surely they would have asked to see who had access," he said.

Mel nodded.

"This is what I showed Detective Lovett." Mel found what she was looking for and turned the phone around to show the men. Both leaned forward, brows drawn together in attention. "These are the time stamps for when the keypad was accessed and the alarm was turned off and on again. The top line is me turning off the system to let everyone in after I found Rose, the one before that was me turning it on after you dropped me off and the one before that was me turning it off right when we showed up." Mel ran her finger down to the next time stamp. "This was a week ago when the cleaning crew came in and turned it off and on again. Which is what I told Detective Lovett. Now, see, the security system is hardwired. It doesn't have a battery backup. It was an extra feature I decided not to pay for since, honestly, I was hoping the house would just kind of be forgotten by everyone."

Mel turned her phone back around and went to a different app.

"Which means the only thing that can turn the security system off without tripping the alarm is when the power goes off. Instead I get an email alert letting me know when the power went off and when it came back on. Neither gets logged."

She found what she was looking for, buried beneath several other emails. It was unopened.

Mel clicked it and turned the phone back around.

"The system went off-line Monday at 1:23 p.m."

"And according to this didn't come back on until 2:32 p.m.," Sam read.

Mel looked at Sterling. This time he pulled out his phone.

"Your security system was off for more than an hour," he said.

"And considering there were no storms in the area and
I was in the hospital—"

"There's a good chance the killer cut your power, probably flipped your breaker, to move Rose's body inside,"
Sam finished.

Mel handed her phone over while Sterling scrolled
through his, looking for a number.

"Does this help?" she asked.

Sterling stood up. Mel could already hear the phone
ringing as the call went through.

He nodded, expression severe.

"Rose's estimated time of death was around one thirty.
If she was killed outside the house, then that means she
probably wasn't killed that far from it. You may have just
narrowed down the search for where she was murdered
by more than half."

SAM LEFT AROUND TEN. Mel said good night right after. Sterling was in his own bed by eleven.

When midnight rolled around, he was back on his feet
and trudging through the hallway to the kitchen for some
water. He wasn't exactly thirsty, but it was something to
do to occupy his mind other than just lying in bed, staring up at the ceiling.

Apparently, he wasn't the only one with the same plan.

The kitchen light over the sink was on. Mel stood beneath it. There was a glass of water in her hands and a far-
away look on her face as she stared out the window.

For a moment, Sterling thought about not disturbing her.
She looked too peaceful.

A far cry from earlier when she'd finally broken down
on his brother's shoulder.

Sterling knew then that he should have brought Sam
into the fold earlier. Seeing the two best friends reconnect

without a word exchanged between them had been a silent reminder that Sterling hadn't been the only one to lose her.

Mel jumped. She must have seen him out of the corner of her eye.

Her hand went to her chest in surprise.

Sterling walked the rest of the way in.

"Sorry," he said. "I was debating whether or not to disturb you. I came in here for a drink."

Mel patted her chest and shook her head.

"No, it's fine. I *am* in your house just gazing out your windows when I should be sleeping." She lifted her own glass. "I also needed an excuse to stop tossing and turning in bed."

Sterling gave her a genuine laugh.

"Great, troubled minds."

He reached over her for a glass and went to the refrigerator for some water. When he was done, Mel had found a new spot leaning against the oven door. Sterling mirrored her stance and leaned against the counter opposite her.

For another long moment, Sterling wanted to just look at her. To wonder about her without that true-blue gaze searching him.

Without the weight of questions pressing against both of them.

But it was Mel who dived headfirst into several conversations he was ready to avoid until the morning.

"Has Detective Lovett gotten back to you yet?"

Sterling shook his head.

"No, but he said the information would definitely help. He also said he'd keep me updated."

Mel sighed again.

And then continued.

"You know, despite the circumstances, it was nice to

see Sam." A small smile pulled up the corner of her lips. "Thank you for calling him in."

Sterling took a sip of water and shrugged.

"Who said it was for you two? Maybe I just wanted someone to come over and complain about some of my beer."

That smile grew.

"Either way, it was nice. So was the beer."

Sterling did a little bow.

"I try."

Mel took a long pull of her water. She didn't look away when she was done. Instead her smile fell. She held his stare with a viselike intensity.

"I went to Huntsville."

She let her words linger for a second. Then followed them up quickly.

"After I left, I went and stayed in a hotel in Huntsville for a week," she continued. "Then I got a job as a barista at a coffee shop. I worked there for six months until a reporter found me. He was trying to make a name for himself and wouldn't leave me alone. It brought everything back up, so I left. A coworker felt bad for me and got me a job at a coffee place with her friend in Birmingham. I lived with a woman named Deirdre and her son for a little bit, then another barista for a bit more, and then met my current boss one day at work.

"I was manager of the coffee shop for a while and wrote articles for my current boss on the side until she offered me a full-time spot as a writer and technical designer. I got my own apartment in a nice neighborhood two years ago and have lived alone since. It's a small one-bedroom, but I can walk to the store if I want, and I also have a spot in the parking garage for my car, which is nice."

Mel hesitated briefly but her words stayed strong. "I

dated one man I met at the coffee shop for five months before I broke it off, have been on three other separate dates that ended in disaster and thought about touring Europe alone until I realized just how much money I didn't have. Dad still doesn't talk to me, but Mom has been calling me on my birthday and Christmas, which is progress for her. I got a tattoo on my right hip last year and finally watched *Game of Thrones* and have been thinking about adopting a dog."

Mel put her glass down on the counter behind her and took a step forward. There was still a foot between them. Sterling didn't move.

"And I realized tonight that I have no right in the world to ask you about your life without at least offering up what I've been doing with mine, so that's why I just rambled to you. Because I *do* want to know about yours."

Mel snapped her mouth shut. True to her word, she'd said her piece.

Now she was looking at Sterling, waiting to see if he'd say his.

But in the low light of his kitchen, staring at a woman he would have been married to for five years now had he had his way, he couldn't bring himself to tell her the truth about his time spent away from Kelby Creek.

She must have seen it in his expression.

Mel did a little nod.

"That's okay," she said. "You don't owe me anything. Honestly. I'll just see you in the morning, okay? Good night."

Mel moved faster than a blink. She left Sterling standing there feeling every way a man could feel.

It wasn't until he heard her bedroom door shut that he poured his water out with a low curse.

He went to bed right after.

Chapter Ten

The town's sirens woke Sterling up.

But if they hadn't, his phone blaring would have.

Their tornado watch had turned into a tornado warning.

Sterling was out of bed in an instant. He swiped his phone, unlocked it with his thumb and was at the guest bedroom door all in one quick movement. There wasn't time for niceties or privacy. Sterling opened the door already calling Mel's name.

She might have been gone from their neck of the woods for five years but Mel had grown up in South Alabama. She knew the drill, too. Her hair was framing a face fresh from sleep, but she was standing at the door, her own phone in hand. The only difference was she'd been quicker on the draw and had her Facebook app open. Sterling recognized their local weatherman, Todd Decker, at the helm. He was talking fast, but Sterling listened to Mel.

"He said it was spotted near Wynn Road heading west. Isn't that near here?"

Sterling didn't waste time. He slipped his hand around Mel's and pulled her along to the hall closet. It was small and lined with flimsy wooden shelves filled with towels, sheets and extra blankets.

Sterling grabbed the shelves as quickly as he could and pulled them out. Mel stood back while he made up the room just as the power cut out. Her phone stayed on, the only source of light. Todd Decker had his voice raised and was pointing to the map. Sterling didn't hear the specifics, but "Seek shelter immediately" was enough.

He kicked the discarded shelves and linens aside and pushed Mel into the slightly bigger space. Sterling had every intention of staying outside the door, but Mel hooked his arm.

"Come on!"

The wind outside was hellish against the house. Sterling folded around Mel to make the small space work and shut the door. Todd Decker's voice fell somewhere to the ground.

"Where's Wynn Road?" Mel asked against his chest.

Sterling hated to tell her the truth.

"We're on Wynn."

It was like the tornado was waiting for him to drop the punchline. No sooner than the words were out of his mouth did the world around them get loud. Todd became a murmur in the dark. All Sterling could do was put his head over Mel's and became a cage around her. Mel only strengthened the hold by pressing into him, arms circling his waist.

All they could do after that was wait.

And wait.

And wait..

HE MADE IT to the house in time to watch the weather report on the tornado tearing through Kelby Creek. He wasn't the only one who was plugged into the news.

"It's saying it dragged from John Riley Drive, past Wynn Road, before popping up around Hartley," his companion reported. "Wynn is where that Costner guy is, isn't it?"

He balled his fists. He was seeing red.

"Yeah. That's where *that Costner guy* is. But, more importantly, that's where Melanie is."

The other man rubbed his chin and shook his head. He was still looking at the live report streaming from his phone.

"They're saying there's a few houses that got damaged and a lot of trees down, but no one can say if anyone's dead yet."

"That would be just fine luck. After all of this time, after all of this effort, and Melanie would up and get killed by a tornado of all things."

He swore deep, low and with a ferocity that caught the other man's attention. He lowered his phone and tried to look hopeful.

"We can still do this if she's gone. We don't *need* her. If anything, this might be a blessing in disguise, you know? The last two times we've tried to grab her, she's managed to get away. I mean, because of her and her friend, Luis is probably brain-dead in the hospital." He tried to motion to himself. It made him look even more pathetic lying there hooked up to an IV on the makeshift bed. "Look at me. If you didn't have your doc connection, I'd be just as bad or worse off. Maybe this is God's way of giving you one."

He didn't mean to lose his temper, but one moment he was on the other side of the room at his desk and in the next he had his finger pressed on the man's bandage at his shoulder.

The man roared in pain but knew not to try and fight back.

"*You* aren't a part of this. *You* are here only because I need you now. *You* don't get to say one way or the other what importance Melanie has to my plan. *You* certainly don't get to say her death would be a blessing." He applied a quick spike of pressure. The other man groaned. "And while we're on the subject of Luis, if I had to pick between you and him, you'd be the one in a coma in the hospital and Luis would be right here, squirming under my finger. Because while he might have dropped the ball, he at least remembered not to disobey my *one* rule. Do you remember what that one rule was?"

The other man was sweating now.

His face was pinched.

Still, he answered.

"Under no circumstance do we kill Melanie Blankenship."

He lowered his face to the paling man.

"*Under no circumstance do we kill Melanie Blankenship,*" he repeated. "And yet, you shot at her. Several times. Is that following the rule?"

"No," the man bit out. "I'm sorry."

"I don't care about your apology, but since I owed your father, I saved your life." He finally lifted his finger and stood tall. "I'm considering that debt paid. If you disobey me or so much as wish death on Melanie again, I'll kill you myself. Understood?"

The other man was quick to nod.

"Good. Now, since you can't go be useful and our favorite lawyer is busy, I suppose I need to be the one to leave this charming hideout." He made sure the buttons of his shirt were in line with his belt buckle and nodded. "I need to see if my ex-wife is dead or not."

Mel OPENED HER eyes against the warmth of Sterling's bare chest. She could feel his heartbeat against her cheek. His arms were wrapped around her and not budging an inch.

And, for a second, she thought it would be nice to stay like that.

Yet the quiet world around them was too loud.

"Is it over?" she asked, her voice as wobbly as her legs. Mel had been through two tornado scares in her life and was lucky enough to walk away unharmed and with no damage. She hoped this was her third time.

Sterling was the first to move.

"I think so."

With one hand he pulled his cell phone from his pocket and turned on the flashlight. That light directed down at her.

"Are you okay?" he asked.

"I think I have more adrenaline in me than when I was dangling in the air after falling through the ceiling at the Meeting House, but, other than that, yeah, I'm okay."

Even though she answered, Sterling brought his hand to the side of her face. His palm was as warm as his chest. It cupped her cheek and tilted her chin up higher so he could look into her eyes. He rubbed his thumb along her cheekbone.

Mel felt several butterflies dislodge at the gesture.

Those butterflies were thrown directly into the storm of fear still raging within her.

Sterling searched her face and nodded.

Then he let her go completely and opened the closet door.

Mel felt an insurmountable amount of relief that the hallway was still there.

Sterling was less enthused.

"If a tree didn't hit this house, I'll give you everything in my bank account."

He shone his phone's flashlight down the hallway toward the front of the house. The power was still off, but the structure looked intact. Mel turned her light on and shone it toward the back half.

There was nothing out of the ordinary there.

Mel walked slowly to the guest bedroom door and peeked inside. There were mud and leaves stuck to the outside of the window but no damage. She turned around and went to Sterling's room.

Mel sucked in a breath.

Sterling was at her side with his light on.

The two windows on either side of his bed were shattered. Giant limbs stuck through where they should have been.

Sterling's light tilted up.

"I had a feeling the maple would fall. At least it didn't come through the roof. It must have caught on the smaller tree that was right next to it." He started to go to the window.

Mel grabbed his hand and squeezed.

"You're barefoot and there's glass everywhere. Hold on."

She let go and hurried to the guest bedroom. She jumped into her tennis shoes and was back in the master bedroom looking for his shoes. Mel found them on the other side of the bed. She paused by the dresser and pulled out a pair of socks and an undershirt and then went to a lower drawer for some jeans. Sterling might have moved, but how he organized his clothes hadn't changed.

"I know you're about to go a mile a minute, and there's no point doing it in your nightclothes," Mel explained, bringing them back and crunching over broken glass in the process. "Go get changed in the hallway so you don't hurt yourself."

Sterling took the clothes with a nod, but his cell phone started ringing.

Mel saw by the caller ID that it was Sam.

She took his phone and shooed him.

"Go put that stuff on. I'll talk to him."

Sterling didn't complain.

"Yes, ma'am."

Sam was talking non-stop as soon as Mel answered the phone.

"We're good," she assured him. "It looks like a tree fell against the house, though. Not enough to cave anything in, but definitely enough to blow his bedroom windows out and damage the siding."

Mel walked across the broken glass again carefully and tried to look out past the branches. It was still raining and way too dark.

"That was the last storm front supposed to come through," Sam said. "But the rain might pick up a little before it's all gone. I'll call Dad and we'll be over in ten. Tell Sterling we'll bring the chain saw, but I think he has the plastic sheeting in the garage that we can use to cover the openings."

Mel's gaze went over to the bed, following a long limb that had twisted and jabbed downward.

Right into the bed.

Her stomach went cold at that.

What if Sterling hadn't gotten up when he had?

"Tell him to bring lanterns." Sterling was behind her. He'd dressed in record time. "I have a flashlight, but I'd rather have something to put down in case the power doesn't come back soon."

Mel opened her mouth to relay the request, but Sam had already heard it.

"Got it," he said. "We'll be over in ten."

Sam ended the call.

"They're bringing the chain saw, but you have the plastic sheeting in your garage." Mel's voice was flat to her ears. She was still looking at the limb. "We're out of danger for another tornado, but Sam said we're still going to get a little rain."

Mel wasn't looking at Sterling, but she felt him stand next to her, as easy as breathing.

She felt a different kind of weight pressing into her chest. All she could see was the punctured sheets and mattress. Leaving him had been hard. Losing him? That feeling burned itself through her heart with such heat her eyes started to water.

Sterling couldn't see that.

Not in the low light, not with her facing away.

Instead, he was trying to find some humor.

"Sam'll be a grinning fool to hear that him staying on me all these years to keep my phone charging at night finally paid off," he said. "That phone alert was no joke. I didn't even know my phone could be that loud."

Sirens sounded in the distance. First responders.

Sterling's phone started to ring.

"I was wondering when Marigold would reach out. I'm sure Brutus will be next."

He started to turn away, but Mel was faster.

She grabbed his hand to get his attention. When he faced her and she knew she had it, Mel did the only thing that felt right.

She pushed up on the tips of her toes and pressed her lips against his with a world of gratitude.

Sterling didn't get a chance to react before she ended the kiss.

"I sure am glad that you're a light sleeper, Sterling Costner," she said with feeling.

Mel slid her hand down to his chest and patted it twice. She sniffled but didn't linger. Instead she let the man go and headed to the door while glass crunched underneath her shoes.

"I'll go get a broom."

Chapter Eleven

Ms. Martha was out in her housecoat. Marigold was in a dress and with a man wearing a casual suit. The Costner men were dressed in rain jackets, jeans and water boots. Deputy Park and half the department were in uniform.

Everyone was helping with something.

Sterling had been fortunate in the fact that the lone tree to fall in his yard had only damaged the side of his house and not his roof, like Mr. Sinclair across the street—he had a tree splitting his one-story and his neighbor's car that had started in the driveway had ended up in the side yard, upside down and crunched.

There was more damage up the road where the tornado had actually touched down and run long, but, as best as they could tell half an hour into everyone trying to assess the damage, no one had been killed. A few, however, were taken to the hospital for cuts or bruises. Marigold's date said he'd heard that an elderly man two roads over had a broken arm from where a cabinet had fallen on him. Not the best news, but a lot better than it could have been.

Sterling repeated that sentiment when the sheriff arrived.

Brutus clapped hands with Sterling's father, asked quickly about Sam's daughter and had a hand on Sterling's back as he surveyed the tree both were about to start cutting away from the house.

"I hate when they hit at night," Brutus said with a deep sigh. "They already have the audacity to be wild, unpredictable devils, and then they go and do it when no one can see a damn thing."

"Night tornados definitely aren't my favorite," Sterling agreed.

Brutus nodded. The power was still off, but Sam had pulled through with several battery-powered lanterns. He'd never been a fan of the dark, so he always made sure to be prepared for it. Something Sterling was going to have to double down on in the future.

"I heard Melanie's here. She okay, too?"

Sterling was glad the dark probably hid the fact that he tensed.

Not so much because Brutus was talking about Mel, but because he still was partially processing what had happened.

Sleep. Tornado. Mel kissing him.

A man could only handle so much at one time.

"She's good. Was already up and ready when it was time to go into the hall closet. She took over cleaning up the mess in the house. Even was smart enough to start moving some of my things to another room so they wouldn't get ruined."

Brutus nodded again.

"That's good."

He went quiet for a bit. Sterling gave him a long look.

"If you want to say something but are trying to find a way to get it out, I'd prefer the direct approach," Sterling said. "I can tell something's bothering you."

If Brutus had been wearing his cowboy hat, Sterling was sure he would have taken it off and placed it on his chest.

Like it was a barrier that could keep him protected from the world around them.

His head was hat-free, though, and he kept his words frank.

"The reason I came by wasn't just to check on you," Brutus started. "I came because Cole found a lead that might just be what we've been waiting for."

Sterling turned so his back was to the house. He was ready.

"What is it?"

Brutus lowered his voice. No one was around them.

"Rose's car was spotted at a gas station the morning of her death. She was in a heated conversation with a man, and they both left in a visible huff. We couldn't hear what they were saying, but it was easy to see the man was Jonathan Partridge." Brutus held up his hand to stop Sterling from reacting prematurely. "Foster is already trying to run him down and, I have to say, it could be nothing, but—"

"But it would a damned coincidence that Jonathan Partridge fought with the late Rose Simon the morning of her murder and on the same day that Mel comes to town and is attacked," Sterling interrupted. He was heated and only getting hotter. "And we all know his feelings for Mel are nothing but hate. Especially after the fire."

Brutus kept his hand up to slow Sterling down.

"I'm not here to say that he isn't involved, or even behind whatever this is," Brutus said. "I'm here to tell you that, until we find Jonathan for some questioning, you sound the red alert if you see him. That goes double for Melanie. Her run-in with him in her hospital room should be the last time she's alone with him until we get this all figured out."

Sterling was huffing now. He nodded.

"What about the gunman in the hospital? Any ID on him yet?"

Brutus shook his head.

"He's in a coma, but nothing is popping on our databases. Foster's been on it, though. I reckon it won't be long."

"I guess they're still looking for where Rose was killed, too, huh?"

This time Brutus nodded.

Sterling made an impolite noise.

The sheriff didn't seem to mind. If anything, he sympathized.

"You know how these things work half the time," he said. "We go from knowing a few things to learning a lot all at once. When it rains, it pours. Pardon the phrase." He nodded to the sky. It had stopped raining, but it definitely had been pouring.

Sterling grit his teeth.

"It's the other half that has me worried," he admitted after a moment.

"The other half?"

Sterling sighed.

"The other times where we only ever know a few things, they never make sense and we're stuck with more questions than answers." He rubbed his jaw, then turned back to face his house at the sheriff's shoulder. "I don't know what's going on, and I can't help if I don't know what's going on."

Brutus clapped him on the back. When he spoke again, his voice had gone from gruff to a slightly softer gruffness.

"When I took this job—the second time—I was so frustrated that I couldn't fix everything wrong and bad about what had happened on my first day. That stress came around at the end of my first week. Followed me to the end of my first month, and near about the end of my first year, my wife sat me down and said something that sounded ridiculous. But boy, I tell you what, it's done wonders for me since."

Sterling faced the older man, genuinely curious.

Brutus's smile was easy to see despite the dark.

"'You can only ever kiss the person right in front of you.'" That smile of his grew into a grin. Sterling felt his eyebrow raise. Brutus laughed. It was genuine. Then he grew serious within the span of a breath. "You can only control so much in this life, Sterling. That goes double for this line of work. Beating yourself up or running yourself ragged to solve everything all at once isn't going to do anyone any good."

"Because you can only kiss the person right in front of you," Sterling repeated.

Brutus tipped his head down as if he was wearing an invisible cowboy hat.

Sterling thought a moment on that.

Then he was smiling, too.

But not because of Mrs. Chamblin's weirdly appropriate piece of advice.

No.

Sterling was looking at his house and thinking about a real kiss.

And a real woman he'd like to share another one with.

Brutus might or might not have picked up on that fact. He cleared his throat and put his thumbs through his belt loops.

"Well, I've got to head on out. I'm glad you're okay, son."

A thud sounded, and the chain sawing stopped. They shook hands, and thoughts of kissing went to the back burner as Sterling hurried to see what his father and Sam had done. He didn't see the sheriff drive away, and he didn't see when Marigold's date drove up with his truck and more tools to help secure the side of Sterling's house. He also didn't see, though he heard, when a few people from up the road came to talk to his father, who was taking a break and talking about the damage everyone had sustained. Sterling also didn't see Mel for a bit, mostly because she said she was focused on moving more of his things so they didn't take on any more water.

And maybe he was using his own focus as an excuse to keep his distance.

Because, as much as he shouldn't, he wanted to press his lips to hers, feel her body against his and forget about the last five years for a while.

So he did the work outside and gave her space inside, and of all the things he didn't see in the darkness, he sure hadn't seen the man across the street.

Watching.

Waiting.

Ready.

THE GLASS CAME up without much fuss. The tree limbs penetrating the bed were a lot trickier. Mel hated looking at the twisting, gnarled things making holes in the mattress through a torn blanket and sheets. She was stuck in a loop of what-if for a man she'd left in the dust.

It was driving her crazy.

When the Costner men finally came in to saw away the branches and tarp up the window, she could have cried with distracted relief, because when they went back outside to deal with the bulk of the tree, it left Mel with a new job.

She stripped Sterling's mattress, inspecting the holes with a quick eye, and put all the linens in a garbage bag. Apart from the gashes, the mattress itself wasn't wet, so she decided to cover the nasty reminders and went to the closet she'd been hiding in hours before. She went through the motions of straightening the closet up, taking out new sheets, and was walking back to the bedroom with her small lantern in one hand and a bundle in the other when something caught the corner of her eye.

In a plastic tub she'd filled with things from the top of Sterling's dresser and nightstand, Mel saw that the wooden box his grandfather had given him had shifted open. Had it been anything else, she wouldn't have put everything down to fix it, but it was his trinket box. A family tradition among the Costner men, a trinket box was handmade by a Costner and given to a Costner. Ray had one from his grandfather, Sam had one from his father and Sterling had said many times he couldn't wait to make one for his son or grandson. It was just something the family did.

They made a box for important things, and they gave that box to someone important to them.

It had always been a lovely notion to Mel, especially since she wasn't close with her parents.

So she bent down and picked the box up to make more room for it.

The lid, already open, slid off.

Mel scrambled to catch it before it hit the floor. She made another noise when she was successful.

Then she looked down at the now-open box.

And froze.

The box itself wasn't large but was big enough to hold a few items. There was a bolo that Sterling's uncle had given him from their trip to Texas when he was a teen, a coin made of foil that Sam had made him for his birthday when he was ten, an old picture of his parents when they'd first started dating, and a ring.

Mel grabbed the lantern and held it down to get a better look.

A thin gold band with a single diamond.

It was beautiful.

She'd also never seen it before.

Mel looked around. She could still hear people working outside.

It wouldn't hurt to hold the ring, would it?

Mel picked it up with slightly shaking hands. She didn't know why. It wasn't like it was hers.

Still, she couldn't deny it was exactly what she would have wanted in a ring. There was a pure beauty to something so simple.

A deep sadness shook within her.

Was there someone in Sterling's life whom he wanted to give it to?

The fact that she didn't know hurt almost as much as if she'd been told there was.

Mel shook her head at herself.

Sadness or not, she did something she shouldn't have.

She put it on.

The fit was perfect.

Her heart fluttered.

When someone cleared their throat behind her, that fluttering turned to heat in her cheeks.

She whirled around, already trying to think of an excuse as to why her nosiness had turned into a ring on her finger.

But it wasn't Sterling behind her.

It wasn't a Costner or a neighbor. It wasn't even a stranger.

No.

It was a nightmare in a suit.

"I gave you a ring once. It was a lot bigger than that." Rider Partridge was grinning. "And we saw how that turned out, now didn't we?"

Chapter Twelve

Mel thought she was dreaming. She had to be, right?

If she was, then Dream Her knew instantly that she was in trouble. There were just no two ways about it.

She was sweating something awful the moment she opened her eyes. The fabric of her blouse was sticking to her skin with a slickness that sent a shiver through her. Her hair wasn't faring any better. It was adhered to her forehead like someone had slapped paste on her. She tried to focus on what was going on and found nothing but the easy details around her.

Light poured through windows without curtains in a room that was as unfamiliar as they came. She was on the hard floor, lying on her back. No one else was in a room except for a woman who was also lying on the floor.

Next to Mel.

With eyes closed.

Mel struggled to get up but found her movements sluggish. Every alarm bell in her mind was blaring. It was the only reason she didn't make a noise. She hadn't been awake long enough to determine if she was in immediate danger. Although it wasn't like she'd just woken from a nice slumber.

Regaining consciousness was more of what fit the bill. Just like she had in the ambulance after the car accident.

She *had* to be dreaming, right?

Mel racked her brain quickly for her last memory.

Just like after the accident, there wasn't a lot to grab.

Mel looked at the woman.

She wasn't moving, and neither was anyone else in the vicinity. Mel took a moment to check herself. The scab from her head injury in the crash was still closed. She was wearing her own clothes but no shoes. Her head hurt, too, but not in a way that she expected. It felt fuzzy. Weird. Otherwise, physically, she seemed okay.

Mel wasn't about to sit still and wait for answers to come to her so she stood, slowly.

The cabin was not unlike other fishing cabins that she'd visited in the South. You could only live so long in a place called Kelby Creek before you actually fished in the creek. This cabin, unlike one you might find in the mountains that was made of charming logs and wood galore, was more function than flair. She was in the main living space with furniture that looked older than her thirty years and a kitchenette in the corner whose heyday had probably been when it was first built. It was also clearly used. There were beer cans littering the surfaces, crushed and tops popped, and the distinct smell of fish in the air. Probably cleaned and cooked right there in the room when there was a catch.

Two doors ran across the back wall, and one was opened to show a bathroom. The other one was closed.

It had a metal clasp at the top with a padlock attached.

Mel felt another shiver go through her at the sight.

The last door was the one behind her. It led outside. Through the window next to it, Mel saw grass, dirt and a dock that hung over water in the distance.

It had to be the creek, right?

Mel hurried to the window to see if there was a vehicle

parked outside when the woman on the floor behind her made a noise. A groan of pain.

She felt like a fool for not checking her sooner.

Then again, who was she?

Friend or foe?

The woman let out another sound and shifted her weight. She moved from being prone on her stomach to turning on her side. The woman opened her eyes. She blinked a lot and groaned some more.

She wasn't a particularly big woman, but she was tall. Lean, too, but she wasn't toned or overly muscled. If she carried strength, it was the surprising kind. Something that came out of nowhere when she needed it. She had a tan but not one that look like she spent all day in the sun, and her brown hair was cut short to her chin. She was wearing a yellow blouse and a pair of jeans that had a few holes worn into them. Mel guessed she was younger, maybe early twenties.

Like her, the other woman didn't seem to fit in the cabin.

She also didn't appear to have a weapon on her. At least not in her hands, and nothing obvious seemed to be protruding from beneath her clothes.

The only move she made was to cradle her head.

Then her eyes finally locked onto Mel's shoes.

The woman was up in a flash, yelling out in pain as she did so.

Mel jumped back like the noise stung her. Her hands went up in defense.

"Whoa, calm down," she hurried. Her throat was dry, along with her mouth. It tasted stale. How long had she been out? Mel pointed to the floor. "I just woke up right there next to you."

The woman was definitely on the younger side. Her flighty look spoke volumes.

She was terrified.

She was in pain.

But, most of all, she was confused.

"What do you mean, you just woke up beside me?" she squawked. "Where are we? What's going on?"

Mel moved her hands to motion for her to bring her volume down.

"I don't know what's going on, but I'm sure yelling isn't going to get us any answers."

That didn't do a thing for the woman. She shook her head and lurched away from Mel.

"Who are you? Where are we?" she rattled off. "Why is my head killing me?"

"I'm Mel, and I have all the same questions." The woman continued to spiral. Mel put her hands out to steady her but stopped before making contact. It focused the woman. She took a visible deep breath. "What's your name?"

"Ella. Ella Cochlin."

That name rang a very small, very far-off bell, but Mel couldn't figure out why. Not when the feeling of urgency was nearly blinding.

"Okay, Ella, what's the last thing you remember?"

"I—I think I was headed to the post office?"

The answer was as sure as Mel felt about what was going on.

"In Kelby Creek?"

Ella nodded.

Well, at least they were most likely still in town.

"What about you? Do you remember anything?"

Mel took a beat to try and recall her last memory again.

"Sterling. My last memory was being with Sterling."

Ella's eyebrows, perfectly manicured, went high in question.

Mel might have flushed had it been any other situation.

Instead, she funneled everything into one question.

What would he do in this situation?

"Do you have your phone?" Mel didn't have hers. She held out hope that Ella might.

It was a hope that died quickly. Ella whimpered out a no, but Mel was already on the move. She searched the room with adrenaline pouring into her veins. Her hands shook something awful.

"Can you see a phone around here or anything that might help us?"

Ella went to looking on her side of the room until they met in the middle.

No phones. No weapons. Nothing useful.

"I may not remember how we got here, but I'm pretty sure we didn't just walk in like we owned the place. We need to leave."

Mel didn't know what had happened from the time she'd been at the house to regaining consciousness in the cabin, but she thought it was safe to jump to three conclusions.

They'd been drugged.

They'd been kidnapped.

And whoever had done both would be back soon.

There was a fourth thought that crawled into Mel's mind, but she decided it the least important issue compared with the others.

Still, she thought it was a bitterness that hurt.

I really *shouldn't have come back to Kelby Creek.*

THE DAWN CAME and the sun rose to show a neighborhood of extremely tired residents. And those who had helped them.

Sterling's dad left when everyone came to an agreement that now it was someone else's turn to deal with the damage, namely insurance companies and a tree-cutting business. Something most Kelby Creek residents were used to dealing with during their erratic tornado season.

Sam, however, stuck around.

"I've gotten the same amount of sleep being here as I do at home with Linney," he joked, when Sterling tried to shoo him home. "I might as well make us some coffee and eggs before I go."

Sterling was too tired to argue, so he followed his brother into the house.

It was cold and quiet. Not the scene of a close call only hours before. They went back to his bedroom, careful to step quietly in front of the guest bedroom door, and looked inside. Sam spoke low.

"Mel sure did a good job in here. Apart from the plastic sheet over the window, you wouldn't know a tree had tried to say hello while you slept."

Sterling had to agree. Not only had Mel cleaned the room, she'd made his bed with new sheets and a blanket to cover the tears and holes from the branches on top of putting some of his more valuable things in plastic tubs and boxes and moving them to the hallway to stay dry.

It was nice.

"Want me to wake her?" Sam added, looking at the door behind them.

Sterling shook his head.

"I told her to get some sleep after we sawed the branches out of the room but she said she'd only go when she was done cleaning," he said. "Considering all the work she did, I'm betting she needs the rest."

Sam didn't argue, and soon they were both back in the kitchen eating eggs and drinking coffee. Sterling had a plate covered next to them just in case their movement woke Mel, but she still hadn't shown by the time their coffees were drained. He fought the urge to check on her with every swallow of his food and drink.

"Is it weird having her in the house again?"

Sterling gave his brother a questioning look. Sam pointed to his brow with his fork.

"You've been looking at that plate of food with a Sterling-specific intensity that I've only seen when Mel is around," he explained.

If it had been anyone else, he might have waved off the question and comment. But it was Sam, so he told the truth. One he'd never told anyone else.

"You know when she didn't come back that day, when I found her room empty, I felt that. Every moment after for weeks and months, I couldn't get over that feeling. Her *not* being there." Sterling set down his coffee cup. "Then I left and I worked on getting used to me just being me. I made new friends and did new things and then realized how much I wanted to come home to Kelby Creek."

He glanced at the empty chair next to him. "But even then, even as the years went by, I'd catch myself looking for her when I went into another room. Making extra of her favorite food on accident. Even sleeping on the left side of the bed because she preferred the right. I just… If I'm being honest, I'm not sure I ever let myself really believe she was truly gone in the first place. Just in another room I couldn't see. Sleeping in late or at the store grabbing those awful gluten-free cookies she used to be obsessed with. Here, but not really here."

"Gone, but not really gone," Sam added.

Sterling nodded. He let out a long, long breath.

"So, her being here now? Just feels like she took the long way home, even though I know it shouldn't, because she's not back for good."

Sam nodded this time. Sterling didn't think for a moment that he didn't understand him. He was, after all, Sterling's first and best friend. The brothers knew each other completely.

Which was why Sam didn't question the fact that Sterling was romanticizing Mel leaving him high and dry. Sam had probably already known that Sterling hadn't let go. Not completely.

"You know, I never understood why she left in the first place," Sam said, instead. "I thought that after everything was settled with Rider going to prison that she would finally be able to feel free. Or start to heal. I mean, we even had plans to do a big movie night that weekend, and she'd already picked out a movie."

That was news to Sterling.

"Wait. Y'all made plans for after the court date? I didn't know that."

"Yeah. I thought I'd told you."

"Maybe you did," he admitted. "I wasn't exactly thinking straight then."

Sterling tried to remember. He couldn't.

Still, it bothered him.

"What movie?"

"Notting Hill."

That bothered him more.

"Her favorite feel-good movie," he said.

Sam shrugged.

"I thought that maybe that's why she picked it. To throw me off so I wouldn't suspect she was about to run."

Sterling looked back at the chair, like it could answer for Mel, when his phone started to vibrate against the tabletop.

There was no ID, but it was a local number.

"Pretty early for a call. Are you working today?" Sam asked.

"No, I took it off." Sterling answered. "Hello?"

"Sterling, this is Carlos."

He looked at the number again.

"Where are you calling from?"

Carlos Park was a little out of breath. There was a lot of noise in the background. He wasn't at home, that was for sure.

"I'm at the hospital. You heard what happened here the other day? I know you've been busy."

Sterling nodded even though he couldn't see him.

"Yeah. A small fire broke out, right?"

"Yeah. Small but, well, it made for some confusion in the lab," he said. "And I think that was the point."

Sterling gave his brother a questioning look. It was returned.

"What do you mean?"

Sterling didn't understand why Carlos Park was calling him about a hospital fire from the other day, especially so early in the morning.

Though, just as he thought that, he turned his head to look at the doorway leading to the hall.

Carlos spoke fast.

"Amanda—I mean, Dr. Alvarez—had a few questions about some blood work that was taken and, well, she realized that some samples had been swapped around."

Sterling stood.

"Swapped around? Are you talking about Mel's?"

"They're looking into it right now but, yeah, they realized Mel's from the day of the car accident hadn't been logged right." There was more movement on Carlos's end of the line. When he continued his voice had gone low. He was whispering. "They got all squirrelly after finding it and, well, I overheard them say something I thought you should know. I don't know if it's what caused the accident or not, but Sterling, they don't think the car accident is what had Mel unconscious."

Sterling was already walking to the guest bedroom as Carlos kept on.

"She was drugged. And given everything else that's happened, I think it might be safe to assume that she didn't do it to herself. Someone's gunning for your girl, Sterling. Hard."

Sterling had the phone down at his side; Sam was right behind him. He opened the guest bedroom door without knocking.

He'd been hoping to see a messy head of dark hair.

Instead he saw an empty bed.

Sam ran past him to the closed closet. Sterling already knew she wasn't there.

"She could have run again?" he offered. But there was no conviction in his voice.

Sterling went to her suitcase on the floor. Nothing but the clothes she'd been wearing the last time he saw her were missing.

Just like her.

Sterling felt red-hot.

He pulled the phone back to his ear and growled.

"We need to find Jonathan Partridge *now*. Mel's gone and—"

A beep cut through the call. Sterling stopped himself to see another number calling. It was also local.

Hope sprang eternal. Maybe Mel *had* left on her own and was calling to say so?

"Hold on," he told Carlos. He switched over. "Costner here."

The phone call cracked.

So did the voice.

It was Mel.
And she was yelling.
"Sterling! Help us!"

Chapter Thirteen

"Mel?"

Sam motioned wildly through the air, letting his big brother know he had no idea what was going on.

Sterling didn't explain since he had no idea himself.

Mel had yelled for help, then the line had gone silent.

The call had dropped altogether after that.

"Let me call you back," Sterling barked to Carlos as the Call Waiting shifted back to him.

He didn't wait for Carlos to respond.

Sterling stared at the phone for a moment, waiting.

Nothing happened.

"Was that her?" Sam's face was drawn with concern. He was no law enforcement officer, but he'd never turned down helping someone when they needed it. Largely in part, no doubt, to how their father had raised them.

"Yeah. She said they needed help."

"They?"

Sterling's phone started to ring again.

"Mel?" he answered. "Where are you?"

This time her voice was low and strained. Whispering with force.

She didn't want to be heard but needed *him* to hear her.

"We're somewhere along the creek. Me and a woman

named Ella Cochlin. I think we were drugged, Sterling. Kidnapped. My head hurts and I can't remember how I got here. We woke up in a fisherman's cabin with a dock. We—we followed the creek and found another place maybe a mile up. I—I've never been here before. I broke the window to get in. I'm on the landline."

Sterling wasn't the best at the details. Sure, it would have been a nice skill to claim and it would have made his life easier, but that just wasn't him. Finding Waldo in a crowd took him double the time of others. Yet he didn't stop until he found him. For every detail he missed, he made up for in dedication to get the next.

That said, not one syllable went unheard from Mel's rushed explanation.

Two women, drugged and kidnapped, a fisherman's cabin with dock access, a mile walk along the stream, a structure with a landline but with no occupants.

Sterling took in those details and made sure to lock his emotions out.

Feeding into his rage and concern wasn't going to help Mel now.

Only keeping her safe until he got to her would.

"Okay, Mel, I need you to listen to me." Sterling was walking back through his house. When he got to his car keys, he threw them to Sam. "Are you and Ella alone right now? Why are you whispering?"

They made it outside. Sam understood his assignment. He ran around to the driver's side door.

Sterling was in the truck in a second flat.

"We haven't seen anyone since we woke up. But—but I think there's someone outside."

It tore at Sterling how Mel's voice wavered.

He pushed past it.

"Where are you now? In the house."

He made a phone motion with his hand, and Sam passed his cell phone over.

Sterling might not have been a whiz at the details, but he was good at multitasking. He dialed in a number and hit Call. He passed the ringing phone back over.

"Ask Sheriff Chamblin where he is and tell him we're coming to get him," he said, moving the phone aside to do so.

Sam took to the directions without fussing as Mel's soft voice answered.

"We just hid in the closet. I dropped the phone. That's why I hung up earlier."

"Well, that's good. You two need to keep quiet, but can you tell me anything about the house you're in first?" Kelby Creek was a small town, but in the past ten years or so, a lot of cabins and houses had been built along the creek. They could be anywhere along the length of the town, and that was assuming they were even still *in* town. The creek didn't stop at the town limits. "How big? What color? Any identifying markers outside?"

"Yeah—uh—it's like an ugly gray? Two bedrooms, I think, but small. No garage or carport. No dock, but the water is close and—"

Mel stopped midsentence.

Sterling pulled the phone away from his face to see if the call dropped.

It hadn't.

"Mel?"

When the woman responded, it was barely a whisper.

"Hurry."

The phone went dead again.

Sterling waited to see if Mel would call back.

She didn't.

SHERIFF CHAMBLIN LIVED near the creek himself and was an expert on the area. After retiring from the department, and before he'd come back to help keep it afloat after The Flood, he'd spent many a day fishing along the water. Even after he was back at work, he'd make time to walk along the creek bed with his fishing pole or take out a small pontoon boat to the parts of the creek deep enough to navigate. He knew the area more than most locals.

It was why when Sam sped them to his house, Brutus was already at the curb with a hand-drawn map under his arm and his gun in his holster. He was ready and willing. Though, the gleam of the sheriff's badge in the headlights that caught Sterling's eye reminded him that there was one person inside the truck who didn't have a badge.

"You stay here and call Robbie or Dad to get you. The sheriff won't mind you waiting in the house," Sterling ordered his brother.

Sam shook his head.

"No way. I can drive while y'all talk all of this out."

"Sam, we have no idea what we're getting ourselves into. You don't have a gun or badge."

He shook his head again and smiled.

"I'm not moving, but I *will* stay in the truck at all times. All the heroics left to you two. Promise." Sterling doubled down on his stern look, but Sam wasn't budging. It helped that his reasoning was concrete. "It's Mel, Sterling. We have to help her."

Sterling nodded at that.

Brutus was less concerned with Sam's presence. When Sterling hopped out of the passenger's seat and threw open the back door, they both slid into the back seat without preamble. Sam kept the truck idling as Sterling dived right in with what he knew. He also addressed the fact that they couldn't easily trace the number since Mel had called him directly and not a dispatcher.

"Also…as you can see, Google isn't helping us narrow it down, either," he added, searching the number in his phone's browser as he spoke. "Sometimes we get lucky with that. Not now."

"That's okay. We know enough to start our own search. Like we know that wherever they are, there's power." Brutus was eyeing the map that he'd smoothed out across the middle seat between them. "Which means it could be a rental or occupied by someone who just isn't home right now. Also, not many people have landlines in more modern builds, so let's take a leap and eliminate any newer structures."

He made Xs over a handful of squares representing houses on the map.

"Mel also said they came to in a fisherman's cabin," Sterling said. "One that was a mile or so off following the creek."

"But where they are now doesn't have a dock…"

Sterling was beyond anxious. He tapped his foot and squeezed his phone. Watching Brutus work through his own thoughts was infuriating. Yet, it also made Sterling proud.

Brutus Chamblin might have seen himself as an interim sheriff, but everyone who knew him saw him for what he really was—a great lawman who loved to fish.

He made a few more Xs, leaving twelve or so boxes still on the map without one.

"Tell me word for word what Mel said."

Sterling did so, careful to not forget anything.

Something that worked out for them.

"An ugly gray?" Chamblin repeated.

Sterling nodded, his adrenaline spiking as the sheriff made circles around two of the boxes on the map.

"There are two places that could fit that description. Two that happen to have a fisherman's cabin between them."

"And which one does your gut say they're at?"

Brutus stared at the map. He rubbed at his jaw.

"My wife went out with me one day to fish and commented on how gray doesn't look good on every house…" He tapped the box on the right from him. "This one. I think they're at the Cooper place—a new rental but older build."

Sam was already driving.

"I actually know where that is," he called back.

Brutus pulled his phone out.

"Good, because we're about to make a lot of calls."

Sterling's adrenaline surged again.

"Time to call in the troops?"

Brutus nodded.

"You bet your ass it is."

HER JEANS WERE wet around the ankles, and the cordless phone in her hand was dead.

"The power is out," Mel whispered.

She couldn't see Ella in the darkness of the closet, but she was sure as the sun was hot that the younger woman's eyes were wide with fear. Ella had barely kept it together when they'd come up to the gray house. She'd cried as Mel had used a rock to smash open a back window, and it had only been after they'd heard the splash of what sounded like someone in the water outside that Ella had managed to reel in the louder tears.

Not that Mel was sitting there in the closet judging her.

She was terrified, too.

Even more so now that the power had, she guessed, been cut.

"What—what do we do now?" Ella's voice reminded Mel of a wrung-out towel. She wasn't crying now, but her words were hoarse.

"We stay here and keep quiet. Sterling will come for us."

"But how?" Ella shifted. The closet they'd rushed into barely fit the two of them. Mel could feel the woman's breath against her at the question. "Can they trace the landline? Is that even a thing?"

Mel didn't know. If she had called 9-1-1 and not Sterling's cell phone, maybe they could trace it faster? Or maybe all they needed was a phone number? She wasn't sure how all that worked.

"He'll find us," she said, still flushed with reassurance that Sterling would come. "He'll find us."

If Ella needed more answers than that, she kept her questions to herself.

A minute or two went by with no other sounds than their breathing. The adrenaline that had encouraged them to run from the cabin to the house they were in was long gone from Mel's system. Now she felt exhausted.

Exhausted and more than confused.

It didn't make sense what was happening.

Why had she been taken? And by whom?

And why was Ella there and the kidnapper not?

Mel should have kept her thoughts more positive. Thinking of their kidnapper must have manifested whoever it was. The alarmingly loud sound of a door opening and glass crunching reached into the closet and turned her blood to ice. Ella's hand made it to Mel's arm and turned into a vise.

"Sterling?" Ella's voice was a new level of low whisper.

But Mel wasn't about to answer her.

She listened so hard that it felt like it hurt.

Heavy footfalls walked along the tile of the kitchen, not

far from where they were. If it had been Sterling, wouldn't he have announced himself? Wouldn't he have called for her?

Ella's grip tightened exponentially as those footfalls redirected. If there had been any other noise in the house, like the air conditioner, the steps wouldn't have sounded so crisp. So undeniably there.

But they did.

Mel's muscles started to strain in anticipation. She held the cordless phone, envisioning it as a brick instead of hard plastic.

Was it the same people from the Meeting House?

The footsteps thundered into the room next to them and made quick work of righting that wrong before coming into their bedroom.

Mel hunkered down on a scream as those steps settled…

Right outside the closet door.

The pain from Ella's grip became secondary to the fear of what would happen next.

Mel almost closed her eyes to help feel an ounce of protection from it.

Yet, just as her lids started to drop, another sound filled her terrifying world.

Dirt and loose gravel dispersing. Tires rocking to a stop, brakes engaging.

More than one car door shutting.

Whoever was on the other side of the closet door must have gotten a dose of their own medicine. The footsteps retreated at a fast enough speed that Mel couldn't follow exactly where they went in the house.

She did, however, lock onto a new set of sounds entering through what must have been the front door.

"Dawn County Sheriff's Department!"

He didn't need to say her name for Mel to know exactly who had arrived.

"Sterling!"

Mel yelled so loudly for the man that Ella jumped next to her.

She didn't care.

When the new set of footsteps rushed to their hiding place, Mel was already breathing out sweet relief.

Seeing Sterling standing on the other side of the opened door with his gun in one hand, his badge on his belt and his eyes on her was only the icing on the cake.

Chapter Fourteen

Sterling moved his service weapon just in time for Mel's arms to wrap around him. There was nothing but fear in him, and then all he felt was an embrace that was wired with tension.

And obvious relief.

Mel let out a breath against him that Sterling felt all the way through his bones.

She let go and stepped back before he could react. Concern scrunched her brow and widened her eyes.

"Someone was in the room with us when you pulled up," she hurried. "They ran out, but I couldn't tell where they went."

Sterling didn't like that.

He also wasn't about to leave Mel and Ella to go look. He needed them safe first.

"Sam's outside with the truck, and the sheriff is around back. Let's go."

Neither woman bucked at the idea. Ella stood and clutched at Mel's hand within a breath while Mel positioned herself behind Sterling. He almost imagined he could feel her hands on his lower back. He pulled his gun up and focused on navigating the exact way they'd come in, hyperfocused on anyone who wasn't the sheriff or his brother. The house was small but had enough corners to watch out for, and he wasn't keen on doing anything close quarters with two civilians with him. Plus, fighting at the Meeting House had been messy.

He didn't want a repeat.

It felt like a slow walk, but later he'd guess it took less than a minute. They weren't even off the porch before Sam was locking eyes with him. He was out of the truck fast, a liar to his word. Sterling wasn't complaining.

Brutus was nowhere to be found.

Sterling stopped and moved Mel, and with her Ella, around him. He spoke to Sam.

"Get in the truck and get them to the hospital."

"We're not going without you," Mel said at the same time Sam said, "I'm not leaving you."

"We'll be fine. The closest cruiser is less than two minutes out and we don't know—"

The sound of a man yelling made everyone turn.

Brutus.

"Sam. Truck. Now."

Sterling heard a truck door open as he turned around and hustled to the side of the house. Mel hadn't exaggerated—the water was close. So close that when Sterling rounded the last corner he saw Brutus stumble from the grass into the creek.

"Sheriff!"

Sterling swept the area with his gun while running over. There was no one around and no obvious sign of injury on the older man. Except for the pained expression on his face and the fact that he was on his side in the shallow water.

"Sheriff?" Sterling repeated, lowering his gun but not holstering it yet. "What's wrong? Who did this?"

Brutus's eyes were almost closed.

Sterling used his free hand to pull the man up to keep his face from the creek.

Brutus made a noise at the effort.

He was hurting.

A lot.

"Sheriff?"

This time the older man answered.

"My—my heart."

Then his body went limp.

STERLING WAS A sagging mess of worry and wilted anger when he came into Mel's hospital room later that day. Had she not been her own sagging mess in a hospital bed, she would have embraced him.

"They say if Brutus had been alone and had the heart attack, they don't think he would have made it." He dropped into the chair next to the bed. The doctor had just left, but she wasn't about to tell him that. Not when his mind and heart were being dragged around at the same time. "Since we already had everyone on standby, the ambulance made it there even faster than it would have normally. The timing of it all probably saved his life. The doc said Brutus was lucky, all things considered. Now we just wait to see if he keeps that streak up."

"Oh, Sterling."

Mel reached out, but it didn't do much good. Once Sam had gotten her and Ella to the hospital in a blaze of speeding glory, she'd gone from feeling afraid and tired to sick and tired. Her first hour of the stay had been a blur. The dizziness had only stopped a few hours beforehand but, still, she wasn't keen on moving around too much. After Sterling had come in with the ambulance and the sheriff, he'd only left her side long enough to talk to a colleague or doctor. When he wasn't in the chair next to her, Detective Lovett or Sam had been. That was to speak nothing of the uniforms in the hallway, guarding her and Ella's doors. They were still going over what happened to Ella. If they'd gotten a better understanding of it, they hadn't updated Mel yet.

Sterling scraped his chair across the tile until his knees were butted up to the side of the bed. Taking one of her hands in his was easy after that. Mel marveled at how small her hand was within his. Also how warm he was.

She tried to give him a smile that had some warmth, too. "He's tough. He'll make it."

Sterling nodded, but there was some hesitancy there.

"I talked to his wife just now, too. Turns out she's been worried about his stress levels since he came back to the department." His sigh dragged his shoulders even farther down. "The man was trying to kiss too many people after all."

Mel's eyebrow went sky-high at that, but a knock on the door marked the second appearance of the day from Detective Lovett.

This time his notebook was gone, and he had a friend.

Cole Reiner waited for Detective Lovett to take a seat. He stood off to the side of it.

Sterling let go of her hand.

Both men saw the movement, but neither commented on it.

"So, I know the doctor already went over everything with you two about the drugs in your system, but, since my wife and I had a personal experience with it a few years back, I thought I'd give you the less technical side." Detective Lovett sounded tired. Still, Mel was enraptured by every word.

"The street name for them is Sleepers. Not the most inventive thing, but it's mostly accurate. They're like sleeping pills mixed with Xanax with some steroids thrown in. With a controlled amount, they can make you lose consciousness fast and stay that way for a fair amount of time. My wife and I were dosed with a very small amount and were unconscious for several hours. We also lost some memory right before we lost consciousness. About half an hour, we guessed."

"Which is what happened to me the second time around," Mel said. "The last thing I remember was sweeping up glass while everyone was outside. Then nothing until the cabin."

Sterling tensed. It caught both men's eyes, but Detective Lovett continued.

"You didn't have a lot in your system, the same with Ms. Cochlin. Just enough to knock you out and keep you from remembering who did it. Which, I might add, is why Sleepers *are* popular with some people. Even though they have a higher, and somewhat unpredictable, fatality rate."

It was Mel's turn to tense.

"And that's why the doctor said I was lucky. When I came into town, I apparently had triple the amount I had in me today. That's why I lost so much time."

Mel fought the urge to touch her neck. There was an injection site the doctor had found there that had bruised. Near it was a small scab from another. They hadn't seen it the first time since everyone had thought she'd simply been in a car accident.

Detective Reiner crossed his arms over his chest. Unlike the others, he didn't look tired. He did, however, seem more than ready to end whatever it was they were caught up in.

"That's one thing we're looking into now," he said. "With the amount of Sleepers you were on, driving would have been almost impossible. But where your car was found was a good twenty miles from anything, and I've searched that road in both directions. There's no marks from running off the road or any kind of reckless driving."

Mel shared a look with Sterling.

"What are you saying?"

Detective Reiner actually shrugged.

"Either Ms. Blankenship here is one of those rare people who drive like a pro under the influence or—"

Mel was surprised she interrupted, but before she could stop herself she finished his thought.

"—or I wasn't the one driving."

Detective Reiner nodded.

Sterling wasn't a fan of the theory.

"So someone was driving her, drugged, to town and then—what?—was involved in a hit-and-run with Rose Simon's car before switching places with Mel and fleeing? It makes no sense."

Detective Lovett looked up at his colleague. Reiner answered.

"We're looking into the possibility that Jonathan Partridge might have been in the car with you."

It was like Sterling had been jolted awake. Mel wasn't far behind.

"Did you find him? Is he the one Brutus was chasing at the cabin?"

Reiner shook his head.

"The theme of this case is that we haven't found anyone. Yet. We're actually about to go to his house with a warrant. It doesn't take much for a judge to grant one for a Partridge."

Sterling had already told Mel about Jonathan's on-camera fight with Rose Simon before her murder, but she couldn't get her mind around him possibly being involved.

"Don't get me wrong, I am no fan of Jonathan's, but why do we think he's doing this, if he is? Revenge against me for not sticking up for his brother? Revenge for the fire? Why wait all these years?"

"You left."

Sterling's words were simple, blunt.

True.

Mel felt her face heat.

"Maybe he wanted you back in Kelby Creek," Sterling continued. "And maybe he finally found a way to do it. Just like with Rose."

A silence settled over them.

Mel didn't want to break it to say what she was thinking.

There was only one reason Mel would come back to Kelby Creek.

And he was sitting next to her.

"How does Ella fit into this?" she asked after the silence became too loud. "If this is revenge for his brother then, I guess, I get me and I get Rose. But why Ella? We talked earlier, and it seems like she's just some sweet girl who was visiting her grandmother and then woke up in a cabin next to me."

"We think she could have been taken on accident," Detective Lovett supplied. "Her grandmother lives a few miles from the cabin you were taken at. She might have been unlucky to see you being moved and was grabbed before she could call for help."

Mel was frustrated. It didn't help that she was starting to feel sick again.

"But why drug us, stick us in the cabin and then *leave* us? Why try to grab me at the Meeting House?" She balled the hospital sheet in her hands. "It just all sounds like bad planning, and I don't understand why. If this was really Jonathan, I can't imagine him being this *sloppy*."

She looked at Sterling for backup, but he stayed quiet.

Detectives Lovett and Reiner shared another look.

"We're still trying to figure out why you came back to town." Reiner's voice was cold. Hard. Mel wasn't the only one frustrated and tired. "Why Rose's car was a part of your accident and then hours later, while you're in the hospital, she's killed and left in your home. Why after five years you show up with an address in your pocket that leads to the Meeting House, right to the people who want to take you. Why the man who showed up at that house had the weapon that killed Rose and, so far, an identity that is just as hard to pin down, as he might or might not ever wake from his coma. Why you were taken from a house in the aftermath of a tornado—was it planned for that night, or was the weather seen as an opportunity?—and why you were taken to a cabin, left alone and then able to escape, all while Jonathan Partridge has been missing for days now."

His voice had gone colder as he spoke. Sterling had become more tense.

"Okay, calm down there—" he started, but Reiner held up his hand in defense to cut him off.

He kept eye contact with Mel.

"I'm just trying to point out that this is not a normal investigation. We have a *backlog* of questions and, so far, less than a handful of answers. That's in large part because we have no idea how you fit into this. And, believe me, we're certainly trying to figure that, and everything else, out."

He stopped there. Then looked at Sterling.

Mel didn't need him to say it out loud, but she knew what he was thinking.

She was involved, and the only reason why her questioning had been the way it had was because of the deputy who wore a cowboy hat.

They trusted him.

He was vouching for her.

Even now she could see it in him, in the way his jaw was set, that he was ready to come out swinging.

Thankfully, Detective Lovett spoke with a cool tone.

"We can't get answers sitting in this room, so it's time for us to head out." He stood slowly. Then he extended a hand to both Sterling and Mel. "Rest," he implored them. "The mysteries of Kelby Creek are too strong for any one man or woman. We need all hands, and those hands are worthless to us if they're hurt and exhausted."

Sterling saw both men to the door.

Mel could read the tension in him without seeing how drawn his face was when he turned back to her. Again, Mel wanted to reach out to him—to embrace him and, maybe, kiss him just like she had before her memory had been blacked out—but another wave of exhaustion took over.

She closed her eyes against it, hoping the dizziness didn't show up again.

When she reopened them, she noticed Sterling had found his seat at her side.

That tension in him had lessened considerably.

"Foster's right. We need to get some rest and recoup."

Mel snorted.

"Every time I seem to open my eyes, I'm missing time and memory and am somewhere I'm not supposed to be. Maybe staying awake for once will do me some good."

It was meant as a joke—though there was some real fear there for Mel—but Sterling didn't find any humor in it.

His hand encircled hers. Together they rested next to her on the bed.

"This time will be different," he said, resolute.

"Why? Because drugging me hasn't worked out for whoever is behind this before, so they're probably done trying that trick?"

Sterling shook his head.

His voice dipped even lower. The deep sound rumbled through his hand and along her skin.

"Because, this time, I'm not leaving your side."

Chapter Fifteen

Mel dropped her suitcase to the living room floor and let out a cuss that was as loud as they came.

"Two. Days," she said, turning around to face Sterling. "Two long days in the hospital with nothing but time to try and figure out why I was in town, why Rose Simon came back and where Jonathan went and we got *nothing*. Nada. Zilch and zippo."

Mel had her hair back in a braid. It was messy but looked nice. All of her looked nice, in fact. Something Sterling had been worried about for the last two days. After Sam had gotten her and Ella to the hospital, Mel had become progressively worse until, finally, she'd gotten better. Little by little.

"I almost overdosed on an illegal street drug with a dumb name," she'd told him on the first night of him hovering. "I'm going to look and feel like a potato sack until it's all out."

She'd never looked like a potato sack—in Sterling's opinion, Mel could never look bad—but it was great to see her now with some color in her cheeks and some fire in her eyes. Waiting for that, and for her exhaustion to finally ebb, had put a stress in him that he'd hated to feel. It was only in her recovery that he'd let some of that worry go back to Brutus. Who wasn't doing as well.

He'd survived his surgeries, but he was far from out of the woods.

"There's nothing to do here," Marigold had told him before they'd left the hospital. "Go home. Everyone from the department will let you know the moment any one of us hears something."

So, Sterling had listened and brought a fired-up Mel in tow. Healed, hungry and ready to go, as per her own words.

"Just think of it as a testament to your skills in stealth," Sterling said. He dropped his hospital bag, courtesy of Sam, by the recliner. "Not even you could figure out what you were doing in hindsight. And you know you better than anyone else. That's skill."

It was just after lunch, and Sterling had already swung them into an unhealthy drive-through on the way home. They'd devoured tacos and theories on the ride over. Aside from the nitty-gritty of the mystery surrounding them, it had once again felt like old times—two teens dropping crumbs in the cab of his truck and shooting the breeze as they did it.

But they weren't teens anymore.

That was certainly apparent when the anger in Mel only grew.

"Well, I really wish I could go back and bonk myself on the head, because what a bunch of crap this has been. One minute I'm out there writing an article about patio furniture and the next I'm riding low on Sleepers and surrounded by people who have no idea what a whole group of *other* people are doing." She fell back into the couch with a loud sigh.

Sterling laughed.

It caught her attention. Her head popped up, hair from her braid escaping.

"And what's so funny? This has to be bothering you.

Probably more than me! I mean, look at us. You help me, a tornado hits your house. You help me again, the poor sheriff has a heart attack." She disappeared from view. Sterling could hear her head hit the couch cushion. "I probably shouldn't be here lest I herald in the second coming of The Flood. Which, might I add, I'm pretty sure Cole Reiner thinks I'm trying to do. He can't get over the fact that I of all people am smack-dab in the middle of this."

She sighed again.

"Then again, if I wasn't me, I'd sure be suspicious. People already thought I was in cahoots with Rider. Once it gets out that I'm just casually where the action is, then it's game over for my already-crippled reputation with this town."

Mel finally had wound down. Sterling could hear it in her voice. She'd gone from fiery frustration all the way down to self-loathing.

Just as she had after Rider had gone to prison and Kelby Creek had turned on her.

Sterling hated hearing it again.

He might have had his own issues with Mel, but they were far outshone by his hatred for Rider Partridge. Mel might have chosen to marry him, but she hadn't chosen to be betrayed by him. To be strung up and tarred and feathered the way she had been.

"All right. All right." Sterling clapped his hands together. Mel's head popped up. He didn't answer her questioning eyebrow. Instead he went to the garage, found two old lounging chairs striped in pink and blue plastic, and passed her on the way to the back door.

The backyard wasn't large by any means, but it was private and, thanks to Sam's husband, now under the watchful eye of two of several security cameras set up around the house.

Sterling set up the first chair facing the back privacy fence and the second one right next to it. He didn't spell it out for Mel and sat down on his chair, taking his cowboy hat off in the process. His holstered gun, however, was firmly secured.

"Been a long time since we did this," Mel finally said. The squeak of her settling next to Sterling did something to him, but he wasn't going to think on it too much.

They'd both been through it within the span of a week.

He didn't always have to think about missing her.

"Remember the first time you made Sam and me do this?" he asked instead. "You said we needed to feed our leaves."

Mel laughed so hard and quickly that she snorted.

"Sam thought I was trying to get y'all to do some drugs, but all I was really doing was trying to make a clever joke about photosynthesis. Also, get a little bit of a tan. My legs were so pale that they were blinding me when we drove around in the car."

Sterling chuckled.

"Sam didn't last long, that much I remember about the first time we did it," he said.

Mel shook her head.

"After the way that boy complained about sweating, I was glad he decided to just let the two of us and these old loungers feed our leaves." Mel's voice changed so quickly that Sterling glanced over at her. She had her shoes off and pants rolled up. She ran her finger along the plastic at the side of her chair. "You kept these. The loungers."

There was something there—something in her words— that took a simple observation and made it punch well above its weight class.

It was appreciation and surprise and hurt and guilt and utter disbelief. Sterling knew it like he knew the sun on his skin was warm that Mel couldn't wrap her mind around someone holding on to something nice about her. Not when she was the ex-wife of Rider Partridge, the connected corruptor of Kelby Creek.

It was easy to blame and be angry at Mel for leaving him—God knew it had still been sitting heavy on his chest—but right then and there, Sterling was listening to a woman who had disappeared on him and finally hearing something else.

A woman who didn't think she was worth saving a good memory for.

And so Sterling did something he hadn't planned on doing.

He let it go.

He let it all go right then and there.

He forgave Mel for leaving, he forgave her for staying away and he forgave her for being the only woman he'd ever truly loved because, in the end, he couldn't blame her for being the perfect woman for him.

She just was.

Sterling went back to staring at the fence and took a deep breath. He ran his thumb over the brim of his cowboy hat and let that breath out.

Forgiving her wasn't just thinking it, so Sterling answered a question he should have already answered before.

"Dad made space for me in the garage when I left Kelby Creek," he started. "Just for the stuff that wasn't as easy to tote around. When I first set out, I only really had a few bags of stuff, which worked out well for me, since I went to Florida." Mel was keeping quiet, but he knew she was surprised at that. Florida had never been a place Sterling was keen on.

"I ended up staying with my cousin Joseph in an apartment near the beach and working a construction job with him. After The Flood, believe it or not, even if you came out squeaky-clean with the investigations, it was a pain just to get a law enforcement interview. So, I helped build fancy houses for a year instead."

He laughed because it was still funny to him now.

"Then Joseph went and married a client, which made the boss mad, and we both got canned. I couldn't be too mad at it since he made me his best man, but I didn't have much fun looking for a new place to live and work." He leaned back and changed his view to the blue sky.

"So I left the sun and sand for the dreariest place I've ever lived, out in Tennessee for a spell. Smaller town than Kelby Creek and, honestly, kind of weird, but I stayed there doing odd jobs for another year. May have been because of a lady I started dating, though. Her name was Rhonda, and she made a mean cup of coffee. Wasn't meant to be, though. We broke up and then I finally made my way to Georgia."

Sterling shrugged and stepped over the real reason he'd broken up with Rhonda and got to the end of his five years away from Mel. "A sheriff from a county triple the size of Dawn County offered me a job. She was a good woman, smart and a fighter. Newly elected and out there trying to make her hometown a better place, no matter who tried to get in her way. One day we were sitting around the break room table when a news story from Kelby Creek came in. It was a good story, and the reporter made a comment that maybe Kelby Creek was finally putting some good out into the world."

Sterling thumped his hat with his finger.

"And that burned a hole through me," he said. "There I was in Georgia, missing the struggle of my home trying to become better. To *be* better. And the sheriff saw that and told me that the job was a fight and to leave only if I was willing to fight it. So, I came home, got this place and have been here ever since."

That was it.

That was his last five years summed up.

Sterling took his cowboy hat and put it on. Mel took a few seconds before she spoke.

"And you brought the loungers here."

He nodded.

"Nothing else I'd rather feed my leaves on."

Sterling didn't know what to expect, but Mel falling into a laughing fit was a sound he more than liked.

"Wow. That really *does* sound like some kind of euphemism for doing drugs. No wonder Sam was so squirrelly about it when I first asked."

Sterling joined in.

MEL WAS WARM that night after her shower. It took a bit to realize that their session in the sun had more to do with it than the thoughts she'd been having about Sterling in said shower.

Her cheeks were rosy, along with her arms. She had a little sunburn going on, yet didn't much mind it.

Not after what else had gone on while she earned the slight heat of the burn.

Something had shifted between her and Sterling, and she had no idea what had been the cause. Not only had he told her about the years of his life that she'd missed, their conversation had been easier after. They'd talked about a lot and also nothing all at the same time. Which was fine by Mel. She'd forgotten how great it felt to just *be* with someone.

And that someone being Sterling Costner?

Mel looked at her reflection in the mirror. She was smiling. Maybe it was time.

Maybe it was *finally* time to tell him.

To explain why she'd gone the way she had. Why she'd just left.

Why she'd never planned on coming back.

Because, really, she'd stayed away for years, and now she was back because of the bad.

What would be the harm of telling him now?

Rider.

It was an automatic response with years of practice.

Mel's head hurt at how loud one name within her mind could be.

But there it was.

There *he* was.

Just as he had been at the courthouse that day five years ago.

Mel hated remembering her ex-husband's sneer as he gave her one last parting speech.

"Sterling Costner is as good as in a prison cell right next to me as long as you stay with him. All it would take was a few words from me to a few people." Rider had leaned in close, his lawyer letting the close contact happen, knowing there would be no repercussions for him. *"And before you remind me that I'm going to prison, let me remind you, my dear sweet Melanie, that I helped destroy an entire town from the comfort of our living room. Imagine what I could do to one single man with nothing more than my righteous anger to keep me company all day, every day."*

Mel watched her smile fade in the mirror.

Their marriage might have been a lie, but Mel had recognized that threat for what it was.

The absolute truth.

Being with Sterling wasn't dangerous for her. It was dangerous for him.

If Rider knew she was here now?

Mel turned away from the mirror.

She was angry.

She wished Rider would have just used his power to attack her, not threaten the people she loved.

Mel let her new anger and frustration lead her into the guest bedroom to change. Marigold, who had spent a portion of time after her shift in the hospital room with them trying to find *something* to help them sort everything out, had been kind enough to go clothes shopping for her, since Mel had only packed for what looked like two to three days. She absently slid into a brand-new matching pajama short set and then went to braiding her wet hair.

Sterling could be heard walking around the kitchen, the hallway, his room. Ambling through the house, trying to get them answers without leaving her side to do so. Trying to keep her safe despite all evidence making her seem like the one who was actually making everything happen.

He was a good man.

A great man.

Someone who deserved a great woman who didn't always find herself in the thick of bad, bad things.

Mel let her wet braid drop across her shoulder. The water started to spread through the fabric of her shirt.

With a fire that burned quick and hot through her heart, Mel wished she'd never met Rider Partridge.

Then, with a scorched heart that turned heavy as quickly as it had burned, Mel felt the real truth she'd been avoiding settle.

She should have never married Rider.

And now the man she should have was paying for her mistake.

Chapter Sixteen

The house was quiet.

Mel was not.

Sterling was in his bed, door open to the hallway, gun on his nightstand and his phone fully charged. Along with the security footage application that was currently monitoring the outside of his house…that he had already looked at several times, since sleep wasn't coming easy.

Judging by the constant movement he heard coming from the guest bedroom, he wasn't the only one.

It wasn't until eleven rolled around that Mel admitted defeat. Her door opened slowly. When she saw him sitting up, lights still on, she gave him a small smile.

"I think I've gotten used to hospital machines beeping and nurses waking me up every two hours," she said in greeting. "Every time I drift off, I jolt awake trying to figure out where I am and where my IV pole is."

"I could sit by your bed and try to make the beeping sounds," he offered. "I'm not sure we should try and replicate the IV part, though. I might deal well with a lot of things, but the last time I had an IV put in my arm and watched, I almost passed out."

He set his phone aside and waved her in.

Mel cocked her head to the side slightly.

"When's the last time you had an IV put in?"

Sterling snorted.

"The last time someone tried to use me as a pincushion."

He lifted his shirt and turned. The exposed skin on his side and beneath his rib cage had a nasty scar across it. Mel came closer.

"Twelve stitches and several 'you're lucky' comments from the ER staff," he continued. "It happened when I was in Georgia and on a call for the department. Let's just say that I met a very unhappy customer who was, thankfully, not as good with his aim with a knife as he was at being drunk and disorderly."

Mel wasn't a fan. She surveyed the scar up close. Sterling could smell his extra body wash from the guest bathroom wafting off her.

"I know we haven't seen each other for five years, but it's still wild to see the reminders," she said after a moment. "Mind some company?"

Sterling patted the spot next to him in bed.

Mel went around to the other side and climbed in. He was surprised to see her slip under the covers, but, then again, he had the house's AC set to slight winter. The temperature outside might have cooled off, but that just meant the humidity was now out in fine fashion. Mel's legs slid across the sheets, a few inches from his own.

As he did with the scent of his body wash, Sterling tried to rein in his focus and ignore the new closeness.

"Not bad for a brand-new mattress someone else picked out." Mel bounced a little. "I'm a little jealous, to be honest. The mattress I have back at my apartment needs to be hauled off to a dumpster and dealt a killing hand. The poor thing was cheap when I got it and had to endure several moves after. Also a stint of time with my past roommate's cat, Busta Rhymes."

Sterling laughed at that. It egged Mel on. She slapped lightly at his shoulder.

"See? That's how you accurately respond to learning Busta Rhymes's name," she said. "When I first heard it and laughed, my roommate called me rude!"

"I would think *not* reacting to his name would have been the ruder thing to do. I mean, you just don't name your cat that and expect people to not say anything and just nod."

Mel nodded with enthusiasm.

"Exactly!" Sterling repeated the name with another long laugh. Mel was grinning ear to ear. "Glad you enjoy that as much as I did when I heard it the first time, because I will, one hundred percent, name my dog that. Just as soon as I adopt him or her."

Her words were resolute.

So much so in fact that they changed the direction of the conversation.

"Is that what you'll do when you go back? To Birming-ham." Sterling was genuinely curious, yet he couldn't deny his words held a weight. Sure, they'd started talking about their past, but they hadn't for a moment talked about the future. "When this is all over, I mean."

It was like they were outside again. Both looked straight ahead as they spoke.

"I don't know," Mel answered. "With everything going on here—with me stuck in this weird web and looking like the one who's at the center of it—it's hard to even think about what's next. I already had to call my boss and take a leave of absence. My job might not be the hardest thing to do in the world, but the need to focus is definitely still there…and I'm definitely having a hard time with that."

She sighed and slid down a little, farther into the bed.

"A part of me wishes I could live two lives," she con-tinued. "One of them could be me going back to my small apartment, adopting a dog, going to the gym and being a loner until I want to be social again. No muss, no fuss. But the other life? The other me? She could do better here. She could figure out what's going on and make peace with this town. Make them see I'm not the bad guy they've always wanted me to be. Then— Well, then they would believe what *I* say. Not whatever Rider Partridge might say to hurt me."

Sterling felt his eyebrow raise at that.

"What do you mean, whatever Rider Partridge *might* say?"

It was a small movement, but Sterling watched Mel tense. She shrugged into it.

"I'm just tired of being a walking reminder of Kelby Creek's long-standing wound," she fielded. "If I'm going to be remembered for something in this town, I'd sure like to *not* be the villain."

Sterling opened his mouth to tell Mel that she *wasn't* anyone's villain, but his phone went off, vibrating across his nightstand.

Mel sat at attention. Her hair brushed against his arm as she tried to look around him at the phone's screen.

"Who is it? Detective Lovett?"

Sterling felt a small jab of guilt.

"No. It's Dad. I forgot to call him after we got out of the hospital." Sterling started to get out of bed. Mel, too. He held out his hand to stop her. "I don't mind you staying. I'll only be a sec."

He took the call with him out into the living room, and Mel must have listened. Sterling never heard her pad across the hallway to the guest bedroom and, after taking longer than he intended with his call before ending it, he walked back to see the door still open.

Then he turned to his room.

And there she was.

Right where he left her, eyes closed and face lax with sleep.

Sterling stayed his feet for just a spell and took in the sight.

"I'm a reminder. A walking, talking reminder that not all wounds are made by weapons and bad people. Sometimes they're made by people trying to pretend that everything is okay."

He heard her words from the day out at the field, slushies in each of their hands.

Everything wasn't okay.

But, for the briefest of moments, Sterling decided to pretend like it was.

EVERYTHING WAS WARM.

Mel kept her eyes closed but stretched wide.

She felt good. Better than she had in a while.

That feeling went away in a flash. Mel opened her eyes as something moved next to her.

Rather, someone.

The warmth she was feeling was a man. A man she was draped over, head against his shoulder, chest against his side.

Adrenaline shot through Mel. She forgot where she was, fear blinding her.

Then that person moved again. The arm he had wrapped around her tightened its hold.

Mel's racing heart started to slow.

She smelled the woods and pine and spice.

The same body wash she'd used on her body.

Sterling.

Mel lifted her cheek gently.

They were in Sterling's bed—she must have fallen

asleep—and the man of the hour was right there with her. His eyes were closed, still asleep. Mel's face heated as she realized just how close they were. She had no doubt it had been her doing. When they'd been together before, she'd been notorious for leaving her side of the bed and wrapping herself around the man. Even in sleep she felt comforted by him.

And even in his sleep, he'd always found a way to wrap her up—to keep her safe.

Mel wished she could stay like that a bit longer, but something had woken her up.

She stilled herself, waiting, before his cell phone went off again.

This time the man woke up. He met her gaze before gently untangling himself.

Mel's face was aflame, but she didn't comment on their compromising position.

She wanted to know why someone was calling when it looked like the sun had barely come up through the crack in the blinds over the new window.

"Costner." Sterling cleared his throat. He sat up, running a hand down his face. Mel could hear a man's voice but couldn't recognize it.

Which she didn't like, considering how Sterling sat up ramrod straight after whatever it was the man said.

"Are you kidding me?" he asked, voice filled with anger.

He was out of bed in one fluid movement.

Mel followed, body still wobbling from sleep.

Whoever was on the phone was talking fast.

Sterling was at his dresser, grabbing a pair of jeans while he listened.

Mel tried to catch his gaze to mouth a question, but he kept moving.

"You know that's a bunch of crap. There's no way," he continued.

Mel ducked to the side, trying to meet his eye again. It only worked when the doorbell rang.

Sterling ended the call, no goodbye to the other party.

"What's going on?" Mel asked.

Sterling's voice was low, only a bit above a growl.

"Go get dressed. I'll take care of this."

Mel wanted more than that but listened.

She hurried across the hall to the guest bedroom while Sterling threw on a shirt. Mel listened to him stomping down the hallway to the front door as she changed and used the bathroom in record time.

It turned out, maybe she should have taken her time.

"This is insane," she heard Sterling almost yelling when she made it to the living room. Her stomach dropped at what she walked into.

A Dawn County Sheriff's Department deputy was standing next to a very intense-looking Detective Cole Reiner. His badge was hanging around his neck. His lips were pulled down in a frown.

"This is what's happening," Reiner said, resolute. "And if you try to stop it, you'll only make everything worse for *both* of you."

Sterling finally noticed she'd come in the room. He turned to Mel with nothing but fire in his words.

"I'm not going to let this happen."

On reflex alone Mel touched Sterling's arm. It seemed to stay his rising rage.

She looked to Reiner next.

"Not going to let *what* happen?"

The detective, to his credit, didn't look happy saying his answer. Still, he said it all the same.

"Ella Cochlin came to the department this morning and

recanted her original statement of not remembering what happened to the two of you." He glanced at Sterling. It was only for a second, but Mel knew then where this was headed. "Ms. Cochlin said that *you* were the one who attacked and drugged her outside her grandmother's cabin while she was out on an early-morning jog. And that your partner drugged you to make it look like you were the victim."

Mel's mouth was hanging open. She felt like she was dreaming again.

"What?" Her voice pitched high, even to her own ears. "*I* attacked and drugged her? That makes no sense. I was the one who was here one minute, then in a cabin hours later. How did she even remember? I haven't been able to recall either time. And who the heck is my partner? Sterling? That's a big side of 'I don't think so.'"

Sterling didn't add on to her questions. She realized it was because he'd probably already asked them himself.

Reiner answered, regardless.

"Ms. Cochlin had far less of the drug in her system. The doctors say she stood a better chance of remembering something. As for the why, we're still looking into that, but I personally think it might have to do with your partner."

Mel gave Sterling an incredulous stare.

"They said that Ella found her phone on her running route near the fisherman's cabin," he explained. "They said there's a picture on it of you, time-stamped early Monday morning. Talking to Jonathan Partridge."

"An hour before your car accident, several before Rose Simon's murder and—may I add—in between those two incidents he also came to visit you in the hospital," Reiner added. "Do you have anything to say about that?"

All eyes went to Mel.

She had nothing to say.

No answers to give.

She was speechless.

Sterling was not.

"Something is going on, but she isn't a part of this, Reiner. You know that."

The detective shook his head.

"What I know is that every lead we've gotten goes right back to her." Reiner addressed Mel directly now. "To you. So I'm going to need you to come to the department with me now. And, if you don't come willingly, then you'll come in handcuffs." He nodded to the deputy at his shoulder.

"Your choice."

Chapter Seventeen

The handcuffs never went on, but Mel got into the back of the sheriff's deputy SUV all the same. A feat considering how riled up Sterling was. He tried to convince Detective Reiner and the deputy that they were wrong up until they started driving to the department.

That Mel hadn't attacked Ella. That she hadn't drugged herself.

That she hadn't had anything to do with Rose Simon's murder.

But his words got lost in the heat of the day.

"I'll meet you at the station," he called out before the door shut behind her.

Mel nodded to him. She felt numb.

And not because she was surprised, but because she couldn't help but wonder…was she the villain after all?

Detective Reiner was texting someone from the passenger's seat.

"If I were you, I'd stop letting Deputy Costner throw himself in front of you," he said, gaze still fixed to his phone. "Just tell the truth and cooperate and we can minimize the fallout as much as possible."

Mel didn't like that.

"I am telling the truth and I will cooperate," she said hotly. "But I'm telling you that this is all some wild misunderstanding. If I really was photographed with Jonathan Partridge, then something else must be going on. *He* must be behind it. Because he's definitely not my partner in crime. I mean, you do know about what happened to him, right? About the fire?"

Reiner nodded. His head was still angled down at his phone. It incensed her, so she continued, trying even more desperately to make her point.

"When the investigation into The Flood turned to Rider, he was given a heads-up that a search warrant was issued for his office half an hour before it was executed. I overheard him make plans to try and go out there and I warned the department before he could destroy any evidence. What I didn't know was that Jonathan was already there and half the office was on fire. Jonathan was caught trying to save some documents and got burned because of it. He blames *me* for the pain and scars and helping the town tar and feather his brother's good image. He said if I'd only stood up for Rider, if I hadn't helped go after him, then everything would have played out differently."

"But you didn't start the fire," Reiner pointed out. "Neither did he. It was an employee of Rider Partridge. One who didn't know Jonathan was inside, last I heard."

Mel shook her head. She crossed her arms over her seat belt.

"It didn't matter," Mel said. "Jonathan placed blame on me because I didn't do one thing to stop the stone rolling down the hill once it had been pushed. Everything after was my fault. Including a fire I never even saw because I was in FBI custody."

They were out of the neighborhood now and heading toward the other side of town. Instead of going through it to the department, the deputy took the county road that went around. Probably to keep Sterling from getting on their tail when he finally hit the road behind them.

"What happened in the past, fire or not, doesn't change what's happening now." Reiner finally put down his phone. He turned to look at her. "You will have the time and more than the opportunity to tell your side of this story. Just like Ella. Just like Jonathan when we find him. Even Sterling is going to get his fair share. We're going to figure this out, one way or the other."

Mel wanted to say more, but what words could really sway the man? Especially if she herself was questioning everything?

So she quieted.

Reiner turned back around in his seat.

Mel wished she were back in bed, warm against Sterling and torn between her desire to stay with him and go back to her life.

But Kelby Creek was proving to be wholly unkind.

"Wait, why are we out here, James?" Reiner made a show of looking this way and that out the window. "Pretty sure this is going to add fifteen minutes onto our—"

Mel saw the car before Reiner did and screamed.

It swerved from the other lane of traffic and went right at the passenger's side.

The impact happened in a blink. Mel's adrenaline and fear surged as she was thrown forward and back by whiplash. The airbags deployed, and a scattering of dust from them was floating in the air when everything stopped. The nasty sounds of whirling car parts and metal settling into places it shouldn't be filled the world around her.

Mel touched her head. The scab from her first accident was gone.

This time she was just shaken, not hurt.

At least she didn't think she was.

The front of the SUV was undeniably bent, but her cage in the back was intact.

Mel unbuckled her seat belt. She needed to help the deputy and detective.

The man known as James was the only one moving.

"Are you okay?" she asked. "Is Detective Reiner?"

James grunted. He opened his door with ease and without a verbal answer. Mel expected him to call for backup or go to the passenger's side or just go check on the other car.

He didn't.

Instead he opened the door next to her.

"Get out." Blood was coming from his busted lip, but his words were clear.

"I don't understand—"

"Get. Out."

James grabbed Mel by the wrist and yanked her out of the SUV in one quick movement. It was one thing to be treated poorly because of public opinion—it was another to be manhandled after a car accident because you weren't liked.

Mel was about to put that into words after insisting they check on Reiner when she finally took a look at the second car.

The driver was already out and walking toward them.

Mel recognized him instantly.

It was the man from the Meeting House.

He had a gun in his hand.

And his eyes focused on James.

"You ready? We don't have long," he said.

James nodded.

Mel started to back up but stilled in mute horror as James pulled his service weapon from his holster.

Then gave it to her.

Mel took it on reflex, just as she yelped when James

took it back. He handed it to the new man, who put it in the waist of his pants. Then James lay down on the ground next to the opened back door. He nodded to the other man.

Mel watched in horror as the man from the Meeting House backed up, took aim and shot James in the chest.

James made an awful noise.

Then the man switched the gun's aim to her.

"Now get in the car or you're next."

Mel didn't move. The man switched his aim again.

This time it was on the front passenger's seat.

"Do as I say or the detective isn't waking up."

Mel looked at Reiner. He still hadn't moved.

Then she looked at the open road behind them.

It was empty.

Part of her wished she'd seen Sterling there, ready to attack.

Part of her was glad he wasn't behind them.

"Okay." Mel nodded. "I'll go."

The other vehicle was an aged blue Bronco. It had damage from ramming the deputy's SUV but not enough to make a difference.

"I don't understand." He pushed her through the driver's side door and across the seat to the passenger's side. He grunted at the effort. "Why are you doing this?"

The man looked worse for wear. He was wearing a button-up, open at the top, and cargo shorts. He shouldn't have been sweating as badly as he was, yet he was drenched.

Mel would bet it had something to do with the fact that thick bandages could been seen through his open shirt.

And the fact that Sterling had shot him.

Twice.

He kept his mouth closed and focused on keeping the gun aimed at her while he put the vehicle in Drive. Mel contemplated trying to crash the car as they picked up speed.

She decided to wait.

She might survive a car crash, but she wasn't confident she could survive a bullet to the belly. He had already shot at her before. What was stopping him from pulling the trigger if she fought back?

"Just tell me *something*," Mel tried again when he didn't speak. The car lurched onto the road but drove fine after. She gave James and Detective Reiner one last look. Reiner still hadn't moved. James had now joined him in that state. "Like why did you shoot him? Why do you want me? *What's going on?*"

All the frustration boiled over into her last question. It came out less of a scared wobble and more of an angry confusion.

It caught the man off guard.

He shook the gun at her, then went back to looking at the road.

"Don't go getting no ideas," he warned. "You won't get answers from me, so you might as well just wait to ask the man in charge."

Mel would have shaken the man had she been able.

"*Who* is in charge and *of what*?"

The man shook his head this time.

"You really don't remember nothing, do you?" He chuckled. It obviously pained him. "I took some Sleepers once, and all I did was hallucinate that the world had flipped upside down. I guess everyone gets hit by them a bit different."

He took an upcoming turn that would point them back to the heart of town instead of near the department. In the process he gave her a quick sidelong look.

"You don't remember seeing him? Talking to him?"

"Him?" Mel's voice broke on the one syllable.

The man gave her a pained smirk.

"I'm not about to ruin the surprise. Plus, it's not part of his plan for me to even talk to you right now." Mel jumped as he took his hand off the steering wheel and then hit the same wheel hard. It made the vehicle swerve a little. "I took two shots and was lying there dying and still I have to make up for messing up the first plan. 'Don't hurt, shoot or kill Melanie Blankenship.'" He blew out a breath. Then started cursing.

"I'd ask what makes you so special, but I'm guessing it's not about you," he continued, very chatty for a man who'd just said he wasn't supposed to be talking at all. "You know, I'd feel sorry for you if I had half a mind to. But I don't." He shrugged. "All I gotta say is you sure know how to pick 'em."

That cold sense of dread that had been building was body-chilling now.

Mel didn't remember what had happened during her Sleepers-induced memory loss, but she had the horrible feeling that she knew who he was talking about.

And it wasn't Jonathan.

"Now I'm going to shut my trap and keep driving," the man went on. His voice dropped low. He shook the gun again. "And if you ask me one more question, I might just pull this trigger, then put my foot to the floor and leave this horrible little town behind. Consequences be damned. Got it?"

Mel felt numb.

She didn't understand.

And, for the first time, she didn't want to anymore.

She kept quiet.

Though not even that lasted long.

They pulled in behind a building near downtown Kelby Creek. It looked nice, even though a For Sale sign was in the street-facing window.

"Why are we here?"

The man killed the engine. Beads of sweat dotted his forehead.

"Just one thing to do before we head out."

He had them in the alley behind the for-sale building, facing the sidewalk. A few blocks up was the official downtown.

Mel didn't understand.

Then she saw her.

A woman walked across the sidewalk in front of them, grocery bags in hand.

The man next to Mel was fast.

He was out of the vehicle, gun drawn.

Mel realized three things all together.

The gun he drew wasn't the one he'd had pointed at her. It was James's gun.

The woman wasn't a stranger. It was Ella Cochlin.

Then, when the man shot Ella and she crumpled to the ground, groceries spilling across the sidewalk around her, there was a third and sudden realization. One that made Mel realize there was one theory she'd been dancing around but hadn't yet entertained.

The man hurried back, jumped in the driver's seat and had him and Mel going back out the way they'd come.

Mel refused to say a word.

She was in shock. She was crying.

She was trying to work out a way from the new hell she'd found herself in.

Because, even though she didn't have all the answers, she finally understood one horrible fact.

She *was* the villain.

Chapter Eighteen

Sterling knew something was wrong the moment his feet hit the parking lot of the sheriff's department.

And not just the obvious.

That much was clear the second Marigold met him at his truck. She was in her street wear but had her badge on her hip. There was an excitement about her and not at all one that was good. There was also an undeniable amount of relief that followed. She didn't waste time on any greeting.

"Half the people in that building thought you might not show," she bowled into him with. "I told them you aren't like that. You're a good one, but I'll tell you, it sure feels good that you didn't prove me a liar."

Sterling didn't understand.

"Of course I'd show," he said, indignant that anyone would think otherwise. "After Reiner took Mel in like that, you better believe I'm going to come defend her. This is ridiculous. Mel—"

"—is missing," Marigold interrupted.

Sterling paused. It didn't last long.

"What? She just left my house with Reiner a few minutes ago."

Marigold shook her head but didn't explain.

"Did you follow them here? Did you see them at all on the road after they left?"

Sterling hated to shake his head.

"No. I—I had to change and grab my holster and badge." He motioned to his service weapon. His cowboy hat, the one that made him feel mighty, was atop his head. "But I was maybe three minutes behind."

"Well, a lot happened in those three minutes."

"Explain."

Sterling didn't mean to be curt, but he definitely wasn't trying to be polite. Not when the stakes suddenly felt like they were rising even higher than when Mel had left at the threat of handcuffs.

"Park just responded to a Good Samaritan call about a wreck and shooting out on County Road 12."

Sterling opened his mouth, adrenaline surging, but she was quick to hurry on. "He found Deputy Reynolds's cruiser with an unconscious Cole in the front seat and a shot Reynolds lying on the road. Next to an opened back door. Mel wasn't there."

That adrenaline rerouted from dread to hope.

The change wasn't lost on Marigold.

"And that's the problem, Sterling," she added. "Reynolds was responsive when Park was calling in an ambulance. He said someone rammed them off the road. And then forced him to let Mel out."

Sterling shook his head. That hope disappeared at the movement.

"So she's been taken. Again," he growled out. Anger was instant. He shouldn't have let Reiner take her. "We have to—"

Marigold did something that she had never done before during their time as partners. She placed a hand gently on his chest. The contact stilled him.

"Sterling, Deputy Reynolds said the gunman was Jonathan Partridge…and that he was working *with* Mel to help her escape. She even took Reynolds's gun before getting into the other car."

Sterling was already shaking his head.

"No way did Mel have anything to do with this. No way she's working with Jonathan. Deputy Reynolds has it wrong."

"He's got a bullet in him. And Mel was being brought in as the lead suspect for conspiracy."

"You don't believe me," Sterling said hotly.

It wasn't a question.

Marigold still answered.

"I trust your judgment and I trust your instinct," she said. "But even you have admitted that there was only one person in this world who ever truly blindsided you. And that was Mel when she left. Those were your words." Marigold took her hand back. "What makes you think this isn't the same thing? I mean, look at everything that's happened. How can anyone not think she's guilty? All roads point to her."

Sterling was ready to plead his case—that Mel wasn't a part of whatever was happening—but he stopped himself.

Mel *had* blindsided him when she'd left all those years ago. And not because he was a man who thought he was so important that no one would ever leave him, but because he'd felt nothing but love from her. Even that morning before she'd left for the courthouse.

She'd woken up in his arms, chatted with him over coffee and then kissed him goodbye like they did every morning.

She'd even had plans with Sam for later in the week.

Then she was gone. All before he was even done with his shift.

Not a word in person. Just a text.

It hadn't made sense.

After being with her this past week, it made even less now.

Sterling felt something with her.

Just as he did then.

He felt love. He felt *her*.

And that's when it finally dawned on him.

"Then— Well, then they would believe what I say. Not whatever Rider Partridge might say to hurt me."

Sterling felt like an idiot.

Right then and there in the parking lot.

A downright fool.

Marigold's eyebrow rose.

"Is Foster here?" he asked, instead of explaining.

Marigold nodded.

"He was about to head to the hospital, though."

Sterling was off in a second.

"What? What's going on?" Marigold was hurrying behind him as he headed for the station doors, but Sterling's mind was running his own theories through the wringer.

It wasn't until he was inside the station and running down the hall to Foster's office that he finally landed on something he should have realized years ago.

The door was open, and Sterling and Marigold rushed on in.

Foster stood behind his desk. His face was pinched. It only became worse when he saw Sterling. The look said it all.

Which was why Sterling put his hand up to stop his friend from saying whatever it was he was about to say.

"You're about to tell me that Mel is guilty of something new, aren't you? That after her daring escape from custody she's managed to do something else, right?"

Foster cocked his head to the side. His cell phone was in his hand at his side.

He nodded.

"Ella Cochlin was just shot downtown," he said. "A witness said they saw the same vehicle Deputy Reynolds described leaving the scene."

Sterling banged his fist on the desk.

"And I bet if we sit here long enough, something else will happen to point us right back to Mel."

Foster shared a look with Marigold.

Then the fates truly aligned. Foster's phone started ringing. He held up his finger.

"Don't move," he ordered. Then he answered the phone. "Detective Lovett."

Whoever was on the other end was talking fast. By Foster's responses, Sterling couldn't get a bead on what the call was about.

But then it ended and Foster's eyebrow was raised high.

"What are you getting at?" Foster asked.

Sterling swiped his cowboy hat off and pressed it into his chest. It was the only thing helping him remain focused on what was happening right now and not go running off to do a one-man search in his truck for Mel.

"There's only two options here," Sterling hurried. "The first is that Mel *is* guilty of whatever this is. That she came to town to partner up with Jonathan Partridge and kill Rose Simon for revenge or whatever working theory you might have. The second? That Mel is innocent, which is what I'm banking on, and if she is? Then why in the world does *every* single road lead back to her? Every single one of them, an almost-indisputable line between her and something wild."

Foster was thinking it through. Which meant that he hadn't completely given up on Mel yet.

So Sterling brought his point home.

"You said you checked in with the prison where Rider Partridge is being held to make sure everything is on the up and up, but are we sure it really is? Are we sure that Rider isn't the one doing what he has done best in the past?"

Foster glanced down at his phone.

He was still contemplating something, though his response was quick.

"That call was from Marco. He's at the hospital. The man you shot at the Meeting House woke up and has only said one thing since." Foster's eyes had widened. Excitement. But not the good kind, either.

Sterling could barely contain himself.

He knew in his heart that Mel was innocent. He just needed everyone else to get on board.

"What one thing?" he asked.

Foster shook his head in disbelief.

"That Rider Partridge was an innocent man."

MEL DIDN'T KNOW the house, but it was by the creek.

A wide one-story that was near the town limits. Not an ugly gray, not a place where fishermen hung their hats. A simple cabin with nice white trim and sky-blue paint on the siding.

And probably the place where she was going to die.

The man next to her parked at the back of the building. He'd grown awfully quiet the closer they'd come to the place. Now he took his sweet time staring at the back door.

Mel knew then, without a doubt, whom he was waiting for.

Still, she felt the cold creep up her spine as the door opened and the man of the hour stepped out.

Rider.

God bless him, he still looked good in a suit. And just as terrifying.

"We could go right now," Mel said into the quiet of

the Bronco's cab. "We could leave long enough for the law to get him. I'd vouch for you. Say you saved me. That'll count."

The man pulled the keys from the ignition.

He almost looked sorry.

"We both know there's not much that man can't make happen. We leave now, he won't even have to lift a finger to catch us. He'll get someone else to do it for him."

Mel felt tears prick at her eyes.

Rider stood there, staring.

He knew that she knew.

"If I leave this car, he'll kill me," she said simply.

The man's answer was just as simple.

"If you *don't* leave this car, he'll kill *me*."

Mel let out a breath that shook and put her hand on the door handle.

In a moment of pure empathy, she paused.

"If I were you, once I get out of this car, I'd floor it out of here anyway," she said. "One thing Rider Partridge doesn't suffer is loose ends. That's why his brother has scars and he doesn't."

She didn't wait for a response.

Mel's shoes sank into the dirt of the drive. Rider stayed just where he was until she crossed the distance between them.

"I'm guessing we already did the whole 'nice to see you after all of these years' thing," she said in greeting. Mel was proud how her voice didn't shake. "But was it during the car accident or after the tornado?"

Rider was a study in contrasts to Sterling. She'd always known that, but right then and there, the details were glaring. Light hair, dark eyes and a body that was lean and short. Maybe that's why his suits meant so much to him.

The same for his shiny shoes that cost more than most people's rent. He'd never be caught in worn clothes or family heirlooms. His hair never was tousled, and even now she could smell the expensive cologne he'd worn during their marriage.

It wasn't that Rider had expensive tastes.

It was that Rider didn't value anything else.

"After the tornado," he confirmed with a smirk. "But don't worry, the most we talked about was my insistence that it was better for everyone if you walked quietly to the car. Once we were in the car you, thankfully, became very quiet."

Mel had wondered why she would have left Sterling's house.

Now she knew.

Rider had threatened Sterling.

Of course he had.

"If you hadn't drugged me I would have asked why you were in Kelby Creek. Or, you know, not in prison."

Rider's smirk never wavered.

It made Mel's stomach knot.

His arrogance was only as powerful as his confidence, and both seemed to be in full swing. He stepped back into the house and waved her in.

"I have to wait for a package, and you know that I'm not a fan of humidity."

Mel glanced back at the Bronco.

Her friend had gotten out. Both guns in view.

She wasn't going to get far if she ran.

Not that running from Rider ever worked, apparently.

"Will I at least get some answers if I come inside?" she had to ask.

Rider laughed.

Once upon a time, that sound hadn't chilled her to the bone.

"Oh, don't worry, Melanie. You're going to get exactly what's coming to you."

Chapter Nineteen

Mel sat on a couch covered in an obnoxious floral print and, of all things, toucans. Rider sat across from her in an oversize armchair that was pastel blue.

It was almost comical.

Almost.

A man in fishing attire, complete with a mesh hat, stood in front of the windows that faced the main road. He gave them a half-hearted glance before returning his gaze out the window. On one hip he had a sheathed knife so big that it reached down to midthigh. Leaning against the other was a shotgun.

Rider didn't address the man. He knew Mel had seen him. Instead he crossed his ankle over his leg and threaded his fingers together over his knee. Calm. Confident.

Mel hated him.

"You look well, *Mel*," he started, laughing into his rhyme. That didn't last long. "I mean, I got worried there for a bit since you never visited me once during the last five years. Never mind you almost disappearing from the internet's radar. I actually lost you for a few weeks after you moved to Birmingham. By the way, can I say how glad I am that you finally got up the courage to rent your own apartment. Sure, sharing saves money, but you're only getting older, and a woman in her thirties with roommates sounds like a sad sitcom no one wants to watch."

Mel's jaw clenched.

She was angry.

She felt violated.

"Usually you don't keep tabs on your ex-spouse," she pointed out. "Especially when you weren't particularly there during the marriage. Never mind the fact that you're supposed to be in prison."

Rider scoffed. He was enjoying himself.

"Now, don't you go getting offended by the truth and then start telling lies to make yourself feel better." He leaned forward a bit and glazed right over her prison comment. "We both know you were happy during our marriage. The perfectly kept wife. Smiles aplenty, heart aflutter. Isn't that why this town turned on you so quickly? Your blindness? Your naivete? Your hope among hopes that the long hours I was pulling were for work and nothing more?" He shrugged. "Just because you say our marriage wasn't perfect, let me remind you that the divorce only came once the FBI did. It wasn't even on the table until then. Face it—you would have stayed with me till death did us part."

Mel felt heat crawl up from her belly and turn her face hot.

Rider knew he'd touched a big nerve.

He held up his hand to stop her from replying.

"Now, maybe I'm wrong. Maybe this town didn't turn on you simply because you married a charlatan. *Maybe* they turned on you because they knew that something was off about you. That you certainly couldn't *not* be involved." He smiled. It was genuine. "They're going to love finding out how right they were."

"You've been setting me up," Mel offered. Her voice had gone cold. Unfeeling. Stating facts since emotion wasn't going to get her anywhere with her sociopathic ex-husband. "You're making me the bad guy."

Rider held up his pointer finger.

"You *are* the bad guy. I'm just giving the town what they wanted five years ago—proof that they were right about you."

Mel shook her head.

"No one is going to believe this. I didn't do anything and I'm *not* going to do anything."

Rider laughed.

"You were on the way to the sheriff's department to get questioned by a very intense Cole Reiner. If our buddy Tate out there hadn't intervened, you'd be in an interrogation room. Again."

Mel wanted to point out that Sterling would have convinced them otherwise—that Mel was innocent—but Rider was already a step ahead.

"They might have believed Sterling's grand stand that he'd no doubt give to defend you, I'll give you that," he said. "But he's the only one who would do that. Which is why everything had to go to plan up until this moment. You leaving the love of your life out of the blue, with a text? Then no contact for five years? Kelby Creek already hated you, but doing that to a fine, country-fed Costner? A good man—a better man than you deserved?" Rider shook his head. "And then, as your final act in Kelby Creek, you're going to kill him? Any doubt left in their heads will fly out into the breeze."

Mel moved to the edge of her seat.

Her emotions broke through in a brilliant burst of fear.

"What do you mean, kill him?" Mel shook her head so hard her hair slapped her cheek. "You don't need to do this. You don't need to hurt him. Leave him out of this. You have me."

Rider uncrossed his legs. His hands went from threaded together to resting on each arm of the chair.

All humor was gone.

"I don't think you quite understand yet, but Sterling Costner is the *reason* I chose *you*."

He was transforming. From a gloating villain to his original title earned from The Flood. The Connected Corruptor. A man filled with charm and armed with patience. A man who was seeing his hard work finally pay off. It was Rider's turn for his voice to go void of emotion. Now, he was just stating facts.

"I was seventeen and interning with our family lawyer when I first realized that Kelby Creek was a double-sided coin," he continued. "The only person who ever won—who ever got anywhere they wanted—was the person who knew which side to call before a flip even happened. I wanted to be that person who knew the winning call before ever moving an inch. So, I was taught an invaluable lesson that I took to heart. Planning is power." A chill went up Mel's spine. He kept on. "It's painful, too. And, if you do it right, requires a lot of patience. Luckily, I have that in spades."

The man at the window moved. He looked down at his phone.

Rider paused to take in the movement, too.

He sat straighter.

Then his gaze was back on her.

"I knew eventually something would go wrong," Rider continued. "Whether on my end or someone else's. There's always going to be that unknown variable that has an unfortunate consequence. I realized that I needed a partner. And a patsy. So I asked you out on a date."

The chill across Mel spread and hardened.

"You married me so you could frame me, just in case?" Mel shook her head. She couldn't believe it.

Rider shrugged.

"It wasn't necessarily personal. I needed a type, and you fit it."

"A type?" Mel felt sick.

Rider might not have been the man she thought she'd married, but she never for a moment thought every single part of their relationship had been a lie.

He explained like the subject was as simple as apples and oranges.

"Someone pretty, smart and capable," he said. "Someone who's also quiet, somewhat a mystery. They're not close with the family they had growing up so they're left craving to create their own. They're nice and ready to sacrifice if needed, but there's only really one or two people that they'd burn the world down for. Bonus points if one of those people happen to be well-liked or beloved by many." Rider held his hands out to motion to her. "And then there you were. Quiet unless pushed, parents detached, notable in public and wildly in love with a town favorite."

"Sterling."

"Sterling Costner. Bless the both of you for not waiting too long after my arrest to finally act on your feelings. Also, bless you both for not keeping it a secret."

Mel hung her head a little. She looked at her hands but was remembering the past.

"You threatened Sterling so I'd leave him in the dust and everyone would know it. You got me to hurt a good man because you knew it would only make Kelby Creek hate me more."

Rider clapped his hands.

"And *that's* why poor Deputy Costner is about to have a very bad day. If you kill him? Your one true defender, a man who's been in love with you since you were teens, then there's nothing you can say that will change anyone's mind. Not with everything else I've planned."

Mel opened her mouth—she didn't know what she was going to say. She didn't understand everything that Rider had done or was doing. She was missing pieces of his clearly elaborate puzzle. But, lucky for her, Rider loved the sound of his own voice.

He stood, shared another look with the man at the window. He faced her again.

"The moment the mayor was suspected of being connected to Annie McHale's abduction was the moment I started planning on how to get out of prison. How to stay out once everyone figures out I had escaped." He lowered himself, bending over and using the couch cushions to prop himself up over her. Mel fought the urge to headbutt him. She fought the urge to yell, too. "Patience is a virtue. Planning is power. And you, my dear, are about to be revealed as the actual Connected Corruptor and the reason why Annie McHale was really in our basement. All because I'm so damn good at both."

Rider rose. This time he spoke to the man at the window.

"Time for a ride."

THE BASEMENT WAS UNRECOGNIZABLE. Just as it was unavoidable.

Like everything about Mel's relationship with Rider, something became apparent about it and the house it was beneath. But only in hindsight.

"That's why you left me this place," Mel said. "Another way to damn me down the line."

Rider hadn't monologued on the drive over. He'd spoken in hushed words to the man with the fisherman's hat, but Mel hadn't understood them. Just the gun in the man's hands.

Now they were back at the house.

Rider Partridge's castle.

He was smiling.

"When you didn't even try to sell it—which would have been met with so many issues that it would have looked like you weren't trying to sell it at all—I had me a party in prison. I'm assuming not many people understand why you held on to this place. It definitely doesn't help public opinion of you."

He motioned to the area around them.

In what had once been a basement filled with a swarm of FBI agents, and at one point Annie McHale, there was now a cold quiet. Several boxes were stacked high across the tile floor while a chair sat stationary against the wall.

"When did you get all of these boxes in?" Mel had to ask. She answered herself before he could. "The tornado. The power was out across this side of town for hours. That's why I didn't get an alert for the security system."

Rider nodded.

"You actually were out in the car while some of this was being moved inside. Unconscious, but I had you sitting up in full view. Constance McCarthy glanced your way when she was hustling by with that yappy dog of hers—can't believe she's still around, to be honest—but I'm not sure she realizes yet that it was you. She'll probably put two and two together later. Just another dash of suspicion to put on you for Kelby Creek."

Mel walked up to the nearest box. It wasn't like an Amazon package or a box you'd get from the FedEx store to move. It was perfectly square, taped up neatly and void of any markings. Rider let her open the closest one.

Her already-knotted stomach tightened.

There was a case of plastic syringes inside. Too many. Vials lined the bottom, along with plastic bands.

"Drugs. Sleepers, I'm assuming."

Rider laughed.

"You sure pick up on things fast." He slapped the corner of the box. "It's hard to sell so many people on the idea that *you* were the one pulling all the strings involving my shenanigans back in the day without a few current shenanigans. Plus, Sleepers can be addictive, and you've had more than your fair share in your system twice now."

He moved her from the stack of boxes, around a few more and to a chair positioned at the back of the room. It was from upstairs, bought months before The Flood and never used after. Lavender cloth, wooden arms and polished legs. There were handcuffs around each side. Rider maneuvered her to sit down. He cuffed her left wrist but not her right.

"Wouldn't it have been easier to just do this?" Mel was back to fighting tears. She was tired. "To just plant something on me? Heck, wouldn't have killing me been easier?"

She hated to say it, but she felt it in her soul.

"Couldn't you have escaped and disappeared and never looked back?"

He checked that her handcuff was secure.

"I may be a patient man, but that doesn't mean I'm going to let my entire reputation be permanently destroyed. So, I spun a web and made you the spider. Making me one of several flies haplessly caught."

Mel continued to hold back her tears.

"Our entire relationship was a lie. None of it meant anything to you."

Mel knew she shouldn't have cared, but at the moment she let the hurt in.

"I thought we were happy at one point," she continued. "We laughed and kissed and took goofy pictures on our honeymoon. I have *good* memories with you, Rider. Honestly good ones."

He crouched in front of her, smile back in place. His gloved hand was soft as it brushed a strand of her hair behind her ear.

"Oh, my Melanie." There was an almost imperceptible shake of his head. "You were a plan."

Rider pulled something from his pocket.

It was a ring, but not her old one.

It was simple and gold and pretty.

"The only man who ever wanted to marry you for something as trivial as love never gave this to you."

Mel felt her eyes widen.

It made Rider all the happier.

"You found this in Sterling's things after the tornado. You put it on and were smiling when I showed up. My guess is it was meant for you, but, well, you know, you left the poor sap, heart in his hand."

He took her right hand and slipped the ring onto her fourth finger.

The fit was perfect.

"Such a shame," Rider said. "In another life you and Sterling might have made it."

He stood and walked to the bottom steps in the most dramatic fashion yet.

"Don't go anywhere. We still have some things to discuss. But first, I need to get some incentive for you."

He didn't say anything else and left.

When Mel heard the door at the top of the stairs close, she took a long look at the ring on her finger.

Finally, she cried.

Chapter Twenty

Night came.

Sterling felt every second of the lead-up. Every second that Mel was missing. Every second that someone else thought she was guilty.

Guilty of her ex-husband's crimes.

That angered Sterling to no end.

And was one of the reasons he was asked to leave the department and stay his ass at home.

"You are the only one here who hasn't even flinched at the onslaught of evidence coming in that, at the very least, might mean Melanie is working *with* a Partridge," Cole Reiner said when he was back from the hospital. He'd walked away from the crash with a broken arm and a well of anger. "Either now or back then. You're too close to this. You're too close to her. She could shoot you in the face at this point and I think you'd take it with the insistence that it wasn't her who'd done it."

Sterling's rage had been boiling at that.

Foster, who had run into a whole heap of red tape about trying to get visual confirmation that Rider Partridge was indeed in his cell and had headed to the prison several hours away himself, had been the only thing that had kept Sterling from making a true scene.

"No one can force you to stay at home, but you're going

to have to leave your badge there," Foster had said when Sterling had called after his verbal tussle with Cole. "He's right, Sterling. You're only starting to make this harder for us and worse on yourself. That only hurts Melanie in the long run."

But no one knew where Mel was.

No one could tell him that she was okay.

That she wasn't hurt or scared or—

Sterling couldn't even think about the worst-case scenario.

He did, however, listen to his colleagues. Mainly because there was nothing else he could do at the department. He went home, changed into his boots and jeans, and dropped his badge at the door.

He kept his holster on, his gun inside.

Then he went to look for her himself.

Sterling drove to every place he could think of that either Partridge might go. That Mel might go. Then he thought about where she would look guiltiest if found.

That's why he went back to the Meeting House a second time just as the sun started to set.

Crime scene tape dressed the barely livable house. Sterling took out his flashlight and searched high and low throughout the structure. He even ducked to look beneath the foundation at the side of the porch.

It was why he didn't hear the man approach.

He did lift his gun in time to make the newcomer stop and raise his hands in defense.

Sterling recognized him instantly.

The man he'd shot at the Meeting House. The one no one had found.

"If you don't come with me, Melanie Blankenship will be killed," he said, no preamble. "You come now, no fuss, and that won't happen."

Sterling didn't lower his gun.

Though he did believe the man.

"Tell me this first—who are you working for?"

He wanted to be sure.

Not just have a theory.

The man, at the very least, obliged. He looked tired, worn. Seen much better days than the ones he was experiencing in Kelby Creek.

"We both know it's Rider," he answered. "And we both know he's back in town. So, let's not keep him waiting or that prized patience of his might just go to hell."

Sterling weighed his options, but it was like putting a feather on a scale against the weight of a building.

There was only one option for him.

"Lead the way."

STERLING GOT OUT of the Bronco and was staring at water.

And a dock that stretched over the darkness. Black glass surrounding the wood and quiet. There was a lone light on one of the wooden columns.

Mel was standing at the dock's end.

Alone.

Sterling gave his driver a long look.

The man nodded to Mel.

Only one of them had a gun now, and it certainly wasn't Sterling.

He wanted to tell the man something—anything—to get them out of the situation but knew there wasn't a word he could say against Rider to one of his lackeys.

So Sterling walked to the dock and focused on the relief filling his chest. If only for the moment.

Mel was alive and, as he got closer, seemed physically okay.

"Mel?"

He slowed his approach, boots thudding against the wood of the dock. Mel was standing awfully still.

She watched him with wide, tear-filled eyes.

"Rider's back." Her words were quiet. A drop in the creek around them.

Sterling stopped, a foot away from her. He nodded.

"I figured as much when the only other option was you were the bad guy."

Mel seemed surprised. She rattled on, voice shaking.

"I think Ella was in on it, too. Haven't seen Jonathan yet, but who knows where he is."

Sterling reached out. Mel took a small step back, her eyes widening again. This time in fear.

"Where's Rider? What's going on?" he asked. "Why are we here?"

Mel pointed down at a spot near their feet.

"He said this was the last stop on the tour."

The spot, like the rest of the dock, was dark from the wood being wet after the storm.

"We're near the house," he realized. The same house he should have known to check when Mel went missing. Sterling hadn't even made it an option in his mind since the house had already been used as a piece in Rider's game. He should have known the man would have doubled down on such an elaborate set piece. Because Rider was that dramatic. And Sterling should have realized that. Just as he finally understood something else. "This dock is close enough to kill someone and move them there by a quick car ride."

Mel nodded.

"This is where Rose was killed," Sterling continued. He sighed. "And this is where he wants you to kill me."

Mel let out a strangled sob.

She didn't correct him.

"I knew when they showed up for me. It's the only thing that makes sense." He gave her a small smile. "I've never not loved you, and I'd never not fight for you. Getting me out of the picture makes sense."

Tears started to fall down Mel's cheeks.

"Oh, Sterling. I'm so sorry," she cried. "It's all my fault. I never should have married him. I should have married you."

Sterling reached out again. This time Mel let him wrap his arms around her.

Mel's body shook against his.

"And I should have asked you to marry me," he said into her hair.

Her sobs became harder.

Sterling pulled away. He put his hands on the sides of her face to focus on her.

"None of this is your fault. Not one moment of it. Not back then, not now, not whatever happens next. Okay?"

The new position opened up room for him to see her hands pressed against her chest.

Sterling saw the ring first.

He dropped his hand to hers and pulled it out between them, cradling it as she shook.

"Where did you get this?"

Mel took a deep breath.

"Rider said I found it after the tornado. He—he kept it and put it on me at the house."

Her eyes searched his.

Sterling touched the ring.

The one he'd bought for her after their first kiss.

The one he'd never told her about.

"I should have been the one who put it on you." Sterling smiled. Mel's chest moved as she tried to control her crying. It wasn't the time, but he finally, truly understood what had happened back then. So much so he didn't even form it into a question. "You left town because Rider threatened me. He was using me against you. He's using me against you now." He let out a deep breath and looked around them. The man in the Bronco was still there. Waiting.

Sterling went back to the second thing he'd seen Mel holding.

He turned her hand over in his.

Beneath the engagement ring and against her palm was a full syringe.

"What does he want you to do now?" he asked.

Mel's tears were flowing now.

"I made a deal—deal with him." She shook her head. "I—I do this to you and—and—" A sob racked her body so hard that Sterling tightened his hold to steady her. It broke his heart when she met his eye again.

There was so much pain there.

And he was about to find out why he couldn't do a damn thing to stop it.

"It's okay," he told her. "It's okay."

Mel shook her head again. She took a moment to compose herself. It was still shaky, but when she spoke it was clear as day.

"He said there were only one or two people in this world that I'd burn everything for, and I thought there was only one. Only you. But, Sterling, he has Sam."

A gut punch unlike any other shook him.

Guilt as fierce as fire followed.

In all the madness, he hadn't once called Sam.

And Sam hadn't once called him.

He should have known.

"What's the deal you made?" Sterling kept his voice calm, low. The fear and rage wouldn't help Mel. It wouldn't help Sam. It wouldn't help Robbie or Linney.

Mel took a deep breath.

"Inject you and I can go back to the house and do the same to Sam. He won't remember what happened and—and I tell the cops everything that I did and admit I was the one who framed Rider after The Flood."

Sterling didn't think it was that easy.

Mel gave him an imploring look.

"He's been planning on me taking the fall for years. I believe him, Sterling. I believe him when he says he's thought of everything and can pin this on me. I believe him." Mel glanced down at the syringe. "I could have said no. But—but it's Sam."

Sterling let go of her hand and ran it across her cheek.

"And we can't let Sam die," he finished.

Sterling closed the space between them and gave Mel a long, deep kiss.

It felt like the first time.

Soft and warm and perfect.

When he broke it, Mel was crying again.

"I don't know what he has planned for you after," she said, shaking her head. "Maybe we can run? Jump in the water and swim away? Send the cavalry to the house? Maybe we—"

Sterling stepped back and took the syringe with him. He stuck it into his arm before she could stop him.

"Don't think for a second I'm going to let Rider Partridge keep us apart any longer. You save Sam, I'll save you. The details in between don't matter right now."

He pushed the plunger down. Small but necessary pain pinched beneath his skin.

Mel put her hands over her mouth.

Sterling pulled the syringe out and held it up in the air, turning to motion to their friend at the Bronco.

He was on the phone.

He nodded.

Sterling turned back to Mel.

She was so scared.

Sterling smiled.

He took her hand again.

"Can you do me a favor?"

Mel's lip quivered. She nodded.

"Anything."

Sterling thumbed the engagement ring.

"I want to ask you to marry me, but I'm afraid I'll forget I did it when this has gone through my system. So." He tapped the ring. "The next time you see me, make Sam give this to me and I promise I'll give it right back. Deal?"

An unfamiliar sensation started to run down his back.

One not so unfamiliar wrapped around his heart when Mel reached for him. Her kiss was quick and hard.

The sound of approaching footfalls didn't help.

She looked over his shoulder.

Then back to him one last time.

She smiled. It was small, tired, afraid, but genuine.

"I'll say yes."

Sterling let her go as the man from the Bronco took the syringe with gloved hands.

"Time to go," he told Mel.

And she did.

And Sterling was glad for it.

He watched as they got into the Bronco and drove away.

Then he tried to hurry, to escape whatever was supposed to happen next, but all he did was go numb at the first step off the dock.

Sterling went to his knees as a man appeared out of the darkness near him.

Sterling balled his fists.

He might be down, but he certainly wasn't out.

Not yet.

Chapter Twenty-One

Mel couldn't see through her tears as the night swam past the Bronco's windows.

She'd killed Sterling.

She'd killed the man she loved because of the man she never should have married.

It was all her fault, no matter what he'd said.

The sob that tore from her mouth shook the man next to her.

He actually jumped.

"Man, I felt that all the way in my toes."

Mel folded in on herself. Her head went to her knees, her arms wrapped around her stomach.

The man didn't speak for a second. His tone changed when he did.

"You coulda run with him, you know," he said. "I mean, I would have tried to stop you two, but I've seen how fast that man is and there's a good chance y'all coulda escaped. Why didn't you? Why didn't you even try?"

Mel shook her head.

Then she was back to sitting up, wiping her eyes with the back of her arm, astonished at the question.

"Because Rider has Sam," she said simply.

The man's eyebrow rose.

When Sam had been brought into the basement, the man

in the fisherman's cap had done it. Mel had yelled at him, angry and afraid for Sam. He'd been bloodied and stumbling. Like a true Costner, he'd tried to assure *her* that *he* was okay while being forced into cuffs on the chair she'd just been freed from.

He'd also been insistent that she not do anything Rider said.

When she'd agreed to inject Sterling with the Sleepers drug so the final piece of evidence could be thrown against her, Sam had all but screamed.

But he wouldn't remember that she'd made the call. Not once the Sleepers went into his system.

He'd just wake up one day, confused and lost without his big brother.

"Oh God," Mel let out. "Sam will never forgive me."

The man behind the wheel wasn't connecting any dots.

"Who the hell is Sam? Is that another lover of yours?"

Had it been any other situation, Mel wouldn't have dignified him with a response to a question so personal.

Now, now part of her world was about to end, so she told the truth.

"Sam is Sterling's little brother." Anger, rage flew hot and fast through her, burning out the urge to keep crying. "Rider said he picked me to marry because I only truly loved two people in this world. Two people he could use against if he ever needed to do something like this." Mel hit the dash. "He gave me a choice—Sterling for Sam, and once I told Sterling that…it wasn't a choice anymore. They're my two people, and Sam and I are Sterling's. We lose saving Sam. Sterling loses more by not saving him. I knew that. I *know* that."

Her hand hurt at the hit. Mel flexed it. She got caught looking at the ring.

Her emotions were tangling together as they drove back to the house.

"Rider has spent his adulthood trying to be the best of the best—trying to be king." Mel shook her head. "He knew that Sterling would make the choice for me, but he'll never *truly* understand why he made it."

She turned to the man.

The gun at his hip wasn't the one he'd used to shoot Ella—the one with her fingerprints on it. Mel didn't know where that gun had gone, but she was sure it was somewhere waiting to implicate her.

"Rider doesn't see us. He only sees how he can use us. He doesn't care what happens when that use is done."

The man met her gaze. Mel was so close to him that his dark eyes reflected a startling movement.

They were driving up to the house.

Rider's castle.

Mel whirled around.

Flames.

They were crawling up the front of the house.

"No! Sam!"

The man stopped the car, but Mel was already out and running.

She tore through the front yard like a bat out of hell. The flames weren't high, but they were eating away at the front porch and exterior of the first floor and main door. So she ran full tilt to the back.

The gate to the yard was locked.

Mel scrambled to jump the wrought iron.

Pain scored her as the iron cut open her shin.

She didn't care.

She didn't need to know Rider's plan to know that Sam was still in that basement.

Still tied up.

Mel landed on the grass and picked up speed to the back door that led into the kitchen.

It was locked, but it gave very little resistance to the rusty fire poker that had lain useless for five years near the fire pit off the porch. The glass shattered with ease. Mel ran it around the rim until most of the glass was gone. She felt more pain as she scrambled through it. A piece had cut her. Just as the fence had.

She didn't care.

"Sam?" she yelled into the kitchen.

Mel regretted it.

Smoke was already spreading through the bottom floor of the house. Her eyes watered while she coughed into her arm.

The door to the basement was the only hurdle she didn't have to jump. It was wide-open.

Mel saved her breath and hurried down the stairs.

Briefly she thought that Sam wasn't there. That Rider had kept true to his word and burning down the house was just another step in the plan to have all clues pointing to her guilt.

Then she saw him at the back of the room.

His head was hanging low.

He wasn't moving.

"Sam!"

Mel rushed over, true terror in her heart.

She could have flown when she saw his chest rise with breath.

Mel tried to wake him, but he was limp. A small blood mark was on his right arm.

Rider had drugged him.

And he was still handcuffed to the chair.

Mel dug her hands into the cuffs, trying to free him. When they didn't budge, she tried it in reverse. They were so tight against his skin there was no wiggle room. She turned her attention to the chair. She pulled on the wooden arm that the cuff was clasped around. It, too, didn't budge.

So Mel pushed the chair over.

"Sorry," she told the unconscious Sam. His body jostled to the floor while the hand attached by the cuff swung above him.

Mel had never been a tall woman but with the chair on its side, she had just enough space to kick her foot forward. The first time she missed, but the second time her heel connected with the chair arm.

To her absolute delight, she felt it give.

The wood might have been expensive, but the frame beneath the fabric only took four solid kicks to break. Several moments later Mel took that broken piece and snapped it the rest of the way off, with the cuff attached to Sam.

His arm dropped like a ton of bricks.

Him helping her help *him* was out of the question.

Mel moved her hair back, sweat and blood soaking her clothes. She was tired. She hurt. But she wasn't about to give up.

Bending low, she grabbed Sam's hands and started to pull.

He didn't move much.

"Come on," she yelled at herself.

Mel adjusted her hold and pulled with all her might. Sam, thankfully, followed this time. It was excruciatingly slow. At this rate she'd make it to the stairs just as the fire did. Never mind going up them.

Somewhere above them, the house made an awful noise.

Mel kept pulling.

She couldn't let Sam die. Not after Sterling had—

"Move."

The voice was deep and commanding. The push at her side was gentle.

Mel was shocked to see the man from the Bronco.

He looked the worst he had since she'd been taken by him that morning.

"Come on."

He scooped Sam up and threw him over his shoulder like a sack of flour. Mel didn't ask questions. She followed him up the stairs and went around him to open the back door in the kitchen.

The smoke was thick now, dark and hot.

They ran into the backyard, coughing.

After a few yards, the man lowered Sam to the ground. Mel was on him in an instant.

Still breathing.

Mel turned her attention to the man. She didn't know why he'd helped her, but she was grateful.

"Thank you," she said, meaning every word. "Thank you so much."

The man shrugged off his deed.

"I'm not a good man, but I can still see people as human beings."

Mel felt absolute fondness for the man.

It was partly why she yelled when the gunshot tore through him. He crumpled to the ground before she could spot who'd done it. Mel threw herself over Sam just in case more shots came.

The shooter merely laughed.

"You know, this is actually perfect."

Rider lowered his gun.

"Did you know that Westley here is who I planned to make your accomplice? Because, as much as you've done in town, you'd need at least one person to help you. It was going to be Dewey, but he went and got himself in the hos-

pital. So Westley here got an upgrade to a big-time role…
and he didn't even know it. I was going to kill him before
that. But now, look at this absolute gift."

The sound of fire crackling behind him, the sight of
smoke billowing high, gave Rider the look of a devil in
his delight.

"The theatrics of the last week have almost made the
last five years in prison worth it."

"The theatrics?"

Mel thought of Rose Simon, dead in their old bed. The
shoot-out at the Meeting House. Abducted after a tornado.
She thought of the sheriff and his heart attack. Detective
Reiner unmoving in the front seat of a crashed car. The
man named Westley whose change of heart had saved a
drugged Sam.

She thought of Sterling and the ring on her finger.

This was a play to Rider. A game. A chessboard where
no one moved their piece without him punishing them for it.

Mel thought of Annie McHale, trapped in the basement
just below their feet. Terrified and alone.

Then she looked up at the man who didn't seem real. A
nightmare come to life.

It was then that she finally saw it.

The lie.

Mel stood, slowly.

Rider found humor in it. The ant that dared bare its
chest at the boot.

He was about to regret that smug look.

"You're called the Connected Corruptor because you
made sure everyone stayed in charge." Mel stepped over
Sam. She stood a few feet from Rider. "Everyone *else*. You
were the tape, the glue. You were a tool. I'm not sure if anyone has ever told you this, but you were never in charge of
anything, and I don't know why it's taken me so long to re-

alize it. Just like I don't think the flaw in your precious plan of making me the bad guy has ever crossed your mind."

Rider's smug smile turned into an angry frown.

She'd struck a nerve.

"What flaw?" he asked.

Mel smiled.

"Make me the villain and I just might play the part."

Mel lunged forward and used her right palm to thrust Rider's hand up. The gun he was holding went off but flew out of his grip after. Mel's attention had already split. Her left hand went flat against his chest with all the force she could muster. Rider, a man who'd never fought—something he paid others to do—lost his footing. He didn't fall, but the stumble was enough of an opening. Mel brought her right hand back again, but this time she balled it and punched him in the face.

She missed but had already committed to ending this. Following her momentum, she spun around and used her left elbow as her next attack.

It landed against his chin.

Rider made a pathetic cry of pain.

That only enthused Mel. She pulled back to continue her onslaught but was caught off guard by movement over his shoulder.

It made her hesitate.

Which was enough time for Rider to show Mel one last time that he never played fair.

The gun she'd knocked out of his hand wasn't the only one he'd had.

Rider pulled it up and aimed. Mel fell back against the grass trying to dodge the shot.

Mel closed her eyes tight.

The gunshot tore through the night air, the sound of flames as its backdrop.

Mel waited for the pain. Waited for the darkness.

Yet it never came.

She opened her eyes just in time to watch Rider fall forward.

Behind him was the movement she'd seen before.

A man with a gun.

"Sterling!"

Sterling dropped to his knees, the gun dropping from his hand.

Mel flew up, kicked Rider's gun clear across the grass and was on Sterling in a flash.

"Sterling!" She wrapped her arms around the man and felt his whole weight press into her. It made them both fall flat.

Mel scrambled to sit back up. She held his back against her chest.

"Are you—are you okay?" he asked. His words were soft. Low.

Mel nodded. She looked down and saw blood on him. She couldn't tell where it was coming from. Instead she answered him, relief that he was here flowing through her.

"Now I am."

"Sam?"

"He's good, too. Just sleeping."

Sterling's head was starting to droop.

The drugs were finally pulling him under.

She barely heard his last words.

"I think I might, too."

Chapter Twenty-Two

Sterling woke up warm.

With his eyes closed, he thought of Mel next to him in bed. He almost let sleep take him back under, but then there was the beeping. Then a dull pain in the back of his head.

He opened his eyes and found himself in a hospital bed, two thick blankets on top of him. Not Mel.

She was on the couch next to his bed.

There was a baby in her arms.

Sterling moved, and Mel's gaze was quick.

She smiled.

Sterling had no idea what had landed him in the hospital, but that smile put him right at ease.

"I'm guessin' something happened," he said after a moment.

Mel's smile grew, but her words were quiet.

"You definitely could say that." She didn't try to stand but did angle her body so she could face him easier. Sterling could see the baby's face now. It was Linney. "Don't worry," Mel hurriedly tacked on. "Everyone is fine now. I'm just giving Sam and Robbie a little time alone. I figured you wouldn't mind."

Sterling had questions, but it seemed like the right thing to do was not ask them now. Instead he watched Mel readjust the sleeping Linney.

He liked the sight.

"How are you feeling?" Mel asked when Linney didn't wake.

Sterling thought about it a moment.

"Laggy," he decided. "Fuzzy. Like I woke up from sleep too fast and I could go back in a second."

He yawned, proving his point.

A look of concern crossed her brow, but Mel didn't sound it.

"The doctor said your dosage was a lot higher than ours. He said you might wake and sleep a few times before finally being able to stay up. Do you want to sleep some more?"

He did, but worry caught him.

"Will you be here when I wake up?"

Mel didn't skip a beat.

"I haven't left you yet."

Sterling didn't say she had before. He closed his eyes and let sleep drag him under again.

THE NEXT TIME he woke, Mel was still on the couch. This time she was asleep. A nurse talked softly to him, and a doctor came in after that. He got up after that, slow but steady, and used the bathroom. He showered and found a change of clothes folded in the corner. He did all movements with caution and was just as slow when he went back out to the room.

Mel was waiting for him. She had a pillow mark lining her cheek. Sterling smiled at it. At her.

"You stayed."

Mel laughed.

"And you got right up to walking around. You must be feeling better."

She stepped back to the couch, and Sterling lowered

himself into the seat next to her. He flinched at the pain in his ribs. Mel didn't miss it.

"I guess that means you might be up to hearing what happened."

"I wouldn't mind a play-by-play."

Mel tilted her head, blue eyes clear.

"What *is* the last thing you remember? For everyone else it's been different."

Sterling had thought about that in the shower. Now that he was feeling more like himself, the answer was the same as it had been earlier.

"You," he said. "Next to me in bed."

Mel's cheeks went rosy. She dipped her chin a little.

"Not a bad memory to take a pause at, if you ask me," he added.

Sterling took her chin in his hand and pulled her to his lips.

She let the movement happen.

The kiss was quiet. Calm.

When it ended, it ended too soon.

"I've been told I'm missing close to two days of memory, but I sure hope I did that sometime in between."

Mel sighed. A smile was still there when the breath was gone.

"A lot happened—not all of it good, but some of it definitely so."

She took his hand in hers.

"But not all of it is mine to tell. We need to bring in some more people to get the whole picture."

THE WHOLE PICTURE went from the two of them in his hospital room to two more. Detective Reiner had a cast on. Sam had a hospital band on his wrist. Mel started as soon as they were seated.

The story started with Cole showing up at the house. It nose-dived after that.

"Deputy Park found me unconscious and James shot on the ground next to the car," Reiner said when she got to his part. "He was wearing a vest but pretty banged up. He told us that Jonathan Partridge had rammed into us and had worked with Mel to escape. Then shot him when he tried to fight back."

"When really it was the man from the Meeting House, Westley, who grabbed me and shot James, who, by the way, volunteered for the bullet," Mel added.

"After that the department got word that the Bronco with Jonathan and Mel had gone downtown and shot Ella Cochlin," Reiner continued. "Around the same time you blew through the department to Foster and pitched your theory that Mel was being set up by Rider, and if Rider was setting her up, then he had to be in town."

Sterling nodded to his own deduction. It made sense, especially since there was no way that Mel had done any of what she'd been accused of doing.

"Foster believed you and drove out to the prison to see for himself."

"Oh, and the man from the Meeting House woke up here in the hospital, saying that Rider was innocent," Mel interjected. "I wasn't personally here for that, but Detective Lovett gave me the full rundown earlier."

Cole nodded.

"By the time Foster made it to the prison and saw that Rider had switched places with a man named Randy Kolt and paid off several guards *heavily*, we realized that you'd gone missing, too."

"Before that Westley had already taken me to a house out near the creek for a bad guy monologue," Mel jumped in. "Then he took me to the house and a basement full of his supply of Sleepers."

Sam raised his hand.

"That's where I come in, apparently. Robbie said they found my car still running outside Sterling's place, empty. That other guy got me, as far as they can tell."

Sterling became angry again. Mel touched his hand.

"The other guy was another Rider lackey. His name was Bailey, and he owned the fisherman's cabin I woke up in after being taken the first time," she explained. "He didn't mind at all doing the things Rider paid him to do."

"His name *was*? Is he dead?"

Cole and Mel shared a look. Sam nodded.

"They'll get to that. This is the part you're going to want to hear first." Sam nodded to Mel. This time they shared the look. It was soft but warm.

Then she told him about their time at the dock. The deal she'd made and how Sterling had been the one to finish it by injecting himself.

Mel's eyes had started to water. This time he took her hand and squeezed.

"I don't remember it happening, but I stand by what we both did," he told her. "What happened after you and Westley left?"

Mel shook her head a little and cleared her throat.

"Bailey showed up to try and kill you," Cole said. He laughed. "You're never going to believe who helped save you."

Sterling had no idea. He said as much.

Sam couldn't keep it in.

"It was Jonathan Partridge," he said, a little too loud.

Sterling didn't believe him.

"No way."

"Yep," Mel responded. "Jonathan Partridge showed up,

helped you fight off Bailey and then drove you to the house while calling in the entire department."

"Hearing you back up the story on speakerphone definitely helped," Cole added.

After that the story became no less wild. Jonathan had apparently gone into the house to make sure no one was in the basement while Sterling had fought the drugs in his system long enough to run outside when he heard Rider shoot Westley.

"The doctors said it was a miracle you hung on as long as you did," Mel said quietly. "Rider didn't plan on that."

But he had. Long enough to save Mel.

That made simple sense to him, too.

The story wrapped up in technical details. Jonathan had run out to greet the arriving deputies and firemen, and Sterling, Sam and Westley had been transported to the hospital. Rider hadn't survived the shot. They all took a moment of silence for that but didn't linger on it.

While everyone was in the hospital, the house burned to the ground. Later a rumor would start that the structure could have been saved but instead the fire department and deputies alike watched it burn, standing on the front lawn, ash falling around them. He'd never know if it was true or not, because no one talked about the house ever again.

Ella Cochlin and Deputy James Reynolds recovered quickly from their respective wounds while Sterling and Sam slept off their drugs. The moment they found out Rider had passed, they both broke down. Ella had been in a relationship with Rider after a chance encounter with him while visiting her brother in prison. Since then she had made her home in Kelby Creek and waited to be another thing that tried to make Mel look guilty. James, however, had been blackmailed for almost as long. He'd been one of the few who had been protected by Rider's omission of facts during the investigation after The Flood. The same went for the man who had owned the fishing cabin, Bailey. He'd died of his wounds inflicted in the fight with Sterling and Jonathan, but Ella had told his story in full.

Then there was the man who had fallen into a coma after the Meeting House. He was the son of Randy Kolt, the man who'd switched places with Rider at the prison. He never would admit why he'd helped Rider, but there was enough on him that he was about to go to prison himself.

The only person left who had helped spin the web surrounding Mel was a man Sterling visited before he was discharged later that week.

Westley looked awful.

It was a miracle he was even alive, though that miracle was mostly due to the fact that Rider Partridge was a terrible shot.

"Three bullets I've taken in this town. I'm going to laugh if anyone tries to tell me Kelby Creek ain't dangerous again."

Sterling had laughed at that and sat with the man awhile. He had already agreed to cooperate fully in the investigation and had evidence that damned everyone involved. Including himself.

All Sterling could do, though, was thank him for saving his brother.

"Don't thank me," he'd said, serious. "You thank that woman of yours. She's the one who ran into a burning building to save someone you loved."

Sterling had left him at that, promising that he and Mel would make it known how Westley had helped, and Mel and Sterling finally went home.

Before he could get down to something else he'd been wanting to talk to her about, someone else came calling for a chat.

Jonathan Partridge had definitely seen better days. Scabbed and bruised and limping, he took a seat at the kitchen table and finally gave Sterling the rest of the missing pieces.

"Everyone assumed I was always with Rider just because I was his brother. Even you, which I think is why I was so angry with you all these years." He said the last part to Mel and gave her a sympathetic smile. "You knew me, and the second Rider was found guilty, you joined everyone else in pointing the finger at me because I was blood. I should have told you in no uncertain terms that I wasn't but, well, pride, I guess."

Mel apologized to him then and there. Sterling, too. Jonathan shrugged it off but accepted.

"I tried to believe he was good, but after the trial and all the evidence, well, I cut him off," he continued. "Every month for five years he called me and punished me for it. Asked if the town still hated me for something I never did. Every month without fail. Made me furious because I never could escape that call. He always found a way. Then, one month, the call didn't come. At least not from him."

"Rose," Mel offered. Jonathan nodded.

"She told me that she was being forced to write a new piece on Rider on the anniversary of The Flood. That it was an entire spread about how Mel was the real Connected Corruptor and that Rose had been wrong. But whatever he had on Rose wasn't enough to bind her conscience. She reached out to me because she's the only one who always believed I had nothing to do with it. Then I reached out to you."

Mel had already heard the story from Jonathan in the hospital, but Sterling put it all together for the first time now.

"You're why Mel came back to town."

Again, Jonathan nodded.

"We decided to meet with Rose at the Meeting House, but on the way into town Rose had a change of heart," he said. "So Mel and I decided to head to the sheriff's department instead. For whatever reason, Rose turned on us. We fought, and Bailey showed up. He managed to drug Mel before we got away, but they chased us down."

"That's when the car accident happened," Sterling realized. "And it was you driving."

"Yep. And what a job I did."

Mel had swatted at him, affection clear in her voice.

"He convinced Bailey that if they took me then and there that his brother's plan of framing me wouldn't work. Instead putting me as the driver would work the best. Then he went to check on me at the hospital."

Jonathan shrugged.

"I didn't know what they'd given her, but when I realized her memory was gone, I panicked and worried that she wouldn't believe me without Rose. So I left to try and get some proof. I couldn't find it, but once I heard that you had gone missing, I went to where I thought Rose might have been killed. That's when I found you."

Mel had surprised them both by hugging Jonathan tight at that. Sterling surprised himself by not being far behind.

Jonathan had laughed when they saw him out to the front porch.

"I know this might come off as a weird thing to say, but I've always thought you two made a much better couple."

He told them 'bye and drove off, lighter than when he'd walked in.

Then it was Sterling and Mel.

She sighed her way into the comfort of the couch. Sterling followed suit.

"You know, while I was talking to Sheriff Chamblin and his wife at the hospital, they invited us over to their house for some good ol' comfort food since he's now officially on the mend," Mel said. "And Lordy if that doesn't sound good after the last two weeks."

She had her eyes closed and was feeling a sigh.

Sterling angled his body to face her and held up something for her to see.

When she opened those blue eyes he'd loved since he was a teen, they went right to the ring in his hand.

"Sam said you gave this to him when he woke up," he started. "He said you swore him to secrecy on how it ended up on your finger. I'm not going to ask about that now, because, well, I'm going to kiss the person right in front of me." Sterling smiled.

"I'd like to ask you to marry me, though, right here and now. Maybe even for a second time, because, well, it's hard not to love you out loud, and I'm tired of pretending I'm okay with not being with you." He held the ring out, heartbeat already in sync with hers. "What do you think?"

Mel looked at the ring. Then her eyelashes fluttered up and those blue eyes were his.

"You can ask me every day for the rest of our lives and I'll always say yes to loving you, Sterling Costner."

She let him put the ring on her finger.

Then she kissed him long and true.

Later that month they'd marry on the back porch of the house, Sam between them as he officiated the wedding. They'd never remember the memories they'd lost but they didn't need them to know they were lucky, all things considered. After the ceremony Sterling and Mel would drive off to their honeymoon, but not before stopping for slushies.

Then it was just like they were teens again, driving around with the breeze in their hair and love in their hearts.

* * * * *

STALKING
COLTON'S FAMILY

GERI KROTOW

To Steve, Alex and Ellen; thank you for always being here. I love you with all my heart.

Chapter One

Rachel Colton stared at her infant daughter Iris's inno-cent face, soaking all the cuteness up from her bright red wisps of hair to her adorable chin. "I love you, dar-ling daughter, but you're making me late for work. Again."

With an expertise she hadn't had before Iris's birth six months ago, Rachel cleaned up the dirty diaper—or more accurately, the contents of said item that had messed up her only clean going-to-court suit—as she spoke to the most important person in her life.

Iris Colton, the wonder baby who'd surprised every-one with her appearance—Rachel included. Those first few moments of realizing she was pregnant last year had been some of the most trying of her life. And yet, here she stood, getting through another morning with Iris, facing another day as Blue Larkspur's brand-new district attorney after several years as assistant DA. There wasn't one minute that went by that Rachel didn't feel the weight of both her job and motherhood on her shoulders. But being Iris's mom was, hands down, the best job she'd ever had.

"Ba ba." Iris's chubby, six-month-old cheeks puffed

out as she babbled and melted all of Rachel's irritation away. She'd come to think of Iris as her "joy baby" because her precious daughter brought her a heaping heartful of happiness each day. Being a new mother was like that—one minute Rachel had no idea how she'd get through the next hour; the next, she wanted to stop time and revel in her joy baby forever.

"We both need to clean up, Iris girl." She held Iris out at arm's length and carried her to the changing table, where she made quick work of getting the infant back into a clean outfit. The sound of the back kitchen door closing alerted her that Iris's nanny had arrived.

"We're back here, Emily!" She smiled at Iris and made silly sounds to keep the baby from squirming until Emily's smiling face appeared at the door of the nursery. Not for the first time, an immense wave of gratitude pulsed through her heart. Emily was the perfect nanny for her baby and had come at the highest recommendation of her mother, Isadora Colton, and her older sister, Morgan. Isa's best friend's granddaughter had Emily as her nanny for her first three years, and Morgan's friend had also employed Emily for a few months before eventually taking a break from her career to stay home. Emily's skills and gifted ability to handle young children put her in high demand in Blue Larkspur. She came with the highest levels of recommendation. Rachel wouldn't have it any other way.

"Good morning, ladies. Oh my." Emily's gaze took in Iris's and Rachel's appearances, from the ruined suit to the soiled onesie on top of the hamper.

"She had a major blowout. I'll put the dirty clothes in the laundry, then I have to do a quick change myself."

"Here, let me take her." Emily reached for Iris at the same moment Iris lifted her arms to greet her nanny. Rachel's heart swelled with relief alongside bittersweet longing. It was a gift to have such a loving, kind nanny for Iris, someone she trusted her daughter with for her often twelve-hour days. But the reassurance of wonderful childcare did nothing to ease the sense of her heart being torn from her chest each time she left her precious girl, knowing she'd invariably miss out on some milestones. It also bothered her that Iris was lacking in the father department, but at least her brother Gideon was a superb uncle and around a lot, most often with Sophia, the love of his life. They'd recently reunited, and the entire Colton family was thrilled for them. Sophia was a pediatrician and both she and Gideon were hoping for a family of their own soon, which would give Iris her first cousin. Rachel had five other brothers in her total of eleven other Colton siblings, but between their jobs and own lives, Gideon remained the one she relied upon most.

It had been a cruel blow to find out that her one-night stand at a legal conference in Helena, Montana, was unavailable to be a responsible father. Rachel had learned the cold, hard truth when she'd tried to call Iris's father, and instead of him answering or being put through to voice mail, another woman who'd identified herself as his fiancée had answered. Which meant he'd most likely been in that committed relationship during their Montana fling.

Rachel had decided on the spot that it was better for all involved that he went on with his own life, and she with hers. The last thing she was willing to do was risk her baby's emotional stability and sense of security with a part-time parent. She'd tucked him away as a bad memory, a mistake, except for the gift of her joy baby. No way would she ever reveal the name of her child's father to her family. Her brothers were protective and wouldn't hesitate to find the man and make his life miserable. Not that she thought of her brothers as criminal stalkers or anything; they were simply very typical brothers who didn't take kindly to anyone messing with their family.

Besides, James Kiriakis had shown more of his true colors the morning after their night of passion; all he'd talked about was the high-profile firm he worked for and how he prided himself on winning his corporate litigations. She remembered the regret that had pierced through the incredible chemistry they'd shared only hours earlier. James's ego-driven boasting had reminded her too much of the worst parts of her father, the long-deceased Ben Colton. As a judge, her father had taken the Blue Larkspur, Colorado, community for every nickel he could, supplementing his legal income with kickbacks from sending offenders of all ages to detention centers. It still stung, twenty years later, that her father had been dirty.

Which validated why Iris didn't need James for a father.

You've got to stop assuming every man is like Dad.

True, but the discovery of her father's nefarious undertakings when he was a judge was a long shadow to not only outrun but a deep wound in the community that she was determined to help heal. Her eleven siblings and she had formed the Truth Foundation for this very reason. Now that she was DA, she'd had to recuse herself from the foundation's work, but there was plenty she could do for Blue Larkspur at the most basic levels. Getting the real criminals locked up while ensuring the innocent got the rehabilitation they needed was a good start.

"I'm going to make you proud to be a Colton, Iris." She spoke to the quiet as she stripped out of the pale gray sheath dress she particularly liked for the way it complemented her figure. As she changed her attire, she tried to ignore the now-familiar struggle to leave her precious infant for another full day at the office.

Iris is safe. I have a good job to support both of us. Our family has our backs. We have Emily.

And that was the crux of it. Emily Chase was the nanny Rachel only would have dared dreamed of, not actually believed existed when she'd been pregnant and the realities of becoming a single parent were sinking in. The last fifteen months had been the most trying yet happiest time of her life. Becoming a single parent had never been on her list of life goals when she'd decided to pursue the law but neither had learning about true love and commitment—in the form of wide-eyed Iris—been the remotest possibility for her.

A text lit up her phone.

Where are you?

Her assistant, Clara, had gotten into the habit of checking on her if she was more than a minute past her self-appointed show-up time for court. Before Iris, arriving thirty minutes early had been an easy parameter to meet. Since becoming a mother, however, she'd scraped the time down with only a handful of minutes to spare.

This morning was going to push that to the limit. She wrestled with a sleeveless shell and skirt, her skin slick with stress sweat. Her ob-gyn assured her that the excess perspiration from hormonal changes while she was breastfeeding Iris was temporary. But being over-heated and feeling as though she was always disheveled never left. As if she was just shy of the professionalism she'd taken for granted before Iris.

A soft groan escaped her throat as she threw together the outfit on the fly, grabbing a bracelet while shoving her feet into too-high heels that were the only match for the navy blue.

She forced herself to get her mind focused on work. Emily had Iris; it was okay. Did all new mothers have to reassure themselves like this, all day long?

No wonder Mom stayed home with us in the begin-ning.

Her mother was an accomplished graphic designer these days but had devoted many years to full-time homemaking. Before her husband's crimes had been exposed and their family driven to near bankruptcy.

As assistant DA, she'd relished putting away the crooks her father had wheeled-and-dealed with years before. Now, as DA, she spent most days proving the culpability of local losers. Her commitment to Blue Larkspur ran as deep as the Colton blood that coursed through her veins.

She was able to serve on her current case only be-cause she'd taken the necessary steps to legally detach herself from the family's Truth Foundation, formed to right the wrongs of Ben Colton. It was imperative that she resign from the nonprofit a few years back, so that she could avoid a conflict of interest to be able to serve as a public prosecutor. But a disgruntled judge or pushy defense attorney could derail her goal to get a crook who'd worked with her father behind bars. That was the thing about the law that Rachel both loved and detested. Justice had to serve all.

Which meant she needed to keep it as professional as possible and show up on time. Today's defendant had made hundreds of thousands of dollars in kickbacks before Ben Colton had died. She'd refrained from investigating him when she was part of the Truth Foundation, of course, but his time was up, now that she was DA. The crook, Brian Parson, had earned enough from the rig he and Ben had set up to support his family with the dirty money for the last twenty years, not to mention all he'd earned as the area drug boss. The Truth Foundation had been supportive of the DA's relentless pursuit of Parson, sitting on its hands so as to not jeopardize the DA's prosecution. It wasn't the first case the Truth Foundation had needed to scale back on, in support of the legal system. Because Rachel had been meticulous about remaining legally unattached to the Parson case, it allowed her to prosecute now, as DA. She relished bringing Parson down. It was time he paid the price.

But he wouldn't if Rachel was late—today's judge was a stickler for promptness and wouldn't hesitate to delay, or worse, throw the case out if she appeared at all unprepared. And what was more evident of piss-poor prep than tardiness?

She hit the speed dial to her assistant.

"Yes, ma'am? Are you here?" Clara's voice was smooth, but she detected a lilt of anxiety.

"No, but I will be. Give me fifteen minutes."

"That takes it to—"

"One minute before showtime. I know. I'll be there."

She disconnected and prayed she'd make it.

"You've got to be kidding me."

James Kiriakis let out a sigh as he stared in aggravation at the large mechanical arm lowering in front of the hood of his black BMW, preventing him from crossing the railroad track before what appeared to be an endless line of shipping containers began to click by. Blue Larkspur, Colorado, was nothing like Denver. He'd mistakenly thought the traffic would be a breeze after the constant congestion in the state capital. Wrong assumption, on all fronts. Blue Larkspur was tiny compared to the state capital but mighty in its desire to get to work on time.

He sent a quick hands-free, voice-activated text to the paralegal he was meeting at the courthouse, his fingers in a death clench on the steering wheel. He frantically used his rearview and side-view mirrors, the action automatic at this point as his heart pounded in time to his spike in stress. James was certain he was awash in cortisol as his body poised for yet another nasty confrontation.

There were no signs that he'd been followed by the one person he was running from. The main reason he'd left Denver, truth be told. It didn't stop the hairs on his nape from rising, though. Since he'd departed the city, the nasty sense that he was being watched, followed, *stalked* hadn't lifted. No matter how much he reassured himself that no way could Bethany Austin know he'd moved, had cleared out his high-rise condo and sold it for a tidy profit.

Could she?

"Relax. You've left it all behind." He did the box breathing he'd read about, the method used by navy SEALs. It eased some of the tension in his shoulders, which only seemed to allow the flow of nagging thoughts back into his mind.

It had to be his tardiness that was making him so much on edge. He'd taken all the steps to excise himself from the hellish predicament he'd lived through these past months. Yet as he continued to watch his rearview mirror, he noticed as a vehicle six cars back pulled out of the waiting traffic, made a quick U-Turn and sped off. His gut tightened at the familiar action and he gripped the wheel to pull himself closer to the rearview mirror, tried to make out the license plate on the unfamiliar car that didn't even resemble Bethany's. It was a blur. Probably for the best. What would he do with it if he was able to discern the plate's letters and numbers? Tell the police he thought an unknown vehicle was occupied by his stalker when he hadn't been able to see the driver?

He sucked in another breath, held it, let it go. Disappointment thumped against his chest, under his sternum. How foolish was he to think he'd rid himself of the awfulness of being stalked with one move?

You're just stressed because you're going to be late.

It wasn't like him to be late to anything, ever. But

since he'd hit an emotional bottom in his personal life—thanks to stalker Bethany—he found himself questioning everything from his ability to discern fact from fiction, to real emotion from passing illusion. It all boiled down to the fact that he'd lived the life of a victim—had *been* a victim—something that, as a six-foot-one former college athlete, he wasn't accustomed to. But Bethany, the woman he'd briefly and most casually dated—they hadn't gone to bed, hadn't gone past two dinner dates—had turned out to be a stalker extraordinaire.

He'd ended it with her, made it clear they were going to be a friends-only deal, right after he got back from a legal conference in Montana. After he'd spent one incredible night with a woman who made him rethink his personal creed to remain single for at least a while longer. Bethany and he had had zero commitment. He'd only agreed to go out on that second and last date because she'd surprised him at his apartment, telling him how much she'd missed him while he was gone. Her nearly frantic behavior raised red flags that night. So he'd called it off. But Bethany never heard anything she didn't want to. He'd been forced to get a restraining order only a month later, but her chilling antics had continued for the next eight months. He'd put up with a stalker for almost a year.

A stalker. He still struggled with it, that he had his own personal harasser.

He'd dealt with ugly scenes before, when he'd stopped dating someone. But he soon found Bethany Austin wasn't any run-of-the-mill, bitter-that-the-relationship-is-over pursuer. Her methods to get his attention had accelerated into Mach speed without lingering in any manageable area within two days of him telling her that they were no longer even friends. From showing up unannounced at his office to breaking into his condo with a key and digital codes she'd bribed from the doorman—now fired—she'd shattered James's sense of well-being.

His repeated pleas that she seek medical attention for her obvious issues hadn't worked. But even after he'd been forced to get a restraining order, Bethany had still found ways to tail him. Showing up at restaurants, retail stores, recreational parks, always unannounced. She was careful to always maintain the exact distance needed from him so that he couldn't report her presence as a violation of the restraining order but made certain he saw her.

If he hadn't found this new job in Blue Larkspur, he'd have gone back to court to tighten the order's restrictions against her. Bethany wanted more than any man could give her, in his opinion. She'd wanted to be in a committed relationship with James after one date, so he'd immediately backed off, insisted they be friends. No matter how much she assured him that she "got it" and only wanted his friendship, no strings attached, it became clear within days that Bethany saw James as the sole object of her affections.

Affection that had turned creepy in a Denver minute.

Getting Bethany physically out of his life didn't keep her from occupying his mental and emotional space, though.

He blamed himself for her continued harassment; he should have pressed charges each time she broke

the restraining order or did any one of myriad definite stalking actions. His empathy for her distress, his
guilt that maybe, somehow, he'd encouraged her, had
always won out.

James was counting on a new setting, miles and
hours from Bethany, to allow him to finally let go of
the constant fight-or-flight drain on his adrenals. That's
what his personal trainer had said was wearing him out
and flooding his nervous system with cortisol.

He shifted in his seat, stretched his back. James
didn't discount that theory, but the observation had
struck a chord. Bethany had wormed her way into the
most dangerous parts of his mind, the neighborhoods no
one should ever wander in alone. Her stalking ignited
his most primal defensive behaviors. It didn't matter
that she hadn't bothered him for months. Some crimes
leave deeper scars than others, and invisible marks can
be worse.

Which is why he'd taken so many precautions as he
left Denver to prevent Bethany from being able to track
him, follow him to Blue Larkspur. She'd always found
him in the past, though, was always able to worm her
way around any security he'd put in place. It was easy
to tell himself that being haunted by Bethany would
never end.

Enough.

He was in the midst of his new start, free from Bethany and all the baggage her actions brought with them.
He raised the volume on his stereo, allowed his favorite
band to drown out any unwanted thoughts.

Today was the first day of week two at a premier
Blue Larkspur litigation firm, where he'd accepted a

not-unimpressive position that practically guaranteed he'd make partner in short order. Otherwise, would he have ever before considered moving out of Denver, quitting the high-pressure, highly successful job he'd worked, representing major corporations for the past decade, where partnership had been offered only three months ago?

He knew he wouldn't have. He'd fought a deep internal battle and decided to turn down the partnership. Bethany's continued and escalating exploits continued to haunt him, even months after she appeared to have given up on him. A change in address was a good solution. He had his family's support, and that was the deciding factor for James.

His mom, Helen Kiriakis, and his siblings were all close, as his father had died when James was six years old. The Kiriakis clan took care of its own. That said, they all agreed that short of them becoming vigilantes against Bethany, James's move was a smart response.

He'd been eager to transition here anyway. The hustle and bustle of Denver was getting to him, and while he still opted to live in a contemporary luxury condo in Blue Larkspur, he was trading big-city life for more of a quiet-city vibe.

And there's a certain district attorney in Blue Larkspur who caught your vibes fifteen months ago.

He ignored his heart's musings. Rachel Colton had refused all of his calls after they'd shared an incredible night together at a Helena, Montana, legal conference. It'd been all over the state news last month that she'd been recently appointed to Lark's County DA, remarkable for her young but solid career. The Colorado bar association's professional periodical had done an impressive profile on her, and when he saw her stunning features beaming out from the page-sized glossy photo his heart had raced. As if they'd shared more than an evening.

He'd been disappointed to read through and see that it included zero personal information. Why he was still thinking about this woman, though, when she hadn't taken his calls was beyond him. He had to blame this one on the stress of being stalked. Why else, when she'd patently ghosted him, would he allow his mind to flash back to their incendiary night? He couldn't deny that she'd cut him off. Or blame her, for that matter. They didn't even know each other, and it had been the classic one-night stand, on paper. What gnawed at him was how harsh her rejection felt. How hard is it to answer, or at least text, with a "sorry, not interested"?

Besides, for all he knew, Rachel could have turned out to be a stalker, too.

No.

He wasn't going to allow the situation with Bethany to mar his entire future, shadow every thought he ever had about another woman. He'd finished dating Bethany before he'd connected with Rachel. In all his past one-nighters, he'd thought of them as hookups, and as much as he respected great sex, he never expected more. James wanted nothing to do with a permanent relationship until he'd made his mark in the world and he knew his career was solid. He'd been feeling a sense of missing out on what was important as he saw his siblings and close friends get hitched, have kids. That was why he'd tried to get in touch with Rachel after their too-brief connection in Montana. Rachel had struck him as more than a one-nighter. Maybe, daresay, the kind of woman he'd be willing to be committed to.

"All in the past, buddy." But it wasn't. Not in his mind, anyway.

He shifted in his leather bucket seat at the mere memory of *that* night. James was great at putting unwanted thoughts and distractions aside from whatever the task at hand, but his body had never forgotten the pleasure the beautiful Rachel Colton had gifted it with.

He'd been unable to shake the sense that Rachel had been different from every woman he'd met before. James snorted, then all-out laughed at himself, banging his palms on the steering wheel.

Why did he think he was an exception to human behavior? He'd still been emotionally vulnerable after evading Bethany and wanted some companionship. That's why the time with Rachel was still imprinted on his mind. Nothing more.

She lives in Blue Larkspur. Had nothing to do with why he'd picked here for his relocation. It'd been more about the first job offer that would allow him to escape Denver. Okay, mostly. All right, there was some hope that if he let Rachel know he'd moved here, she might bite.

It still bothered the heck out of him that he'd basically been chased from his own life. And yet, he'd also grown tired of his job as he'd done it for so long. It was time for a change.

The train cleared and he tried to clear all thoughts of women out of his mind as he made the last half mile to the courthouse. Not willing to chance there'd be an open spot available in the main, smaller courthouse parking lot, he parked in a garage a block away and sprinted, laptop bag slung over his shoulder, to the front steps. He zigzagged between people also heading to the same single entrance.

Exhilaration pumped through his veins as he hit the top level, skidded to a—

Bam!

"What the—" A female voice continued into a rather succinct, albeit quiet, stream of profanity that would have made James laugh if he wasn't doing all he could to remain upright, to keep from landing on his ass or worse, atop this stranger. His efforts were futile, and it was with horror that he realized he couldn't stop his fall.

Fortunately his hands landed on either side of the person he'd slammed into, and as his knees hit the unforgiving stone ground, he didn't know what was more surprising: the searing pain of marble-on-kneecap or the sexiest blue eyes he'd ever known staring up at him in complete shock.

"Rachel." Her name came out on the *whoosh* of air that expelled from his lungs.

"James?" Her intense gaze jolted him back to their time in Helena, to when she'd begged him to be this close. To when he'd wondered where she'd been all his life. Sure, he'd expected their paths might cross ever since he'd searched for her on the Internet, when he'd wondered why she was completely icing him out. And he'd all but decided to look her up. But literally running into her wasn't part of his plan.

She never returned your calls or texts.

Not. One.

Even the harsh reminder couldn't make him move, stand up, walk away from Rachel Colton and get to work.

Work. His new job.

"Aw, crap."

Chapter Two

The last time James had been on top of her they'd been in a swanky, minimalist executive suite, and his breath had carried the distinct scent of single malt mingled with her own essence. As she caught her breath, no doubt sucking in his exhales, she smelled peppermint and something…green.

"Let me guess, smoothie for breakfast?" She shoved at his chest, wanting him up and off her *now*. She needed to be in court three minutes ago.

His eyes widened the tiniest bit, which she took as surprise. "What?" Recognition lit up his irises which only annoyed her further. He gave her a slow grin. "Do I have kale in my teeth?"

"Get off!" She pushed harder, struggling to get back on her feet. Anywhere but this close to the man she'd worked every waking hour to free from her mind, ever since that last, lingering kiss well over a year ago.

He adroitly got to his feet and grabbed her elbow, helping her up. Too flustered to fight the unwanted assistance, she figured the quickest way to get away was to keep it simple. She leaned against him, fought to regain balance on the blasted stilettos, to get her breath back. This wasn't any kind of pleasant surprise; it was a scary-as-all-get-out shock. What the heck was James doing in Blue Larkspur?

Fear stabbed through her racing thoughts. Did he know about Iris?

James was a powerful attorney, wasn't he?

No. No way could he come in here now and change the life she'd built. One where Iris was protected from any upset. Like meeting a father she'd never known.

Rachel wasn't worried that she'd have to share her baby with James, was she?

Are you?

"Thank you." Once on her feet she turned away and made a straight shot toward security, James on her heels. Which made her angry at herself for picking the too-high shoes that she hadn't worn since before Iris was born. If she'd stuck with her black flats, no matter that they didn't match the suit, she'd never have been knocked down. She would have made it through security moments before this buffoon—James—had barreled into her. But today was an important court day, as was every day for the DA. She wanted to look her best. To feel her best. So she'd picked the sexier fashion choice.

A scream welled in her throat and she bit her cheek, threw her laptop bag on the X-ray machine's belt and walked through the metal scanner under the keen gaze of the security guard.

"Wait!" The urgent note in his deep voice reached out, grabbed her focus away from getting into court.

She spun back to him so quickly that she teetered for a brief moment before stilling. He leaned in, as if ready to catch her.

"Folks, keep it out of the surveillance area." The guard was not impressed.

Rachel waited for James to clear security.

When she faced him this time, she made no disguise of her contempt as she batted away his smile, his attempt at a friendly greeting.

"James. It's been, what, fifteen months? And while I appreciate that you remember me—"

"You remembered me, too." Issued like a challenge, as if he was out to prove a case. "Otherwise, how would you know the exact amount of time that's passed?"

"Right." She looked at her smartwatch, which dinged with a frantic text from her assistant. "I'm due in court, and I'm late."

"Meet me for dinner."

"I've got to—"

"Please." His hand was on her forearm, his intensity undeniable. She glanced at his left hand, which rested on the laptop case slung across his shoulders. No ring. Sure had to be some long engagement. Or maybe…

No.

"I'm sorry, James. I'm unavailable." She tugged free of his light grasp, and this time, he didn't try to stop her from going through security. The twinge of emotion that tore at her heart was her annoyance at being late for court.

It had nothing to do with disappointment.

"You're going to have to work harder to get this loser behind bars." Her assistant looked at her across Rachel's massive desk, a tablet balanced on her lap.

"I know that, Clara. Don't you think I do?" Rachel

sighed, unable to forgive herself for being late, for not giving her best impression in court this morning. Her mistake had made the judge raise his brows at her. His Honor had seemed more congenial than usual to yet another one of the men who had profited by her deceased father's criminal doings. Ben Colton had been a judge who willingly took bribes to incarcerate innocent people. As a juvenile detention center administrator and board member, Brian Parson had facilitated kickbacks to Judge Colton for providing prisoners who were given harsher sentences than called for and become a very successful, menacing drug kingpin. "We're dealing with not only the slimiest of scum but the richest, too. Brian Parson won't go down without a fight, but we've got him by the…throat." She tried to keep it classy as DA, but sometimes her words got away from her. "I'm just lucky the judge hasn't recused me from the case yet."

"He can't, not since you've resigned your position with the Truth Foundation. Plus, you've never worked on his case before, even when you had my job."

"No, I didn't." She'd made it clear to the then-DA that unless Parson was up for trial she didn't want to be privy to any information about him. She'd never expected to become the DA this soon, though.

Being able to work this side of the cases that the Truth Foundation helped bring to light was important to Rachel. It had cost her years that she could have been working closely alongside her siblings to right her father's wrongs, but she was doing her part to keep Blue Larkspur safe. Parson was a notorious drug kingpin in the area and could go to jail none too soon, as far as she was concerned.

Rachel let out a long breath, wondering what Iris was doing. She missed her baby. A quick glance at her watch told her the baby was taking her afternoon nap. "I know that, but I absolutely can't be late ever again. I'm going to undo all my brothers and sisters have accomplished in twenty years in two months if I'm not careful."

"Stop it. I may be overstepping, but none of this is your fault." Clara was ten years younger and a newly minted lawyer, just as Rachel had been in the same position. Rachel knew her assistant aspired to someday have Rachel's position. Rachel sincerely hoped Clara achieved it. Being DA wasn't all that she'd thought it'd be, and it wasn't just because her father, as well as his widow and kids, had become Blue Larkspur's pariahs after his death. The pressure and quickly evolving cases kept her on her mental toes, which she loved. But combined with the stress of raising an infant, being a new mom, it felt like a bit much at times. Rachel suspected she'd want a quieter position when Iris got older.

"Now you're smiling."

"I've got to call Iris before we go back in session."

Clara nodded, never slow to get a hint. "I'll meet you back in court in fifteen minutes." As Clara opened the door and walked out, the receptionist arrived, holding a huge bouquet of creamy white tulips in a vase that didn't look like a typical florist's inexpensive type.

"These just came for you, ma'am."

"Thank you." She nodded at the corner of her desk, doing all she could to appear unaffected by the gorgeous spring bouquet. Mother Nature had dumped ten inches of snow just last week, not atypical for a Colorado spring, so the reminder of warmer weather wasn't unwelcome. Though she suspected the sentiments might be.

As soon as her office door shut, leaving her alone, she sprang from her chair and whipped off the note card from its stake above the blooms. Her fingers shook as she removed the classy white stationery. "Have dinner with me. James."

He'd left his cell number below his signature. His handwriting was definite, the slant distinct. And her libido responded as if their time together had been only last weekend, not over a year ago. It had to be because he was Iris's father, a purely biological reaction.

She pulled up his contact information in her phone, noting that this was a new number. Her hands shook as she updated his profile. Before she could allow herself to think, Rachel did a most uncharacteristic thing and texted him one word.

Yes.

"I DON'T WANT to be the one to tell you you're letting your past run your life, bro, but have you considered your Spidey senses are tingling because you're in a new place?" Jake, James's older brother, had a point. James spoke to him via his wireless earphones as he stacked books on his office shelves. The shipment from Denver had arrived this morning.

"I haven't had any thoughts of Bethany since…"

"When she crashed your farewell party?"

James groaned. "Yes." The reminder of how she'd shown up at the upscale restaurant, in front of the senior partners and staff, still gave him heartburn. Bethany had worn a dress more suited for a private lover's night out than a business function. He experienced the embarrassment all over again as he remembered his shock at her behavior. In front of all of his colleagues, no less. She'd sidled up next to him, squeezed his butt and tried to kiss him. Since his former firm knew about the restraining order, the office receptionist made a quick 9-1-1 call and Bethany had been removed from the premises in cuffs. But not before the jovial celebration had been doused. "I should have pressed charges then." She'd been let out on minimal bail and an agreement to do community service.

"Stop blaming yourself for her behavior, James."

"I know you're right."

"I always am." They both shared a laugh. Jake was older by five years and also a lawyer. He'd set up his own family practice in the same Denver suburb they'd grown up in. "Seriously, try to let go of what you've been through here. The cops told you that Bethany has a history of stalking boyfriends, right? You're just another bozo on the bus, James. She'll forget about you and latch on to someone else when she finds it impossible to find you. The odds of Bethany following you to Blue Larkspur have to be equal to the odds of you switching to family law."

"Nil." James liked the thrill of the chase for justice in a commercial setting.

"You're such a softie."

"I am." James knew his limits. Jake was well suited for family law as he'd been the one to help his mother and younger siblings when their dad, Stefanos Kiriakis, died. James had never been able to shake the trauma of losing a parent when he was only six. As he grew, he more fully comprehended the legal mess his father had left for his mother. He didn't have a will, which in itself was no problem, as the law provided that his mother and Stefanos's children would inherit the meager coffers left behind by his father. Still, his mother had had to fight off several unscrupulous, distant relatives who battled to gain family heirlooms that in the end provided James's family with the minimal security they needed to eat and keep a roof over their heads. His mother had sold the jewelry and artworks, all to keep her family going.

Back then he'd been too young to understand anything but the intense sadness that permeated the family for several years, at least until he was an adolescent. He was very conscious of the fact that he avoided involved relationships with women for this reason. He never wanted to leave any child in the lurch the way his father had, no matter that Stefanos's mistake was unintentional. "Give me a cold, calculating business suit over a family dispute any day."

"Speaking of which, how's the new job?"

"So far, so good. I thought it'd be slower in a smaller city, but the partners aren't afraid to stack my caseload."

"Have you been to court yet?"

"Only to observe. I begin trying a case next month."

"That's a good amount of time to get your feet wet, to allow you to get settled."

"Definitely."

They spoke for several more minutes about the family, their mother and, of course, the Rockies. Both brothers were baseball fanatics.

When they disconnected, James's mind immediately went back to this morning and how he'd literally run into Rachel Colton, the one woman in town he'd been hoping to see. If it wasn't the definition of serendipity, he didn't know what was—although they were both lawyers in the same small city, there'd been no guarantee they'd see each other again anytime soon, not unless he reached out. Which, he had to admit, he might have procrastinated about. And best news of the day, the week, the past two years? She'd agreed to meet him for dinner tonight. He'd shared neither fact with Jake. Which meant only one thing.

He was hoping for the best of outcomes tonight. First, that Rachel wouldn't think he'd moved here just because she lived here. It was especially important to him that she didn't believe he was any kind of stalker. He knew too well how that felt. Second, he'd be thrilled if Rachel would realize what they'd shared in Montana was more than a mountain fling. That maybe it was worth their while to spend some time together.

It was a great feeling, hope. A lot better than the gnawing fear of being followed.

"I can't thank you enough for helping me out here, Mom." Rachel undressed in her bedroom closet while Iris lay in the middle of her queen-size bed, gurgling with what sounded like glee as her grandmother gave her raspberries on her belly. Isadora Colton was chronologically seventy-two but cut the figure and had the activity level of a woman twenty years younger. Her shoulder-length blond hair with barely a whisper of silver threads was still soft, and a favorite of Iris's. The infant tugged on the long strands with her pudgy hands.

"I would have been offended if you didn't call me. I don't get to see this rosebud enough, do I, Iris?" Iris responded by grabbing another baby fistful of hair and yanking, prompting a deep belly laugh from Isa. Rachel didn't have any memories of her loving mother being so playful with her or any of her siblings. The sixth of twelve Colton kids, she'd been enlisted to help with the younger ones as she become old enough. By the time Rachel was in middle school, Isa seemed exhausted from child-rearing and was often distracted. Rachel remembered a parent who was caring but had little patience for youthful antics. In hindsight she realized worry over her husband and family had consumed Isa's every waking moment.

Ben Colton had enjoyed the esteem and privilege that came with being the local judge for years. His noted career had kept their family in the spotlight, always the ready example of Blue Larkspur's thriving community. They'd remained in the public eye, though, as it turned hostile. An investigation revealed Ben had accepted bribes. He'd been on the take from local private prisons and juvenile detention centers to ensure they remained filled. All Judge Colton had to do was assign the harshest penalty possible to a convict.

A tenacious reporter had uncovered the scandal just before Ben's untimely death in an auto accident twenty years ago, right as Rachel turned fourteen. Her prior idolization of her father and desire to follow in his footsteps had been shattered, but when she emerged from the grief and shame, Rachel knew that there was no path for her other than the law. She vowed to never become corrupt like her father, and in fact, along with her siblings, had been instrumental in helping establish the Truth Foundation. The organization's goal was to exonerate wrongfully convicted people, including those their unethical father had sent to jail.

It was to her dismay that as district attorney she couldn't continue to work on making certain all victims of Ben Colton's crimes received the justice they deserved. Rachel had recused herself from all of the Truth Foundation's legal dealings, with assurances from her siblings that she need not worry, they'd handle it. Plus she was the new Lark's County District Attorney—she'd be serving justice across the entire community, not just Ben Colton's victims.

"What am I doing?" Her gaze froze on the two dresses she held from hangers, knowing that she couldn't go on this date—no, not a *date* date, it was only to find out more about Iris's father—with James. No matter that her heart had flipped along with her stomach the second she'd locked gazes with him. She had to stay the course, though, and not get sidetracked by James's too sexy looks. First she had to figure out why he was in Blue Larkspur, and then see how much he'd heard from the locals about her…and Iris.

"You're getting back to the life you deserve." Isa stood next to her, expertly balancing Iris on her slim but strong hip. Isa Colton never missed a yoga or spin class and could out-lift her daughters nine times out of ten.

"Mom, you are the last to talk. You've never even dated since Dad died." It used to be hard to mention her father's demise, but after two decades, it was a natural part of their family history. Grief, however, was a different story. Despite his wrongdoings and faults, she still loved her father, the man he'd been before corruption sunk its sharp teeth into his soul.

"And that might not be the best example for you to follow."

Whoa! Was Isadora Colton—family matriarch and the last word for most Colton disputes—showing a crack in her stoic veneer?

"Mom?" She searched her mother's expression, which was resolutely set in a joyful smile reserved for her grandchildren.

"Oh, don't act so surprised, Rachel. You're a woman who knows what's important in life. You've shown remarkable grace in the midst of a surprise pregnancy and now an unexpected promotion and election to DA. More importantly, you're much younger than I was when Dad died. There's no reason for you to be alone for all of Iris's childhood. If I had to do it over again, maybe I would have been going out with my girlfriends while you babysat your brothers and sisters. Right, Iris baby?"

"Is there someone you wished you'd dated, Mom?"

"Back then? No, not really. A man or two caught my eye, but, well, I was so ashamed by what had happened and we were so busy keeping it together after your dad died that dating wasn't anything I seriously considered. And when my parents died only a year later, I was swamped with grief, again." Her mother turned away and bent down to retrieve a soft elephant rattle Iris had tossed onto the floor earlier.

Rachel knew that while losing her grandparents had been a gut-punch loss to all of them, it had affected her mother the most. Isa had thankfully inherited enough money from her parents to support the Colton clan until all of the kids reached adulthood. It had taken savvy reinvestment and a much tighter budget than they'd ever been accustomed to, but Rachel remembered all the years of struggle as the best family time ever, save for the fact they were grieving Ben Colton and Isa's parents.

"What about now, Mom? Is there someone special?"

Isa's eyes flashed, and for a second, Rachel thought her mother was about to confide in her. But then her walls went back up. "Look, enough talk about me. This is your night. Who again are you meeting?"

"Just a new lawyer in town. It's not a date."

"Uh-huh. Well, I'm perfectly prepared to sleep over if you decide to have your own kind of pajama party on your 'not a date.'"

"Mom!"

"Stop it with the false modesty." Isa nodded at the navy dress with the plunging neckline. "Wear that one. It's the least like your stuffy court suits. Add the diamond earrings I gave you last Christmas and the necklace from Grammy. Put some color on your cheeks and rev up the lipstick while you're at it. That bright pink brings out your blue eyes best. Iris and I are going to go rustle up some dinner while you finish primping."

"The breast milk is in the kitchen freezer." She kept all the milk she pumped at work available for times like these, when she had to be away. Sadness tugged at her peace of mind. Maybe she should cancel the date. She'd only be able to nurse Iris for so long—

"You can nurse her when you get back in, before she goes down for the last time." It was as if her mother read her mind. "I've got it, Rachel. Relax. Twelve kids, remember?" Isa's delicate brow raised in amusement as she sauntered off, singing a medley of sixties soul to her granddaughter.

"I do, Mom." She looked at her phone. "We've got to go." Her car was in the shop due to an unexpected issue and Isa was going to drop her off and pick her up. "Let's get Iris in the car seat. I feel like a teen again, needing my mom to drive me to a date."

Isa laughed. As they left the house and then strapped in Iris, Rachel was glad that the baby wouldn't be visible from outside of the car. In case James arrived at the restaurant entrance at the same time she did.

A nibble of doubt sprinkled with guilt gnawed at her insides. She'd deliberately lied. James was not "just another" lawyer. He was the father of her child.

Had the time come to tell him?

Chapter Three

"Hi, James. I'm so sorry I'm late. It seems to be a theme today." Rachel stood next to the table he hoped might be the location for the start of the relationship they'd never begun. She slid into the seat across from him. So smooth was her appearance that he barely had time to register the dark blue dress that clung to her curves, her impossibly long legs, her slim feet tucked into heels even higher than this morning's. Besides, he was too preoccupied with her face. Rachel's classically high cheekbones accented her sapphire eyes. Eyes that he'd never forgotten. Especially the way they'd flashed indigo when she...

Stop. Keep it out of the gutter, dude.

"No problem. Does work always keep you late?" He figured it was a definite "yes," since she was DA.

She opened the menu, gave the waiter her drink order when he silently appeared. "No, not all the time. The office works well enough most days. This afternoon I had car trouble of all things. My car wouldn't start, so I switched with my mother's. She's, ah, um, she lives nearby." Odd. Rachel wasn't the type to get flustered.

At least, not the Rachel he'd met in Helena. There was something she'd stopped herself from saying.

"So your car's in the shop?"

She grinned, and the sight of her dimples hit him in his solar plexus. Rather, the memories of how many times he'd made her smile like that during their time together in Helena was what sucker punched him.

"I've got six brothers, and a couple of my sisters are great with cars, too. My car should be fixed by the time I get in tonight. One of my brothers, Gideon, promised me he'd take care of it. He's always looking for an excuse—" She grabbed her water glass and took a large gulp.

"An excuse to what?"

A soft flush rose up her throat, her cheeks, and he had the distinct impression she'd kept herself from saying something she'd regret. Which was ridiculous since they barely knew one another. How did he know what her actions revealed, or hid?

Except for how she'd reacted to his touch, his kisses…

"You know what I mean. Be around me. Check out my house—I bought it pretty recently—and see what changes I've made. Stuff siblings do." She stared intently at the menu. He reached across the small table and gently tugged on the middle of it.

"May I?"

"May you what?" Her quizzical gaze struck a chord of compassion in him. She really was out of sorts. He could only imagine the private and public pressures of her job.

"Fix this so that you can read it. Unless you like an

extra challenge?" He turned the menu right side up, and at first, he wasn't sure if Rachel was going to bolt from the dining room or break down in tears. So many emotions played across her usually confident, serene face.

What he didn't expect was her laughter. It came out in a surprised gasp, not unlike when he'd undressed her—

Whoa. His desire for her kept making his thoughts jump the gun. This was a first date, what would have happened if she'd answered his calls last year. Not an invitation to pick up where they'd left off.

Slow and easy, that's what he'd promised himself when he moved here and again after running into her earlier. He'd decided that if Rachel were amenable, he'd like to pursue their relationship on more than a physical plane. To see if they might cultivate a friendship. Or, well, something in parallel with the sexual chemistry they obviously shared.

"I'm not good at hiding my feelings, am I?" She put the menu on the table. "There's a lot I need to talk to you about, James, and well, can I be frank here? I don't know where to start." The votive candle flame in the table's center reflected in her eyes and he felt a tug in his gut. Why hadn't he driven to Blue Larkspur sooner, figured out why she hadn't answered him?

Because you didn't want to come off like a stalker. No, that was the last thing he'd ever want.

"Why don't we start with where we left off?"

Her raised brow reflected desire and surprise. Too late, he realized how the words must have sounded.

"No, no, I'm not trying to get you in the sack again.

Not that I don't want to, I mean." He reached for his water, took a gulp. Where was his composure? "I'd never put that kind of pressure on you until we're both on better footing with a friendship. I think we deserve a shot to get to know one another more than a weekend at a legal conference affords. I've thought of you a lot since we met, Rachel. For whatever reason, you didn't return my calls back then, but this is now. We're both in the same city. I'm asking you to give me a chance." His voice cracked on the last word. Sweat trickled down his back, and nothing had ever seemed more important to him. Who was he? This had to be from the stress of the last several months with Bethany, changing jobs, the move.

"That's fair." Were those tears glistening in her eyes? Or was it the crystal votive reflecting in their blue depths? Before he could discern which of the two, a movement in his peripheral vision drew his gaze. When he focused on the distraction, recognition froze him to the spot. Dread like no other twisted with the bile in his stomach.

A woman whose profile exactly matched Bethany's walked past the dining area, toward the direction of the piano bar at the far end of the spacious restaurant. Was this the fallout from being stalked for months on end? That he'd imagine seeing Bethany at every turn?

Or was it worse? Was Bethany really here, in Blue Larkspur, at the very restaurant he'd invited Rachel to? Was he unconsciously sabotaging his chance with Rachel?

"James, is something the matter?"

"I'm not sure, but if there is, I'm going to take care of it. Stay here."

He'd explain later. After he told Bethany to stay out of his life.

WELL, THAT WAS ODD. Rachel knew she'd behaved like a flighty squirrel since she'd arrived, but had her behavior put James off so much that he'd needed to flee the table? She'd been almost fifteen minutes late, which had totally stressed her out before she even arrived at Ricco's. Punctuality was the key to her peace of mind, something that Iris tested on a daily basis.

She regretted starting the evening off on a rude note, when James was being so accommodating, so…attractive. She hadn't stopped thinking about him since Montana, either, but blamed it on him being Iris's father. Since finding out he was engaged, there had been no way she'd considered him in any other manner.

She lifted her phone so that she could see the screen saver. Iris's face filled the display, her irresistible smile lighting up her big green eyes, which were focused on her Uncle Gideon as he took the photo.

Her stomach grumbled and she put the phone back down on the table. She hadn't eaten since she'd chowed down on the salad in her bento box, six hours ago. The best way to deal with any new situation was to focus on what she knew, so she studied the menu. Right side up this time. Her choice was made easy since her favorite, lobster ravioli, was tonight's special.

The waiter reappeared with her wineglass and what looked like a scotch for James. She'd been so flustered when she arrived that she hadn't heard his drink order.

All she'd been concerned with was keeping her eyes from devouring him. Vulnerability wasn't her favorite emotion and James stirred it up in her big-time. And she hadn't told him the truth yet.

He was Iris's father.

Seeing him this morning had been such a surprise. She still hadn't processed it—Iris's father was here, in Blue Larkspur. A ball of nervous energy had consumed her by the time she arrived at the restaurant.

"Have you made your decision?" Their waiter looked at her with polite expectation. Before she replied, James returned and sat down, his expression unreadable.

"I know what I want, but do you need more time?" His courtesy was like a warm hug after her chaotic thoughts. With a little bit of a sexy squeeze.

"Actually, no. I'm ready." Rachel knew she lived up to her family's description of "control freak" with zero question. Normally she arrived at a restaurant with her choice made, having already perused the menu online. There hadn't been time today, though. Not a spare second between Iris, work and her car. This had to be what was making her so aware of James, of the way his athletic build filled out his white dress shirt and black slacks.

But then he flashed her the same smile that had gone a long way to convince her to step out of character and spend a wild, passionate night with a stranger almost fifteen months ago. He nodded for her to order first, unaware of her thoughts, much more significant than any food order. It hit her that while they'd only spent that one night together, James felt like someone she'd always known. An important part of her life.

Well, duh. He's your daughter's father.

"Ma'am?" The server's prompt brought her back, and first she, then James placed their requests.

With them alone again until their meals arrived, she couldn't keep what she knew was anticipatory awareness from flitting across her mind, triggering the warm curl of attraction in her belly, between her legs. It was a constant reminder of how excellently they were matched.

Physically. You don't really know him.

Not yet.

"Before we go further, I need to understand why you didn't take my calls." James fired the first verbal shot. "I saw that you'd reached out to me a few weeks after we met, but when I called you back you never picked up."

"Are you certain you're not a prosecutor?" She tried to make light of their situation. For now. It was going to get superheavy right about the time she revealed that he was a parent. Guilt sucker punched her yet again. No matter that James was engaged, possibly married by now. He needed to know he had a child. "And what exactly brings you to Blue Larkspur?"

"Nice sidestep, Rachel. Fine, I'll go first. I needed a change and received a compelling offer from a large corporate firm in this county. It's number three in all of Colorado."

"Oh, Schmidt, Thungston and Turner?" She rattled off the firm that employed many of her law school classmates.

He nodded. "That's the one. And while I recall that you're not a fan of corporate law, the practice has taken on many cases that are unusual for a firm with its success and reputation."

She knew this to be true. James's new employer wasn't afraid to help out smaller ventures as needed and often filled in the gap between small-business law and full-on corporate litigation. But it wasn't enough for her to get her hopes up that James wasn't as power hungry as she'd ascertained when they first met.

And it didn't matter. She was going to do the right thing and tell him about Iris. But as for more between them—

"James, are you married?"

His head reared back ever so slightly but just enough for her legal scrutiny to catch the movement. "Absolutely not. Why do you ask?"

This wasn't a time for tiptoeing. Not when she was going to reveal that the most precious thing in the world to her, her daughter, was also his.

You don't have to tell him.

She did, though. He deserved to know.

"You're correct—I did call you a few weeks after we'd met. And frankly, wondered why you hadn't called sooner."

"I wanted to, believe me. But I was out of the country." Her expression had to be doubtful because he leaned over the table, nose to nose, his eyes reflecting honesty. "My sister got married in Edinburgh."

"Oh."

"The entire time I was in Scotland, I couldn't stop imagining you there with me. We'd only had that one night—hours, really—and yet I couldn't shake you. You were different."

Stunned, she sought for reprieve from the possibility she'd made a mistake and found none. If he was being truthful, if he'd been gone when she'd called, then—

"Wait a minute. I called you no more than three and a half weeks after we met." This date she knew by heart, as it had been the earliest her doctor had assured her that the pregnancy test result was valid. Positive.

"You didn't leave a voice mail." He tilted his head. "I always check."

"I would have left a message, but a woman answered before it switched to voice mail. James, she told me she was your fiancée. I didn't leave my name or try to call you after that. I…couldn't."

It was her turn to observe James's discomfort as his eyes sparked with rage and he leaned forward, his gaze sincere. "I've never been engaged or married." He took a swig of his drink, collapsed back in his chair. "It seems we're destined to share more than pleasantries tonight."

"What—"

A huge boom sounded, and the floor under her feet reverberated. Before she had a chance to react, strong hands yanked her from her seat and she found herself facedown on the floor, James on top of her. Protecting her.

She gulped for air, unable to utter a sound as she heard screeches of panic from all corners of Ricco's.

Another *boom* was followed immediately by its force shaking the building. Her head turned to the side, she saw ceiling tiles hit the floor amid other patrons doing exactly the same—taking cover from a deadly blast.

"Get ready to move as soon as we can." James's voice

was steady in her ear, her only anchor as panic threatened to set in. The image of Iris's laughing eyes, her
gurgling laughter, melded into a single thought.

I can't die.

Chapter Four

Screams rent the air. As he observed from his location under their table, James saw patrons react on instinct, hitting the ground on their bellies, covering their heads with their hands. Others raced for the main exit. All the while he was aware of the precious charge under him— Rachel. If anything happened to her, he'd never forgive himself. Especially if the cause of these explosions were from what he thought. *Who* he thought.

The blasts suddenly ceased and his stomach sank at the large group near the closest exit. It'd take too long to get out through that door. He stood up and looked around the dining room, spied another neon EXIT sign in the far corner of the room. Already, several people were running through the more distant door.

"Let's go!"

James reached for Rachel's hand at the same time she got to her feet. With zero fuss she took his lead as he ran around several tables and out the back door. The fading daylight was bright but welcome as they sprinted from the building across the paved lot. Cold wind hit his cheeks. Rachel's dress was thin, offering no protection. But he couldn't worry about keeping Rachel warm, not yet. He had to get her far from the restaurant as quickly as he could.

Only when they reached the edge of the asphalt did they stop, leaning into one another as they caught their breath. James folded Rachel into his arms and she clung to his biceps, her fingers digging in as if she was drowning. He willed warmth and reassurance through his hands, holding her to him.

He put his forehead against hers. "Are you okay, Rachel?"

She blinked, her eyes still glazed over in shock. "Yes, yes, I'm fine. And you? Are you hurt?"

He shook his head, sucking in air like her. "No, no injuries. I'm good." They were both good. Relief began to douse the flames of fear, the rush of adrenaline.

"What on earth was that?" Her voice shook and he knew the reality of what had happened was hitting her, digging past the shock. "Oh my gosh, James. I've got to get home, back to…" She pulled back and her frantic gaze searched the lot, presumably for her car.

"I'll get you home." He quickly dialed emergency services and reported what had happened. He didn't think he'd be the first to call it in, since the loudness of the blasts must have reached for at least a mile or so. But the weight of responsibility that cloaked him made his shoulders ache. And not from an old college injury, aka his torn rotator cuff. If he'd seen Bethany, she was behind this.

The dispatcher took his information and confirmed that they already had units en route. "One more thing, I saw a possible perpetrator." He described Bethany in detail, hoping against all odds he was wrong. That the woman he'd spotted was no more than a doppelgänger.

Rachel's gaze never wavered from his face as he gave a definitive description of the entire event, including providing a description of a bar patron she'd never noticed. Hyperaware of her scrutiny, he felt his gut tighten. Sure enough, once he disconnected, she wanted answers.

"James, what just happened? And who is the woman you were talking about? Is that why you got up from the table so quickly?"

He placed a hand on her shoulder, hoping to dispel her concern. "Don't worry. You're not stuck here. The police and bomb squad are on the way."

"Stop it. Answer my questions." She shrugged out from under his touch, the stubborn streak he was more familiar with emerging. Gratitude hit him sideways. *She was okay.* Rachel was uninjured. If the explosion was Bethany's doing—

He pinched the bridge of his nose, forced himself to calm down enough to answer Rachel's valid questions. But his hands shook as his anger soared. He was furious with himself for dragging her into this nightmare, if indeed his stalker was behind this.

"Let me answer your questions one by one. The explosives first. My guess is it was something like an M-80, possibly homemade due to its strength. But it wasn't a legit bomb, or we wouldn't be here to talk about it, not in as small a space as that building. A strong firecracker, nothing more."

"How can you be so sure it was a firecracker? And what woman were you telling the dispatcher about?"

Blue eyes emanated determination, control. Like a shark assessing its victim. Her scrutiny was the antithesis of *pleasant*. James needed no further reminder that Rachel was a gifted prosecutor. She had to be tops at her job or she wouldn't have been elected to it so early in her career.

"I can't be certain it was an M-80 or cherry bomb, but my past experience matches what just happened." He ran his hand over his face. "I'm so sorry, Rachel. I put you, the entire restaurant, in danger."

"That's ridiculous." She moved closer, put her hand on his arm. "How can you blame yourself for some random explosion? Unless you're some secret agent posing as a lawyer?" A ghost of a grin flitted across her face.

Tell her.

Confronted with Rachel's generosity of spirit, he had no choice but to level with her.

"I moved to Blue Larkspur to take a fantastic new job. And yes, I'd hoped that maybe you and I would reconnect. But another big reason I moved was to get out of Denver. I needed to go anywhere else a good distance away. I thought heading to the other side of the state would be the end of it."

"It?" She looked like she was pulling teeth and he cursed his lack of directness.

"I've been stalked by a woman I briefly dated before I met you. I thought I'd taken every precaution to keep my transfer confidential, but somehow she's apparently found out."

"How do you know for certain she's followed you here? Because you think you saw her in the restaurant?"

Sirens sounded and snippets of panicked conversation from several small groups of patrons floated around them. Rachel reached for his waist and leaned against him, her body telling him that she wasn't a threat. She supported whatever he was going through.

He tightened his arm around her waist. Her gesture gave him hope that this horrible scourge that Bethany had been in his life could, and would, pass. Eventually.

"I've been stalked for the better part of two years by a woman who has told anyone she can that she's my fiancée or even my wife on several occasions. I believe she answered my phone the day you called. She's the woman who said I was engaged. I should have realized that there had to be a valid reason you wouldn't take my calls. The good news is that I haven't seen a whiff of her for at least three months. But now I think she was biding her time."

"Has she harmed you before? Set off other explosives?" Rachel kept close contact with him but exuded intense energy. He swore he saw the cogs whirring behind her beautiful eyes.

"No, not a bomb per se. This wasn't a bomb, either, but I'm not an explosives expert. Blue Larkspur PD will be able to identify the cause soon enough. It's probably nothing more than a powerful homemade firecracker, meant to scare, to instill terror. She knows how to make them. If it's Bethany, it's because she wants to throw me off balance again. She set one off in the hallway outside my condo door back in Denver. I have a restraining order against her and I thought she'd finally backed off, moved on to her next target. I was wrong."

How many times had he told this story? *Too many*.

"Wow. That's a lot. I'm so sorry, James." Her gaze

remained steady on his, her compassion licking the deep wounds.

"Thanks. All of this being said, you've probably figured out that you can't see me again. To be fair, I don't want you to see me again, not until I know Bethany isn't a threat."

His chest and throat tightened with the crushing disappointment of his decision. The woman he'd put hopes on for being the best thing about Blue Larkspur was out of his reach.

He'd thought dealing with Bethany for so many months, constantly looking over his shoulder for her, had been the worst days of his life. Nope. Not even close.

Saying no to any hope of a future with Rachel was his rock bottom.

"R ACHEL!"

The familiar voice reached her but still in the midst of trying to corral her emotions, she didn't trust her ears. What would her mother be doing here?

"Rachel!" At the second yell she turned from James and faced Isa, holding Iris.

"Mom! What are you doing here?" She ran to her mother's side, leaving James. "Baby girl!" Iris had her arms up, her face an expression of pure happiness at seeing her mother again. "Come here." She enfolded Iris in her arms.

"We hadn't gone home yet."

"Let me guess, the toy store?" She smiled at her baby.

"Toy aisle at the supermarket. I needed a few items. But then… I got a phone call, I mean, I found out that the explosion happened, and I had to get here, to make sure you're okay. I wouldn't have gotten out of the car if it didn't look safe." Isa pointed at her vehicle, only a few yards away.

"You sure have your ear to the ground, Mom."

"I had to see for myself that you're okay. Is that your date?"

James.

"Um, yes." James must have heard them as he walked up and stood alongside Rachel. "Mom, this is James Kiriakis. James, my mom, Isa Colton."

They exchanged the briefest greetings, and she noted that both her mother and James had the same strained smile. Did she look just as frazzled?

"Is this a granddaughter?" James's gaze flitted over Isa, bundled up in a pink snowsuit, the hood snapped to only reveal her cherubic face.

"Yes, this is my mom's first grandchild." Rachel shot her mother a stern look. Isa was no dummy and she remained quiet. Rachel prayed James's curiosity was cursory. Her prayer was quickly answered as sirens permeated the air.

"Nice." James's reply was distracted as he searched the street for the response team.

"Mom, why don't you and Iris get back in the car and stay warm until I'm ready to leave?"

Not one to miss a hint, Isa smiled. "Sure thing." She took Iris back and retreated to the car. Rachel let out a breath and stood next to James, wondering how on earth she'd just survived not only an explosion but an explosive situation.

James had family he didn't know about yet.

As THEY WAITED for the police, Rachel realized James was blaming himself for everything.

James wouldn't meet her gaze; the combination of despair, resolution and determination etched on his face aged him well beyond thirty-six. She remembered he was two years older than her along with many other details she shouldn't have hung on to. Facts she didn't need to know about a man she thought she'd never see again. Definitely not if she was going to remain detached, perhaps just co-parenting with.

Nothing more, certainly nothing romantic. Because being with him again for such brief, albeit intense, interactions was enough to inform her that she wasn't ready for a relationship with any man, especially James.

But James's palpable frustration blew away her resolve as effectively as the explosion had ruined their quiet dinner conversation. And she had lots to offer him as far as dealing with stalkers went. Memories of always looking over her shoulder for the boyfriend-turned-stalker through her entire senior year of college tried to resurface, but she'd experienced enough life since then to know it was behind her. James was still going through his hell, though.

In for a penny...

"James, listen to me. You are not going to go through this alone. You're living in Blue Larkspur now, part of our community. It's a small city, yes, but we pride ourselves on being a city with a small-town feel and an urban flair. We look out for each other around here. I know what you're going through better than you realize. I had a stalker in college, and it took months to convince him that he was wasting his time. I was fortunate in that he never got violent, but it honestly didn't make the ordeal less scary. He finally stopped after I moved back here, and he moved east. Plus, he got the help he needed."

He swung his gaze from the arriving cruisers to her. She recognized the pain in his eyes, the wariness.

"That sucks, Rachel. I'm sorry you've been through this, too."

"I know more now and have a different perspective, thanks to working in the DA's office. Crimes like stalking require tireless reporting and persistence in not only getting the culprit to back off but getting them the help they need so that no one else becomes a victim. If I hadn't had my family around me, my friends, the support of the university, I don't know what I would have done."

He gave a curt nod. "Yeah, it's a multifaceted issue." His tone was pure attorney, but his stance was 100 percent defeated victim.

She reached out and gave his shoulder a quick squeeze. "You'll get through this, James. And no way are we going to allow Bethany, if it was indeed her, to interfere with our friendship."

His face turned, and when their gazes met, a sudden shock of bonding, laced with awareness, coursed through her. They stood for what seemed like hours but couldn't have been more than a few heartbeats, lost in each other.

Red flag, girlfriend. The chemistry here is bigger than you.

Sirens screeched as the cruisers neared, and she forced her gaze away. What was wrong with her, getting all hot in a parking lot after she'd just been through a potentially life-threatening event?

Two words. *James Kiriakis.*

Blue Larkspur FD's main engine pulled into the lot and she used all of her energy to refocus. To look at anything besides James. "They're not messing around with the response."

James put his hands on his hips and shook his head. "Nor should they. Whether it was a firecracker or bomb, both have the potential to become a whole lot more than a one-building event. Someone could have been hurt in the rush out of the restaurant. Thank goodness it's been a rainy spring so far. It takes less than a firecracker to start a forest fire when it's drier."

"Did Bethany get charged for the illegal use of fireworks in Denver?" Short of looking up the case file for herself, she had to rely on James's account.

"Yes, but her attorney got her off with a fine. But that doesn't seem to affect her behavior. She broke the restraining order several times, always let off with community service and a fine. It's my fault—I should have insisted that she have the full charges pressed against her. But I felt sorry for her and always petitioned the court for leniency. My mistake. If this really was her, she's broken the state fireworks law. Again."

"Maybe they'll catch her, and the charges will hold this time. If she has any extra explosive ingredients in her possession, she's in violation of terrorist laws, too." Colorado did not take its fireworks laws lightly.

He sighed. "I'm not holding my breath. Bethany's as intelligent as she is determined. It's how she's wriggled out of all previous violations related to stalking me. That, and a good lawyer."

"You mean a slimy lawyer." She hated disparaging her own vocation, but there were good and bad players in all professions. A good defense counsel for Bethany would, at minimum, suggest the woman get medical help for her ailment, if she had one.

"Yup." Her fingers itched to soothe the furrows on his tanned brow. She drew in a breath, held it and resisted the over-the-top gesture.

"Fill me in, James. You saw her right before you ran out of the room, didn't you?" She knew the answer but needed to know what he was thinking.

His attention on her had splintered when they were at their table. He'd been distracted, not hearing her as she'd tried to engage in small talk. She'd thought maybe it was because she'd been late, made him think she was going to stand him up. Now she saw it'd been his internal struggle after seeing Bethany. Or at the least, a woman who looked an awful lot like her.

"Yes." He rubbed his nape.

"And you second-guessed yourself."

"Yes. I can't be certain, but I thought I saw a woman who looked just like Bethany walk through the dining area to the bar. She had the same build and facial profile but very different hair, so I wasn't sure. I knew I wouldn't enjoy our time together until I proved I was wrong. I went and looked, but before I got there, she was gone." James spoke with regret. "If only I'd reacted sooner—"

"If it was her, from what you've told me, she's very resourceful. It sounds like she wanted you to know she was there, to know she set the minibomb off. If it wasn't her, you had no way of knowing something so nefarious was going to happen."

James's gaze met hers and she thought she recognized appreciation in its green depths. Rachel understood. When her father's misdeeds had been fully revealed, she and her siblings had sought reassurance from their friends that no one blamed them, only Judge Ben Colton. Not everyone had been supportive, which was why she wanted James to understand she was on his side.

Especially if this Bethany character was all that had kept them from reuniting, from James finding out that he was a father.

Iris.

"Hey, Rachel." Chief of Police Theodore Lawson, an attractive older man with a full mane of silver hair, stood next to them. Theo was an imposing figure no matter where he went, but especially when in his element as police chief. "I'm going to need you to tell me what you witnessed."

"Hi, Chief." The chief was a permanent fixture in Blue Larkspur. Rachel couldn't remember a time when he hadn't been a friend of her family's. Even in the dark days of first finding out about her father's criminal activity and then Ben's tragic death, Theodore had never exuded an air of judgment or blame. He'd shown nothing but the utmost compassion and support to all of her siblings. Most importantly, to their mother, Isa.

A flicker of a memory flashed across her mind, momentarily distracting her. When Isa told her about having second thoughts over remaining alone for the rest of her life. Another memory triggered, from when Rachel ran into her mother with Theo at the local coffee shop. They'd been chatting away, oblivious to her presence until she announced herself. She'd thought it was coincidence that the two were there at the same time, that they'd simply run into one another. But had it been more?

"I'm the one who called it in, Chief. James Kiriakis." James offered Theo his hand, and Rachel shoved her musings on her mother's romantic life to the side.

"Did you, now?" Theodore nodded and accepted James's handshake. "Well, then, come along. This shouldn't take much time."

James nodded at the chief, then looked at Rachel. "I'm sorry about our first date... I'll make this up to you."

"Please." She waved him off, as if it were customary for a date to end on such an explosive note. A date. He'd said it was a date.

"First date, eh? I wondered where Iris was." Chief Lawson grunted but she saw amusement in his gaze. "You don't have to end it now. Just give us fifteen minutes."

Rachel nodded, alarm bells clanging in her mind. Was he going to ask who Iris was? But as she searched James's expression, there was no indication he was paying the chief's words much attention. He was focused on how to stop his stalker, she surmised. How to survive the present was more than enough for James. She got it. Hadn't she been unable to take her siblings' advice all those years ago when they'd told her to stop obsessing about her stalker? To let the cops handle it? It had been impossible for her and it was clearly the same for James. He wanted all of this behind him.

At least the current traumatic incident had kept James from paying too much attention to Iris.

Self-loathing reared and she had to work to not gag at how she was behaving. Grateful that James had something else to worry about that kept him from asking the question she dreaded most. Where was her integrity? She couldn't second-guess her original decision to forget about James, and to keep Isa from him, no matter how difficult it may have proven, with his having a fiancée.

And yet she knew the time was closer than ever for her to tell James about Iris's paternity. No matter the consequences.

Chapter Five

James found Chief Lawson to be incredibly professional while maintaining an aura of relaxed expectation. But James wasn't fooled by the man's obvious years—he put him in his late seventies or early eighties, impressive to still be on active duty—as his astute gaze and pointed questions indicated he missed absolutely nothing.

"That's enough for now, James, but I want you to stop by the station first thing in the morning and give us all the information, legal and otherwise, that you have on Bethany Austin. If this proves to be her, the more details we have, the better. In the meantime, I'll have my department cross-reference your statement with Bethany's record, and contact your former local PD."

"Thank you, Chief." They shook hands and James searched the parking lot for Rachel.

"She's over there, under those aspens." Lawson nodded at Isa's car, and paused. "I've known her family for a long time, James. A lifetime, you could say. Rachel Colton is as good as they come. She deserves the best."

"Good to know." James heard the subtle warning in the chief's statement. Rachel hadn't been kidding when she'd said Blue Larkspur looked out for its own. He headed toward Rachel, wondering what she was thinking. She leaped off the large, sturdy picnic table where people probably enjoyed eating takeout outside when the weather cooperated. Before he could get anywhere near the car, she reached him.

"That didn't take long. Here." A smile lit her face and she handed him his coat. "The coat checker brought out the rack so no one would freeze."

"Why didn't you wait in the car?" He nodded at Isa, still in the driver's seat.

"I'm fine." Concern had replaced panic in her wide blue eyes. "Did Theo agree that it's probably Bethany?"

"Thanks for this." He shrugged into his long, charcoal-wool coat. "Actually, Theo didn't comment much. He said they had half a dozen firecrackers go off in different businesses over the last few days. They've caught three juveniles, thanks to cameras, and he's going to look over Ricco's security report. We'll have to wait and see."

"Blue Larkspur High is out for its spring break." Rachel slid over from the center of the picnic table and patted a spot next to her. "Have a seat."

He complied, not wanting the evening to end. "It might not have been Bethany. It'd be a relief if it wasn't."

"But the woman you saw walk into the restaurant?" The wind grew stronger and caught at her golden hair, whipping strands across her face. He longed to cradle her head in his hands again, press his lips to her full, luscious, strawberry ones.

"It could have been my overactive mind. It's a common malady amongst attorneys, wouldn't you say?"

She grinned. "Absolutely. I hope, for your sake, that's

all it was. You said she hasn't bothered you in months. It would be a long shot to expect she'd follow you out of Denver, wouldn't it?"

"Let's hope so." He checked his phone and saw that it was about the time their meal would have wrapped up with coffee and aperitifs. Instead they stood on cold asphalt while a leftover winter wind blew. "I am sorry about tonight, Rachel. How can I make it up to you?"

"Tell you what. Why don't you let me make us dinner? Nothing fancy, just a quiet night in. Away from mischief makers with fireworks." Did he detect a tremble in her voice? Why would she be afraid or nervous about having him over?

"I'd love that, and I promise I'll make certain no one's following me." He said it teasingly but knew he'd continue to put himself through all the checklists that he'd learned about since becoming a stalker's target. Which he obviously hadn't done well enough when driving to Blue Larkspur in the first place, no matter that he knew he'd been religious about all of the safety precautions. The only people who knew he'd moved here were his family, the Denver police, a few colleagues he trusted and the real estate agent who'd sold him the condo. He'd spent any free time getting settled and working out.

"You don't have to come over this week if it's too much, with being new to town and now this. But I'd like to have you to dinner." She arched her brow and motioned her hand in a circle. The last thing he wanted was for her to think his scowl was directed at her or in reaction to the thought of dining at her house.

"I'd love to see you again. But like I said, I can't risk that Bethany might be on my tail."

"Nonsense. If it is her, we'll deal. But she's going to figure out who I am, and that may be enough to keep her at bay. No one wants to tangle with a district attorney. My new job does have a few perks." White teeth flashed, and her chuckle gave him respite from his constant worrying.

"Since you put it that way, what about tomorrow?" The words flew out of his mouth, proving his mind had zero control over his actions. He held his breath, hoping he didn't scare her off by being too eager. Where was his usual savoir faire, which he'd cultivated after years of defending big corporations against heady lawsuits?

Her wide smile was its own reward. "That's great. See you tomorrow night, my place. I'll text you the address." She looked over her shoulder at Isa's car. "I've got to get home."

He watched her get into the car before he turned away and headed toward his own. No matter what Chief Lawson thought about the probable culprits, James couldn't shake the ugly sense that it had been Bethany he'd seen, that she was at the root of this. Somehow she'd found out he'd moved from Denver to Blue Larkspur.

Which meant someone had betrayed his trust, or Bethany had found a weak link in his chain of what he'd thought was an impenetrable security wall. Neither option was palatable.

BETHANY SAT ON a battered aluminum picnic bench next to a combo gas station/convenience store. She was across a wide boulevard from Ricco's and watched the result of her brilliant actions. The fancy clothes and blond wig she'd worn to gain inconspicuous entry were bunched in a bag in her car, which she'd left parked in a big-box store's lot on the other side of the restaurant. Right now, Bethany knew she looked like a teenager in a huge baggy sweatshirt under a down vest. Skinny jeans and lace-up lumberjack boots completed her anonymous alias. She'd picked the clothing up at a local Goodwill, eager to blend in with the locals.

Bethany was pleased with what she'd accomplished since James's first working morning in Blue Larkspur. Was that only yesterday? She'd been keeping tabs on him since she'd found out he was moving here a week ago. Once she'd figured out where his new place was, that spiffy contemporary condo downtown, she'd promised her boss she'd be at work tomorrow. She'd planned to get back to Denver and keep her job, with frequent weekend trips back here to Blue Larkspur. To win James back.

Except her employer had gotten sick of her frequent bouts with the "flu" or "food poisoning." She'd been fired over the phone today. Which was perfect, because this gave her several weeks of unemployment. By her estimation, she wouldn't need that long to convince James that he'd made a mistake. A mistake she was willing to forgive.

Following James was easy, too easy. The security team he'd consulted at the same time he'd filed the restraining order against her was long behind him in Denver. It helped that she'd borrowed her stepsister's beater. It kept James from identifying her via her usual, more familiar vehicle. Not that he'd know it was her—she had eight different wigs and twice as many outfits equally distributed in the back seat of each. Bethany chuckled. She'd become an expert at quick costume changes. The battered car with tinted windows helped—she didn't draw attention as she undressed.

She'd like to undress in front of James. He'd never allowed their dating to get past flirting, but she knew he wanted more, wanted all of her. She hoped he would know the special cherry bomb she'd created was from her, especially for him. Hadn't he told her she lit up a room? He had. The night they first met at the fancy bar near his firm. Bethany had found many men in that bar before, but it had never lasted past a date or two. And trailing them was too much effort. Besides, whenever she hung on to a guy for too long, she got in trouble and it wasn't worth it.

Except when it came to James. He was special.

James, James. He was smart but not necessarily discerning when it came to where he lived. Of all the places he could have left Denver for, he picked this crap-kicking place? The highway sign read "Welcome to the City of Blue Larkspur" but in her mind, Denver was the only city in Colorado. She smirked as she sipped the super-sugared concoction she'd bought in the stop-and-shop place. A Blue Larkspur Latte Bomb, according to the sign. Fitting for today and what she'd just made happen.

A thrill whistled through her midsection as she watched the restaurant patrons pour out of the building. It wasn't what she'd expected. She'd meant to let James know she'd never left him by using the same explosive she'd made for his Denver condo. When she'd needed to get his attention same as today. But she couldn't drop it in the dining area without being caught, so she'd settled for the women's restroom off the bar.

It hadn't occurred to her that James would be able to recognize her, but she'd watched through the cracked restroom door as he stomped around the bar, acting like he'd seen a ghost.

A giggle escaped her before another memory stifled it.

That unexpected interloper. Rachel Colton.

She hadn't planned for another woman in James's life so soon. Hadn't he learned from Denver? That he shouldn't waste his time with anyone but Bethany herself?

District Attorney Rachel Colton was nothing more than another one of James's passing interests. It was Bethany's job to know everything about James, so she'd followed Rachel home after she'd seen how James had interacted with her on the court steps when the conniving woman had slammed into him, definitely seeking his attention. Bethany had been sitting on a nearby bench—disguised, of course—and witnessed the whole event. Dressed as a street sweeper, she'd gotten close enough to overhear their conversation while Rachel clung to James's jacket collar the way a praying mantis grabs its partner.

James knew Rachel. Rachel had acted all huffy, as if their fall was his fault. The drink turned sour in her gut and she shoved a scream down deep into her chest.

Keep your cool. Patience.

James turned heads, male and female alike, as he was a fine specimen of a human being. But those people didn't know him like she did. Didn't know that he was a very sweet man under the lawyerly veneer. Bethany knew James Kiriakis better than anyone. Once they had more time together, she was certain he'd see what she knew in her bones.

She was the only woman for him.

This date must be very important to Rachel, because she'd had to figure out how to get not only to work this morning but to the restaurant without her car. Bethany thanked the video she'd found online about how to dilute the fuel in Rachel's tank for at least making her rival's life more difficult. Next time Bethany would make it impossible for Rachel to be with James at all.

Her butt was sore from sitting on the metal bench, her drink near its end. The fire engines were gone, and she counted only one police cruiser left in the parking lot.

And then she saw them. Her skin tightened across her face and her belly, and she gripped the plastic cup until it collapsed, crushed under her fist. James was walking Rachel across the lot. She acted like the kind of rich bitch Bethany wasn't. Bethany knew what mattered in life. True love. Like she had with James.

Without further thought she sprang up and bolted to her car, got in and started the engine.

It was time to follow Rachel again.

RACHEL HAD NEVER been so relieved to pull into her driveway. Isa had left her to her thoughts during the drive from Ricco's, and Iris was asleep in the back seat. Rachel's white Jeep was back in its usual spot, parked next to the trees that separated her property from her neighbor's. Gideon and one of his buddies had dropped it off for her. She sent Gideon a quick text to thank him for taking care of her, again. Rachel relied on her brother more than was probably reasonable, but it was the Colton way. They all depended on each other.

"Mom, I can get Iris out so that you can leave right away."

"Nonsense. I left some things in the house, anyway."

"All right."

The car was still running as shivers continued to race down her spine, despite her seat warmer and heater being on full blast. Rachel had always considered herself intrepid, willing to dive into any case, take on any bad guys. Before she became a mother, that is. Iris had changed everything.

When Isa stopped the engine, shivers ran down Rachel's spine. The leather car seats were still warm, but the reality of what she'd just been through sank in further as she peered through the windshield into the dark night.

What if James's stalker was watching him all the time, as he feared, and had seen her with him? What if she'd taken note of Iris or Isa?

She opened the door to exit and heard a soft rustling to her left. The noise was immediately followed by a definitive *snap*. Her nape prickled with dread and she peered into the shrubs that surrounded her home, up close to the house walls but not touching, as she didn't want to invite any critters to make nests under her siding or on her roof. More sounds drew her attention to the tall aspens that lined the short drive. She let her shoulders sag down in relief. Many nights found deer or fox traipsing through the neighborhood, and with the wet spring, she'd not seen any yet as she'd been mostly inside with Iris.

"What is it, Rachel?" Isa, still in the driver's seat, spoke.

"It's just an animal." She slammed the door shut to warn off the wildlife as much as banish her jumpy nerves. Nothing like taking charge to put fear on the back burner. Before she reached the back driver's side door, Iris's cry rang out. Just great. She'd woken her innocent baby with her own fear.

No. She was not going to let anyone or any threat infringe upon Iris's life. Rachel gathered the infant into her arms, where she quickly lay her head on her mother's shoulder and snuggled in.

Walking into her brightly lit home was the medicine she needed. She kicked off her heels and padded barefoot into the living room.

"I'll be right back, Mom. Let me put her down first."

"Take your time." Isa was distracted with her phone. Her mother sure spent a lot of time texting these days, more than Rachel ever could recall.

Iris went down with zero fuss after Rachel nursed her. She walked back into the living room to find a steaming mug of tea waiting for her on the coffee table.

"Ah, thank you, Mom."

"Not such a great date after all?" Isa always intuited Rachel's mood.

"No. I'm sorry I didn't text you right away. I had no idea you were so close, at the store. I didn't want you to worry, and I figured Theo might mention it. If you talked to him." Could she be any more obvious? *Mom's love life, if she has one, is none of your beeswax.*

"Well, I appreciate that you thought of me." Isa regarded her, compassion lighting her eyes. "Care to fill me in, now that we're home?"

Rachel kept her description of escaping what she'd thought was a bomb explosion to the barest facts, not wanting Isa to freak. Fortunately her mother got distracted when Rachel mentioned Theo.

"Theo does not know the meaning of slowing down, I'll tell you. He should be retired by now."

"He is the chief of police, Mom."

"I know, but he needs to learn to take better care of himself. I told him that this morning."

"Did you?" It was great to be able to turn the tables a bit and put her mother in the hot seat.

Isa drained her mug, stood up and gathered up her things. "I did. To continue on in the vein we spoke about earlier, I was hoping this date would lead to more. Maybe not with the same man, but don't you want to have a full family life? For Iris?"

"Mom, Iris and you are my family. I also have eleven siblings, remember?"

"Oh come on, you know what I mean." Isa paused. "Have you given any further thought to reaching out to Iris's father again?" Suspicion tugged at Rachel's nerves. All she'd told Isa was that circumstances had made Iris's father unavailable. Did Isa have an inkling that James was Iris's father?

She knew her family might have suspected she'd been involved with a married or otherwise-committed man, since she'd made it clear she was not going to contact him for "personal reasons." To their credit, they never questioned her, never made her feel judged. They'd done what Coltons do best—bonded together to make sure she, and now Iris, knew how loved they were.

"I have, actually. And… I just may." She couldn't tell her mother about James. Not yet. Not until she saw how he handled finding out about his daughter. "But I do have another date tomorrow with this same guy. It was the least I could do, after the explosion."

"The things you have to put up with these days to find love." Isa let out a long sigh. "When your dad and I met, it was easy. At a work party, where we found out we had a lot in common. And the chemistry!"

"Mom."

"I know. You don't want to know, but doesn't twelve children tell you something? After I met your father, that was it. All I cared about was the next time I'd see him. He was focused on his career and wanted a partner to share it with. I loved being a paralegal but always wanted to be a mother. It happened a lot faster than we'd planned, but that was okay. It seemed perfect timing, for both of us."

"Life was less complicated forty years ago, Mom."

"Yes and no. People are still people. Human beings with both assets and flaws. We all know your dad's."

"I'm sorry, Mom." She knew this was hard for Isa, to talk about Ben's steep climb and exponentially precipitous fall.

"There's nothing for you, or any of you kids, to be sorry for. Maybe if I'd been further along in my life when we'd met, like you are, I'd have paid more attention to the warning signs. I was already almost thirty but very coddled by my parents and immature, now that I look back. You're head and shoulders ahead of where I was at your age."

"You were having your third and fourth child by my age, Mom. What did you mean by 'signs'? Did you mean red flags?"

Isa nodded. "Yes. Ben was the type to just skirt the edges of the rules. Do you know what I mean?"

"I think so, but I'd appreciate examples." No matter how much they hurt, no matter that Isa's admission stunned Rachel. It wasn't a secret what Ben had done to the community and his family. And Isa had never shied from admitting the truth about Ben once she knew it. But Isa had never mentioned any indications of Ben's dark side existing before their marriage. Rachel and her siblings were close and kept one another informed about Isa's life as needed. She knew that her sense of obligation to protect her mother from life's unpleasantness wasn't unique. Her sisters and brothers all wished Isa could have somehow been spared the havoc Ben's criminal actions had caused.

Her father had been a bad man, no question. But it didn't change that she'd loved her father—he'd always be her dad—but her job, her vocation, her passion was to set things right.

Isa was poised to leave but stood stock-still. "I don't know, Rachel. There's no good rehashing the past."

"I'm not asking for your lovers' secrets that you shared with Dad." *Ew.* "It's just that with going on this date tonight, it's got me thinking. I need to know what you wish you'd picked up on before you got married."

"Ben preferred to work jobs that were under the

table." Isa referred to income that wouldn't be reported to the IRS. Illegally tax-free. "You're a DA, honey, and I know you'd never dream of breaking the law like that. But back then, it wasn't an unusual circumstance. We didn't have two nickels to rub together in those early years. So I let it go, overlooked it. But then he got his first big job, making a salary he'd never dreamed of. Yet he still looked for ways to cheat the system. Always." Isa balanced on the sofa arm, her expression distant and gaze unfocused.

"At the time I believed him when he said it was 'just what affluent folks do, Isa. It's not illegal, just protecting what's ours.' He was very showy, you know. Loved the spotlight at all costs. And he insisted on only the best when it came to material things—from our home to the cars, our clothes. Nothing but top-shelf."

"I remember having nicer things right before he died." She and her siblings had riding lessons and fancy summer camps on the West Coast at an exclusive California beachfront property.

"Yes, we sure did. He was furious when he found out I'd been buying baby clothes at the consignment shops and Goodwill. I'll never forget it. I did the family household budgeting and showed him the figures. Do you know the very next week that man had a raise, doubling our income? Of course, now I realize it was the first time he took a bribe."

"Mom, stop." She'd seen Isa's face stamped with regret too many times. "None of it was your fault. You were doing the best you could, and why wouldn't you believe him? He was your husband. You can't blame yourself for his crimes."

"I'm not blaming myself for your father's transgressions, trust me. But I know that in a twisted way, I was complicit. It was easier to shove my head in the sand and focus on raising our beautiful children than facing such an awful reality. At this point in my life I realize it wasn't right to look the other way. I'm so relieved and grateful that you and your brothers and sisters are working toward restitution for all of his victims and others wrongfully convicted. The Truth Foundation is helping me make amends, you know."

"I do, Mom." And she did. Rachel still had survivor guilt that she and her siblings had lived such a nice life at the expense of juveniles or adults who received longer sentences or ones they didn't deserve. All to fill private and youth detention centers that in turn lined Ben Colton's, and his family's, pockets.

"Take one bit of advice from your old lady. Always trust your gut and follow through on any doubts with the man you love. Always."

"Thanks, Mom." They hugged, then Isa slung her tote over her shoulder and left. Rachel watched her get in her car and drive off before she closed and locked the door.

Just as she was ready to jump into a hot shower, Rachel remembered that it was trash day tomorrow. She turned off the water and shoved her feet into slippers, threw a coat over her robe. She pushed the button for the garage door and waited for it to open before she wheeled the trash and recycle bins down the drive.

Rachel froze on the spot when she saw the muddy footprints at the front of the drive, behind where her brother had parked her repaired car. Icy tremors shot through her gut. They weren't prints from deer, fox or a bear.

They were boot prints.

through her gun. They weren't prints from deer, for

one treat.

They were bone prints.

Chapter Six

"She's a woman I'd love to get to know better. I think we might have reunited sooner if Bethany hadn't intercepted her call over a year ago." James looked out the window of his corporate law office as he spoke to his older brother. Birds flitted between aspen branches and the April rain made everything slick. The view was a far cry from the Denver office tower he'd worked in for over a decade.

"Wow, bro, that's a lot to deal with in the first week you move to a new city." His senior by five years, Jake wasn't one to hold back. "Are you certain it was Bethany you saw in the restaurant?"

He swallowed the hot coffee he'd grabbed moments earlier. "I'm positive. And then the explosion, just like when she shot off the homemade M-80 in my condo building last year."

"That woman doesn't understand the constraints of a restraining order. I thought maybe she was running on anger, at the humiliation of being dumped by you. But now I wonder if she needs help, bro. I'm sorry you're dealing with this."

"Yeah, me, too." He looked at his watch. Five more

minutes and he had to get back to his caseload. "I thought a geographical move would be the end of her stalking, but somehow she's found out I'm here."

"Maybe she hasn't. Maybe it wasn't her. Give it a bit before you assume. Although the explosion is too close to home—I get it." He heard his brother's chair squeak, meaning he was leaning back from his computer desk. "Tell me more about this DA you took to dinner."

James confided a lot in Jake. But his sibling didn't need to know that part of the reason he'd moved here was to maybe—well, okay, *definitely*—run into Rachel again. He'd looked her up and knew before he moved that she was the new DA, and hoped that she was single. At least, there was no mention of her relationship status in the media or on social accounts.

"The local DA happens to be an acquaintance I met at a conference over a year ago, is all."

"Uh-huh. 'Met?'" Jake knew James was holding back—why else be evasive? But James couldn't waste energy on Jake's opinion. Not now, not when he had the pressure of making a good impression in his new job and figuring out if Bethany was really here. If she'd found him again. Just the possibility made the coffee burn like acid in his esophagus.

"Look, if more comes of it, I'll let you know."

"So you're seeing her again? Soon?"

"Yeah. Tonight, actually."

Jake's laugh rolled across the connection and tugged a grin out of James. "This is the first I've heard of you doing a second, no, make it third date in, like, forever. Since Bethany."

"Yeah, well, Rachel's not Bethany. And the first time I met her wasn't really a date."

"Good thing she's nothing like Bethany." Jake's voice had sobered, reminding James that he wasn't dealing with a jealous high school crush. Bethany had put him through his paces back in Denver, between showing up uninvited at work events, slashing his car tires and those of any women he was seen in public with, and leaving threatening notes in his mailbox. The restraining order had sent her into her hole for a while, but now he wasn't so certain he was rid of her.

"Yeah."

"Talk to you later, bro."

"Bye." He disconnected and stared out the window, but all he saw were mental images of Rachel last night—how beautiful her smile was, how it warmed him inside out, even as they'd stood in freezing weather while waiting for the building to be cleared.

His phone rang and he glanced at the caller ID, which displayed a number he did not recognize. He'd usually leave it but, being new, didn't want to miss any number of possible callers, from the cable/internet provider to the new health insurance he was setting up.

"James Kiriakis."

Silence greeted him. He listened. "Hello?"

The sound of breathing was soft but detectable. Someone was listening to him. And in the background the definite strains of the cloying '70s tune Bethany had insisted was "their song."

His stomach clenched with anger, but he kept his cool long enough to hang up, write down the number, then block it.

He'd need a new phone number. *Again*.

Worse, James had changed his number along with his address. If it had been Bethany on the line, she had his new number. Which meant she knew he'd moved.

And the area code of the caller had been that of Blue Larkspur, the same as James's new number. Definitely not out of Denver. She'd found him.

Icy dread worked up his spine as James realized his biggest fear. He didn't need Chief of Police Theo Lawson to validate his hunch.

Bethany was back.

"OUCH!" RACHEL DROPPED the baking pan back on the oven rack and quickly shoved her fingers under cold running water. She'd forgotten to use a potholder.

With Iris's sudden teething and working an hour later than usual, she'd backed herself into a corner with getting dinner ready in time for James. Iris had fallen asleep in her baby swing, which Rachel had set up next to the dining table and had a clear view of from the kitchen island. Iris was at the end of being able to use the swing, as she was outgrowing it. The baby's nap was a reprieve of unknown duration. There was no telling when she'd wake up, so Rachel was trying to get the chicken baked, rice steamed and veggies stir-fried all at once.

Why hadn't she ordered out? James would never remember what he'd had for dinner the night he found out he was a father, she was certain. All he'd recall was that his daughter looked exactly like him, minus the green irises, and Rachel had kept her from him.

Not one to ever balk at a challenge—it just wasn't

in the Colton gene pool—she'd never considered post-poning this second meetup. Having James over sooner rather than later was the absolute right thing to do.

She mentally replayed their conversation as she shoved silicon-coated oven mitts on. Rachel still couldn't believe what he'd revealed last night. He'd been stalked, and it sounded like it was the stalker, Bethany, who'd answered his phone when Rachel found out she was pregnant. Self-recrimination loomed, threatening to batter her normally positive esteem into smithereens. So many doubts and questions about her motives railed at her. Why had she so easily accepted that James was engaged? Worse, what difference should that have made? He was her baby's father, period. He had a right to know.

Her phone rang with the distinct tone she had for her mother, but the noise still made her jump. She was letting James's stalking issue get to her.

"Hey, Mom."

"How's Iris doing? Poor thing. Growing new teeth tuckers a little soul out."

"I'm not so sure about tuckering her out, Mom. She's sleeping now, but she's also in her swing and the house has been pretty quiet. She was hell on wheels when I got home from work, though."

"I can come over and help you through the night with her. The Lark's County DA needs her rest, even on the weekend."

"Uh, I'm fine. I appreciate the offer, though." She pierced one of the chicken breasts with an instant-read thermometer. "And thanks again for driving me to Ricco's. I don't know what I would do without your support these last months."

"You'd do what you have to. That's what mothers do, dear."

"Well, the shop Gideon took it to thought maybe a squirrel or other rodent got in there and chewed a bunch of random wires. That would have taken a long time to fix. As it is, they flushed the fuel tank and it's up and running. The mechanic said she's checking something out about the fuel, but I know I didn't put the wrong type in." Of course, her mind had been all over the place, between work and Iris.

"That's odd for this time of year. The rodents, I mean. It's been rainy, sure, and still below freezing some nights, but not so cold that critters curl up on engines."

A hint of doubt edged into Rachel's thoughts. She'd thought it unusual, too, as "critters" finding shelter in vehicle engines, gas grills or garages wasn't unheard of—in the winter. Spring was making its mark these past weeks, warming up the Colorado Rockies enough to ensure most their precipitation was of the liquid variety. As for the fuel tank, she hadn't given it a lot of thought as her heavy caseload required all of her mental faculties today.

"You still there, honey?"

"I am, Mom. Look, I've got to get dinner finished and on the table."

"Ah. This isn't anything about your date last night, is it?"

"What are you thinking, Mom? Let me guess. Theo

said something about when he interviewed James? What did he tell you? Spill it, Mom."

"Nothing. Well, okay. Theo thinks James is a very nice young man."

Rachel laughed. "Neither James nor I are particularly 'young,' Mom."

"Wait until you are seventy-two and then tell me thirty-four isn't young."

"Hmm."

"I'll let you go. Listen, if that sweet little grandbaby of mine looks like she's not going to give you any sleep, call me. Have a nice dinner!"

"Bye, Mom. Love you."

"Love you, too, sweetheart."

Rachel disconnected and stared at the phone for a second. She could have been honest with Isa. Her mother was the least judgmental person she knew, and she'd be thrilled to know Rachel was planning to tell Iris's father about his daughter, no matter who he was. But she needed the mental and emotional space to first let James know and then see where it was going to go. His attitude about wanting to get to know her better might cool as quickly as the sautéed veggies.

The chicken was done, so she set its pan on two cork trivets to cool and made haste with the zucchini and summer squash, already sizzling in the drizzle of olive oil she'd given the heated pan. The rice wasn't a problem as it cooked automatically in her favorite kitchen appliance—her electronic pressure cooker. Finally she let her shoulders relax, took a sip of the herbal iced tea the nanny had made a huge pitcher of.

The doorbell rang, followed a split second later by

Iris's piercing scream. So much for letting James in, allowing him to adjust to his surroundings before introducing his daughter to him.

"Come here, sweetness." She unstrapped Iris from the swing, hugging her. "Time to meet someone for real this time. No quick intros." Iris settled into her, gumming Rachel's shoulder. The bell rang again, followed by a soft knock. Rachel hurried to the front door.

Butterflies attacked her insides and her stomach swooped, just as it did going down a class-A roller coaster. Life was going to change for her, but more importantly for Iris, in the next few moments. Without her hood, Iris's red hair was a dead ringer for James's locks. Rachel's hand shook as she reached for the handle and opened the door.

"Good evening." James's smile lit up his face, dispelling the sterner expression she'd noticed last night. He held out a potted orchid and box of fine chocolates. "Thanks for having me." His gaze was on her, her face, until Iris let out another shriek.

"It's okay, my baby." She looked at James, whose puzzled expression went from surprise to disbelief to thunderous rage in two seconds flat.

Maybe she didn't know James Kiriakis so well.

Chapter Seven

James knew people claimed to have "out of body" experiences. But he'd never fully comprehended until he stood in front of a woman he'd come to with hopes of a deeper relationship, to find out she already had a family. And a *kid*.

"Are you babysitting? Or is this your child?" He looked past her into the house. "I never thought to ask you if you were in a relationship, or married, did I?" His fists balled and he fought to not turn and stalk to his car. Finishing this off here and now was best for all of them.

"I'm not going to talk to you while you're like this." Rachel's attorney countenance showed in the steel glints sparking from her eyes, the way she held the kid as if prepared to make a run for it. "Calm down."

"Oh, I'm calm." His jaw ached from clenching, and the knot between his shoulders intensified into a throbbing mass of pain. He looked past her, tried to see into the house. "Where's the father?" Did he know Rachel had been out with him last night?

He was done being anyone's fool.

"COME IN BEFORE you come to any conclusions, James."

Rachel hated how James's initial pleasure at seeing her had turned to betrayal, and now anger, in the space of a heartbeat. Before she said anything she'd regret, she turned away from him, hoping her refusal to take on any of his anger would dispel the ugly tension between them.

"Aaaagh!" Cranky Iris was back, her cheeks red and eyes watering.

"It's okay, baby." Gently bouncing Iris on her hip, she grabbed a frozen washcloth from the freezer. Cool relief shot through her veins. At least he'd come inside. He could have easily taken off, ghosted her for good. Instead he stood on the other side of the island and observed the überdomestic scene with an air of ticked-off detachment. His gaze never wavered as he set the plant and the sweets down.

"What's wrong with it?"

"Her. Not 'it.' Her name is Iris, and nothing's wrong. She's teething." At his continued stare she added, "Her baby teeth are coming in. It makes her gums swollen, her jaw and ears ache, and her nose has been superrunny."

"Are you married or with someone? Were you with someone when we met in Helena? What about last night, when we met for dinner? Does your family know you were there?" His questions weren't a surprise, but she couldn't help a small smile.

"What's so amusing, Rachel? That I misread you or that I'm standing here, thinking that I've been made a fool?"

"It's not any of the above. You sound so much like a lawyer. Let's sit down for a minute." She sat on the sofa and he took the loveseat opposite, his movements stilted.

"Naaa!" Iris didn't want anything to do with the washcloth. Rachel ignored her and continued to rub the frozen fabric over the bright pink gums until she relaxed and began to chomp down on the pain-relieving remedy.

"There we go." She smiled at Iris and then looked across at James. "I freeze wet washcloths. They work better than any kind of fancy teething ring."

"Huh." He gave Iris the briefest of glances, as if he thought looking at the infant would burn his eyeballs, before refocusing on Rachel. "Is she your only kid?"

Her only kid? Anger blazed deep in her heart, where her mother love lived. It set off mental warning alarms. *Whoa, girlfriend, rein it in.*

James didn't know who Iris was, or if he'd figured it out, he was in shock about it. She had to play fair and give him the benefit of the doubt. It was on her that he didn't know.

"Yes, Iris is my one and only. For the record, I've never been married nor with anyone long-term. I was happily single the night we met in Helena. I still am."

"So you decided to have a baby on your own? I'm not judging, just asking. I have several friends who've decided to go ahead and have a kid with or without a partner. It just would have been nice if you'd have been up front with me about your family from the start." His dismissive tone tossed invisible barbs that dug into her conscience.

Rachel bit her lip, knowing she couldn't keep her calm demeanor in place much longer, but breaking

James's obvious denial too soon wouldn't be productive, either. Maybe she was relying too much on her prosecutor skills, but it would be best for him to figure out as much as possible on his own, at his own pace. Since he was an intelligent man, it wouldn't take very long.

"Iris wasn't planned, James. She was a complete surprise. I didn't know you were averse to children."

"I'm not opposed to dating you because you have a child. I wish you would have trusted me enough to tell me, is all."

"Rachel is six months old, James." She watched him, waited for him to digest not only the age but the fact that she was speaking slowly, deliberately. "I found out I was pregnant about fourteen months ago."

He nodded. "January last year."

"Yes. A month after the legal conference."

He stilled; his facial muscles froze in place. Except for a single pulse visibly pounding at his temple. His gaze muddied. "A month after, you said?"

She nodded.

"Wait a minute, Rachel. You're not—"

"James, this baby girl—" she held Iris facing him, so that he could see his daughter's features "—is yours."

REALITY HIT JAMES like an ice bath after a college football game. As his university's quarterback he'd sustained countless injuries that healed exponentially faster with the aid of freezing temperatures. The knowledge had never dulled the excruciating pain of putting his game-heated body into the tubs, though. At least he had the edge of the stainless steel to hang on to. As he stared at Iris, there was no thought his mind could grasp at to put him on solid ground.

He had a *daughter*. If what Rachel said was true.

Unless… *Oh no*. Dismay dropped his stomach fifty stories in three seconds. He'd been so wrong about Bethany; was Rachel a different kind of stalker? A single mother who'd do anything to gain a father for her kid?

"She's really mine? That's a strong declaration, Rachel." He meant for the words to come out strong and not a little accusing. Instead, he sounded like a limp version of himself.

"It's the truth." She held the baby up, allowing Iris to pump her legs against Rachel's thighs. "Look at her eyes, James. I've never met anyone besides you with that shape to them. And her cheekbones. Exactly yours."

He'd never given his eyes or facial structure much thought, only knew that he resembled his father, and his siblings. His father's genes came from a long line of Greek Americans, the first of whom had emigrated from Greece in third-class steerage. No one was tougher than his Mykonos-born great-grandfather, what little he remembered of the man. If what Rachel said was true, Iris was the image of her paternal ancestor.

"I'll need a paternity test. For both our peace of mind. Unless you've already done several?"

To her credit, Rachel didn't play the indignant game. Her eyes narrowed and she gave a curt nod. She was a lawyer, though. It was her darn job to stay unruffled, even when caught in a lie. "Of course. Maybe you want to wait to get to know her until you have scientific proof?"

"That's probably for the best." She'd given him an excellent exit opportunity. All he had to do was get up, walk back out that door and drive away. Back to Denver if he wanted. Or maybe to the East Coast. Some of his siblings lived in Philly. He could just go, keep driving, away from Bethany and her reemergence, away from Blue Larkspur, away from Rachel and the baby doing some kind of Irish jig on her lap.

But he couldn't move. It was as if he was stuck to the loveseat with NASA-grade epoxy. Worse, he couldn't stop looking at Iris.

His Iris?

Iris. It was a word for "rainbow" in ancient Greek. Had Rachel named the baby in a nod to her father— him?

He was an attorney, darn it. Of all people, he knew the power of suggestion. It was one of his many trial tools, used to convince a jury his client was right, on the side of justice. So it should be easy to dismiss what now looked like his grandmother's hair color—Kiriakis flaming red—and his facial features as anecdotal. Yet something about the baby was so familiar…as if they'd always known one another. The same feeling that drove him to keep calling Rachel, despite her rejection of him. The urge to take the job in Blue Larkspur, on the off chance Rachel was still available and had changed her mind.

A breath in, a breath out. As his respiration returned to normal, it was easier to take stock of the situation. Rachel sat quietly, playing with the infant. Most likely his child. He couldn't ignore that Iris looked almost exactly like his sister's twin girls. Yeah, the Kiriakis genes were strong. He and his cousins had all looked alike as kids.

"You never told me—" He held up his hands in surrender. "No, wait—that's why you called me, when you said a woman answered."

"Yes."

Anger welled. Deep and lasting. Not at Rachel or this beautiful little girl—that was *his* child—but at the woman whose determination to make him hers cost him more than a year with Rachel and the first precious months of his daughter's life. It was one thing when Bethany had come after him, another when he'd been concerned that she was targeting Rachel. But Bethany had kept him from his own child.

His. Own. Child.

"James?" Concern laced her tone.

He tore his gaze off Iris and met Rachel's unflinching yet compassionate gaze. It was as if she thought he was…fragile.

His gut twisted. What the hell had happened in the last year and a half? He'd been on top of his legal game, looking forward to a Denver corporate law career. Then he'd met Bethany, and things started falling apart. His liaison with Rachel had been a bright, happy spot. Until she'd ghosted him. *No, not true.* She'd reacted naturally to the lie she'd been fed.

"Sorry. I'm okay, really. I know I probably look off-kilter. It's a lot to digest."

"I know. But I can only imagine what you're feeling right now. Iris has been with me, a part of me, since I've known you. I've definitely had a lot more time to adjust to my new reality. And for what it's worth, it's been a joyride. Right, Iris, baby?" She kissed her before giving him a rueful smile. "Why don't you stay for dinner at least? I know it's not what you'd imagined it'd be, but since you're new in town, it won't hurt to make a local friend. We can be friends until you get the paternity test results. Then we'll talk about co-parenting, if you're even interested."

"Okay." He agreed without reservation. If Rachel was a conniver, she was over-the-top good at it. And her behavior, her actions last night and now, confirmed that she wasn't going to force the issue. By all appearances, Rachel was confident that things would work out for her and Iris.

So where was he in the equation?

IRIS GOBBLED UP the applesauce that Rachel had mixed with a tiny amount of rice cereal, slapping her tiny hands on the plastic high chair tray. She was at the center of the small table, with Rachel at the head and James across from her. If Rachel was one given to worry, it would be wasted on James's reaction to finding out he was a father.

"She's a good eater, I'll give her that." He'd finally tucked into his meal, though she noticed he'd left some of it uneaten. In his shoes she was certain she wouldn't have been able to eat anything.

"I've been so blessed with her, no kidding. She's always been a good eater, from the first time the delivery nurse put her on my breast. She latched on like a champ." Used to telling this story to the women in her life, she halted as she fed Iris, the spoon full of mushy food in midair. Suddenly the word *breast* had a different meaning. As when James had held hers—

"Aaaah!" Iris's squeal happened at the same time her arm swung out and hit Rachel's hand, turning the innocent baby spoon with a bear-shaped handle into a catapult. The sauce splattered across the table, and on James's face.

"Oh man, so sorry about that!" She stood to get him another napkin but he motioned for her to sit.

"If I can't handle a bit of baby food on my face, what kind of court attorney would I make?" He used his napkin to wipe his brow, his shirt. And then, to Rachel's surprise, James stood, not to walk to the kitchen sink and continue the cleanup, but to move his chair close to Iris's high chair.

"May I?" He held out his hand for the spoon. Their eyes met, and she saw the acceptance instead of the resistance that had flashed when she'd first announced Iris's paternity.

"Of course." It was almost too easy to relinquish the feeding duties. Sure, she shared so much of raising Iris with her mother and nanny. But James was a stranger to her baby, even to her. One night of incredible sex did not a relationship make.

It made a baby, though.

Hunger made her stomach gurgle and she realized she hadn't eaten but one or two bites. While she had the opportunity, she shoveled the dinner down. James's rich laughter warmed her, drew her focus from her plate.

"What?"

He was smiling at Iris as he answered, successfully

scooping the remaining food into the baby's mouth. "You ate that as if it's your first meal in days."

A grin tugged at her lips. "Maybe not my first meal, but it's my first full dinner. Even with all the help I have from my family, I like for Iris and I to have the evenings to ourselves. We have a dinner-and-bath routine, but since she's started on solid foods, it's been a challenge to eat my meal before she's in bed." Often she skipped it, waking up famished the next day, when having a full breakfast was out of the question. "Smoothies are my go-to, and then I do get a decent meal at lunch, most days."

"Really? Because the last I checked, there's no busier lawyer than a district attorney."

"Long hours include a lunchtime, trust me." His focus on her self-care made her toes curl and she bit her lower lip. From James's perspective they'd gone from one-night-stand acquaintances to survivors of an unexpected blast to co-parents. All in less than forty-eight hours.

"Have you been able to find out if it was Bethany last night?"

He shook his head. "No. Chief Lawson said that unless they can find her on the restaurant's security footage, all they have to go by is my sighting. Which to be fair, was of a woman with very different hair and makeup than I've ever seen her in." He sighed. "Sometimes I think I'm losing my mind. Seeing her where she isn't. You know, like when someone you love dies?"

"I do know." Those first months after her father's fatal accident, she swore she saw him in crowds or heard his voice in the other room instead of the television.

"But your stalker's not dead, and if there's any chance she knows you moved here, it's not unreasonable to be on guard."

"There's one other thing you need to know. And I need to call the chief and report it. I had a hang-up call on the way here. It's classic Bethany."

"I get hang-ups all the time. And solicitors. Maybe someone was about to sell you a new source for electricity."

"Ah, I wish I had your optimism. But I'm certain it was her—she played the same song she always does on her crank calls."

"I'm afraid to ask what the song is."

He told her, and she sucked in a deep gulp of air. "I remember that from when my mother played it after my father died. It's kind of a creepy song, saying they'll love you until you're both dead and six feet under."

"Exactly. And perfectly Bethany."

"Look, you'll report it, and the chief will put his best officers on it. There are many ways to catch a stalker these days and tracking her phone will help."

"I'm sure she's using burners."

"You're probably right. But come on, no going negative. Let's enjoy the rest of the meal." She knew she was probably off-putting with her extreme-bubbly affectation, but she'd do anything to get the hopeless look off his face. Surprise sideswiped her, making goosebumps dance across her forearms. How could she care about his feelings when honestly, she hardly knew him?

Because she knew the truth, and a paternity test would prove it to James. It wasn't personal that he was resisting it. Although, seeing how he was feeding Iris, making soft encouraging noises as the baby chowed down, she knew that somewhere inside his walled-off heart he knew the truth. At least, his DNA did.

"What do we do now?" He showed her the empty bowl. Iris was as content as she'd been in days, staring at her daddy. Whether or not James believed it yet, Rachel knew the truth and suspected that with some kind of baby intuition, Iris did, too.

"We sit and finish our meals, then she gets her bath. James, you don't have to do—"

"Rachel, the lawyer in me knows that I need to wait on a paternity test. And I'll use the lab you've recommended." She'd given him a card for a facility downtown. "But for some reason I can't explain, I believe you. If we find out I'm not the father, we'll deal with it then. I don't think it'd change the fact that I want to get to know you better."

This struck a chord of fear into Rachel deeper than any stalker could. It meant that James wanted to be with her for her, not just because he thought she was his child's mother.

"I'll go get her bath going." She stood and all but ran to the nursery. Before James saw the utter panic on her face.

BETHANY DIDN'T LIKE having to park a block over from the woman's house and was thankful she'd worn all black. Still, the light didn't disappear until after six as spring had reached Colorado. Only the shadow of the Rockies allowed her to slip up next to the darkened side of the house, which turned out to be her lucky choice tonight. It gave Bethany views into the living room and kitchen area, and a back bedroom with a crib.

Maybe she'd misread Rachel Colton's body language and she was some kind of relative of James's? A sister she didn't know about, with his niece or nephew? It made her feel a bit bad about spiking the woman's fuel so that her car wouldn't start. But James needed to understand that everything about his life was Bethany's business. No one was going to get close to James without her approval.

Aggravation made her itch all over as she peered into the window and watched James talk to the baby girl as if she was someone he knew. Bethany had been infuriated when James arrived here. She hadn't expected that. It was a Saturday night. James liked to watch or attend baseball games. She'd been certain he'd drive back to Denver and go see the Rockies take on the Phillies in a doubleheader tomorrow. She'd arrived at his Blue Larkspur condo too late this afternoon, after she knew he'd be out of work—he'd already left, and that's what she'd assumed he'd done. She couldn't risk tailing him from work, as the city was too busy that time of day. But he hadn't gone to the game, not if he was back in this hick excuse for a city in time to have dinner with Rachel and her brat.

Watching James play with the baby made her womb contract, she was certain. It wasn't her IBS; it was a sign that James was meant to be the father of her babies. Judging from how he was such a natural with the infant, she knew she'd found the right father for her future children.

All she had to do was get him alone, get all distractions away from him.

Which meant she had to find out why James was spending so much time with Rachel Colton. If she was James's sister, or a friend from his past, she'd come up with a strong but safe message. But if this was James's idea of a new girlfriend, all bets were off.

Bethany was going to annihilate anyone in her way.

Chapter Eight

"Rachel, your brother is here to see you." Clara spoke from the door to the DA's office, a full twenty feet from Rachel's monstrous red-oak desk. She still wasn't used to the perks of being the top prosecuting attorney in Lark's County. A tickle of concern broke her concentration from the case she had to present at the end of the week.

"Which brother?"

"Gideon." The tickle turned to full-fledged alarm bells. Gideon was the sibling she was closest to, and despite being single-birth Coltons, just a few years apart, she and her younger brother got on as if they were twins.

"Send him right in, thank you."

Gideon entered no more than thirty seconds later, an expression of concern on his classically handsome face. His blue eyes, an exact match to hers, flickered with the energy he put into his work as a social worker. It was perhaps the single reason they were so close— they shared a unique passion to serve their community. Of course, her new paycheck was the most she'd ever dreamed of making, and Gideon was doing well in his position, too.

"Hey, what's going on?" She rose and rounded the desk to hug him, then motioned for him to take a seat as she sat next to him in the matching chair.

"Sorry to bust in on you like this, but I had to see for myself that you're okay."

"Wha— Oh, let me guess. You spoke to Mom."

"I did, and one of my coworkers was at the same restaurant that night. I heard firsthand how awful it was."

"It was scary at first, sure, but I'm pretty certain it ended up being nothing more than an oversize firecracker." For her the scarier part was that Bethany might be the cause, and had her sights on Rachel, too.

"I'm glad you're okay." His eyes narrowed. "But I know you, Rachel. You're not telling Mom everything. Who is this James dude that you met for dinner? Are you going to see him again?"

"Dang." She let out a laugh. "I should have known you were picking up on my vibes."

"Spill it."

"You can't tell Mom, or anyone else. I need you to promise."

"I have to be able to tell Sophia." His eyes softened and a small smile graced his square jawline. Gideon had rekindled his relationship with the strong, no-nonsense pediatrician recently while working with her to save a little boy's life. Satisfaction curled in Rachel's belly. There was nothing lovelier than knowing her brother was happy.

"Okay, well, I don't see a problem with that. She's used to keeping confidences just like we are." She paused, knowing her next words would interest Gideon, who until now played the major male figure in Iris's life.

"Tell me, Rachel. Neither of us have that much time." She realized he was here on his lunch hour, and she needed to have hers soon, too.

"Okay. The 'James dude?' He's Iris's father and he's in the city. Actually, he's moved here."

"What? And you didn't tell me, or any of us?"

"Hold on. I didn't know it until a few days ago. He didn't move here to find me. At least I don't think he did."

"But you must have told him that Iris is his?"

"Not right away, I didn't. That's what the dinner at Ricco's was about. I had to feel him out, see what his deal is. The explosion cut that date short, so I had him over on Saturday night. I told him then."

"He believed you?"

"Yeah. I mean, he resisted at first, as anyone would with such big news. But I know it's his child, and he will too, after he gets the paternity test. Although I daresay he's already convinced Iris is his. It's hard to overlook the hair color and stubbornness." She grinned but Gideon wasn't picking up on her sense of humor.

"Wow. This is a huge turn of events. I'm proud of you, sis, even though you should have told me as soon as you knew this jerk was around."

"He's not a jerk and what's there to be proud of?"

"You're stepping out of your comfort zone. No offense, but you like things neat and tidy. Controlling, some might say." He grinned. "I know you said you tried to tell him about Iris already, but did you, really?"

She hadn't given anyone in her family one iota of information about James or the circumstances of their meeting, for good reason. Her brothers were too protective for her liking. Which could translate to a black eye for James. A snort escaped her at the thought of her brothers acting like some kind of gang. They were all softies at heart, with their family's security being the one exception.

"No, no, you've got me there. I didn't try hard enough to tell him, when I should have. When I was pregnant." She explained what had happened, how a woman she now believed to be Bethany Austin had answered and said she was James's fiancée. Gideon listened in his unique attention-to-detail manner as she dumped the entire story, leaving no stone unturned.

"Let's distill this down, sis. You've got your kid's dad in your life, and I hope for his sake he'll become involved in Iris's life the way a father should." At her movement to fight him on his dramatic concern, he held his hand up. "Hang on. Let me finish. Besides finally getting the truth out in the open with this man— James—you find out he has a stalker? And you've entered her sights?"

"Yes." There was nothing to deny, even though she wanted to. Anything to avoid the fear that circled around her consciousness all day since the explosion.

"You've got to go to the police, Rachel. Talk to the chief directly. I don't give a rat's butt if this James dude wants you to or not. A stalker is nothing to mess with."

"He's not what's kept me from reporting any of this. He has a restraining order out on her, for heaven's sake."

"Then, I don't understand why you're here in your office and not down at BLPD headquarters. You and Iris need round-the-clock protection."

WHEN RACHEL HAD called James and asked him to meet her within the next hour, alarm bells had gone off. Was she going to end their brief relationship already? Refuse him access to Iris? He'd agreed to meet her ASAP and told himself to stop jumping to conclusions.

"Thanks for meeting me here." Rachel's eyes were unreadable behind her oversize sunglasses, but her posture, hunched over her coffee, bundled in the long raincoat, suggested she was still wary of him, his intentions. "I realize that you probably need time to process everything I told you, but I have to ask you something."

"Okay." He sipped his black brew, full strength, even though it was the middle of the afternoon. They sat at a table outside a popular Blue Larkspur coffee shop, a block up from the riverfront.

"I'm going to go to the police with the additional incidents I believe Bethany Austin might be involved in. Above and beyond the Ricco's explosion."

"The explosion and your car's sabotage?"

"There's another thing. The morning after you were over, I took Iris into the backyard for fresh air. We had a break in the rain and it was sunny… Anyway, there were footprints on my back deck and patio, similar to ones I'd found in my driveway after our night at Ricco's. That night after Ricco's I blamed the prints on my overactive imagination and thought that maybe they were from neighborhood teens playing tag or hide-and-seek at night. They do that every so often. But after seeing the prints on my patio, I'm not so certain. Plus the shrubs and plants near each of my windows had been disturbed. Then there's my gas tank. The mechanic called me today because she'd sent off a fuel sample when she serviced my car. My engine failure had nothing to do with errant rodents but was caused by someone tainting my fuel."

Her mouth was in a grim line and she didn't need to elaborate.

"I wish you'd have called me. Of course you have to go to report this, all of it. I'm so sorry I've involved you in my mess, Rachel. And Iris…" He choked on the little girl's name. His daughter. He had to get the DNA verified for legal purposes but he knew that girl was his, as clear as he knew Rachel wasn't lying.

Slow down.

But no matter what his lawyer instincts said, he knew in his heart what the truth was. The DNA test would only validate his instincts.

"Iris is fine." Two lines appeared between her eyebrows. What had he done that puzzled her?

"I want to get the paternity test over and done with." The words sounded harsher than he'd intended. "For all our sakes."

"Of course you do." The wariness was back in her voice and she leaned back in her chair, putting more space between them.

"I have an appointment later today to take care of it, at the lab you recommended. They told me it'll take up to five days." He said the last part so she'd have the information, but what he didn't mention was that he was paying to have the results expedited. By this time tomorrow he hoped to know if he was a father.

You already know.

Rachel stood, and he followed. "And I've already sent Iris's in. We're in good shape as far as that's concerned, then. Look, I've got to go—I'm due in court in forty-five minutes. I'll let you know what Chief Lawson says."

"I'd appreciate that."

She gave him a nod, then walked toward the center of the city. He watched her departure, unable to take his gaze off her slim figure, the way her legs looked in what must be her courtroom shoes. Sexy, strong, the most attractive woman he'd ever met.

More importantly, the smartest person he probably knew. And she was most likely the mother of his child. What did his divorced friend call it, raising kids with his ex? The same term Rachel had used on Saturday. *Co-parenting.* He and Rachel were going to co-parent Iris if the paternity test proved his gut instinct and her claim correct.

She turned a corner and disappeared from view and he had to fight the urge to catch up, walk alongside her. Instead, he took their empty cups to the recycle bin, pulled out his phone to see what was waiting for him back at the firm.

Anything to ignore the sensation that the term *co-parenting* elicited. It wasn't pleasant, the idea of only being Iris's daddy and working with Rachel in what would be a more businesslike relationship.

James wanted more.

"THANKS FOR SEEING ME." Rachel sat in one of the comfy chairs in front of the chief's desk at BLPD. "I hate to bother you when there's so much on the station's plate these days."

"Please, Rachel. I know you're the DA, and rightfully so, the best Blue Larkspur could ask for. But you'll always be family to me." His eyes twinkled and belied the hard-core crime and hardened crooks he'd dealt with in his decades-long career.

"I'll get right to the point. Somebody put a thinner in my fuel tank last week so that my car wouldn't start. The mechanic says it's a deliberate act, and while it could have been bored teens, she doubted it."

"You use who for your auto repair?"

She named the shop. "I've known her since high school. Laurie used to fix our family beaters when we were all still teens and saved me so much money as I hustled tables through college and law school. She knows her stuff, Chief."

"Go on." He was taking notes on a bright yellow legal pad, using the same brand of all-wood pencil that she preferred. It made her heart warm to see someone else who needed the tactile motion to get his thoughts together.

"This part is harder. I haven't even told my mother yet."

Theo's brows raised, but he didn't say anything. He understood the heft of her statement. Rachel was close to Isa and kept little from her. Their bond had cemented at a time that most mothers and daughters struggle, when Rachel was fourteen. The same year Ben died and the broad-scale damage he'd done to the community had come to light.

"I, um, well." Rachel stopped, took a deep breath. It wasn't usual for her to be timid or without words. "Iris's dad is here, in town. You met him the other night, at the restaurant explosion. James Kiriakis. He moved in from Denver, for a job. He has a restraining order on his former girlfriend, Bethany Austin, that he took out when he resided in Denver. He's certain she's followed him here, that she's in Blue Larkspur. You already know all of this, right?"

"Right."

She spilled the rest of it. The sense of being watched, the odd sounds around the house. "And there's one more thing. When I got home after the explosion, I thought I heard animals in my yard. Until I found footprints on my drive. They were similar to the patio prints."

"Has James mentioned if he's been contacted by Bethany?"

"We only spoke today, briefly. He had a crank call with the song Bethany thinks is theirs. He didn't mention anything else." She'd been tempted to reach out to him sooner but knew he'd need time to process. And she hadn't known if he'd received the results of his paternity test yet.

"Do you have a problem with me talking to him about this, Rachel?"

"Not at all. He knows I'm here speaking to you. I'm sorry for all this extra drama. You don't need an additional action item today, I'm sure."

He chuckled. "At my age, I'm happy to be able to continue to do the work I was cut out for."

"Did you ever consider doing anything else? Or, if I may utter the word, retire?"

"A few times. Especially after a hard case, one with kids getting hurt. Yeah, I looked at contracting—you know, that HGTV kind of stuff—and I thought about teaching at the police academy. But when it comes down to it, I'd miss the community, the people."

"I understand." She'd worked in public law her entire career.

"I know you do. Not many would have the courage or means to rectify the sins of their fathers, Rachel, but you and your siblings have. The Truth Foundation is the pride of Blue Larkspur."

"As much as Ben Colton is its dark stain."

"I knew your father, and while I was always suspicious of many of his dealings, his original motives were from the heart. He wanted to provide for his family. Raising twelve kids isn't easy or inexpensive."

"But it's not an excuse to take bribes and put criminals away for longer than what's fair, or convict innocents." She shook her head. "My only regret with accepting the DA position is that I can't work on the Truth Foundation any longer."

"You're doing a lot of good right where you are, Rachel. Give it time. The case against Clay Houseman is about to get interesting. We've got evidence that substantiates he's been involved in the illegal activities he was arrested for, unrelated to Spence. But he's still claiming to be responsible for crimes that Spence is serving time for." Theo referred to Clay Houseman, who had recently been arrested for a variety of transgressions. But suspiciously after his arrest, Houseman claimed to be responsible for drug crimes that Ronald Spence, a longtime criminal and prisoner, was incarcerated for. It was suspected that Spence had somehow bribed or threatened Houseman into pleading guilty for Spence's offenses. Spence was the last case that Ben Colton presided over, after Judge Colton had admitted to previous wrongs and vowed to uphold the law in all his future endeavors. Rachel was certain her father had done the right thing, that Spence was guilty no matter his continued claims of innocence, all these years later. Caleb led the Truth Foundation in its investigation of Spence, to determine if the man's claims of innocence had merit. The foundation was all about justice and the absolute truth, no matter any family member's personal opinion.

"I can't be involved in it, Chief." While she'd taken steps to be removed from the Parson case, when it came to Spence and Houseman, she couldn't be partial.

"No, but your staff can. If he gets convicted, there's a good chance we'll find out that we need to free Ronald Spence."

Frustration rushed heat into her cheeks. "I don't know how I feel about that, to be honest. Spence may not be guilty of what Dad sent him to prison for, but he's no innocent victim, either." Ronald Spence had gone to jail for drug smuggling, the last case Ben Colton had heard. Drug dealers decimated families and the overall sense of well-being normally enjoyed by Blue Larkspur citizens, but now the Coltons were not positive whether Spence was actually guilty.

"No. This is one time I wish I could still be on the Truth Foundation as well as DA. It'd be like waving a wand and fixing everything all at once. Except I don't have all the information on Houseman, and I doubt anyone does. Just as with Spence—all drug lords are the slimiest of pond scum."

"You've got that right, Rachel." Theo sipped what had to be a cold break-room coffee by now. "As you said, this isn't your concern. I'm sorry I brought it up."

"No apology necessary. It's a family thing." And he was part of their family, wasn't he? A decades-old friend. Except…

"What's up, Rachel? Do you have another question for me?" Theo must have caught the speculation in her expression.

"I was wondering exactly what your intentions are with my mother." As soon as the words were out, she heard how intrusive and rude they were. She held up her hands in a surrender gesture. "No, wait, don't tell me. That was out of line. And definitely none of my business."

Theo's usual noncommittal expression faltered, his cheeks reddening. His eyes cast downward at the legal pad in front of him. Rachel felt like a heel for being so obtuse. Theo was older than her mom, and their generation did things with a lot more subtlety than hers. Could she have been any crasser in her query?

After a long, silent moment Theo cleared his throat and looked back up. He was still blushing, but his gaze was clear and steady. "It's okay, Rachel. I do happen to care a heck of a lot about your mother. But it's got to be on her terms and her time."

Stunned that he'd responded at all, she blinked and gazed down at her phone, suddenly unable to look at him. His sweet, tender heart was on his crisply pressed dress-shirt sleeve, and a rush of affection for the man who'd become a strong, positive figure in her life stole her words. She bit her bottom lip to keep from blubbering as she spoke.

She copied what she'd seen James do when she'd

proclaimed he had a daughter and let herself take a couple deep breaths.

"It's okay, Chief. We're all doing our best, aren't we?"

"Yes indeed. Give me a chance to continue to investigate the explosion. We'll find ties to Bethany Austin if they're there. She's now a suspect if all that James told you, and the events you've relayed, prove true."

"It will come out in the wash, I'm certain." She couldn't explain why, but she trusted James's claims. And not only because of the incidents that had happened to her, with her car and the footprints around her home.

Hold on, girlfriend. She knew it wasn't wise to trust a man she'd spent so little time with. But her heart didn't seem to care. She stood and gave Theo a smile. The man really was a dear, though she wouldn't express it right now while he was in his Chief mode.

"I'm afraid you're right." Theo nodded.

"Thanks so much, Chief. I hope this doesn't amount to a hill of beans, but if it does, I wanted you to have everything I've pieced together. There's nothing more important than keeping Iris safe."

He nodded. "Agreed. I'm on it, Rachel. I appreciate that you've trusted me with your personal life, too." He paused, and she thought she saw a mischievous twinkle in his eyes. "But can I say one thing?"

"Shoot."

"Isa is going to be over the moon with all of this. It's her deepest wish that you find someone to love you and Iris. Provided my impression of James as an upstanding man proves true."

"Uh…thank you? And if I can say something? I'd

love it if you became a permanent member of our family." She scooted out of the office before he could reply, not wanting to risk embarrassing him again.

Only a few days ago, she'd be on the phone as she walked, texting or calling Gideon to relay the family gossip. But as she headed for the courthouse in the sunny afternoon light, she was struck by another impulse. Her fingers itched to text James.

Nope, not happening. But boy oh boy, she wanted to.

Chapter Nine

The week flew by with work responsibilities and Iris's teething antics. By Friday night, all Rachel wanted was to spend some quality time with Iris, get her to bed and veg in front of her favorite Netflix show. There was a new rom-com she was interested in, even though she didn't need or welcome romance into her personal life. Raising Iris and being a DA was enough, thank you very much.

An image of James smiling, sitting at her dining room table, jolted her off the precarious and defensive pedestal she'd constructed. She and James would be friends. Co-parents. It was going to have to be enough, wasn't it?

"Look at you!" She finished drying Iris off after a fun bath time complete with not one or two but eleven mini rubber duckies of various colors, all gifted to Iris by her adoring aunts and uncles. Her tiny hand still clutched a bright blue one, and Rachel had to avoid getting clocked by her daughter.

"Uuuuu ma ma!"

"What? Oh my gosh, did you say—"

The doorbell rang and the chimes seemed particularly jarring, interrupting a very special baby milestone.

"They can wait, sweetie. What did you say?" And who would be dropping in after eight o'clock on a Friday night? All of her siblings worked long days and hard weeks. The Coltons gathered when anyone who wanted or was available showed up at the main house where Isa still lived. Isa made wonderful meals, but help from all the children turned the former delicious-but-humble food into several-course, gourmet events.

Iris giggled but spoke no more. Disappointment stabbed at Rachel's heart, and to her surprise, tears welled. The combination of all of the past week's emotional upheaval all added up. First James came back into her life, along with Bethany Austin. Houseman's testimony confirmed his guilt for Spence's alleged crimes, raising the probability of Spence's release. Spence was a man she wasn't comfortable with being back on the streets. Her powerlessness hit her in the face and her shoulders felt as if she'd spent all day hauling rocks. Bone weariness settled over her and she blinked back more tears.

Iris's big blue eyes gave her an uncannily adult look, as though her daughter knew what she was feeling.

"It's okay, baby girl. Mommy's just got some hormones and emotions zipping around." Rachel's milk production had slowed down since Iris was eating increasing portions of solid food. Her GP, a nurse practitioner, had warned that Rachel shouldn't discount her hormones from wreaking havoc as her body adjusted to Iris's gradually diminishing need for breast milk. She'd nurse for at least twelve months, but there was no hiding from time. Iris wasn't the tiny infant she'd brought home. These past six months had raced by, and—

Ding dong ding.

"Dang it!" She bundled Iris more tightly into the bath towel, tucked the hood sewn into the corner around the baby's head.

"Coming!"

Gathering Iris in her arms, she headed for the front door. She'd meant to get surveillance cameras she'd ordered online for the front and back entrances installed, but it had to wait until Sunday. Gideon had promised to come over and install them for her. Isa had recently had a system installed. As DA, Rachel would be able to write the expense off and, frankly, should have installed the security measures sooner. Evidence that someone had spiked her gas tank, and that maybe the same person had been snooping around her property, combined with Bethany Austin's probable role in it had pushed her to decide to act now.

Still, the boxes of unopened cameras sat in the corner of the foyer, worthless to her in this moment. Looking through the peephole, she let out a shocked squeak and opened the door.

James's profile was stark against the bright white of the front porch light.

"James!"

"Hey, Rachel. Iris, how are you, baby?" He cooed at Iris as if he did it all the time, not as though he'd just met her last week and was seeing her for only the second time.

"Come in. I don't want her to get chilled." She stepped aside and opened the door wide. Only then did her gaze catch on several stacks of items that surrounded him. "What on earth have you brought?"

He flashed a quick grin before getting to work, hauling in his bounty. "I realize I'm months late and you may already have a lot of this stuff, but I've brought Iris a few things." He spoke as he paraded back and forth from the porch and into the house.

"Here okay?" He indicated a spot next to the stairs. Rachel nodded.

"I'd help you, but Iris is still damp from her bath. Let me get her dressed."

"Go ahead. It'll give me time to set up some of this."

Rachel didn't want to even ask him what, exactly, needed to be set up. If the oversize colorful boxes were any indication, James had decided to play new daddy and Santa Claus all in one fell swoop.

JAMES GOT TO work as soon as he had all his bounty inside. He hoped to be rid of the packaging before Rachel returned with Iris. His stomach jumped with giddy nervousness at the thought of Iris's eyes growing wide at her new toys.

His fingers stymied his progress, however, as they behaved like they were all thumbs. When had plastic packaging become so difficult to open?

Scissors.

He needed help opening the heavy-duty seals. Looking around the living room area, he saw no sign of a tool to help him. Finally, he spied a pair of scissors in the kitchen knife block and helped himself.

Fifteen minutes and ten open packages later, he smiled at his creation. Wait until Iris saw this!

"What on earth?" There was no missing the disapproval in Rachel's tone as she spoke next to him, Iris in her arms. His baby girl was in pajamas and looked cute as all get-out.

"Did you buy out the store, James?"

Rachel's surprise was evident but it wasn't the happy kind he'd expected as she gaped at what he'd worked on. The kid-sized kitchen had what he considered the most fun potential. The pink-and-orange appliances were perfect replicas of Rachel's kitchen. His lungs pressed against his rib cage as he watched her gaze move over the play kitchen, the pile of plastic utensils and dishes, and on to the fully equipped play construction bench. Because his girl was going to be completely self-sufficient. By the time she was an adult, he hoped she would be able to cook, bake and put together a wooden deck with minimal effort.

"Check this out." He held up a miniature plastic cordless drill not that far off from the real one he owned. "The drill bit really turns!"

"Okay. But James—" He could hear the concern in her tone and had to fix it. "It's, it's a lot. That's all. Not in a bad way, necessarily. I'm just…surprised."

"It's not finished. There's a toddler-sized table and chairs, and I grabbed some lawn equipment. A lawn mower and snowplow, plus they had this little gas grill that I thought would be perfect as the weather warms up." He tried to see the toys from Rachel's perspective and noticed the large pile of cardboard and plastic.

"I had a hard time getting started. I guess I'm nervous." *Stop talking, bro.* "I can move it wherever you want it. I got both the kitchen and workbench sets because I don't want Iris to ever feel she has to conform to being anything other than who she is."

"How thoughtful." Rachel looked like she'd swallowed a bird.

"What is it?"

A low giggle sounded and at first he thought it was Iris, but the baby had her fist in her mouth, chomping down as she had on the frozen washcloth last week. The only source of glee had to be Rachel. Whose laughter made her shoulders shake like aspen leaves in a breeze.

"James, Iris is barely seven months old. She won't be ready for any of this for another six months to a year, at the least."

"She'll be pulling up on stuff soon, right? As soon as she starts crawling." He'd been doing some reading. If Rachel saw the stack of parenting books he'd pored over after work this week…

"I suppose you're right." Bemusement gave her cheeks the same rosy glow as Iris's. Awe sucker punched him. He didn't think, no, he knew, he'd never seen a more beautiful image than Rachel holding Iris, both of their attention completely focused on him.

"Kiriakis kids walk early, by the way. My nieces and nephews all started by nine months."

"Okay, well, good to know."

Defeat tried to smother his happy buzz, but he shoved it away. He wasn't about to let Rachel's reluctance get in the way of bonding with his daughter. "I figured you already had all the baby things you needed. Since I missed out on that, I wanted to get a jump start on her next development phase."

At Rachel's sharp glance, he decided to elaborate. She'd find out soon enough. "I've read the latest editions of *What to Expect the First Year* by Heidi Murkoff and

Caring for Your Baby and Young Child by the American Academy of Pediatrics. And I've been an involved uncle to five nieces and nephews. I'm not a beginner." But he was a new parent, no question.

"You've had a lot to digest since we ran into one another again."

He sighed. "I'm a hot mess, aren't I?"

"No more than any of us are. Right, Iris girl?" Her response was generous. If he were her he didn't think he'd be so accommodating. He looked at how comfortably Rachel held Iris, and when he smiled at the baby, he was rewarded with a lopsided smile.

"She has my mother's smile." The statement came out in a whisper, but he didn't care. This was his daughter and not only was he going to make up for every second he'd missed, he was going to fill them with fun. No way was Iris ever going to have the heartbreak that his childhood had.

"Oh." Rachel stared at him until he caught her gaze, then looked at Iris. "I was wondering about her smile. And her feet. Look at these tootsies." She held a foot in her hand. "No one in my family has that wide of a space between their big and second toes."

Warmth beyond his understanding burst inside his chest and he held out his arms. Iris had his feet! "May I?"

Rachel handed Iris over, and in the second where they both held her, their gazes met again. If anyone had ever told him he'd be comfortable in any kind of family situation that remotely involved him, he'd have howled with laughter. But that was before Rachel. Before he held this precious gift that was his baby daughter in his hands.

"Rachel, I want to make this up to you. To Iris." Rachel turned away, her expression guarded. He allowed Iris's weight to settle against his chest.

"I take it you've gotten the DNA results back by now?" Rachel spoke from the toddler kitchen, where she knelt as she tested out the faux appliances. He smiled at Iris who took a second to register the gesture before she responded with her toothless grin.

"Actually, yes. They are proof of what my heart, and your red hair, already told me." He spoke to Iris as he carried her toward the sofa, laughing when her tiny hand reached up and tweaked his nose. "Honk."

Rachel straightened and turned toward him. He couldn't read her mood, not until she moved closer and picked up a baby blanket from a recliner, clearing the seat cushion.

"Well, then that's settled. Legally and heart-wise. Here, use this chair. She likes to be rocked this time of night. It's her bedtime." He complied, acting as casually as he could, not wanting to upset Iris's routine by carrying on a deep conversation with Rachel. He couldn't help but notice that while her lips remained in a soft line, her brows level, there was a spark in her eyes.

Hope.

ANGER TIGHTENED BETHANY'S gut as she stared at her phone, furious at the images of the past half hour. How dare Rachel allow James into her home this late at night! And then, to top it off, she handed over her baby to him. What a lazy mother. Just like hers, who'd foisted her kid off on her younger sister and Bethany's grandma before taking off for the big, wide world. At least Bethany's aunt and grandmother had fed her most nights. Unlike Mom, who barely fed herself. If it didn't have a clever name like Harvey Wallbanger or Sex on the Beach, her mother didn't want it.

Bethany's only mistake in her tracking of James was that she hadn't sprung for an audio feed when she purchased the special cameras from the spy store. She'd left no fewer than five of the tiny lenses on various pieces of Rachel's furniture and fireplace mantel, to give her as full of a picture as possible without a moving camera. No audio meant she had to guess at what they were saying, but she already knew the deal. That Rachel was using all her wiles to snare James in her web.

James was too nice; she'd warned him about that. Unlike the other men she'd tried to hook up with, to make a family life, James hadn't dropped her like a wet cat. He'd insisted they stay friends. That's how she knew he still loved her. He just didn't want to disappoint her with his long work hours, and now that she knew he'd had to change jobs, it was all the clearer to her what had happened. James was struggling at work and didn't want to drag her into it. So typical of him, to be that thoughtful!

Still, it'd be better if she could hear what they were saying. Although not having audio kept her from having to deal with the brat's crying. The kid's mouth sure was open a lot, and Rachel was always holding or feeding her.

Maybe she could go back to the spy store… *No*. There wasn't time. She'd had to drive clear to Colorado

Springs and back for the equipment, because thanks to that pesky restraining order, she couldn't risk leaving any kind of digital footprint around James's apartment. Rachel's house was another matter, in Bethany's opinion. She couldn't help it if James was at her place all the time. If the cops caught her, she was going to claim she'd been tracking Rachel, as a concerned citizen. Rachel was a public servant, so Bethany thought her justification made sense. And Rachel was around him a lot—too much. Way too much.

No, she couldn't worry about getting audio equipment. Not yet. Plus, where would she have a package shipped right now? No way was she risking having it sent to her permanent address in Denver, and setting up a P.O. Box in Blue Larkspur required an ID. Nope, not happening. So she'd gotten all she could with her limited cash funds at the brick-and-mortar location.

She grinned to herself as she mentally ran down her equipment. Wireless cameras that Rachel wouldn't be likely to find, check. Nearly invisible sensors at each door to let her know when Rachel or the babysitter, or Isa Colton, was coming and going, check. Getting James to see that Bethany was the only woman for him—almost a check but not quite yet. It looked like she was going to have to get this woman out of the picture first. Some scare tactics were in order, but Bethany had to bide her time.

Time wasn't her friend right now, though. Paying cash was getting to be a pain, as she didn't dare use her ATM card anywhere near Blue Larkspur. She was down to her last few hundred dollars, too. When her cash ran out, she'd have to use credit or debit.

She refocused on the screen in front of her. A thrill shot through her and made her laugh aloud in the small car's confines. It had been too easy to plant the cameras, one in the living room and one in the kitchen, covering the entire front of the house. She had a third for the kid's bedroom but the darn babysitter had prevented her from placing it. Bethany had had to run and hide when the nanny came back into the house unexpectedly. Bethany had put a neighbor's package that she'd stolen on Rachel's porch and rung the bell. The babysitter hadn't taken the package to the correct address as Rachel had hoped. Probably because the kid was sleeping in the crib. Rachel had looked at the brat but didn't have time to linger. She didn't care about a stupid kid.

Unless.

She watched the video feed as James held the baby and made funny faces at it. Maybe he liked babies. Bethany wasn't ever going to have kids—she'd made sure of it and had her tubes tied when she was still in her twenties. She'd convinced the ob-gyn that she carried a horrible genetic disease with DNA results she'd stolen from a work acquaintance who'd confessed her family's plight. But if James was set on having a baby? No problem. If he wanted this kid, she'd make that happen. Women got their tubal ligations reversed all the time. It wasn't cheap, but James would pay for it. Whatever it took for Bethany and James to make their own baby.

It looked like Rachel Colton was the only thing in her way.

Chapter Ten

"How do you know she's still sleeping?" James asked the question a little too casually as they sat across from each other in the living room.

"You mean how do I know she's still breathing, right? That monitor over there." Joy lit a fuse in her heart as she pointed at the kitchen counter to the small white device The ice wall she'd worked hard to keep between her and James was melting a little too quickly for her liking. James, like her father, loved the better things in life, the best things money could buy. Exhibit A, the top-of-the-toy-line household playset in her living room. But how could she resist opening up to him, to his obvious desire to be Iris's dad? And it wasn't for her, but for Iris.

Keep telling yourself that.

"Yeah, something like that." His sheepish grimace proved her suspicion. "I don't know how you don't worry about her 24/7."

"To be honest, it never ends, the worry part. It's normal from what I've heard. My mom says it's part of being a parent and we'll go to the grave with it. But it does get easier, trust me. You'll get more comfortable with taking care of her, get to know her so well that you'll figure out what she needs before she does." She found herself giving him the same speech her mother had given her in the first hours of Iris's life. "That first night in the hospital, I was certain I'd never be able to manage it all. It's overwhelming at first. You're at the beginning of your journey. I get it."

"While we both have to do the maturing becoming a parent requires, you had the physical side of birth to deal with, too. It's impossible for me to imagine how exhausted you must have been, how you might still be. I can't thank you enough for bringing her into the world." James's voice and words caressed her from the inside out. Again, she chalked it up to gratitude that Iris would have a dad. This had nothing to do with her non-relationship with James.

Co-parents. That was the keyword of the day.

"What made you change your mind, James?"

"About being involved in her life?" He smiled. "I hadn't decided not to be, in truth. I was in shock, you know. Finding out about Iris was like having a grenade thrown at me."

"Are you certain you're ready to begin the bonding process, James?" Toys could be returned. Her baby's heart, not so much. Although she knew he was the father, that the DNA proved it, she feared James would get cold feet. Wouldn't anyone when faced with the overwhelming responsibility of raising a soul from infancy until independence?

He shook his head in one decisive movement that she knew was meant to shut down her doubt.

"I'm not waiting one minute longer to get to know my daughter."

It was a huge turn-on that he was 100 percent committed. She envied his ability to have faith it would all work out.

She observed James's quiet manner and couldn't deny his level of commitment. He appeared to have every intention of being present for Iris.

"For what it's worth, I always knew how the DNA results would turn out." She tried to bring some levity to a most serious subject.

"There was nothing to wait for, except for Iris's sake, and her birth record. She needs to know that she wasn't ever anything but loved from the moment I found out about her. I know you've loved her from the start—it's evident."

She shook her head, but not as sharply as he had. "You know, it was odd, scary and very exciting. All at once. A very big surprise, to be sure. Gosh, when I saw the plus sign on that pregnancy test, I about fainted. I've always been careful with birth control, and we were that weekend. I was certain the test was a false positive. But, well, Iris is here." She smiled.

He grinned back. "Yeah, I remember being extra-careful. Maybe it's true—some things are just meant to be."

She blushed. "Yet nothing is one hundred percent. I did panic and of course got checked for STDs."

"I was clean, like I told you. Still am."

"Thanks for the update." She didn't want to go *there* with him, because they had to remain friends, period. Co-parents. "I don't blame you for doubting me, though.

You only knew me from one night. And you did try to reach me for so long… I should have figured out that maybe you weren't engaged anymore."

"I was never engaged, as you now know. I never have been. I'm sorry for any pain my apparent lack of interest has caused. I blame myself for allowing Bethany so close in the first place. If I'd listened to my brother, my friends, I would have shut her down from the get-go. Now she's out of control and has stolen time from me and Iris that I can't get back. *We* can't get back." Her toes curled with aching need at the heat in his eyes. A need that she couldn't fulfill if she wanted to be a good DA and the best mother for Iris.

"I'm sorry about all of it, James."

She eyed the stack of unopened security cameras on the floor and silently reminded herself to check in with Gideon for a good time on Sunday to have him install them. The sooner, the better. Although, sitting here with James, no secrets between them any longer, she felt safer than she had since she found out she was pregnant.

"What happened with Bethany in the beginning? When you first met her?" They both knew where it was now.

"We were acquaintances, then friends, and we dated exactly two times. I never took her to bed, if you're asking that. I don't know why, because she was willing, and I've never been one to turn down some fun. But she was too clingy, and her laughter seemed almost desperate, if that makes sense."

"It does." She respected that he didn't even try to pretend that he hadn't been a player. "Did you date anyone since who she's tried to interfere with?"

"Here and there, but no more than a dinner. I'm putting myself on the line here, Rachel, when I tell you that since we met, you and I, I haven't had the usual interest in dating around. It was a combination of meeting you, then you rejecting my calls and, of course, constantly having to look over my shoulder for Bethany's next twisted act. It made even me, the self-avowed forever-single guy, gun-shy."

"That makes sense. Since we're being on the level with each other, I have to admit it's nice to know that you didn't reject me. I believe you, James. That Bethany was the one who answered your phone when I called. It makes total sense in the context you've provided."

He ran his hand over his head, scratched his nape. "I couldn't risk bringing another woman into my mess, and I didn't want any other woman but you. I know I'm coming on too strong here. You don't even know that I'm sincere about Iris. How could you? But I'll prove it to you, Rachel. I will."

She heard declarations of all kinds on a daily basis from defendants and witnesses. Hadn't she become immune to emotional ploys? When James spoke, though, looking at her with his sexy green eyes, she couldn't breathe. And instead of appealing solely to her parenting concerns about Iris having an involved father, James stirred up the intense desire she'd thought she'd left behind in Helena with their unbridled sex.

As the moment stretched into minutes, the tension between them increased. Rachel swore there was a cord attaching them, belly to belly, tightening with each gulp of air her lungs fought for. Unable to handle the heat that was swirling in her most intimate places, she stood, walked toward the kitchen. Away from James. Before she gave in to the question in his eyes.

"I've got an early start in the morning." She lied. Saturday mornings were for sleeping in as long as Iris allowed, then heading out to either her sister and brother's Gemini Ranch or the Colton homestead to enjoy wider spaces and time with Grandma.

"Please don't shut me out. Give me a chance." James was right next to her at the kitchen counter. She hadn't expected him to follow her, to be so close, where she only had to lean a bit, on her tiptoes, and her mouth would be able to catch his—

No. Dad charmed Mom just like this.

She didn't move, and James took a step back. "I'll let you get some rest. Can I come over to see Iris tomorrow?"

"Of course. Text me when you wake up, and we'll work something out." She risked a glance at him, but the heat of the moment had passed. Her gut sank, and the rest of the evening loomed large and boring. Which left her…confused. Shouldn't she be relieved? "I think we need to come up with a joint custody agreement, for both our and Iris's sakes."

He nodded. "I agree."

"Okay. Well, that's settled."

"And for the record? I never needed to see the DNA results, Rachel. I knew Iris was mine almost from the second I laid eyes on her."

EARLY THE NEXT MORNING, James marveled at how his life had changed on the proverbial dime. It was still all so new to him. Like Christmas, or a special birthday that kept recurring. He couldn't wait to tell his family. He wanted to do it in person if at all possible, but with Bethany's threatening presence he was unwilling to leave Rachel and Iris. So he might need to tell Mom, Jake, and his other siblings over the phone. Maybe he could arrange a video chat session soon. After he was more settled into his role as Iris's daddy.

"Thanks for helping me with the car seat." He sat on the passenger side as Rachel drove the three of them out to the Colton family home, now solely Isa's. After exchanging several texts this morning, he'd figured out she was planning to spend the day here and asked if her family knew about him. Only her brother Gideon did.

"You'll be a pro in no time."

"Let's hope so, for Iris's sake." They laughed together, then settled into a comfortable silence. He used the time to absorb his surroundings, take in the stark natural beauty that was Colorado.

Unlike the rainy days that had characterized April since his arrival in town, today the sun reflected off every new bud.

"I'm glad you're getting to see this all in spring. I happen to think it's one of the most beautiful times of year here." Rachel must have sensed his appreciation.

He took in the mountains, always standing sentinel, visible or not. "I never want to live anywhere but Colorado. It'd be difficult to not have those to view."

"On that we agree, then. Look, James, if you don't want to tell my mother that you're Iris's dad today, you don't have to. We can say you're a colleague who I'm introducing to the area."

"And I just happened to stop by and ask to spend the entire day with you, butting into your family time?"

"Well, when you put it like that…"

"I've been trying to figure out how and when to tell my family, too. I have no problem with telling the Coltons the truth today. But it's your call. Iris is my daughter no matter when we let our families know." On cue, Iris let out a wail. "That's definitely a Colton trait. Kiriakises don't cry."

They both laughed.

"Guilty as charged. I'm from a long line of very loud, expressive people," Rachel said.

"Why is she crying? I thought babies liked car rides."

"She does, but she doesn't like feeling left out of the conversation, do you, baby girl?" He saw that Rachel used a rearview mirror attached to the usual one to look at the infant without having to take her eyes off the road.

"I'm going to have to get a bigger car. My sports coupe days are over." He lazily thought about the kind of four-wheel drive he'd trade his BMW in for.

"If you're expecting any sympathy, none here." She pointed at the large nylon bag on the floor next to his legs. "Can you get her purple unicorn out of there? It looks like a blankie but has a stuffed animal on the end."

He hoisted the diaper bag onto his lap as she rounded a bend that revealed the subdivision that her mother lived in.

"Whoa. I thought you said your mom lived in the suburbs. This seems farther out of the city. You grew up here, even after your dad—" He stopped himself. *Crap.*

Why had he let it slip that he'd been checking up

on her family? Rachel was nothing like her father as far as he was concerned. Not with her prosecution record while assistant DA and her most recent cases as a newly elected DA.

"Well, it's a story of timing, as most are. My dad's criminal activities had just come to light when he was killed in the car crash. Before he died, and before there was time for him to be disbarred and face the prosecution he definitely would have, he'd tried his last few cases. Immediately after he passed, my mom was strapped for cash and we had several lean times. But then my grandparents died, leaving Mom with enough money to invest so that she was able to take care of us. Her wise financial strategies also enabled her to refresh her graphic design skills and set up her own business. So it all worked out."

"How old were you?"

"Fourteen. Hard to believe it's been twenty years."

"Forgive me if I'm overstepping, but I've read up on the Truth Foundation, too. Impressive."

Rachel's white smile flashed, but she kept her eyes on the road, hands on the wheel. "Thanks. Yeah, I'm really proud of what we've accomplished. It killed me to have to quit it for now, but my siblings supported me in my decision to run for DA. They told me I could do my part by restoring and maintaining justice in Blue Larkspur."

"They're right." He shifted in his seat so that he could check on Iris. Her tiny profile was backlit by the passing scenery as she looked out her window, absently kicking her pudgy legs and clutching the stuffed unicorn. "Is she always this easy to placate?"

Rachel's laugh filled the car. "Absolutely not. You know how she was wailing a few minutes ago? She once did that for two hours straight, when I drove to meet a college classmate in Aspen. She fell into a deep sleep five minutes before I pulled in. My girlfriend and I spent the entire visit in the car with the heater on, eating takeout. Needless to say, Iris woke back up for the ride home."

She shook her head and laughed as she pulled into her mother's parking garage, and she killed the engine. Taking her sunglasses from the center beverage holder and shoving them atop her blond head, Rachel looked at him.

"Sure you're ready for this?"

"No question."

"Then, strap in, buddy. It's always a fun ride at the Coltons'."

Chapter Eleven

"Give her to me this second. Did you miss Grammy, honey bunny?" Isa enveloped Iris the minute they were in the door, only pausing for the briefest moment to take James in with her shrewd gaze. To her mother's credit, she didn't ask or say anything. Relief calmed her nerves as Rachel kissed her mother on the cheek.

"Hey, Mom."

"Come on in. We're going to have a cookie party!" The scene around the oversize kitchen island was typical for a weekend afternoon. Gideon stood behind Sophia, the woman Rachel was positive was his soon-to-be fiancée, and rubbed her shoulders as Sophia dropped cookie dough onto baking sheets covered with parchment paper. While Rachel's other siblings were nowhere in sight, she knew that several would be popping in throughout the day, which would allow James to meet them on a casual basis. The less fuss made of her bringing a guy home, the better.

"There's my goddaughter!" Gideon dropped his arms from Sophia's shoulders and walked over to plant a kiss on Iris's red head.

"Hi, sweetie pie." Sophia spoke to Iris from the is-

land before giving Rachel a broad grin along with a surreptitious wink. "Hey, Rachel." Gideon had obviously
told her about James, which Rachel had expected. She
was so happy for her younger brother, reuniting with
the love of his life.

Would she ever want to open her soul to anyone more
than she did to Gideon?

You already have. Maybe, but this wasn't the time
to psychoanalyze herself.

"Hey, Sophia. Everyone, this is James. He's..." The
words stuck in her throat. He was more than a friend,
but definitely not her boyfriend. To her utter astonish-
ment, she discovered she'd wanted to say he was.

"I'm Iris's father." James picked up where she'd faltered, hands on his hips, confident. "Not the deadbeat
dad you probably think I am. I didn't know about Iris
until very recently."

"Well. Mystery solved." Isa bounced Iris in her arms,
swaying back and forth. The image tugged at memories
of when her younger siblings had been little enough for
her mother to do the same with them. "The real questions are, where are you from and how much are we
going to see of you?"

"Mom!" Rachel never thought of herself as the indignant type until now. Gideon let out a guffaw that he
covered with a series of exaggerated coughs, and Sophia bit her lip and bent farther over her task, moving
her face out of view.

"It's okay, Rachel." James spoke as if he dealt with
intimate domestic conflict instead of corporate law. "It's
a fair and needed question. For now, Rachel's agreed to
allow me to see Iris. We are going to work out a joint

custody agreement, and my intention is to be as much of a father to Iris as I possibly can be."

"No matter your relationship status with my daughter?" Isa didn't so much as blink. The woman had gone through losing her husband twice. First to his lawbreaking ways, then to death. She'd raised twelve kids, all of whom became contributing members of society. Telling her granddaughter's father to pound sand wouldn't be out of her bag of conversational skills. In Isa's worldview, it didn't matter that James hadn't known about Iris sooner. That was on Rachel. But now that he knew, Isa would expect nothing less than total commitment.

"Absolutely. I'm committed to Iris. Rachel is not going to raise her alone," James answered without hesitation. As if he'd turned into the man she'd hoped he was when she'd met him in Helena but had dismissed the possibility in a Denver minute. During that brief night, his descriptions of his fancy car, the tailored cut of his suit that only a top designer label afforded, had conveyed that James was into material things and financial success. Just like Ben Colton. And she knew the ending of that story with painful clarity. But the James she'd come to know since he'd moved to Blue Larkspur didn't fit her initial impression. Not at all.

The skin of her nape prickled with doubt. Was there a chance she'd misread James? Had she misinterpreted the pride in his voice when he'd spoken of his success at supporting his corporate clients? Instead of being the showy big earner, was James perhaps not as much like her father as she'd feared?

"James and I are going to co-parent Iris." She glanced at him for confirmation. Her stomach flipped as she forged through her self-recrimination one more time. "The only reason James wasn't here sooner is because I didn't tell him about Iris."

"Rachel!" Isa's tone was as good as a scolding. "I thought you told him but he wasn't interested in his daughter."

"Mom, I never explicitly gave you reason to think that."

Iris appeared oblivious to the gravity of the conversation, holding out her arms toward James.

"Aaaagh!" she gurgled at her father. Isa carried the baby to him. Isa handed her granddaughter over to the man she barely knew, a silent communication in the gesture. "She knows you, that's for certain."

Rachel knew she'd never forget this moment. The exact time the three of them had become a family. Without the encumbrance of romantic love, that is.

James received Iris with aplomb, as if he'd been carrying her the past six months instead of the past few days. Iris, for her part, snuggled up against his chest and rested her chin on James's broad shoulder.

"You little stinker." Rachel couldn't stop the laugh if she'd wanted to. "She wouldn't rest for the drive up, but now she's ready for a nap."

"Not allowed! Not until she's fed." Isa looked at Rachel. "Do you have some bottles with you?"

"Yes, I'll get them." She walked over to where they'd dropped the diaper bag and small cooler, producing a bottle of the breast milk she'd pumped before driving over. "I knew you'd want to feed her."

"I'll take her back, James, if you don't mind." Isa held her arms out for the baby, but Iris abruptly turned her face away from her grandmother and cried out. "Well, that's a first." Rachel knew Isa didn't take it personally, though, sure her mother was secretly thrilled that the mystery of Iris's father was solved, and said parent appeared to be every part the man she'd want raising her granddaughter.

"She prefers James over me already." Rachel still held the bottle, which she thrust out to James. "Here you go."

He took the bottle and baby to the nearest island stool and perched on it. Without preamble, Iris started eating.

The quiet was fleeting as the front door opened and a rush of voices carried into the kitchen.

"That'll be your brother and sister. At least one pair." Isa left for the foyer and Rachel exchanged glances with Gideon and Sophia, who still appeared ready to burst out into laughter.

"What?"

Gideon grinned and slowly shook his head. "I have to hand it to you, James. If you can make it through an Isa Colton interrogation, you're practically blood. Welcome to the family."

"Your mother's one tough cookie." James slugged back several gulps of water from the large glass he'd carried out to the spacious back patio. Rachel held a stemless wineglass that she'd only partially filled with sparkling water. With Iris taking her nap in the room Isa had set up just for her—and many more grandchildren to come— it was the perfect time to escape her family's scrutiny.

"She is. But you handled her perfectly. Thank you for being so understanding."

"Hey, she has every right to ask the questions she did. I know you might not agree. You're her daughter. But as an outsider I have to say I'm impressed with her direct manner and steady demeanor. Is she a lawyer, too?"

"No, she's a graphic designer. But she was Dad's sounding board and knows the cases he judged as well as he did. You can't get anything past her. When we were kids, it was something I hated. But now I hope I can be half as good a mother as she was for all of us. None of us were made to suffer any more than absolutely necessary after Dad died. Mom picked up all of the pieces and kept her head held high."

"And your brother, he's Iris's godfather?"

"Yes. He's done a great job of being around a lot. He was determined to be the father figure—" She stopped.

"That I wasn't?" His brow rose.

"Partly, yes. Now that you're here, he doesn't have to be so obsessive about it. But I was going to say he didn't want to be like our dad. Dad was a wonderful father in that he loved and provided for us. But the way he provided turned out to be wrong. What we can do now, is to prevent it from happening to other kids."

"Gideon sounds like my kind of dude." The words escaped his mouth without hesitation.

"Like any Colton, he can be way over-the-top when it comes to sticking up for his own." She cast her gaze over the mountains, grateful for the great weather that gave them a break from the spring rains. It was nice to be out on the patio without needing a winter parka.

"No such thing if you ask me." James leaned forward, forearms on his thighs, their well-sculpted shapes matching the rest of his athletic frame. "Sure is beautiful out here. What made you get a place in your neighborhood?"

"My job. And yeah, I agree it's really pretty here. I've spent my share of teenaged angst moments on this patio, thinking through my life and what I want out of it."

"But you picked the city life?"

"I did. When I bought my house, I was the assistant DA and I thought I'd be doing that job for years yet. I had no idea different members of the council would ask me to consider running for DA."

"Why not?"

"Well, first off, I'm young. As old as thirty-four can feel some days, especially days when I find out I'm being watched by your stalker." She shot him a reassuring grin, hoping to ease his concern about coming into her life and exposing her and Iris to Bethany's threats. "It's early days for a DA, especially in a place like Blue Larkspur. Folks here can definitely be free thinkers, but they're apt to stick with tradition, the familiar. I replaced a septuagenarian male, and before him, the DA served until he was nearly eighty. I'm breaking the mold, per se."

"More like re-creating it from what I've read on your court record to date. Having the Colton name couldn't have always been a help."

"It hasn't been easy, you're right. My father really messed up his life and so many others', and even ours for a bit. But it helps that he worked hard to right his wrongs during the last cases he heard."

"I'm thinking your work ethic and integrity, not to mention legal brilliance, is the real reason you're already a DA. I'm in awe of you, Rachel Colton."

"Flattery will get you everywhere."

"Will it get me a kiss?"

She froze, suddenly wishing she were as small as the spider who worked his way across one of the paver patio tiles. "I'm sorry, James. I can't see there being any point in us being more than co-parents." Yet when he reached out and grasped her hand, his thumb caressing the inside of her wrist in slow, lazy circles, her body's response let her know that she was fighting against her truth.

Rachel still wanted James, in every way possible.

She licked her lips, heard his intake of breath and looked up to see his pupils dilated no matter the bright sunshine. Apparently James still wanted her, too.

But in what ways?

Does it matter? She knew it was risky kissing him out here. Her family could be watching, and if they noticed the display of affection, they'd jump to the wrong conclusions. Think there was more between her and James than Iris.

"Stop thinking, Rachel. What have you got to lose?"

Everything.

Maybe it was the bright sunshine and spring's promise of warmer days. Or the way Isa's garden, bursting with wildflower blooms that included her favorite creamy columbine, was beginning to fill the air with its honeysuckle scent. All of a sudden, kissing James seemed not only right but the *only* thing to do.

Careful. The risk of getting her heart broken would always exist. So why not enjoy life where she could?

"Okay." She waited for James's eyes to widen, his mouth to curve into a smoldering smile. More of a gambler than she'd ever dreamed, Rachel leaned in for his kiss.

JAMES HAD WANTED to feel her lips against his since Helena, since he'd nearly squashed her on the courthouse steps over a week ago. Which made the feel of her soft mouth under his as sweet as the taste of her. It was all he'd remembered from their too-brief liaison and more. He felt her tongue's dance on his lips, then in his mouth, and knew the same thrill she'd given him before. But this was different. No longer singles finding passion on their own timeline, they were parents.

A chuckle eased up his throat. Rachel pulled back. He really adored her wide blue eyes, the way her irises were etched in black. "I can't say a man has ever laughed at my kisses before."

Her hands rested on his chest, the breeze lifting her long hair from her face. "I'm just glad you're not shoving me away like you did on the courthouse steps."

"What else did you expect me to do? I was late for court." They both laughed before she leaned back. He didn't want to see the quick embrace end, but they were in her mother's backyard with the potential of any of her Colton relatives popping outside. "We're lucky no one's staring out the window at us."

"Would it bother you if they had?"

"No. My family isn't always the best at minding their own business but it's all out of love. Usually."

"I thought your brother might be willing to take me on if need be."

"Gideon?" She swung her arms in circles, twisted from her waist. When she realized he was watching her, she stopped, gave him an apologetic smile. "Sorry. Carrying Iris around, lifting her car seat, putting her stroller in the car adds up on my back and shoulders. I only get exercise in when Iris is napping or after she's gone to bed. Sometimes at work over lunch, but not very often."

"I'll be able to help you with that. You'll have more free time to work out if I'm with Iris."

"I don't want free time from Iris." Their gazes held. James wasn't going to push it. This was too new and Rachel deserved however long she needed to see for herself that he was true to his word. He was committed to being Iris's full-time dad.

"I understand."

"But I'm not going to keep you from her, of course."

"I know. I trust you, Rachel." It gave him pause, thinking that he trusted another woman when he was still being stalked by Bethany. But Rachel wasn't Bethany nor was she like any other woman he'd ever met.

"You trust me, eh? Then, tell me what you were laughing about a few minutes ago."

"Huh? Oh, that. I couldn't help compare our kisses in Helena to this one in Blue Larkspur."

"Oh?" Her brow rose and she appeared ready to call for her brother.

"No, no, it wasn't a criticism. Same sexy kissing, trust me. But we're both different. We're parents now. There's more weight to it, if that makes sense."

"Yes, it does. And yes, we are definitely parents of that beautiful little girl. Before I got pregnant, I thought I didn't want kids ever, or at least not for a very long time. I'd considered freezing my eggs, you know? Now I don't know how I ever lived without her." She hesitated, the shadow of concern evident in how she puckered her lips, the worry lines at her brows. "James, I don't want to give you the wrong impression, or ever lead you on. You and I are two very different people."

"Meaning?" He fought against the sense that he stood on shaky ground. Was she about to tell him that his trust was unwarranted? That she'd changed her mind about how involved he could be with Iris?

"Meaning you're all about your job. About the more tangible things in life."

"Whoa, pot calling the kettle and all that. You didn't make DA at thirty-four because you're anything but career-driven."

"Yes, I'm career-minded, no question. But look at it objectively. I'm giving my all to putting criminals away, people who are a threat to society. You're a corporate lawyer. Your motives are completely different."

Anger flared, and he banked it with the realization that this wasn't about him, not really. He stood on a platform of eggshells, of letting her know he wasn't her father.

"I'd say my purpose is the same as yours. Sure, it's corporate law and often involves very lucrative corporations. But we're after the bad guys, too. The scum of society who are on the take, going after something they didn't earn. Stealing."

"What about the individual civilians you've kept from receiving settlements for wrongs the same corporations have committed?"

"You're talking about the Lucid Scents case." It had made the national news due to its sensationalist spin. A man had sued James's client for damages related to a particular cosmetic—a cologne that he'd applied to areas of his body that scents were never meant to reach.

Misuse of the product had caused a mild rash, but the claimant insisted his subsequent mental distress had caused him to miss days of work and he was now unable to use any similar product at all, for fear of further skin irritation. The whole thing had been ridiculous, and James had been stunned when the judge didn't throw the case out. But then he'd learned that the judge wanted to make an example of cases like Lucid Scents. Sadly, too many fraudulent cases were on the court docket these days. It had looked like James was going to lose the case, as the judge wanted to show that large corporations needed to care about every customer, not just the majority. Who, in this case, didn't react to their product.

James knew he'd been lucky to win. The claimant's lawyer was a known ambulance chaser, and it was obvious he'd found a case and corporation he thought would become his big catch. Except James had been Lucid Scent's attorney and won the case for the corporate giant.

"That's the most obvious one, sure. And the easiest one to find with a web search. But you have to have represented many of a similar vein." She crossed her arms at her chest.

"Actually, no, that was a unique case. I've done mostly corporate litigation for firm versus firm cases. I'm not the soul-crushing guy here, Rachel. I think you're mistaking my drive to succeed for something else." Like her father accepting bribes for cash to give his family life the appearance of financial success.

"You're right, I wouldn't know about a lot of your work. The records aren't as available as my cases."

Ouch. A blow meant to sting. Of course his cases

were often under the seal of nondisclosure, something Rachel didn't deal with unless minors were involved or very sensitive state and/or government information was at risk of being made public.

"I'm happy to provide you with any details that I can. How far back do you want me to go?"

"Forget it. This is silly." Rachel's easygoing nature had vanished, and she turned toward the patio door. "I'm going to check on Iris. Why don't you walk around out here, familiarize yourself with the layout of the yard? Over there is the play set, sandbox and swings that have been there since we were all kids. They need to be replaced, but there's no hurry. Iris isn't crawling."

"Yet. She'll be walking before she crawls if she has her way." He spoke to her retreating form, trying to recapture their more easygoing connection over their daughter. But Rachel didn't respond. The door clicked closed and he was left alone. He turned back to the handsomely landscaped property, tried to let the calming view take away the ugly sense of loss. He didn't have anything substantial with Rachel, save for having fathered a child with her.

Why did he care so deeply about her opinion of him?

Don't ask a question if you're not ready for the answer.

Chapter Twelve

Rachel swiveled her desk chair from the wide window that overlooked the entire city of Blue Larkspur, where on a clear day she was able to pick out hers, and her mother's, subdivisions.

"This is ridiculous." She spoke to her empty office, a rarity, and tried to focus on her laptop screen. Work was what she'd always used to avoid uncomfortable emotions and situations. Like how her father had betrayed the community twenty years ago. As assistant DA she'd thrown herself into case after case, doing whatever it took, working however long hours, all to fix Ben Colton's crimes. And to ease her broken heart a little more.

Her concerns over her father and the Colton legacy had taken a back seat, though. Ever since James showed up in both her life and Iris's. Almost another full week had passed since Rachel had introduced James to her family and he'd stepped into his role as Iris's father with aplomb. She'd been able to stay a little aloof from him emotionally by focusing on each day as it came, sharing parenting duties with him around both of their work schedules. But at night, when the lights went out and she was alone in bed with herself, her thoughts, she had a more difficult time escaping the changes going on in her heart. Which in turn made her fear of committing to a man like her father, no matter how cursory, rear its head and appear in full Technicolor. Not that she was thinking about a relationship with James—nothing further than co-parenting—but it was only natural her thoughts would wander at times, imagining what they'd be like as a couple. Wasn't it?

"Judge Reed wants to give you extra security." Clara stood in front of her, waiting patiently for Rachel to look up from her desk, where she'd been daydreaming.

"Tell her I appreciate it, but Chief Lawson has already put extra patrols in my neighborhood." She hadn't told her assistant or anyone at work about the potential threat from Bethany Austin. Her relationship with James, and whomever he brought with him, was private. And since Gideon had installed the security system, she was feeling much better about being home alone with Iris. Not to mention leaving Iris with Emily each morning for work.

"She's not going to take no for an answer. Brian Parson is still well-connected with Blue Larkspur's criminal syndicate and he's threatened you three times, counting today." Clara referred to when the defendant had looked directly at her and said "I'll see you in hell, Rachel Colton."

It wasn't usual for a suspect to do that, not once they were in trial proceedings. But it happened. All part of her job.

"The first two times don't count. He was still thinking he was above the law. As for today, he's afraid. We have a solid case against him. This time he's going to be convicted of first-degree murder."

Parson was heavily involved in the area's worst drug trafficking to date. She couldn't prove his ties to Clay Houseman, who was close to getting arrested, according to Theo, but she suspected most crime in Blue Larkspur was related to the syndicate founded by Ronald Spence. Thankfully Spence was still behind bars, but he'd pleaded his case to the Truth Foundation over the years. He proclaimed his innocence, that he'd been framed by Ben Colton. She wasn't sure she believed him, though. Not because she wanted to exonerate her father, but because the evidence pointed to Spence's guilt. And Spence was the bad player she was most concerned about, not some lower player in the drug ring like Parson.

"I'll pass your message to Judge Reed's staff, but expect her to shoot you down on this." Clara didn't budge.

"Fine. But remind them that these criminals don't want to draw the kind of attention to themselves that threatening or harming a government official would bring. They're all a bunch of evil scumbags, but they're business first. No way will they risk their multimillion-dollar revenue in Colorado by targeting a rural county DA."

"Okay, got it. I'm on it."

Rachel tried to get back into her case prep after Clara left the office, but she couldn't let go of the feeling that maybe she shouldn't have been so dismissive of Judge Reed's offer for protection. It wasn't just her, but Iris, too.

And there was the issue that had plagued her since last evening. A bouquet addressed to her, with no return address. The prettiest spring wildflowers, not unlike the ones in her mother's garden. Except for the single long-stemmed rose in the center, which was black. And the note, written with a sloppy but legible hand. "Stick to being a DA and leave James Kiriakis alone."

It had to be from Bethany. If it had been related to her job, James's name wouldn't be on the note. Unless the sender was from one of her cases and had invested in finding out about her most personal details, which she doubted.

She shivered despite the silk cardigan she wore atop her blouse and skirt. While Gideon had been great about setting up the security cameras at both her front and back doors, they hadn't helped when she'd searched the video feed last night in hopes of identifying the flower deliverer. The person had worn dark clothing complete with a hood over their head, a baseball cap brim obscuring their face. It was impossible to tell if the figure was male or female, no doubt what they'd wanted. It especially made sense if it was Bethany, as it still hadn't been determined whether she was actually in Blue Larkspur.

She should at least mention it to the cops, she supposed. It would be their manpower that provided the extra patrols.

As she wondered about whether or not to call Clara back in, her phone lit up with a text from Theo. Serendipity!

Please call me when you can.

Restless with her indecision, she shut her laptop and grabbed her purse.

Ten minutes later she walked into the chief's office, needing the reassurance of his consistency. After her father died, the ability to trust men—and, really, anyone—had perished with him. But Theo's constant presence in their lives, the way BLPD had worked steadfastly to uncover Ben Colton's crimes, had provided the security her life otherwise lacked.

The love of her siblings had been huge, too, and of course Isa's unwavering commitment to her family. Yet the gap left by her father had left Rachel needier than she'd have ever wanted. Academics, the Truth Foundation and the law gave her reassurance, a steady compass point.

Theo had been part of it all along.

She knocked on his door, ajar, revealing the octogenarian at his desk, poring over his computer screen.

He looked up over his glasses. "Rachel, please come in."

She opened the door wide and all intentions of reporting the flower delivery to Theo took a mental back seat as she spied her oldest siblings, Caleb and Morgan, already sitting in the office. As partners in the family legal firm, Colton and Colton, it wasn't unusual to see them working together. But not in here, not since she'd been elected DA. Colton and Colton was the driving force behind the Truth Foundation, and Rachel hadn't seen her oldest siblings in a work situation recently. Caleb was dressed in his usual suit, well tailored and looking like he was about to go into court. But his brighter-than-usual blue tie showed the influence of his fiancée, Nadine. Morgan wore a classic red A-line dress, their grandmother's pearls around her neck. Isa had insisted each daughter pick an item from her own mother's jewelry box.

"Wow, I wasn't expecting this. What's going on?" Alarm bells rang. Caleb was thick into investigating Randall Spence. Was there new information, new evidence that he was dirty, unlike Spence claimed?

"We asked the chief to call you. You didn't have to come in." Morgan smiled. "But I'm glad you did, sis." Her blue eyes matched Rachel's, although Morgan's hair was long and brunette instead of blond.

"Hey, Rachel." Caleb, always the more serious of the twins, offered a quick smile, his brown eyes warmer than they'd been in years. Since falling for his ex-wife's cousin Nadine, he exuded a more relaxed vibe. His expression was stamped with concern, though, which made Rachel's shoulders tense.

"Have a seat." Theo nodded at the usual chair she sat in and she noticed that Caleb sat on a folding chair. It never ceased to give her pause that the folks literally keeping a community secure made do with the least. She never thought of herself in this light, but to be fair, her experience and degree would earn almost three times as much in the private sector. But she'd never pursued the law for financial gain, or even power. "I'm glad you stopped in instead of calling. It'll be easier to figure out our options."

"What options?" She took in all three expressions while her siblings and Theo appeared to be measuring her up, too. Whatever this was about, it wasn't good.

JAMES STARED AT his phone as dismay scrunched his stomach into a painful ball. Chief Lawson was unavailable, "in a conference" according to the BLPD receptionist. He'd checked in with Denver PD, too, but hadn't been able to find out anything on Bethany's whereabouts. She hadn't been seen in Denver, at least since he'd moved. He wanted to go over his options again, remind the chief how persistent Bethany Austin could be. He had to make sure BLPD knew who he believed they were dealing with.

"You look so sad for our most recent hire." Adam Jones, an attorney hired the month before James, stood in front of his desk.

"I'm good. Wrapping up loose ends in Denver, is all." The last thing James wanted or needed was for his new employer to find out about Bethany. He wasn't ashamed that he was a stalking victim, and he wasn't in denial that she was back at harassing him and now Rachel. But if he could keep her separate from work, it'd help his peace of mind.

"I hear you, man. I moved here from Helena and it's taken me almost a full month to close all my utilities, get my apartment professionally cleaned, you know the deal. All the little stuff nobody thinks about until it has to get done."

James ignored the sensations zinging around his insides at the mention of where he'd met Rachel. Where they'd conceived Iris.

"I do know. I have to say I think I'm going to like Blue Larkspur a lot. I already do. Which makes me antsy to get Denver business settled."

"You won't have to return there, will you?"

"No, no. My family's there, and my brother's been a huge help." He wasn't lying on this; Jake had offered to do whatever he needed to assist James in escaping the hell that Denver had become for him. Even with Bethany's lack of activity the last several months, he'd still looked over his shoulder.

And now he had to check his surroundings in Blue Larkspur. Constantly.

"Why don't we grab a beer sometime this week? There's a great place just outside of town that has an IPA I like."

"I'm not sure about this week yet, but definitely soon. Thanks, Adam."

"Sure. If you need anything, let me know. I've only been here a month longer than you, but I think it's fair to say we've landed at a great firm."

"I agree."

Alone again, James knew that the best thing about Blue Larkspur for him wasn't his new job, its partners or even the city that already felt like home.

It was the woman who'd enchanted him, and the beautiful baby girl they'd made together. Bethany was in over her head this time. He wasn't going to give up until she was stopped.

"OKAY, SO SHOOT." Tension screeched across Rachel's nerve endings as she sat next to her siblings. It was the same reason she never read mystery or thriller novels; she couldn't stand not knowing the entire story *yesterday.*

Theo spoke. "I know you're recused from all Truth Foundation cases, but we've had some developments that you need to know about as DA. I wanted to give you a heads-up so that you have time to sort what you can and can't be involved with going forward."

Caleb leaned over, looking past Morgan. "The Truth Foundation has been involved in investigating Ronald Spence's case, as you know, for the last twenty years."

Morgan nodded. "Since Dad died. But now the chief has arrested Clay Houseman. Spence tipped us off after requesting to speak to the chief."

"We brought him in for—" Theo cleared his throat and used his glasses to read off his computer screen "—drug dealing, racketeering, threatening a minor, and added resisting arrest and attempted murder on a police officer when he pulled his gun and shot at one of our own."

Rachel listened, allowed it to settle. "What does this have to do with Spence?" As far as she was concerned, nothing would ever clear the man for the damage he'd rained down on Blue Larkspur. Nothing. Spence had been a drug kingpin when Blue Larkspur went through its worst time. Hundreds of teenagers were lured into using his products, which were whatever illicit drugs he could peddle. Homelessness, crime, addiction all addled the normally friendly city. Spence went to jail on certain charges but Caleb and Rachel had read his files forwards and backwards. If the charges that put him behind bars hadn't stuck, he had committed plenty of other offenses to be prosecuted for. She found the timing of Houseman's plea suspicious, too. Years after Spence went to jail, and for the exact same crimes. As DA she'd read reports that indicated Spence might still be guilty.

Theo folded his hands on his desk, gave Caleb and Morgan each a glance before focusing on Rachel.

Oh crap. This isn't going to be good.

"Houseman confessed to all of the current charges, and more. He says he was the one who committed each and every crime that Spence was charged for and convicted of."

"That's ridiculous! He can't give a blanket confession like that and expect it to hold up in court. Tell me you see this for what it is." Nothing more than another example of how Spence still somehow held sway over the Blue Larkspur crime network.

Theo shook his head. "It wasn't a general comment, Rachel. His lawyer made sure he confessed to each and every charge that Spence was convicted of. We haven't had time to look into their exact connection, but Houseman might be the fall guy for Spence."

"Spence is claiming that he was framed, as you know, but now he's got weight behind his claims." Morgan watched for Rachel's reaction as she spoke, disappointment etched on her face. "I'd hate to see the Truth Foundation's reputation go up in flames. Because it will if Spence walks. He's always claimed he was the victim of circumstances and faulty witnesses, like a lot of the actually innocent people our dad put away."

Morgan's dismay was justified. Spence had always claimed his blamelessness and had appealed his sentence repeatedly. Rachel strongly suspected Spence had never given up his position of power in the crime organization, but they'd never been able to prove it while she was the assistant DA.

"If Houseman's indictment holds, Spence is going

to be freed." Caleb summarized the Colton family's biggest fear. If their hunches were right, one of the bad guys was going to be out on the streets.

Nausea surged and Rachel collapsed back in her chair, wishing she could run off to the restroom and shut herself in the diminutive stall. She didn't want her siblings worrying about her. A sour stomach was the good ol' standby that had plagued her in her teens and throughout adolescence whenever she was faced with what seemed an insurmountable obstacle. Her GP had broken the code on it when she told Rachel it might have been caused by her repressed grief and anxiety.

Morgan placed her hand on Rachel's forearm. "I'm sorry, sis. It was a shock to us, too. From all perspectives it's a certainty that Spence might be guilty of many crimes, but we haven't been able to find enough evidence of his culpability to turn it over to the authorities and possibly outweigh Houseman's confession."

"And I don't need to hear any details about that." Rachel was always eager to put a bad player behind bars but this was directly related to Ben Colton's crimes. She'd never risk her status as DA to prosecute if she didn't have to. "Even though I think that in the instance of Randall Spence, there isn't a judge around who won't recuse me out of hand."

"This is a hard pill to swallow for all of you." Theo's deep baritone reverberated his compassion in the closed office.

"I'm fine, really. It's just— I mean—" What could she say to reassure her siblings she was okay but not lie to them, either?

"I've gone through his case file, the court records at

least a dozen times since I was in law school. No matter how much Spence shot his mouth off about being innocent, the case against him was solid, and the DA at the time had done their homework. He shouldn't be up for parole for at least another decade, and now you're telling me he might stroll out of state prison in a matter of months?"

"Weeks, from the court schedule I saw." Caleb's tone held compassion even though he didn't shy from reality.

"*Days* are what I just found out," Theo added.

"Of course. You know more than I do since I'm recused from all things Spence and the Truth Foundation." She mumbled as she remained slumped, needing a few moments to let the sick feeling pass. Court schedules were full but high-profile cases were often pushed through more quickly. Clara kept her apprised of those that were most pertinent to the DA's office but had to leave this one off the list today. "I take it you caught him only this morning?"

"Yes." Theo was the largest, most experienced presence in the room and yet he'd gone quiet, allowing the siblings to share their combined grief. Rachel had learned long ago that the sorrow over Ben Colton's demise, both legally and morally, would never go away, but she'd learned to live with it. It didn't take away the difficulty of facing it again and again, however. Events like today's news were bound to reopen the heavily scarred wounds.

"Does Mom know?" Isa's expression that combined sadness with gritty determination flashed across her mind.

"Not yet. I'll go over after work and tell her." Morgan looked at Caleb. "We were both going to do it together but—"

"It's Nadine's birthday." A slow flush crept up Caleb's neck.

"Nice to see you join the rest of humanity, bro." Rachel welcomed the opportunity to tease her brother as it also allowed her to think about something other than her still-iffy stomach. "I'll meet you there, and I'll bring Iris. I can get off work early today."

"You don't have to do that."

"I want to do it." Rachel looked at Theo. "I think it would be good if you could be there, too. Mom draws on you for support."

"I, um, sure. Of course I'll be there." Whatever made Caleb's cheeks red was catching, as Theo's face reddened, too.

"Great. We'll all meet there at five, then? Is that too early, Rachel?" Morgan quickly took charge, which was a relief instead of igniting the usual sibling competition, especially among the three Colton attorneys.

"Works for me." Rachel had no idea how she'd get all her work done before then, but nothing like the threat of a bad guy being let loose on the streets again to motivate.

As she walked out of the police department, a text dinged.

Okay if I come over after work to see Iris?

James. James would be able to help.

BETHANY'S NECK MUSCLES were cramping again. Keeping an eye on Rachel Colton was a pain in all of her body parts. All she had was the tablet she'd stolen from the community college campus from an unsuspecting student who'd left it in her backpack on a picnic bench. The same young woman had unlocked it with a passcode Bethany was able to discern as she'd watched the woman all yesterday morning.

Her personal phone and laptop were off-limits since she couldn't risk being found by law enforcement. She didn't think James had done anything more about the restraining order, like reporting that he thought she'd been the one to set off the explosion at the restaurant. If he had, wouldn't she have found out when she called her mother, who would have warned her of increased police surveillance around the family, on one of the burner phones?

Finally, finally, she got to watch James without Rachel's ugly puss in the frame. Rachel had left James alone with the baby. And James, because he was the nice guy Bethany knew better than anyone, was being really nice to the kid. But once he saw that Rachel wasn't the woman for him, Bethany was sure he'd let the kid go, too.

Rachel Colton might be a DA, but she sure was a dumb bunny. Bethany thought her flower arrangement would be enough to warn the annoying woman away from James. But no, James was here less than twenty-four hours after Bethany had delivered the bouquet. A grin made her tight facial muscles relax for a millisecond. It had been smart of her to nab the flowers from the highway medians on the outskirts of town. The black rose had been in a pile of garbage she'd found in a dumpster that the local Goodwill shared with a restaurant, along with a crumpled Over the Hill banner. She'd been searching for some more clothes to use as disguises when the rose stem had scratched her wrist. It was a sign, she was certain, that she was supposed to use it to scare Rachel off.

But if the woman had been afraid, she'd not shown it. She'd actually stood on her porch and dumped the flowers into the side bushes and left the vase—also a dumpster find—on the porch. Talk about lack of appreciation!

And now it looked like Rachel Colton was using James as her personal babysitter. How dare Rachel saunter off and leave her brat with James while she went off to do whatever? Her vision blurred and she clenched the tablet, hands shaking.

Calm down. Focus on James.

What she saw was real. Rachel was leaving the house, alone. Which meant Bethany had to follow her, because she'd lost track of the couple and kid last weekend when they'd gone away for the day. She needed to know every place Rachel Colton went.

Weekdays sure were simpler, when both Rachel and James went to their jobs, and Bethany could count on them being in the same places for hours at a time.

Since she had to follow Rachel, she wouldn't be able to check in on James as often, not unless wherever Rachel went had a strong Wi-Fi signal. That was the other thing Bethany relied upon: free internet so that she could log in to the camera system. The surveillance app she'd purchased saved up to six hours of recorded video, but that was it, leaving at least two-hour gaps in the middle of the night. Bethany didn't like gaps when it came to James or the people in his life.

She waited for Rachel to get into her fancy-ass car and back out of the drive, counted to three, then started her engine and followed her out of the subdivision. Bethany's gas gauge had enough left to take her thirty miles or so.

She wasn't a praying person, as she'd learned long ago that she alone was in charge of her fate as well as the fates of those she cared about. But she whispered some words anyway, hoping she had enough gas until she could get back to where she'd hidden her cash and refill the tank.

The drive didn't take as long as she thought it would. In fact, she had plenty of fuel left to return to her favorite stakeout site in Blue Larkspur. But Rachel had pulled into a very, very upscale neighborhood, by Bethany's standards. Who needed this much? And the house she approached was set back from the road, but Bethany had seen enough of the homes on the drive in and knew that this had to be Rachel Colton's family home. Her mother was Isa Colton, a local graphic designer, and her father had been a crooked judge who the family had created a nonprofit around, trying to fix their father's bad deeds.

Bethany laughed. Too bad Ben Colton was dead. He sounded like the kind of man she'd get along well with. One who understood power, what a deal meant. Unlike James, who'd broken the deal of their relationship. Oh sure, he'd claimed they'd never been more than friends, but Bethany had reminded him that he'd made it seem they'd be together forever. And they would.

Just as soon as she got Rachel Colton out of the way.

Chapter Thirteen

Rachel pulled in front of her mother's house, as her siblings had already jam-packed Isa's driveway. She killed the engine and rested her arms on the wheel, needing a few seconds to calm down before walking into what was bound to be an emotional cesspool with her family.

The empty passenger seat and baby car seat in the back underscored that she was on her own, without her family. James wasn't technically related, but as Iris's father, he was a de facto support she was coming to rely on, maybe too much. He'd agreed to meet her at her house early and was eager for more time with his daughter. It was a relief to know Iris was safe with him, that the baby's routine wouldn't be interrupted by a tension-filled scene at her mother's.

Whenever the subject of her father's criminal activities came up, it brought out the worst in her siblings. They each wanted to protect their mother but had different approaches. Not to mention that they didn't each have the same daily reminder of what Ben had done. Caleb and Morgan certainly had the most to deal with, as far as the community was concerned. All of the siblings were involved with and supported the Truth Foundation, but most of them had dispersed career-wise and found other ways to give back, whether to Blue Larkspur or the world at large.

Rachel knew the meeting was going to be rough. Otherwise she wouldn't have asked James to be with Iris this quickly on his own. Emily couldn't stay late today, and Rachel had been in a bind. The Colton meeting didn't need the distraction of a possibly cranky baby, and she didn't want Iris exposed to the negative vibes that were bound to come up.

Her stomach still roiled with uncertainty.

Your heart is hurting, too.

For once she wished she could blame her unease on being a new mom, fearing for her baby's safety with a man she'd only known a couple of weeks.

It wasn't that, though. She completely trusted James. He'd bonded with Iris in the best way possible, even though both he and Rachel had heavy work schedules and were still getting used to being around one another on a regular basis. Plus she'd asked Theo to do a background check on James, just to be sure. It was clear. James was as he appeared—an honest, sincere man chock-full of integrity.

Which brought her to what continued to tug at her peace of mind. Everything with James, from their passionate introduction to revealing his paternity, had come more easily than she'd expected. As if it was all meant to be and had been this way for a long time.

Rachel didn't know how or when exactly it had happened, but James had become as important a focal point in her life as Iris. She thought of him as family, whether she wanted to acknowledge it or not.

"Enough." She spoke to the empty car, grabbed her bag and exited. As she walked the gauntlet to her mother's home, she clung to the fact that all her siblings wanted the same thing she did. To keep Isa and their family safe, and to keep the ugly touch of any drug dealers out of Blue Larkspur.

A hard goal to achieve if the ringleader was let out of jail.

"You are your daddy's girl, aren't you?" James tickled Iris's cheek and was rewarded with a dimpled grin. A low laugh erupted from his belly and he wondered how he could have been so afraid to be with his daughter alone. Until now, Rachel had always been with him to help out as needed. He knew it had taken all of her trust and self-discipline to leave their baby with him. Her faith in him touched him as intimately as her kisses had in Helena.

She had some kind of important meeting with her family that she didn't think he'd be interested in, and he got it. Sometimes families needed to be alone.

He took Iris's bib off, since she'd just eaten a hearty dinner, and lifted her from the high chair. The pride warming his chest was silly, but so what? Just two weeks ago he'd had no clue how to work a car seat or high chair or any other infant paraphernalia, and now he felt like an expert.

He carried Iris down the hallway to the baby's bathroom. The table where Rachel left her keys and incoming mail was to his left, just off the nursery, and he made sure to avoid bumping into it. A note sat on the whitewashed surface, his name in bold marker shouting out at him from the crumpled sheet of paper. "Stick to being a DA and leave James Kiriakis alone."

The slant and style of handwriting made him stop in his tracks. He'd seen it before.

Bethany.

He tried to engage his reasoning ability, honed by years in law. But when faced with the possibility that Bethany was not only stalking him again but making trouble for others, logic became unattainable. Now she was warning off Rachel, had become a threat to his daughter.

Blood heated his face, made his ears pound with his frantic heartbeat.

Iris squirmed in his arms, shook him back into the present. He looked into her precious eyes, fixated on his, and let out a long breath. Iris was safe, with him. Rachel was safe at her mother's house. She'd texted when she'd arrived and told him she'd do the same when she left. Bethany was the unknown.

Be prepared.

It didn't matter that he'd taken every precaution to not be followed each time he came to Rachel's. If the message on the table had been delivered here, Bethany knew where Rachel lived. Even if it had been delivered to Rachel's office, the sender knew that he and Rachel were involved somehow. Did Bethany know Iris was his daughter, too?

Anger inched up his spine, his nape and crushed his head in a steady throb. The need to protect burst from the center of his chest, and he held Iris close, knowing that nothing was more important. It had happened so quickly, this sense of knowing she was his. That they were part of a family of their own making. He, Iris and Rachel. He'd never let anything hurt them.

Nothing.

"HI, RACHEL!" THE chorus of voices greeted her when she walked into the house, the front door visible from the dining table in the great room's arrangement.

Five of Rachel's siblings, including the oldest twins, gathered around Isa's large, scratched table. The triplets, Oliver, Ezra and Dominic, were absent, and she longed for their grounding presence. Two years older than Rachel, the three were always involved in international intrigue of one sort or another. Oliver was a venture capitalist, Ezra was in the army and Dominic was an agent with the FBI's International Corruption Unit. It wasn't a surprise that they weren't around, but still, it was never the same without them.

Same for the youngest Colton siblings, her sisters Alexa and Naomi, also twins. Born eight years after Rachel and six years after Gideon, they were the "pleasant surprises" that Isa and Ben had joked about when they were younger. Alexa was a US Marshal and like her triplet brothers, often unavailable. Naomi didn't show up for many of the gatherings, either, but she didn't work for the government—quite the opposite, as she was a reality TV producer. Naomi missed many of their family get-togethers due to being off-site or on location.

Rachel understood the impossibility of having them all under one roof more than once every year or so. Twelve adults spread across the country—the planet!— with different interests and ages made coming together in person difficult. But it didn't ever take away from the solidarity and love that they shared as Coltons. That unconditional Colton bond wrapped around her, around Isa's dining room table, no matter how many of them were physically present.

"Mom." Rachel gave Isa a quick peck on her cheek before sitting down. It seemed a rather formal place to gather, as they usually opted for the kitchen and its large island. But as she met Morgan's and then Caleb's gazes, the cold truth of their new reality knifed through her center.

"Hi, everyone."

Morgan and Caleb didn't respond, as they'd gone back to discussing whatever was on Morgan's smartphone. Did they have an update?

"Hey, Rach." Her brother Jasper sat next to Aubrey, his fraternal twin. Both were four years younger than Rachel.

"How's life at the ranch?" She referred to the twins' Gemini Ranch.

"The usual." Aubrey grinned. "Usual" in a Colorado spring meant lots of calving and foaling, highlighted by the muddy marks on both Aubrey's and Jasper's jean jackets.

"I take it from your glow that Luke is well?" Rachel teased her about the love of her life, Luke Bishop. A Neapolitan by birth, he'd been on the run for years from the Camorra criminal organization. Rachel silently acknowledged that while her life might seem chaotic, she wasn't alone. Each Colton sibling seemed to have their own personal challenges to deal with. At least Aubrey's had come with a happily-ever-after.

"I'm fine, *grazie*." Luke spoke from his seat next to

Aubrey, but his gaze barely met Rachel's as he was mesmerized by her sister. Nothing like true love. She wasn't jealous, or anything like it. Simply happy for her sister.

"Where's my niece?" Aubrey interrupted her thoughts.

Rachel shifted on her seat, at a loss for the best response.

"Does James have her?" Gideon's quiet request was a lifeline, his voice steadying. Rachel hadn't felt on solid ground since James had knocked her off her feet in front of the courthouse.

"Yes." At the raised brows and attempts at surreptitious glances, she relented. "This meeting is not about me, or Iris, but yes, James is getting more and more involved in our lives. I mean, in Iris's life." She looked at the wall for the thermostat that controlled the temperature throughout the sprawling Colton homestead. "Mom, do you still have the heat on?"

"Of course I do. It's April in Colorado, isn't it?" Her siblings laughed and Rachel couldn't help from joining in. Her mother was the quickest with a comeback, always.

"I don't mean to be a jerk, but it seems excessive. Is anyone else in here hot?" She lifted her long locks from her nape, stretched her neck in an effort to somehow cool the heat that made her skin feel like aluminum foil around a baked potato.

Rachel's gaze shifted to her brother Gavin's face, prominently displayed on Isa's iPad. Gavin was six years younger than Rachel and a total loner, happiest when pursuing a hot lead for his next article or podcast. He'd been interested in journalism since he'd been a kid. "Hi, Gavin. Wish you were here."

"Rachel. I am there. Virtually, anyhow. How's being the new DA treating you?" Even through the screen she saw how his eyes glinted with brotherly affection and more. Gratitude took her agitation down a level, the distraction from why they were all here acting like a cool breeze on her hot skin.

"It's good. Looking for a new story? Don't look at me." She shot him a smile.

Rachel went around the table, greeting Nadine and Sophia, too, before the meeting began.

"Good evening." Theo's voice boomed into the room from the front foyer and his purposeful steps echoed across the great room.

"Theo." Isa smiled and indicated he take the seat to her left. Was that a blush on her mother's cheeks? And a smile trying to shift the chief's mouth from its grim line?

"Let's get it going, everyone." Caleb waited for the room to quiet down before he continued, "Mom, I hope you don't mind that we asked Theo to be in on this family meeting. It involves our family, him and BLPD." Caleb sat to the right of Isa, her gaze rapt from her seat at the head of the table. A polished attorney, Caleb couldn't shake his training even with his immediate family. Rachel suppressed an inappropriate grin. This felt a little too much like the county courthouse for her liking. But they weren't here to talk about the Colton Christmas-gift exchange.

Caleb met each of their gazes with a nod before proceeding.

"We've asked you all to join us, and we've sent texts to the others, to let you know some sad news for the family. Spence is going to be released from jail in the near term, possibly as early as the end of this week. As expected, there are significant reports and rumors that Spence has orchestrated all of this. He may still be pulling the syndicate's strings from behind bars."

Gasps and several swear words sounded from all present, but Rachel was used to her siblings and their various reactions over bad news. It was her mother's reaction that she cared most about.

Isa kept her gaze downcast for so long that the room grew silent, and she wondered if her mother was saying a prayer or had been shocked speechless. But when Isa's gaze swung up, all Rachel saw in the blue depths much like her own was steel.

"We always knew this could happen. Prisoners get released when it's determined they weren't guilty."

"But Mom!"

"You've got to be kidding!"

"He's a crook!"

So many spoke at once that Rachel couldn't hear her own response. Which involved the swear words her siblings had previously used. Sure, she'd already heard the bad news earlier, so it wasn't a surprise. But being in the company of her family unlocked the box in her heart where she carefully stored all things related to her father's demise.

Ben Colton's sudden death in a tragic car accident and the aftermath of grief was actually easier for her to remember, because her father had had no power over his passing. But choosing to accept bribes from criminals in the same league as Spence was something she'd never been able to forgive him for. She knew many of her siblings were still working on the forgiveness part, too.

Ben had had his hands full and the pressure on as each of his kids arrived and Isa realized she couldn't balance twelve children and a career all at the same time. His initial salary as a small-city judge hadn't been enough to put decent groceries on the table, much less keep them all clothed and the bills paid. Since she'd had Iris, Rachel had a new understanding of what it meant to be a parent and she was able to muster some compassion for her father. But she drew the line where he'd repeatedly broken the law and continued to accept increasingly higher bribes.

"Hold on, everyone." Isa held up a hand. "I'm not saying it's okay, or the right decision, but this isn't about my opinion. Or any of yours. The law is the law, and it seems Spence is going free, right?"

Heads nodded.

"Well, then, we'll have to keep the Truth Foundation on it, assure he doesn't make the tiniest deviation from what's legal. Meanwhile, can we find out more about Clay Houseman?"

As her mother shifted her focus to Theo, Rachel had to keep her jaw from hitting her sternum. Shouldn't Mom be looking at Morgan or Caleb, or even her, no matter that she was recused from all Truth Foundation activity?

"Theo, your department is going to keep an eye on Spence, aren't you? And you must have info on Houseman that even Caleb and Morgan don't know, right?" Isa's respect for the chief was evident.

"We work closely with your foundation, Isa. But no,

we can't tail someone who's being released as a free man. Not unless he breaks the law or reports come in that he has. Unfortunately, Spence may disappear into the crowd unless he does something overt, traceable."

"Which he won't because he's smarter than that. He's always been wily." Isa's use of the old-fashioned word forced a smile from Rachel, which she welcomed in the midst of the distressing news.

"Mom, we're doing everything we can to monitor the situation. You have nothing to worry about." Caleb beat Morgan to the bottom line. Morgan reacted by chewing on her pen cap, an old habit ever since they'd gotten brand-new packages of the blue ink pens at the beginning of each semester. Nostalgia pushed into Rachel's awareness, and she blinked back tears while searching for a distraction from the heavy emotions.

Aubrey and Jasper quietly observed the scene while Gavin pecked away on his tablet. Gavin seemed constitutionally unable to turn off his reporter persona. Sensing her stare, he looked up and shot her a conspiratorial wink. She bit her cheek to keep from grinning. A swell of love for her entire family squeezed tight around Rachel's center.

Isa leaned back in her chair and let out a long sigh. "This is tough, but nothing like what we've been through in the past, right? I can see that you're all worried about me. Stop. Just, stop. This is affecting you more, because you've all been so invested in the mission of our Truth Foundation. The truth of this matter is that if Spence is still dirty, it's going to come out. He'll face justice again. It's all in how you spin it at the Foundation."

"We've already reached out to a PR person who does contract work. And we're looking into hiring a full-time social media person." Morgan spoke.

"The morning coffee club doesn't go on social media a whole lot." Gavin referred to the older seniors in their seventies and eighties who gathered every morning at Blue Larkspur's most popular diner for breakfast, a cup of joe and local gossip. "They're going to get riled up when they find out, if they haven't heard already."

"That's the breaks of small-city life when it has big-time crime." Rachel let her thoughts out, and quickly looked at Isa to make sure her mother wouldn't take it wrong. "I love Blue Larkspur—it's my home, too. But since becoming DA I appreciate more than ever that we face the same challenges as large cities. It's often worse because we don't have all the law enforcement needed to handle them. Morgan, you're smart to hire PR professionals. We have to spin this for the Foundation's, for Blue Larkspur's benefit. Otherwise we're no more than a social media meme promising justice but delivering zilch."

"My only regret is that we can't say the DA supports us." Caleb reminded her that she was recused from the Truth Foundation's work. "But your personal support is appreciated."

Rachel hid another grin. The Coltons were all very much individuals but shared a common passion for their life's work, whatever it was. Just as Gavin couldn't stop being a reporter for a short time at the family dining room table, Caleb couldn't put his eldest-son and legal hats on the shelf.

"My main concern, besides keeping Blue Larkspur

safe, is that all of you, especially Isa, are safe." Theo spoke. "Isa had a security system installed recently, so how about the rest of you? Your other siblings who couldn't make it tonight?"

Theo went around the table and took notes as they each responded. Rachel's stomach churned as he got closer to her. She knew she had to tell her family about the note, which made it more real, scarier.

"Rachel?" Theo prompted.

"Gideon installed cameras at my front and back doors two weekends ago, and they work great. But, well, I've got another problem." She had her family's attention. Even Gavin looked up from his tablet.

"James's ex is a stalker. Not in a joking or casual way. It's gone on for almost two years. She's been arrested several times in Denver since he obtained a permanent restraining order against her. Which she's never followed, frankly. Anyway, when he moved to Blue Larkspur, it was partly for his new job—"

"And to step up to fatherhood," Gideon interrupted. Rachel glared at him.

"For your information James didn't know about Iris." She briefly filled them in on how she'd called James and thought he was engaged. "James is certain it was Bethany who answered his phone. It was when he was still trying to be nice to her, be her friend. Before her threats became dark and twisted."

"We get it, Rach." Aubrey spoke up.

"Right. So, you know about the explosion at Ricco's downtown. I was there, with James. It was our first meeting since he's been back."

"You mean 'date.'" Jasper smirked.

"No, no date. I agreed to meet with him to try to feel him out—"

Gavin guffawed when she said "feel" and the rest of the siblings cracked into silly laughter. Isa hid her mouth behind an elegantly manicured hand and Theo looked down at his notepad.

Rachel's face heated and she fought to keep her temper as a newly discovered emotion pulsed through her veins. *Protectiveness.* Not only for her child, which she was used to, but toward James.

Like a tigress, the urge to slash out at anyone who threatened her baby's father was primal, unmistakable.

"I get it, everyone. You need some comic relief. Please, allow me to provide it at my expense." She tried to infuse her request with exasperation but found herself giggling, too. No one could make her laugh as quickly or hard as her siblings.

"Sorry, not sorry, sis." Jasper's reply was echoed with nods. "Go on."

"Okay, may I finish now? James thinks he saw Bethany in the restaurant moments before the explosion. Add in that I've had some suspicious things happen. Gideon knows about the fuel thinner that was added to my gas tank. Theo knows about the muddy footprints on both my front and back house entrances." She sucked in a deep breath. "What none of you know is that yesterday I received a threatening note in a package that had a bunch of flowers."

She detailed the note and her suspicions, told them her security video had revealed zilch. "I'll get that note to you ASAP."

"Thanks, as soon as you do, I'll send it to the lab."

"There's one more thing—I keep having the sense I'm being watched. The latter is probably my overactive imagination, but the first rule in self-defense is awareness. I've had the being-watched feeling several times over the past two weeks."

"Since James has come back into your life, you mean." Isa's quiet proclamation made everyone turn to her. "We used to call that something else in our day, didn't we?" Isa winked. At Theo. Who blushed like a middle-school boy caught fantasizing about his current crush.

This time Rachel let the table dissolve into giggles. No sense fighting it. Her only regret was that James wasn't at her side, because he deserved to know what they were up against. If they were going to effectively co-parent Iris, it went without saying that their number one job was to keep their baby girl safe, wasn't it?

The sick sensation was back, stirring up her stomach acid.

Were any of them safe with a stalker around and a dangerous criminal about to be put back on the streets?

Chapter Fourteen

"Hey." The touch of Rachel's hand on his shoulder woke James from his uneasy rest on her sofa later that night.

"Hi." He swung his legs down onto the floor and forced himself awake, wondering how he'd drifted off when he needed to be alert for any intruders. The memory of finding the scary letter jolted him to standing. Rachel blinked, eyes luminous in the lamplight, and took a step back.

"You okay?"

"Yes. And Iris is good—she fell asleep before I could finish *Goodnight Moon*. She ate all of her dinner and loves the new boat." He'd brought a windup bath toy for her, noting that she previously only had rubber duckies and soft squirt toys.

"You did say we need to encourage her engineering gifts." Rachel's soft smile about undid him. Would she be receptive to another kiss, to more?

Security.

He shook his head. "I did, and we do, but I need to talk to you about something serious, Rachel."

"Shoot." She remained standing, as did he, a foot between them.

"When were you going to tell me about the note from Bethany?"

Her eyes widened before she looked up at the ceiling, and her chest rose on an inhale.

"I thought you were here to spend time with your daughter. To bond. Not to snoop through my stuff."

"You left it on the hall table in full view, Rachel. And really, it's not the point. Is this what you were meeting with your family about?"

"No." A quick shake of her head. "Not at all."

"Do they know? Do your brothers know?"

"You speak as if you're worried more about the Colton men than women. We're all a formidable bunch, James."

He'd gotten her hackles up and he hadn't meant to, not about her family. "I don't blame them for being suspicious of me. If my nephew's father showed up months after the birth, I wouldn't be very welcoming either, trust me. But we're in this together and your safety, Iris's, is what matters most to me. Please answer my question, Rachel. Does your family know about the note? About Bethany?"

"Yes, I told them about the note tonight. I was planning to tell you sooner, but this meeting came up..." She threw her hands up in the air. "Let's go talk in the kitchen. Want some tea?"

He wanted something stronger, but becoming Iris's dad and now the ever-present danger from Bethany negated any desire for the tiniest sip of a single malt.

"Sure." Following her to the kitchen, he gave her a more detailed rundown of his evening with Iris as Rachel made the hot drinks.

"You're kidding? She actually tried to wind the bath-tub boat by herself?" The sparkle in Rachel's eyes confirmed that she thought their daughter was advanced for her age, too. "She can hardly hold a spoon steady yet."

He sipped his ginger tea. "I'm telling you, she tried to turn the little lever and chattered at me until I did it for her. She misses absolutely nothing." His chest warmed and it wasn't solely from the drink. Being a father was already his favorite job ever. Although, sitting with Rachel, the scent of her reaching him across the counter—strong, sexy, slightly floral—he had to ask himself if he wanted to be more than Iris's co-parent.

"I'm sorry I didn't come to you first about the note, James. I should have. You've had so much come down on you at once. Finding out you're a father, moving, starting a new job. And lest we forget, the constant reminder that Bethany's trying to destroy your life again. I didn't think it was fair to dump it on you, is all."

"One note?"

"There's more I need to fill you in on." Her eyes reflected her contrition. It was impossible to be angry with Rachel when he knew her motives had been in the right place.

He listened as she rehashed everything that had happened to date, including the footprints, her car trouble. "My family laughed and tried to joke about it when I told them I keep thinking someone's watching me, but that's their way of breaking the tension. They're worried, too. I can't leave my house without looking over both shoulders, I can only imagine how you feel after dealing with this for so much longer. And the cameras

Gideon installed aren't enough, not if I can't conclusively identify who left the note with the flowers."

"There's only one solution to this, Rachel."

She shook her head. "I'm not leaving my own house, James. As much as it all points to Bethany, there's a decent chance I'm being warned off by a local crime ring." She told him about her case docket. "There are at least half a dozen culprits but definitely one in particular who'd like to scare me off a strong prosecution."

He wished they were talking about anything but the potential danger surrounding them. His body reacted as if they weren't in the crosshairs of predators. Whether it was Bethany or one of Rachel's suspects didn't matter. A threat to his family was just that. A threat.

She sipped her tea, a lavender concoction that mingled with her scent. His awareness of her every move shot to his crotch. Unlike the previous times Rachel had aroused him, though, this time he wasn't flashing back to how it had been in Helena. Or even that kiss in her mother's backyard.

James wanted to know what Rachel felt like moving against him now. Tonight. It was almost scarier than having a stalker. Accepting she had so much power over him.

"What are you thinking?" She'd picked up on his mood. Always.

"Come on. I have a great poker face."

"You do, except I know you well enough that when I see those lines at the corners of your eyes, you're either angry or ready to break out laughing."

He grunted. "It's both. I'm beyond mad that anyone would try to threaten you or Iris."

"And the second?"

He stared into her eyes, unable to articulate that what he wanted to do wasn't just a physical need. Come to think of it, neither had it been in Helena. Sure, they'd had a solid dose of insta-lust, no question. But it hadn't been her killer bod or beautiful smile that had attracted him, not at first. Rachel's intelligence, the way she seemed to vibrate with a strength and passion he didn't see in other women. Those had been the draw.

"James?" She licked her lips, leaned in toward him.

James cupped her face. The softness of her cheek under his thumb pad sent zings of sexual awareness down his arms and straight to between his legs.

"Babe." He leaned in and kissed her across the breakfast counter. Unlike the exploratory, almost languid kiss at Isa Colton's house, when their lips touched now, it was the bridge to their all-consuming connection. He needed more; no, not more. He wanted *all* of her.

Rachel's tongue met his at the same moment he plunged his into her mouth, and James let go of all restraint. He crushed her lips with his mouth, his hands around her head.

"I need you, Rachel." His voice hitched, his heart slamming against his ribs.

Rachel stepped around the counter and tugged at him, evidently wanting him off the barstool. "What do you want, James?" Eyes half-lidded, her lips red and swollen.

"This." He stood and turned the stool around so that the back was against the sturdy nook. He sat back down and grasped her waist to lift her, but she already had a leg over him, wriggling the rest of the way to straddle him. The contact of her softness against his arousal was at once the sweetest and sexiest moment of his life.

"Like this?" She gyrated her pelvis in an ageless

move of seduction. Except where Rachel was concerned, no seduction was needed.

"More like this." He strung his fingers through her hair, clasped his hand on the base of her head and pulled her mouth to his. As their kiss deepened, he pushed against the small of her back with his free hand, then trailed it up, up her spine, unsnapping her bra and reaching around her front in a single move. Her breast, heavy as it filled his palm, was hot. On fire, like him. He tweaked her pebbled nipple and she cried out, nipped his neck with frustrated love bites.

"James, please. Please. Never stop this. Never."

"It's a deal." He plundered her mouth again, needing every lick and taste of her. Wanting more, knowing it would never be enough. Not with Rachel.

"I have to taste you, all of you."

"Let's go to my bedroom."

"Wait, what about Iris? What if we wake her?"

She gasped out a giggle. "I have a baby monitor on in my bedroom, too. Look, she's fine." She pointed at the video monitor on the counter where an image of their baby sleeping on her side, the sound of her soft breathing, verified Iris was all right. "I ran the vacuum, made all the usual loud noises when she was tiny. She sleeps like a rock."

"Good to know." He tried to not be rough as he held her ass in his hands and lifted both of them from the stool. Her legs automatically circled his waist, and he thought his knees might buckle from the heady desire that rushed through him. It didn't escape him that the dining table was closest, the sofa nearby.

"Stop thinking, James." She saw his gaze wander

and looked over her shoulder at the sofa. "Not this time. Take me to my bed, babe."

JAMES LET HER down so gently it belied the next moments as he quickly shucked his clothing while she scrambled out of hers. They allowed one another a chance to take in each other's full nudity, but urgency strummed through every single nerve ending as she looked at him and pointed to the side of the bed.

"Condoms are in the nightstand drawer. Not that it helped last time." Her breath hitched and she saw his reflexive breath when his chest rose, displaying his strawberry blond hair, which dusted his magnificent pecs. Not the most stunning part of him, though. She trailed her gaze south, took in the full length of him. Her mouth watered in sync with the dampness between her legs as she trembled with need.

"Are you sure, Rachel?" His slightly raised brows revealed that while he was sincere in needing her consent, he also knew what he was doing to her.

"James I've never been more certain about anything. I have to make love to you. If you don't come here—"

He prowled the two steps to the bed and covered her with his sinewy length before she finished, covered her mouth with his. Had she ever met a better kisser? A better stroker? A better lover?

No.

Her mind wanted to go over how wonderful a father James was, how that had surprised her, how he wasn't the corporate shark she'd judged him to be, but his hands and tongue turned her mind to mush. Well, not mush but a sensuous center that put her entire body, her soul into a pleasure zone she'd never visited before. The time in Helena had been hot and fulfilled not only her fantasies but all of her sexual needs. Now, tonight, she knew James. He knew his child.

James knew Rachel's every need.

"Oh my, that's—that's…" She gasped for air as his fingers plunged into her slick, wet folds while his thumb circled her most sensitive spot.

"Stop thinking, Rachel." His laughter rumbled low in his throat but he needn't have repeated her earlier admonition. Waves of an intense orgasm made her back arch, her insides spasm against his fingers.

Before she came down from the climax, he'd donned a condom. Braced above her, a forearm on either side of her head, his eyes were emerald points of need, his open mouth irresistible. Their lips met at the same moment he entered her.

Nothing about sex or mutual satisfaction was new to Rachel, and James's evident expertise mirrored it was the same for him. But as they moved together, watching each other for what heightened their pleasure the most, she caught glimpses of a place she'd never been before. Paradise. Heaven.

James waited until she began her second climax before she heard his breath hitch again, the deep groan emanating from his chest. They each cried out as the waves hit them, and Rachel knew what was different when she made love to James.

They shared more than a physical, or child, connection. Theirs was a heart pact. When or where it had happened, she didn't know, but what Rachel was certain of was that she'd never have a connection like this with anyone else.

Chapter Fifteen

They lay next to one another, holding hands for long moments after. James was at a loss for words, a rarity for an attorney and definitely for him.

"That was incredible." Rachel spoke first. He dug deep for the strength to rise up on his elbow and look at her. He never wanted to talk to her without seeing her every reaction, the way her eyelashes framed her expressive eyes or how her mouth quirked into a dimple on her left cheek.

"More than incredible, I'd say." He stroked her hair back before allowing his fingers to travel around her face, down her throat, between her breasts. "You're the most beautiful woman in the world, Rachel."

She turned her head to meet his gaze and tugged on his short hair, leaned up for a lingering kiss. "You make me feel that way, for sure."

"I'm not leaving, you know."

She smiled. "I'm glad. I wasn't sure if you'd like Blue Larkspur enough to stay."

An icy splash of reality cut through his sensual reverie. "It has nothing to do with the location." He rolled away, sat on the side of the bed. It wasn't the time to try to express the jumble of emotions tearing his heart wide open. And he wasn't going *there*, to the part of him that knew wherever Rachel and Iris were was where he belonged. Instead he tried to focus on what needed to be done, here and now.

"Hold that thought." She scrambled off the bed, disappeared into the bathroom for a few minutes before returning in a too-sexy, red-and-white-flower-print silk kimono. He liked the way the hem flirted with being just shy of indecent, revealing her robust, creamy thighs. James had zero attraction to superskinny women. Rachel's curves and softness were the ideal of femininity to him.

"So, moving here had nothing to do with Blue Larkspur's geolocation?" A soft smile played across her luscious lips.

"I can't have this conversation with you right now, Rachel. My first priority has to be keeping you both safe. I'm moving in with you and Iris. And not because we just made love." He put his jeans on. "I'll be sleeping on the couch tonight. I have to leave early tomorrow morning, to get to my condo and shower before work. Tomorrow I'll come here straight from the firm, packed for the duration. You and Iris are never going to be alone. Not until your cases are closed and we know for certain if it's Bethany or not. If it is Bethany, then she needs to be caught. Helped."

"Whoa. Hang on a sec."

As she ran her fingers through her hair, his own twitched to feel the silky locks. How could he be hard for her again, so soon?

"You don't have to move in here. Gideon installed the cameras, and I'll upgrade to a better security system."

"Not enough. No matter who's stalking you, they mean business. This isn't kid stuff, Rachel."

"Don't you think I, of all people, know that? Darn it, James! Self-serving criminals, including my own danged father, have wreaked havoc on my life since I was a kid. My father was crooked for years before his death. In fact, you could say I was born into crime."

Regret yanked at his resolve to detach from what they'd just shared so that he could be the protection she and Iris deserved. "Stop it. You're not your father."

"Yeah, look how well being his daughter worked out." The lines above her brow deepened and she blew out a frustrated breath. "Spence is free to be the awful man he is and hurt the innocent citizens of our town again." She crossed her arms in front of her. "No matter how much good the Truth Foundation does, it'll never be enough."

"Rachel." He took a step closer, not missing the irony of having to walk on eggshells after sharing the most cataclysmic orgasm of his life with her minutes earlier. He stood still, steady. "It's not your responsibility to fix the wrongs of your father."

Her eyes blazed. "That's just it, James—it *is* my job. Whether it's with my family's nonprofit or as an elected official on a government salary, I'll never stop making amends for what he did. You can't pay back those who served years of unnecessary time."

"I'm sorry. I'm not trying to do anything here but support you. My dad died when I was still a tiny kid, so like you, I lost him too soon. But I don't have the crappy legacy your father left you with. And to be honest? I'm not half the person you are. That's what I liked about you from the start, Rachel. You don't back down from what you know to be right."

She shrugged and nodded. "Thanks for that. I know I'm being uptight, but it's hard not—"

The sound of breaking glass, quickly followed by a solid thump, reached them. James held his hand up to Rachel.

"Stay here." He ran out of the room, to the nursery. Iris was safe and sleeping, but he took her from the crib anyway. Rachel was on his heels and he nodded at the master bedroom door. "Back to your room. Fast!"

Once in her room again, he handed the baby to her. "Don't go anywhere until I tell you it's clear. Where's your phone?"

"On the nightstand." She was already there, clutching the still-sleeping Iris in the crook of her arm as she grabbed the phone with her other hand.

"Call 9-1-1. If you hear any kind of trouble, go out the sliding door and run to your neighbor's."

"It's Rachel Colton, DA." Fear coursed through her as she identified herself to the emergency services dispatcher. She hoped that when she'd said "DA," the dispatcher would alert the cruisers in her area more quickly. Theo had already assigned extra patrols on her house, so she was certain the response would be faster than normal.

"Stay on the line, ma'am. I'll have a unit there in two minutes."

"Thanks." She wrapped her arms around Iris, kissed

her sweet head. The baby snuggled in closer, knowing her mother's embrace without waking. Rachel thought that if the crashing sound hadn't woken her daughter, then Rachel's pounding heart would.

It was impossible to hear what was going on in the front of the house, and she had to fight to keep herself from escaping through the master bedroom's sliding glass doors. If there was a prowler on her property, she'd be putting them both at risk. But her instinct to run was primal, and her entire body shook with the adrenaline rush.

A dark shadow appeared at the patio door and she gasped, until the motion detector light activated and she made out Theo's form. She unlocked the door with shaking hands.

"You both okay?" In pure cop mode, Theo's gaze assessed her and Iris for injury.

"Yes, yes. James went to see what happened."

He nodded. "I know. He's out front, giving the officers a report. My team's combing your living room."

"I guess you don't need me to keep the line open anymore." She went to disconnect the call to 9-1-1, but Theo stopped her and took her phone.

"Chief Theo Lawson. Who's this?"

Rachel waited as he confirmed the call had been handled and disconnected.

"What happened?"

"Put the baby down and I'll show you."

"I'm not leaving her alone back here. Not yet."

"She's safe, Rachel. You're safe. It's over."

James came in through the bedroom door, took in

the scene of Rachel stubbornly holding on to Iris, nodded at the chief.

"I gave my report, and they're going to take the brick with them."

"A *brick*?" Her voice rose in pitch without effort. "What we heard was a brick through the front window?"

"No, your transom over the front door." James walked to her and took Iris from her arms. "Let me hold her and get her back down while you go with Theo and see what happened."

Rachel didn't want to let go of Iris but realized she completely trusted James. If he thought it was safe, then it was.

She followed Theo into the front room, to the foyer. Shards of glass were scattered randomly across the high-gloss hardwood, and as she looked up she saw the center pane of three that made up the rectangular window was a gaping hole. An officer took photos of the scene, then placed a plain brown brick into an evidence bag.

"Why would someone do this? And why the door instead of the front picture window?" She couldn't keep her voice from shaking.

"They wanted to scare you, to get your attention." Theo's familiar voice soothed her.

Rachel squatted near where the brick had landed. The small scar in the varnish was a reminder that they were lucky no one was injured. "Was there a message with it?"

The officer looked at Theo.

"Show her," Theo said.

The officer turned the rectangle upside down, and she made out the two words painted in bright red.

BACK OFF.

"Wow. No mistaking the meaning." Nausea swirled with anxiety in her belly. No matter what, she had to keep her baby safe. The officers present would file their reports but that took time. Time that her internal warning system told her was running out. "Iris and I are going to have to leave town. Or maybe she should stay with my mother."

Theo looked at her with compassion, and something else. Knowing. "I understand your logic. I'd want to do the same in your position."

"But?"

"But short of leaving the state, whoever this is, one of your defendants or Bethany Austin, they're going to follow you wherever you go. No place is safe for you until they're caught."

"Well gee, Theo, color me reassured." She knew she was being caustic, but her daughter's life was on the line. What if Iris was crawling already and had been on the floor?

James stood beside her. "The baby's back down, and I have the monitor." He held up the device that they usually kept on the kitchen counter. He looked at Theo. "I told Rachel earlier that I think it's a good idea that I stay here until we make sure we know who's behind *all* of the criminal pranks."

"Excellent choice. In fact, the best one, short of having an officer check in on you and Iris hourly." Theo chimed in so quickly that suspicion raised its head in Rachel's thoughts.

"I could go to my mother's…" She trailed off and was grateful James and Theo gave her the space needed to figure it out. Going to Isa's wasn't acceptable. She didn't want any bad guy following her there. Plus, the Colton house was too far from downtown Blue Lark-spur. Rachel relished living this close to the courthouse and her office. Not to mention the police.

"I have to say, BLPD was here almost before I'd finished requesting help. I know that you have a team spending more time in my neighborhood, but still, I appreciate the quick response."

Theo nodded. "Yes, that's another solid reason to stay here, in your own home."

"I'll be here." James stood next to her, a steady presence as two more officers appeared and began taking evidence samples with tiny brushes, putting them into small, tightly sealed plastic bags.

Rachel's head pounded, and the heavy weight on her chest made it hard to focus on anything but curling up on the sofa and going to sleep. She had zero fight left.

What harm would it do to have James live with her and Iris? It would give him more time with his daughter, too. Win-win.

"Okay, you two are right. I'll have a professional security team come and install a top-of-the-line system tomorrow. I'll pay for any expenses that exceed the DA private-home budget out of my pocket. James, of course you're more than welcome to stay here. While the sofa in the front room is a queen sleeper, I have a perfectly comfortable guest room. Use that."

Theo cleared his throat. "I'd be more comfortable if James stayed in the front room, close to the window and front door. An intruder would have to pass him first. Combined with our amplified patrols, it'll give you just about the highest level of security possible."

"What's the highest?" She'd thought it would be what Theo had already proposed, what James had insisted upon.

"When your harasser is either arrested, behind bars or dead." Theo minced no words and didn't wait for either of them to reply. "My team will be out of here within the hour. Go ahead and finish up your usual nighttime routine. We'll make sure the broken window is boarded up. Get it fixed as soon as possible, Rachel. If you can't find anyone, I'm happy to come out tomorrow after work and help."

"That won't be necessary. I'll take care of it." James spoke up. "I'll call in a personal day tomorrow."

Relief flowed through her tense shoulder muscles. "That's not necessary. You've only just started your job! Emily takes great care of Iris and has alerted me to any little change she notices."

"I'm not saying to tell her not to come. I'll need her here to watch Iris. I can work on my cases remotely. I'm not due back in court for two weeks. My job is wherever my laptop is. You, on the other hand, can't work from home. Am I right?"

She nodded.

Theo grasped her shoulder and gave it a firm squeeze. "I'll leave you two to it. Rachel, do you have any plywood in your garage?"

"Actually, yes. There are some small pieces on top of the workbench. Gideon left them after he built a platform for the back camera. The light and garage opener switch are to the right of the entry." She heard the heavy door open.

"I'm going to check on Iris for a sec." James spoke. "But when I get back, let's sit down and go over your case docket. I want to know as much as possible about each one, including the names of the defendants." He turned and she watched him retreat down the hallway.

Comfort conflicted with resistance as she processed the fact it'd be a sight she'd better get used to. James was moving in—and not just into her house.

Chapter Sixteen

"I think you'd be fine sleeping in the guest room at this point. It's been well over a week since the brick." And the dead-flower delivery, which he noted Rachel didn't mention.

They sat at the dining room table, a pot of tea between them. Iris was in bed, and the routine they'd established had begun to feel normal to James.

Each night after Iris was down, they'd spend two to three hours scouring Rachel's case files, both as assistant DA and DA. And every night Rachel went to her bedroom alone and James camped out on the sofa.

"Your sofa's just as comfortable as the guest bed. Besides, I'd get zero sleep back there. I need to be up front." He knew he'd never get any rest if he wasn't near the house's main entry.

"You're a lawyer, not a police officer or security specialist."

"I'm in this with you. I've already missed out on too much time with both of you. I'm Iris's father. Nothing is coming between me and her." *And you.* He couldn't say the last but the urge to protect Rachel was as much a part of him as needing to breathe. He'd convinced himself that it was only because she was Iris's mother. That, in his effort to make up for lost time, he'd gone a little overboard, especially when they made love last week. He'd thought they'd gone to bed together again because they had a shared attraction. At least that's what he'd tried to convince himself. Because if that wasn't the primary reason, if he was developing feelings at a deeper level than ever before, James needed to move carefully. The last thing he wanted to do was push Rachel away by being too impatient and rushing whatever this connection between them might grow into.

"You're in that overthinking place again. Here. Have some tea." She'd mistaken his sudden quiet for something completely different, a good thing. It seemed a mutual decision to avoid physical contact, and he knew it was for the best. Yet her presence, her scent, her quick smile made it difficult to convince his body to take a step back.

"Thanks. I still don't know how you think this helps with clear thinking." He'd come to enjoy the spicy aroma and taste.

Laughter made her eyes sparkle, offered a relief from the heaviness of what they were fighting together. "Did I say that? It was just to get you to drink it. Ginger tea is my go-to since having Iris. I like peppermint, too, but it's best to keep it an occasional treat while I'm still breastfeeding."

"It never occurred to me that you have to be careful with something like herbal tea."

"Yeah, keeping it decaf isn't enough of a safety precaution."

"How long will you breastfeed?" He'd been mesmerized by how reverent the ritual was between mother and daughter, honored that Rachel didn't hide it all from him.

"I'd like to nurse her the entire year. Iris is ravenous and, as you know, needs more solid food each day. I'm not sure if she's going to want to nurse the entire twelve months. My mother says I quit around eleven months, only latching on for a bit at a time toward the end. Not that I totally rely on her anecdotal evidence. She had twelve kids, after all." She laughed and he joined in.

"You're such a great mother, Rachel. I don't know how you do it—nurse her morning and night, pump and freeze milk at work, oh, and be a full-time DA." His words came out without any forethought, unusual for him. But he'd been changing, becoming more comfortable around her. He knew his mental filters existed for good reason; he'd been burned by women before.

Rachel's different.

She shrugged, a blush on her smooth skin. "I never comprehended the work, the hours that a baby takes. But it's as though she's always been here, you know? Before Iris, I couldn't imagine having a child, not this soon. Although at thirty-four, I suppose I should have started thinking about it. Now that she's here, I can't for one instant imagine my life without her."

"Same. I don't have to do all the physical lifting you do. My gosh, you carried her for over nine months, labored with her, had her. But I feel the same as far as feeling she's always been a part of me."

"Yeah." Rachel nodded, tapped her hand on the stack of files that sat between their laptops. "We still haven't narrowed down any suspects."

"There are two I'd place as most likely to have thrown the brick. Your most recent case and Bethany."

"My money's on the Parson case. You're convinced it's Bethany. I can tell. And I appreciate that, James, because let's face it, you've been traumatized by her. I understand trauma. Why do you think my dad's crimes still haunt me?" Her hand reached across the table and covered his. A brief touch, but it burned. He fought to keep his palm flat down instead of turning it right side up, grasping her hand, pulling her toward him.

"Your father was a complicated man. But he was *your dad*, Rachel. Bethany was barely a friend. At this point I feel I owe her nothing, except to see that she gets the help she needs."

"If it turns out it's Bethany, we'll both make sure that happens."

"If it's a criminal you've prosecuted?"

"Then we turn to Theo and BLPD to weed out all the other jerks who helped this person harass me." Her beauty was stark against the exhaustion he'd noticed creeping in since they'd met in the restaurant. Sure, Rachel had new-mother exhaustion. But she'd had a verve in her step that he hated to see hammered away by the incessant threats.

"I'm going to do everything to catch whoever it is, Rachel."

"I know you are." She looked at her smartwatch. "I've got three cases tomorrow. How about you?"

"I'll work here 'til noon, then I'm in court through the rest of the day, too."

"See you same time, same place?" She stood and took both of their mugs in one hand, the teapot in the other. He moved the files to the opposite end of the table, away from Iris's high chair and where they'd all have breakfast together tomorrow morning.

"I wouldn't miss it." As he prepared for another night on the sofa, the sense that he was exactly where he was meant to be hit him harder than the thrill of winning any of his biggest cases ever had.

But there was at least one, possibly two criminals who weren't afraid of harming Rachel or Iris. Until they were stopped, his heart would have to wait.

RACHEL'S BED SEEMED humongous as she tried to get to sleep. Knowing James was in the front of the house brought as much comfort as it did frustration. It wasn't sexual frustration, either. Sure, that was a part of it, but whatever was going on between her and James was getting deeper, stronger. If it was just her heart on the line, she'd deal with it. She was a prosecuting attorney, the daughter of a man who'd betrayed the community. Risking her heart was scary but doable.

But not her daughter's.

Her phone vibrated on silent mode, and she was grateful for the distraction.

"Mom! What are you doing up at this hour?"

"Please, it's not that late. I had a project I needed to put to bed and I'm having a cup of chamomile in the tub."

Rachel laughed. Isa had been a bath lover from long back. "Maybe I should take one."

"Oh, trouble sleeping?"

"No, yes. I mean, well, maybe."

"I'm sure you're worried after all the goings on at

your place. Theo assures me that you'll be fine. Between the PD and both you and James, the crooks don't have a chance."

"Thanks, Mom. I'd like to think that, too."

"So let me guess. Is it James? Please tell me you're still not making him sleep on the sofa. Your sex life is none of my business—"

"No, Mom, it's not." Her cheeks heated before she heard her tone. "I'm not ready to give in to it, Mom. I have no way of knowing if James is really interested in me because I'm me, or because of Iris."

"They're one and the same, honey. You can't separate the two—you come as a whole package. And whatever you do, don't base your relationship with James on mine with your dad. Your father made a lot of mistakes, no question, but we had a lot of happy times together before he went to the dark side."

"You've certainly worked through your grief and blaming yourself for his actions. I'm proud of you, Mom." She was. Her mother was the strongest person she knew.

"After twenty years, it's about time, isn't it?"

"Yes."

"I know I've said it before, but please believe me when I say that life is short. Don't waste any more time than you have to when it comes to a man you care about."

"You may be right, Mom." She couldn't think about her future with James. Not while she was looking over her shoulder every minute of every day.

"You sound a little sleepy. Any chance you'll get some rest now?" Isa asked.

Rachel yawned. "Yeah, I think I just might. Thanks for calling, Mom."

"Night, night."

They disconnected and Rachel lay back on her pillows, glad for the call but suddenly wide-awake. Again. Were her feelings for James that obvious to everyone?

Chapter Seventeen

"Please, Rachel. Trust me on this." James reversed out of her mother's driveway, deftly switched gears on the manual transmission and drove them out of the subdivision. The weekend after the brick crashed through Rachel's window, James had surprised her with what he said was a "relaxation day." They were in his BMW, which seemed incongruous to the way he'd told her to dress. Both were in outdoor gear, as if going on a hike. But she hadn't noticed trekking poles in the trunk or back seat when they'd loaded all of Iris's paraphernalia and strapped her into her car seat earlier.

"I'm still not over the fact that you planned this with my mother behind my back. Although my mom sure loves any chance she can get to spend a day with Iris." She gave him a playful punch to his upper arm to make certain he knew she was kidding. "Actually, it's kind of nice to have something other than work to worry about."

And being stalked, no matter by whom. They'd pored over her caseload, checked and rechecked the backgrounds of the criminals she prosecuted. But little progress for their hours of labor. Their research had underscored the cunning presence of the underbelly of the community she loved and never wanted to see suffer at such brutal hands.

James's hand on her thigh spun her thoughts from investigative mode to her confused heart. He kept his focus on the road as he spoke.

"You need a break. And we need time alone together. Co-parents should be on the same page, know one another well enough to be a team."

"Sure. But what does that have to do with this mystery...day." She'd almost said "date." And he'd not made a move to take her back to bed since last week, when her world had forever changed with his lovemaking. No matter whether they somehow became more than co-parents—a place she couldn't let her heart go, not when she was in mortal fear for her daughter's safety—she knew deep down that no one else would ever be able to elicit such a primal, passionate response from her.

But life was about more than sex, even more than romance. She was a mother with a daughter to provide for and the DA for a county that deserved all she was able to give. Wouldn't becoming emotionally dependent on James be a distraction she couldn't afford?

"Rach, please let go. Trust me. It's going to be fun." He squeezed her thigh.

"I don't know how you do it. You always know my mood. Okay, I'm letting go." But as she looked out the window, saw the direction he was taking them, her anxiety edged in. "Wait a minute—if we're not hiking, and I know you wouldn't bike without your mountain bike, please tell me we're not rafting. Isn't it too early in the season, anyway?"

"Okay, I won't tell you. And no, there are a couple

who open earlier." The flash of white on his tanned skin reflected how thrilled he was to have planned this. And his complete ignorance of her white-water revulsion.

"James, I don't like to white-water raft."

"Because of what happened when you were twelve?"

"Let me guess. One of my siblings told you about my bad, nearly traumatic, rafting event as a young girl? All of them think I don't raft because I'm being stubborn. But they weren't the one left scared to death."

"I can confirm or deny nothing." James's smile was small but it was enough to trigger her emotions from that fateful day decades ago.

Shame, embarrassment and a sense of betrayal fought for first billing as she twisted in her seat to make her point. "I don't know which of my brothers or sisters told you, and I know it was one of them because Mom wasn't on the trip and doesn't know how traumatic it was for me. But I'm going to kill them when I see them."

"Careful with such a strong word." He maneuvered a mountain turn as well as his voice soothed her. She hated to admit it, but simply being next to him, in any capacity, calmed her. Except when she thought of sitting in a rubber raft.

"James, we flipped that day. Gideon and I got out of the water only because of luck." The rest of her siblings there had been old enough to basically stand and walk out where the river calmed, which was right after where both rafts had collided and flipped. Caleb and Morgan were seventeen; Oliver, Ezra and Dominic were fourteen; she was twelve, and Gideon was ten. The younger kids had stayed home with Isa, who would have had a stroke on the spot if she'd seen what Ben Colton's idea of fun had turned into. Rachel had never set foot on a river raft again.

"You made it out safe due to luck, or good safety precautions taken by your father?"

The reminder that Ben had loved his children, his family, the best he could, did little to stop the fear that pushed up her throat, tightened every muscle in her body.

"He had trained us well. I give him that." A harsh laugh escaped her. "It's ironic that all of my siblings still enjoy a day on the river."

"Why do you think you're the one that took it the other direction, Rach?" He was pulling off the highway now, and she did her best to ignore the road signs that screamed where the white-water rafting exits were.

"I don't know. It was terrifying, James. One minute we're bouncing along, yelling our heads off. My dad was in the raft with us—me, Gideon and Ezra—and the others were with his friend. Our rafts weren't supposed to get that close to each other, but there's no controlling the river rapids during snowmelt. Of course, today they won't let you on that stretch unless you're sixteen or older."

"Were you having fun until your raft overturned?"

"I was, yes. Yes. But it didn't just flip. I don't know what everyone else told you, but I remember we smashed into one another so hard my head knocked back and hit my dad's helmet. Then we capsized. I was under the water for what felt like hours, but I know couldn't have been more than a few seconds." It had been so cold, compared to the warm spring day. Exactly like today, in fact. "I'm a good swimmer. We all are. Mom and Dad didn't skimp on Red Cross swimming lessons."

"But you think your father took a shortcut with the rafting trip that day?"

"Maybe. I don't know. You don't have to be with an official guide or anything. And it would have cost a lot for all of us to go if we'd paid. Dad's friend had the two rafts that we used."

"So this is why Isa wished me luck earlier."

"You told her where we were going? And she didn't tell you not to bother? She wasn't there but she knows I don't raft."

"Yes and no. She didn't say anything but 'best of luck.'" She watched his profile as he merged onto a busy road. His profile reminded her of Iris's. Already, she could tell that her daughter, their daughter, was going to have her daddy's nose. Long, straight, definitive. And she had the same shape to her eyebrows.

James shot her a quick glance as he stopped at a light. "What?"

"It's remarkable how much Iris resembles you, do you know that?"

He chuckled, which for James was a soft grumble low in his throat. As sensuous as his tongue on the most intimate parts of her body. Too hot for comfort, Rachel's finger felt for the window button and lowered hers. James's brow rose, but he didn't acknowledge the bright red that she knew had to be visible on her face.

"I've been sending my family so many photos of her that they're going to all block me. But my mother, she's over the moon about her and keeps saying that Iris is an exact mini-me. I'll have to get some of my baby pictures the next time I'm home."

"We're already halfway to Denver." The nearest white water to Blue Larkspur was a few hours away, on the way to Denver. She looked out her window as the light turned green and they inched forward in with the long row of cars. "We should have brought Iris with us." It hadn't been more than an hour, and she'd started missing her baby before they left. James didn't display any regret at leaving her for the day, from what she could tell.

"I miss her, too." Surprise zinged through her center, warmed the spot under her rib cage.

"You do?"

"Of course I do," he said. "Granted, I missed out on a lot, but it doesn't make my bonding experience any less intense. I used to listen to my siblings talk about how hard it was to leave their babies for that first day of work, both my brothers and sisters, by the way, and while I thought I empathized, I had no clue. None at all."

"It's impossible to know the joy, love and abject terror having your own child can bring into your life. Not until you're a parent. That's my experience, anyway."

"My family wants to have both you and Iris over for dinner sometime soon,. As soon as I told them about Iris, and you, they were over the moon."

James never avoided questions or confrontation, from what she knew of him. She'd give him a pass, for now. Maybe he needed the break from the long hours with Iris. No matter that Emily was with their daughter during the workday, it was often a two-person job when it came to the tiny girl's care and feeding. How many times had she wished she had a partner to share the weight of the load?

"Next month, maybe?" She mentally skimmed her schedule, wondering where it might fit in.

"If not sooner. I'm hoping we could get out of work a little earlier on a Friday and drive up there. My brother has a huge house we can stay in, and my mother lives less than five minutes from him."

"I'll, um, have to check my calendar once we're home. Some last-minute meetings were planned yesterday and I don't know which days they're on."

"Great." He pulled under a large blue-and-yellow sign that proclaimed Colorado River Rapids as the world's most challenging. Her stomach dipped.

"I don't know about that sign. Isn't it false advertising? The snowmelt hasn't been as much as they'd hoped this year. But it's early yet, barely begun." *Please, please don't let this be awful.*

"Which should make our ride more on the relaxing side, then." He followed the parking attendant's arm signals and aimed for a spot that seemed miles from the entrance, on a grassy stretch of land next to the paved lot. "There's a lot more visitors today than the last time I was here, last year."

"This time last year I was just getting over my morning sickness." Not wanting to drive home the fact he'd missed it, she scrambled for a new topic. "Maybe there are more people here because it's a smoother day, and a good time to bring families of all ages." But a heavy downpour was predicted later, too. Which meant a possibly rougher ride. She had to stay off her weather app.

"Hmm." He maneuvered to back into his appointed

spot, and even though his car had a rear dash cam, he relied only on his visual reference. With his arm across the back of the seat and him turned toward her, looking over his right shoulder through the rear window, it was impossible to ignore the scent that she'd come to associate with him. Fresh, sometimes minty, always pure James.

Go in another direction. Her current train of thought would lead to where any thoughts of James invariably did. Would he still be around, interested in her as more than Iris's mother, over the next months, years? How did she feel about that? How would she take it if he found someone else to partner with, possibly marry? Would Iris get along with any possible stepsiblings?

"Tell me what's on your mind, Rach." He shifted from Reverse to Drive. Had he noticed the emotional upheaval on her face?

"Why don't you use your rear camera?" *Good one. That'll distract him—not.*

"My camera, eh? Okay, I'll play along. It isn't accurate. I trust my eyes better than a backup camera." He finished parking and cut the engine.

"It's kind of scary, when I think about it."

"What, that I used my vision instead of a screen?"

"No, that we're more alike than I want to admit. We need to see the proof ourselves. About everything. You know, obsessive." She couldn't stop her chattering if she wanted to. The throngs of people heading toward the rafting tour office triggered a sense of inadequacy. Why couldn't she get past the accident from so long ago? Her siblings had.

"I'd like to think that's what makes us good attorneys."

"What's that?"

"Our attention to detail." He spoke slowly, eyeing her as if she were a bat caught in a net.

"Oh yes, yes, it does help with legal work." And other things. It meant that they didn't settle for second-best, that neither would be here alone with one another unless they very much wanted to.

He faced her in the car, as physically close as they'd been in a week, save for when dressing, bathing or feeding Iris together. "Look, I don't want you to be absolutely miserable all day. This is my bad. I thought that once you got used to the idea, you'd be able to enjoy it. We can forget the rafting and take an easy all-day hike. I know several spots—"

"Are you kidding me? And have my family find out that I chickened out? No. Freakin'. Way." She reached for her door handle. "I'll be fine. Where do we line up?"

ANGER SEETHED IN Bethany's intestines. Twisting, cramping, taking away any illusion that she had much time left to prove herself to James. To get rid of Rachel Colton.

Except it couldn't happen today, because when she'd been following the three of them over to Rachel's mother's house, her car had begun to sputter. Bethany couldn't afford anyone noticing her or her beater, no matter that she was careful to always follow at a decent distance. If she'd been smarter, she'd have spent her money on a GPS tracking device and stuck it to James's or Rachel's cars, instead of blowing her cash on the spy cameras. But it would have been torturous to not know what they were doing in that house.

She couldn't see the bedrooms or nursery, but there

was enough action in the front room to let her know that James and Rachel were getting too close. There hadn't been any sign of touching this week, but she didn't like how their heads had bent over the same computer screen too many times. Probably working on some dumb legal case that Rachel made up just to get James's attention. Women did that all the time with the men Bethany fell for. Rachel wasn't the first woman to get in the way of Bethany's love life. But she'd be the last.

It still infuriated her that James was being used by Rachel as a babysitter, too. He was at that house all day with the nanny and kid. Bethany saw the cops pull up last week, late at night, while she sat in the tree, two houses over. It hid her perfectly. She parked her car at a supermarket two miles away and walked into the neighborhood after dark. Usually she climbed down and went back to her car to sleep through the hours she'd learned that Rachel slept.

Not that she'd gotten a lot of sleep, not since it had occurred to her that the brat might be James's. But the thought of Rachel having that kind of hold on James made Bethany so angry. And gave her more reason to take care of Rachel Colton.

The night the cops showed up, something odd had happened at the house. A bunch of police cars had shown up. The cop presence had prevented her from getting out of the tree until early the next morning. She'd gotten lucky. The noise and big trucks gave her something to hide behind. It had been a real pain, acting like a perky jogger as she circled and left the large neighborhood. And she'd been tired for the rest of the day. But she'd gotten away, as she always did.

Except that one time with the explosion in James's Denver condo.

She still didn't know why the cops were called to Rachel's that night, though. Probably another thing Miss DA did to cause more trauma-drama and get James to take pity on her and her squalling brat. Oh yeah, she'd heard that kid screaming more than once. James was going to be so much happier without the kid and clingy DA.

Soon, James.

It was a major bummer that her car had kept her from following James and Rachel, but there was a silver lining to the lousy day. Her vehicle had died, but not until she spotted the run-down, mom-and-pop place outside town. If not for the gullible auto mechanic who'd been so eager to help, she'd be getting around on some bike she'd stolen. It had only taken one calculated act to convince the guy that it was worth making her car run smooth again for the little cash she had left in her pocket.

She hauled her stuff back into her trunk and tried to ignore the cramps in her lower back. It was getting old, her routine of hiding her clothing and personal items in an abandoned homesite each and every time she watched or followed James and Rachel. But it was a necessary precaution in case she was pulled over. There was no need to give any clues away that she was living out of her car, that she fit the description of the woman they were looking for.

Maybe she'd missed out on whatever James and Rachel were doing at Isa Colton's place. But it wouldn't stop her from checking out Rachel's house.

She smirked to herself. The local cops were stupid. Their patrols around the DA's home were so regular that Bethany was able to beat them at their game. Walk by the house in between the cruisers, peek in windows when she could. But she'd had to be more careful this past week, since the incident that made all those police show up a week ago.

If only her video feeds were enough. It was one thing to see James on her tablet screen but nothing like seeing him live, in person. He looked drawn, fatigued, if the grainy footage was accurate. She'd put the life back in him soon.

Very soon.

"YOU CAN CHANGE your mind, Rachel. Don't be stubborn on my account." He felt like such a jerk, as if he'd mentally wrestled Rachel into white-water rafting. In a sense he had, not realizing how awful her past experience had been. Now that he did, he wanted to do anything but stir up her anxiety. She'd had more than her share with Bethany stalking them. But despite her misgivings, she refused to back down.

"No way. You're right, James. I need a break. This will be fun." She spoke through a forced smile that would usually make him laugh, but he was too worried about her anxiety.

"Get your helmets on after you fasten your life vests, please." Their welcome guide was a petite woman whose commanding voice belied her stature.

Rachel expertly donned her vest, but he noticed her fingers were trembling and she kept biting her lower lip.

"I mean it. Let's do something else." Guilt wrenched at his gut. "This was stupid of me."

"Stop it, James." Her stubbornness soaked through each word. He paused after tightening his helmet and faced her. Under her helmet, blue eyes sparked determination. "I'm a grown woman. If I didn't want to do this, I wouldn't. Besides, I think it's about time I stop allowing every single thing about my past run my life." Her eyes widened at her last, and she blinked. "I can't believe I said that."

A warm sense of identification with Rachel punched out from under his ribs, spreading across his abdomen. "I can. It's admirable that you've been so active in righting your father's wrongs. You've done more than anyone I know to repair and protect your family legacy. Many would have walked away." Hadn't he been in that category before he'd gone through the hell of being stalked, the joy of becoming a father? Chasing the next court win, the next raise?

"Including help spring a criminal from jail?" Her mouth twisted.

"You mean Ronald Spence?" He needed her to know it wasn't her fault that the shady character was about to walk free. "The Truth Foundation, and your involvement before you became DA, isn't going to lose its purpose or integrity because of this. Spence is who he is, from everything I've read. He'll show his true colors soon enough. If it turns out he's the innocent man he claims, all the better."

"But if not, he's got the potential to harm many. His connections are...vast." Her gaze darkened. "Maybe, instead of accepting the invitation to run for DA, I should have focused on the Truth Foundation, taken a private job."

"No. You're right where you're supposed to be." Standing with little more than inches between them, he was dumbstruck by his own words, exactly the thought that nudged him day and night. Was this where he was meant to be? Next to Rachel? Because that was where he wanted to be more than anywhere else. Save for being with his baby girl. He opened his mouth to tell her, then shut it.

Not the time, bro. Not with Bethany still out there.

"Maybe you're right. I don't know, and good job on distracting me from my nerves, by the way." Her grin belied her shaking hands. He leaned in and gave her a hug. Her body stiffened for a split second before melting against his. "Thanks for your patience with my neuroses. I have a lot more than a fear of rafting!"

"You're perfect, just the way you are." He stopped short of calling her babe. But only with effort.

Even with two layers of flotation device between them it was easy to know why it always felt natural to be with her. Rachel not only shared his enthusiasm for the law and debating various sides of an issue, his love of the outdoors, and now his adoration of Iris; Rachel understood him at a gut level. He'd never dated or been with a woman long-term who seemed to be able to read his mind. Making her happy had somehow become his life's mission.

"Mmm, this feels so good." She gave him an extra-tight squeeze before stepping back. Her eyes had brightened, the worry lines that framed her mouth gone.

"Looks like we're up." He walked to the ticket desk

and displayed the verification code on his phone. He'd paid online.

"Kiriakis, party of two? Both adults? Experienced rafters?" The clerk looked at each of them.

"No, we're both pretty inexperienced."

"Not true." She looked up at him, determination etched in every line of her expression. "We can handle up to Class III. Just nothing more, please."

"Okay, will do. I need your wrists, please." The cashier wrapped the bracelets snugly on their wrists before pointing at an area where several small groups of people stood, awaiting their individual raft guides. "Before you go join the group, go to the gear cage. Select a wet suit, booties and life jacket that fit. Your guide will give you your oars."

The next two hours were full of preparation for the half-day trip. A staff member ensured their equipment fit correctly and took them through a few drills so they'd know the strokes they'd need on the river.

James watched for any signs that Rachel had changed her mind and wanted to back out. He'd call it quits at the least indication of doubt from her. The regret churning in his gut over his callous decision melted away as it appeared Rachel not only was willing to go through with it but she also seemed to be enjoying herself. The tension released from his shoulders and he unclenched his jaw, wiggling it.

Finally, they were free of the dangers that stalked them in Blue Larkspur.

Chapter Eighteen

"Okay, you're all about to have the ride of your lives. Water conditions today are good, with the runoff just beginning. It won't be the fastest ride ever but it'll be thrilling nonetheless." Their guide was paid to be enthusiastic, but Rachel thought he could ease back on the "fastest" and "thrilling."

With James's constant gaze on her, she couldn't let him see her trepidation. Which had dissipated loads since she'd first realized his surprise day trip was rafting. So far, the staff had been positive and supportive, and she didn't expect anything different once they were launched into the river. And it was April, for heaven's sake. Not the height of summer, when the river's fury would be at its strongest.

"You doing okay?" He spoke quietly as they were herded along with the other groups onto a bus.

"I'm good. Honest. I'm ready. If we had to do one more white-water or man-overboard drill in the parking lot, I was going to jump in the river on my own."

"Yeah, it seems a little much, but it won't when we navigate the rapids."

"I've heard that this part of the river is a lot of fun, and pretty tame. Are you sure you won't be bored?"

"Getting to spend the whole day with you? Never." The flash of—attraction?—in his eyes piqued her awareness. Except, the light in his gaze when he looked at her wasn't passing desire. It was something she wasn't ready to identify, not until she got her heart screwed on straight.

The bus pulled up to a concrete boat launch, and the rafters were quickly assigned rafts and guides. Rachel's curiosity rose when she realized it was only going to be her and James in their raft, plus the guide.

She nudged James's ribs. "Why is everyone else going in groups of six or eight?"

"Not sure. That's what we were supposed to be in."

"Hey, folks. I'm Chet." A fortyish man with an athletic build approached them. His grin was a mile wide and he literally took bouncing steps. "You must be the Colton group."

Rachel shot a glance at James. She didn't remember the ticket taker saying her name, but James must have included it when he did online registration.

"We are, but I thought we were in a bigger group."

"We had several large groups that requested Class I or II max today. The staff said you wanted Class III, and the company aims to please. Come right over here and we'll get started." He led them to a place away from the main crowd, to a smaller four-person raft.

Rachel's insides began to quake, but she ignored the overreaction. It was simple anticipatory butterflies, nothing more. The drills, combined with all the equipment she'd donned, gave her a sense of safety she didn't have as a kid on the river.

You can do this.

James tugged on her vest, kept her back as the guy bounced ahead several steps.

"This isn't what I booked. Let's reschedule."

"James, it's okay. Really. We'd be bored silly on a Class I or II ride all day. And honestly? Being with you is all I care about." *Whoa.* Had she just said that? Trying to cover up her gabbing, she gave him a wide grin. "Let's go with it."

"Okay. Yes, let's do it." White teeth flashed before he leaned in and kissed her. Quick, definite, warming.

They caught up to Chet and, within minutes, were in the raft and floating on the wide, flat river. Chet wasn't a talker but stayed on the front bench while leaving them to the back one. It was easy to imagine being alone with James, telling him all of her deepest secrets and dreams.

Focus on the ride, girlfriend.

Trees loomed from both banks, many sporting the bright green buds that heralded spring. The first half hour was the kind of ride that would have gotten Rachel back on a river sooner than in over two decades. But she knew that it could change with little warning.

Not unlike her life over the past several weeks.

"Get ready to rumble, folks. Follow my signals." Chet shouted over his shoulder at the same moment she saw the rocks jutting from the river. Because the water was still low, many more boulders were visible than would be in a couple of months. Chills ran over her, and it wasn't from the weather. The wet suit kept her warm and dry.

"You've got this." James spoke in her ear so that Chet wouldn't hear. She tried to give him a brave smile and he winked. Tears welled at the simple gesture.

The rapids came on fast and hard, and Rachel focused on Chet's oar, where and how he was placing it, and copied his moves. The raft twisted and bumped, making her stomach dip. They raced past rocks that knifed out of the water and she hissed in her breath, prayed they'd clear. They did, but then they were catapulted toward a large wall of granite, faster and faster, with no reprieve in sight. Just when she thought their paddling was in vain, the raft turned left, avoiding the hazard, and they were once again on calm water.

Joy erupted from deep inside, and she let it bubble over in fits of laughter with a few whoops thrown in. "That was a rush!" She looked at James for confirmation. His smile matched her elation. Before she could stop herself, she leaned over and gave him a kiss, full on his lips as he'd done earlier. Rachel would have lingered longer at the way his mouth tasted, but the boat jerked, throwing her on her bottom.

"Please stay seated at all times, folks." Chet barely looked back at them.

"What are we, cattle?" She muttered the words for her own benefit, but James's chuckle told her he'd heard and agreed with her assessment. Awareness infused her from her throat, across her breasts and between her legs. Only James's laugh could turn her on as quickly as his tongue.

His profile against the rugged river was something she'd never forget. He caught her staring and grinned.

"Enjoying yourself, are you?"

"I am. I can't thank you enough."

"No thanks necessary. I'm glad it's not a total bust."

She looked around at the changing scenery. They'd left the wide, deceptively serene river behind them and they were moving faster through a narrower passage. Mountains rose on all sides, and as she looked forward she saw what she'd heard someone call the cattle chute. As in, they were going to move a lot faster through a bottleneck.

"Okay, get ready to ride through the chute, folks."

Rachel would have thought she'd be alarmed as they picked up speed, helpless to stop the raft's forward momentum as jagged rocks emerged from the water on either side. One oar in the water at the wrong angle and they'd be capsized or worse. But as she sat next to James, thigh-to-thigh, shoulder-to-shoulder, she knew she'd never felt more secure. Plus she'd studied the topographical map on display at the rafting center and knew that there was a lot more wide, calm water than rough in this particular part of the river.

"Look, up ahead." James pointed, the sun sparking gray flecks in the depths of his green eyes. The same as Iris's. "See that thin line? It looks like a tree trunk?"

She followed his finger out to maybe a quarter-mile ahead of them and saw what looked like a straight tree, but as she lifted her gaze higher, higher, there were no branches, no treetop.

"What is it?"

"It's where the river forks. We're going to the left,

to the quieter side. The line is the way the rock was carved out eons ago."

"That's wild." She breathed out her wonder as the increasing waves jostled the raft, pushing her into James's side. His arm came around her shoulders and they looked at one another.

"Is this okay?" The pure concern and awareness in his gaze, from the way he seemed to soak in her image to his steadying grasp on her upper arm, further stoked the desire that she constantly carried for him alone.

"It's perfect." She closed her eyes and lifted her lips for his kiss. This time they lingered. Let Chet do his job.

Suddenly the raft made a hard right and they were both thrown to James's side of the inflatable craft. A scream escaped her as she clung to James with one hand and the side of the craft with her other. With her feet no longer under Chet's bench, she had nothing to anchor her to the inflatable. Terror squeezed tight on her fight to stay in the raft.

"Stop!" James's shout to Chet sounded her mental warning alarms. Still on her knees in the space between their bench and Chet's, she righted herself and got on the seat. She tried to shove her feet under the front bench. Chet's weight crushed the inflatable seat and made an L-shape, but Chet was leaning so far forward that her feet weren't getting the grip they needed. She bounced high in the air, then hit the raft hard as the current increased.

They were going to capsize.

"Chet!" James leaned over and grabbed the guide's shoulder, tried to yank him back. But Chet was on some kind of mission, his focused paddle strokes steering them exactly where they weren't supposed to go.

To the Class VI rapids only the most experienced white-water rafters dared attempt.

In an instant, the images of him and Rachel being separated from the bigger groups, the way Chet had seemed to appear out of nowhere, and the threat Rachel's current defendant, Brian Parson, made in court fit together. Fury mowed through him and he prepared to act. This wasn't going to end like Rachel's childhood rafting incident.

It could end worse.

"Use your oar!" James pointed left and Rachel complied, grasping her oar's handle and paddling to counteract Chet's deadly maneuvers. James mirrored her actions on his side of the raft.

Their movements fought with Chet's for what felt like hours. Water sprayed in his face and he strained to see if their efforts were turning the boat. His shoulders burned along with every muscle in his body. Rachel kept up, but even his pride in her efforts wasn't enough to sustain the energy they needed to fight Chet's frenzied strokes. The water's frigid temperature was evident as it repeatedly hit his face.

Keep going, keep going.

While they were able to slow Chet's forward momentum they weren't able to get the raft turned to the left.

"James!" Her scream tore through him.

"Rachel! Hang on!" He grabbed her arm and settled her in the raft's center. She put her oar between her legs and gripped the raft's bench in front of her.

Now or never.

James dropped his oar and dove for Chet, grabbed him around his neck and pulled him backward. Chet's arm swung back, oar in hand, and sideswiped James on the head, against his cheekbone. Bright spots danced in his sight, but he didn't loosen his hold on Chet, who kicked his legs out, one foot landing square in James's face. He tasted blood but didn't stop. He couldn't. Rachel's life depended on him.

The fight rocked the raft more than the river and his hands were wet, cold and bloodied as he struggled to stop Chet. The raft cleared the rapids right before they passed the fork in the water and their ride leveled out, flat again.

James pinned Chet down, the man gasping for air.

"Why did you do that?" James shouted, needing answers. "Who are you working for?"

Chet didn't answer, and the roar of the river prevented further discussion.

It was too late. The raft headed for the wrong side of the fork, to the right, to the stretch of Class VI rapids. James remembered the map's description, in bold red letters.

ONLY FOR ADVANCED MASTER RAFTERS

Chapter Nineteen

Was this how her life would end? After a lifetime of striving to follow in her father's legal footsteps minus the criminal turn, she was going to die in a river-rafting accident?

Images of Iris flashed in her mind, of the day she was born. Of when she'd first met James, how everything had seemed fresh and all possibilities were on the table. And the sight of James with Iris, holding their daughter, his smile reaching out to Rachel and triggering the idea that they had an instant-family connection.

At least Iris would have many aunts and uncles to help raise her, keep Rachel's memory alive.

"No!" The shock in James's voice forced her back to the present, to the sight of Chet purposefully jumping out of the raft into the seething frigid waters. James immediately tossed in the safety line, but his attempt to rescue Chet was unwanted. Chet grabbed the line, tugged hard as if to bring James in the water with him, before raising both hands, showing they were empty and he was not interested in getting back. The fork and knife-edge stone outcropping neared, and she was certain they were about to witness Chet's body being smashed to bits against the granite.

A woman somewhere screamed and with a start she realized it was her. She was screaming, out of control as James put a hand on either of her shoulders, one still holding his oar.

"He's headed for that bank." He pointed. Incredulous, she watched as Chet appeared to float atop the water, using his vest and the current to get him where he wanted. Chet stood up in about a foot of water, the current near the shore remarkably calmer, no matter it was less than one hundred meters from the raft and teeming water. Facing them, he offered a smile she'd always remember as the look of pure evil. Along with a rude hand gesture.

Chet had wanted them to drown!

Brian Parson's threat rang through her mind. *"I'll see you in hell, Rachel Colton."*

"Listen to me, Rachel." James tapped on her helmet to get her attention as he enunciated slowly while he yelled, waiting for her to nod and acknowledge his words after each sentence. The raft stopped heaving, though it moved more quickly as the current shifted.

"We can do this. Follow my lead," he shouted.

"But Chet!" Chet needed to be apprehended. "I'll call Theo!"

"No time. There probably isn't any service, anyway. Look." He pointed toward the right side of the river, to a bank where a group of three men stood, throwing a line to a bright orange speck—Chet. "He planned this. This was one of your defendant's men. We'll call Theo when we're safe."

"Could it be Bethany, James? I can't tell if they're all men from here."

"It doesn't matter who it is. All we need to focus on is staying above water and safe."

Safe.

James's words confirmed her fear. The sheer rock cliff that careened toward them was going to kill them.

"James! I can't do this!"

"Do what I do, and we'll get through it, okay?" His eyes blazed with intent. It was impossible to argue with his determination. "This is fast but a good place to catch our breath. We'll get through the rapids."

She nodded.

Before they had to begin paddling through white water she took her phone, in its waterproof case, and snapped as many shots of Chet and the other men as possible. When James saw her, he grinned.

"I'm at least good for proof!" She yelled over the roar of the water, increasing in decibels with each second.

"We'll need it to call in for our pickup. Put it away, fast!"

Rachel complied, but her exultation that she'd captured decent shots of Chet and his fellow culprits deflated as quickly as the water turned from fast but smooth to dangerously choppy. She'd no sooner zipped her phone securely into the fanny pack she'd worn over her wet suit than James was touching her shoulder, indicating how she needed to hold her oar.

The next two hours were the scariest of Rachel's life. Or at least, they should have been. Except she had the steadiest guy next to her, no matter how rough the ride got. As they progressed downriver, she knew that if she let her concentration slip the least bit, she risked upending the trip for both of them—literally. While they were in wet suits and wore vests, there was no one around to throw them a line, no other rafts in sight. She vowed that as soon as there was a chance she'd try for a signal and call Theo.

Finally they turned a long, slow bend and she allowed herself to look around at Colorado's spring beauty in full display. The midday sun reflected off the water, its clear depths belying the miles of rapids they'd traversed.

"How did Lewis and Clark do it?" She marveled at the rawness, centuries later, of their surroundings.

"They hiked a lot of it, carrying a canoe." His dry response made her smile.

"If you'd told me we'd be joking after that…"

"Now would be a good time to see if we have reception, call in to the tour company. I can do it." He had his phone out and Rachel couldn't stop tears of relief from welling when she saw he'd made a connection. She listened as he gave a rundown of what had happened and requested a pickup somewhere near a place called Miner's Exit within an hour or so.

When he disconnected, his eyes were full of concern. "I need you to call Theo, tell him what's happened. Send him the photos. Hurry."

"Of course. Good thinking." She'd been so relieved to have cleared the rapids that she'd momentarily forgotten what got them in this exact location to begin with. As soon as she'd left Theo a voice mail and sent the photos, the familiar crawl of discomfort up her neck, across her chest returned.

"Why did you tell me to hurry? And what's Miner's Exit?"

"Miner's Exit is our last challenge today."

Her heart threw itself against her rib cage. "What are you saying? You mean there are more rapids?" Her throat was raw and she fought against the disappointment that squeezed at her tear ducts and hoped James thought any wetness on her cheeks was from river water.

"Babe, you're doing great, and I know you can handle the next stretch."

"Can the empowerment coaching and give it to me straight, Kiriakis."

"There's a reason Chet, and whoever employs him, sent us to this part of the river. It's notoriously unpredictable, no matter the time of year. Since snowmelt hasn't started in earnest yet, the rocks are an issue."

"So we paddle around them." Like the other rocks they'd avoided, some just inches below the surface.

"Some of the rapids have crevices that few have survived, if they go under. Our entire focus is to stay in the raft."

"Isn't it always?"

"More so this time, Rachel."

Regret and sorrow flooded her thoughts. "I'm so sorry, James. I got you into this. This is the work of Parson, I know it."

"You're kidding me. It could be Bethany. Who knows? Either way, I'm the one who planned a rafting trip and didn't cancel after I found out your repulsion to white water."

"How would Parson or Bethany even know we were coming here?"

"I used my cell phone and laptop from your house. You know better than I do how resourceful the local crime rings are. It's easy to intercept a call, and if someone was monitoring your home, they could have hacked my computer."

"But everything's encrypted."

"I had to phone to verify my credit card. Their site was down that day for maintenance. That has to be it. It wasn't Bethany—I can't imagine she's that computer savvy. Her expertise seems to be more with shock actions, like the explosive. But a crime syndicate has many resources. They intercepted my call, I'm almost positive. It's the only way this makes sense." He shook his head. "I regret every bit of this, Rachel."

"Please don't. It seems we have an issue."

His eyes filled with surprise. "Issue? You mean besides being stalked by my ex, and now one of the criminals you're going to put away?"

"Nope. The problem with us, as I see it, James, is that we get one another in trouble every time we're together."

"Iris is anything but trouble."

"But she wasn't planned. We can't ignore that, no matter how much we love her now. We didn't plan to be the victims of bad guys, but we are. Folks like that are going to do what they're going to do. It doesn't matter at this point. All I care about is getting home safe. You're going to get us there."

"You trust me?" He spoke with a tentativeness she'd never heard in his voice.

"Implicitly." She looked downriver, to where the wide calm appeared to drop from sight. To where they'd face life-threatening rapids. "I suggest we use our special mojo, whatever it is, and finish up this ride in style. I completely trust your judgment. Wherever you tell me to paddle, I'm on it."

JAMES HAD TOLD Rachel the truth; he'd ridden through a similar stretch of the river more than once. Maybe as many as four times. But it hadn't been on Class VI, he was certain. And he'd been a heck of a lot younger, and there had always been a guide with his group.

He quietly planned his strategy, humbled by Rachel's complete reliance on him. His insides were tight as wet knots and he made himself take a few deep breaths, consciously relaxed his shoulders.

Not for the first time he wished the rapids, or the threat of facing the criminals, were the worst of his concerns. Rachel was his biggest worry. One look at her pinched expression, the way her eyes flashed stubborn sparks while her body quaked with fear, sent a shock of terror through him. It was his fault that Rachel was being pushed to her mental limits. Today, the past few weeks, the time she'd been pregnant and then a single mom without his help, it all added up. He vowed to get them to safety and protect her and Iris no matter the cost to his life. If he had to quit his new job to guard them 24/7, he would.

"Less staring at me and more looking at the river, Kiriakis." Her voice trembled but without her customary spunk. Surprise sent a warm shock through his chest.

"On it, Colton."

The change in tempo was deceptive as they slowed to a comparative crawl after being rushed through the gorge.

"Maybe the rapids won't be so bad today." But Rachel's white knuckles betrayed her attempt to remain positive.

"Hey." He covered her hands with his. "You've got this. The Arkansas River has nothing on us."

She smiled with trembling lips and wide eyes, and he wondered if her confidence in him was warranted.

"James!" The craft swayed, and they were in the rapids.

The next forty minutes were the most challenging James had ever experienced. As before, Rachel stayed with him, not once complaining or setting her oar on her lap in exhaustion.

His shoulders and triceps started to complain when they had about three minutes left, from what he'd calculated it should take for the trip. But instead of the usual aches and pains of a grueling workout, a searing pain in his right shoulder was his only warning before he lost his grip on the oar. His left hand held on, but he couldn't direct the raft the way he'd been.

"What's wrong?" Rachel screamed more than yelled, her voice barely perceptible above the din of the current.

"My shoulder!"

"Tell me what to do!"

"You're doing it!" He had to focus, ignore the pain, keep Rachel safe. It was all that mattered.

RACHEL TRIED TO ignore the fear and panic that fought to take over her thoughts, tripping them into existential dread. The river was unforgiving, and her body was at its limit.

"Left, left!" James directed her like a coxswain, his

direction always spot-on, but the inflatable raft wasn't a crew shell and her efforts were all the more difficult thanks to the personal flotation device the river trip guide had buckled her into.

You can do it. Almost there.

The mantra was harder to hang on to and on the verge of becoming laughable. The possibility that she and James wouldn't make it through these rapids pricked and stabbed at her hard-won positivity.

"No!" She paddled furiously, using the adrenaline that seemed to come from nowhere.

"Slower, easy." Sternness laced his shout and she knew she'd overcompensated. "That's it."

"How much long—" Her request was denied more quickly than any court proceeding as the raft lurched into another stretch of churning water. The harsh motion sent James, unable to balance with an injured arm, into the space between the two benches. The momentum of his weight tipped the craft precariously on its back edge and James slid into the frothy water as she was tossed backward, hitting the waves bottom-first.

V-shape, legs up, let the current take you. Her body had somehow absorbed the safety video and she stared at her feet, up in front of her, her arms at her sides. The PFD kept her buoyant and she lifted her arms up, out of the way of submerged rocks.

James.

"James!" She tried to yell, but the spray and exertion of the last hours captured her breath, making her voice tiny. The current spun her, lifted her, dropped her like a rock.

And then, quiet calm. She'd made it through the rapids! Sunlight dappled the water lapping the beach almost directly in front of her. Several people stood there, waving and shouting. Fear smothered her exultation. Were they Chet's buddies?

Something large bumped her and she turned her head, afraid to look. But when she saw James floating next to her, his grin wide, it immediately dispelled her trepidation.

"You did it, Rachel!" He whooped and pumped his fist, then grimaced.

"*We* did it. We made it."

"Here!" Shouts reached them, and she saw the familiar rafting-company logo emblazoned on a truck, the safety lines being tossed toward them.

"Grab one of the ropes, Rachel." James grabbed her hand and they half swam, half floated together until she was able to grab one of the lifelines. "Let me hang on to you, while you hold on to the rope. We're there, babe!"

Chapter Twenty

"We're not going to agree on this." Rachel wiped Iris's mouth of the butternut-squash-and-cereal blend she'd chowed down on for dinner. "You're convinced Bethany is behind everything bad that's happened to me, to us, and I think it's more likely the work of Brian Parson and his fellow thugs. My siblings regularly post what they think are funny memes about white-water rafting to my social media page. I set my privacy settings tight but nothing's impenetrable, not at all. I'm certain he pulled strings to sabotage our raft."

It'd been two weeks since the white-water-raft event, and since then, Brian Parson admitted he'd "turned on" his network to "send the DA a solid message." He'd said "Get me convicted at your own risk." She'd gone on to rest her case against him, and he'd been found guilty of all counts of racketeering and assault and now faced additional charges of kidnapping, attempted assault and possible attempted homicide for the rafting event. Chet, the pseudo raft guide, and his jerk associates, like the rats they were, had scattered and disappeared, still at large. Theo expected they'd show up again before long. It was a matter of time for such lowlifes.

James methodically rinsed and loaded dishes into the dishwasher as they talked across the island. Rachel had rolled the high chair to the counter so that she could more easily hand the removable tray to James for cleaning. "Here you go."

His hands were sexier while soapy, and for some reason, that inexplicably annoyed her. "You really should have let me do the dishes. How's your shoulder?"

"Good as new, almost." He grinned. The orthopedic doc who examined his shoulder after their boating adventure had instructed James to rest it, take ibuprofen and ice as necessary. He'd been in daily physical therapy, which he swore up and down had worked miracles.

"You and I are alike. We don't want to ever take a break from work. We're lucky we enjoy what we do so much. But that means it's never a good time to get things done for ourselves."

"You mean like your intention to get back to a regular workout routine? Which, by the way, other than for your stress levels, you absolutely don't need." His words stroked her awareness, raised the tiniest hairs on her forearm, her nape. And got the fire in her center burning for him.

"No, I mean like rotator cuff surgery for reinjuring that same shoulder. I get that you don't want to even think about being laid up for a few days. But they said it won't be as bad as when you were in college. Surgical techniques have improved." That's what he'd told her right after. But once they got back into their regular routines, James had pooh-poohed any reference to his injury, saying it had pained him most in the moment, after all the paddling they'd done.

"I'm not committing to such major surgery right now. No way." He placed the items they didn't put in the washer in the rack atop the counter and dried his hands. "We've both got too much going on."

"Since Parson is locked up, you mean you're not considering it until Bethany is out of our lives, don't you? Have you considered that maybe Parson has been responsible for all of our troubles this last month or so?"

"No. I wish we had concrete evidence on Bethany, and I know you do, too. You're going to have to trust me on this one, Rachel. I know her ways. She's behind your fuel-tank contamination and the restaurant explosion, I'm positive."

"But we haven't had any incidents for two weeks." Not since Brian Parson claimed responsibility for the brick through her window and sending Chet to sabotage the rafting excursion.

"I'm not considering moving out until we know for certain Bethany's been shut down. She hasn't shown up back in Denver since I left, so it tracks with her being here."

"Her mother doesn't seem worried, according to Theo." Theo had investigated Bethany's history personally. "She told him that Bethany has had periods of disappearing like this throughout her life."

"And I've no doubt they line up with the other men she's harassed. Her behavior has escalated over the last five years, remember. She'd been known for doing a nasty thing or two, like showing up unexpectedly at a place of employment, before moving on to her next victim, that is, another man to date. The man before me had a dead rat left on his doorstep. The only reason the police think she stopped is because she met me. She won't stop until she's forced to."

Rachel watched him finish up in the kitchen, with Iris settling against her, sleepy and ready for a quick bath before bed. She'd miss talking to him like this, after dinner, as the day wound down. Doubt seeped into her heart. James wasn't her father. Maybe she should think about the "more" he'd mentioned more than once.

"Here, I'll take her while you run her bath." He held out his arms, but she noticed that his injured one wasn't outstretched as far.

"Why don't you relax tonight? You did the dishes. I'll call for you when she's ready to go down."

"Fair enough." The fact that he didn't argue confirmed that he was still hurting. Rachel bit back a grin but not before his gaze landed on her mouth.

"Tell me."

"I never thought it was possible, but I've met someone as stubborn as me."

"Iris?" His feigned innocence tugged on her funny bone and she laughed.

"Oh, she's got both of our genes, I'm certain." She stood only a foot from James and he leaned in and planted a kiss on the baby's head, as he often did. But tonight she couldn't take her gaze off his profile, his mouth, his scent.

As if he read her mind, he didn't pull back all the way but instead kissed her full on the mouth. His lips were firm, the kiss validation that he felt the attraction between them, too.

His eyes were heavy lidded, his pupils dilated when

he pulled back. Iris reached out and grabbed a hunk of Rachel's hair.

"Ow, baby!" She looked away, needing the break between them, from his intensity.

"Rach." Imploring, his request reverberated with need.

"Yes?"

"I've never stopped wanting to be with you. I know we've had this silent agreement to keep our distance, but—"

She held up her free hand. "Wait. We'll finish this conversation after Iris is asleep."

"I want more than talking, babe." His laughing reply followed her down the hallway to Iris's room.

BETHANY COULD BARELY make out their figures on the screen when she was this mad. It had taken her days to work out a way to get more cash without being traced, which meant she'd had to go back to Denver and ask her mother for a money order. Her mom was useless most days but had agreed to keep this visit a secret when Bethany had promised she'd buy her mother a new car with her next job. She'd been fired from her most recent place of employment but the lack of a paycheck didn't bother her. She'd have James in hand soon enough.

All she had to do was get James away from the brat and its mother, Rachel Colton. When she and James returned to Denver, everything would be wonderful and she'd be able to find an even better job, making more money. And James was generous. He'd contribute to her mother's car fund.

Mom had said that some detective type had been

sniffing around, but she promised she hadn't ratted Bethany out. Her mother knew what was best for herself. Not only would Bethany's promise of new wheels disappear, but Mom might need an attitude readjustment in the form of a crack to her head. Bethany had given her mother some lessons over the years, mostly in the form of cutting her off financially. She'd only had to drive one lesson home by hurting her mother a few years back, when she told the cops where her daughter was hiding out.

Yeah, she'd fixed her mother but good that time. But it was nothing like what she planned to do to Rachel Colton and her kid.

Not even close.

JAMES COULDN'T STOP thinking about Rachel's lips, her soft skin, the way her inviting smile told him that she wanted him, too. He walked around the living room, knowing he should have gone for a run earlier today when he'd had the chance. But he hadn't been able to shake the sense of danger that clung to him, even after that loser Brian Parson admitted he'd orchestrated Chet's life-threatening ruse. A week out and the terror still woke him at night, bathed him in cold sweat, his heart racing to beat the nightmare of continuous white water and being unable to find Rachel.

His gaze caught on the fireplace mantel, where Rachel kept several knickknacks including a beautiful photo of her and Iris. He fingered the glazed pottery she'd mentioned she liked to collect from local Colorado artists. One vase in particular had the same shade as her eyes. He lifted it absentmindedly, killing time until she put their baby to bed.

A *plunk* caught his attention and he made sure he hadn't tipped the vase, spilling any contents out. No. It remained upright in his hand. Investigating further, he saw a small black button on the oak shelf and picked it up. And realized it wasn't a button, but a tiny glass lens about the size of a dime with a short wire coming out the back. His mind tried to convince himself it wasn't what it obviously was.

"James!" Rachel called to him from the nursery. Iris was ready for bed.

"Coming." He pocketed the camera, and quickly scanned the rest of the room for more. Sure enough, he found two more, one on the top edge of the television, and one in the corner of a bookshelf. Maybe Rachel had placed them there, the usual nanny cam. He hoped she had.

RACHEL STARED AT the three small disc-shaped cameras in James's palm. They stood in the hallway, outside the nursery, where Iris had fallen asleep to her father's voice reading *Goodnight Moon*.

"Those aren't mine. My brother installed outside cameras for me at about the same time you arrived in town. The security specialists I hired upgraded that system. This isn't their work." She ran her hands over her head. "Oh my goodness, James. I've been so busy between getting you acquainted with Iris and my case-loads that I never noticed these. We've got to check the kitchen, the rest of the house. What if there are some in the baby's room?" Her pitch rose of its own volition, and

Rachel fought tears as her body began to shake. Neither reaction was from fear, but from deep-seated anger. How dare anyone get this close to her, to her child?

"Let's go into the living room and call Theo."

They sat next to one another on the sofa and she put her cell on speaker. She had Theo on speed dial as "Police Chief." She'd entered him into her phone years ago, as he was such a close family friend. Never would she have guessed she'd come to rely on him as much as she had these past weeks.

From how her mother behaved around the chief, she had to wonder if Isa was relying on Theo for far more than friendship these days. But there was no time to ponder family concerns tonight. She had to keep her focus narrowed on the safety of her immediate family. If anything happened to Iris, she'd never forgive herself. *Don't go there.*

It took Theo a bit to answer, and when he did, she heard laughter—and it sounded suspiciously similar to Isa's. Rachel wouldn't begrudge anyone some fun, but with her family's safety on the line, indignation rumbled under her breastbone.

"What can I do you for, Rachel?" Theo's voice vibrated with humor, too, as if he and whomever he was with had shared a great joke. Her initial annoyance melted into sweet relief. Theo was the one man she'd been able to rely upon since her father's death, besides her brothers.

You can rely on James. She paused, her words stuck in her throat.

"Rachel? You there?" No hint of laughter this time.

"Theo. Yes, yes, I'm here. I'm sorry to bother you

at this time of night, but I'm afraid there's a new development—an answer, really—to the question of how whoever's stalking me, or James, or both of us has figured out our movement patterns." She summarized what James had found.

"Do any of your windows or doors show signs of a break-in?" Theo was in full-on cop mode again.

"No, I checked." James spoke. Their gazes caught, and she realized he'd been busy while she was giving Iris her bath. "Every single window and door is secure. And judging by the dust that was on them when I found these camera devices, they've been here awhile."

"At least since the brick necessitated the woodwork repair on the transom." She relied on Emily to pick up around the house, but emphasized that the nanny's focus should always be on Iris, not cleaning. "I've been meaning to get a housekeeper, but it's not the right time."

"Good thing you haven't yet, Rachel. As James said, the dust lets us know the cameras have been there for at least a couple weeks. Plus your house is a newer build and they don't get as dusty as the older places." The way Theo broke it down into its simplest facts reassured her, almost as much as knowing James was still staying in her house.

"I agree. The air filters on my HVAC are top-of-the-line and keep the dust to a minimum. My guess is that these cameras have been here for several weeks." Fear worked its paralyzing grip up her spine as the ramifications of being watched for so long pressed in on her. Warm hands clasped her shoulders and began to knead. *James.* She mouthed "thank you" to him and then relaxed under his deft touch.

They continued to talk to Theo for the next several minutes, telling him the various cases they'd reviewed, listing possible suspects. But it all came back to Bethany.

"Listen, Theo, I understand that I'm looking at it through my unique perspective, having been stalked by Bethany Austin for so long. But I'm thinking that she placed these cameras." James's fingers stopped their magic on her shoulders as he gave all his attention to Theo. She immediately missed the connection of his skin on hers.

"It's possible James is right, Theo, but my money's still on Parson's criminal connections. It would explain how they knew our movements, and if there are mics embedded in the cameras, it all but confirms it. They would have heard James make the reservations, no need for a cell phone intercept."

James stood up and went to where he'd left the cameras, on the kitchen counter.

He frowned as he peered at the discs, sealed in a plastic bag. "I can't tell if there's a mic in these or not."

"Leave them be, and I'll have an officer stop by to collect them as evidence. Our tech expert will take a look at them. In the meantime, continue with your security measures—make sure all blinds are closed, leave all outdoor lights on 24/7 and expect an officer to stop by periodically to visibly check on you."

"Got it. Thank you, Theo." She almost added "Hi, Mom" but thought better of it. If it was Isa's voice she'd heard at the start of the call, her mother didn't want her to know she was there or she would have spoken up. And if it was another woman, Rachel didn't want to know. As the call ended, she recognized the sensation squeezing her heart. Regret at the thought of Theo caring for another person instead of her mother. She shook her head, silently told herself it was the stress of worrying about Iris's safety that had her thinking the errant thoughts.

"What's wrong?" James stared at her, his eyes bright with compassion.

"You mean minus being targeted by a bad person? I'm wondering if I should take Iris to my mother's, but the last thing I want is for whoever's doing this to go after her, too."

"If it's Bethany, she wants me, not you. Her pattern has always been to frighten, not actually harm anyone."

"I'm sorry I didn't back you up in front of Theo, but I don't think it's Bethany any longer, if ever. James, Theo's right. The reach of these thugs in a small town like Blue Larkspur is vast. Strings are pulled with the blink of an eye. For all we know, Parson knows you've been stalked and has made all these incidents appear to be related to Bethany. It makes sense, as I was working to put him away for a solid few months before you arrived in town. If it is him, then there's nothing to be concerned about as he's been found guilty on all charges, and after his harsh sentence yesterday, it should send a message to all the crooks to back off. That threats aren't going to keep justice from being served. You found the mics, so there's that, too. For all we know, they're not operational any longer."

"You could be right." James used the classic I-don't-agree-but-whatever line with a shrug.

Heat pierced her heart, but unlike moments earlier, it wasn't passion. "Excuse me?"

"You've blown off every suggestion I make that Bethany is behind all of this."

"That's not true. But why does it matter who's behind these acts when the bottom line is that harm could come to our baby?"

"No harm is coming to either of you as long as I'm here."

"Really? Because last time I checked, your presence didn't keep that loser Chet from almost getting us killed on the river. And what about the brick? And the explosion the first night we had dinner?" It didn't matter that she heard how strident her accusations sounded; the dam holding back her fear had burst open. Cold knowing washed through her veins, making her shiver.

She was a DA. It didn't matter that it was a new-to-her position. She'd worked in the prosecuting office long enough to know that a determined criminal could get what they wanted more often than not. Especially one connected to an established criminal ring, like her most recent defendant. Hadn't she seen it first with her own family, when her father had succumbed to the pressure to break the law?

"Hey, I hear you. It's been a scary, chaotic time. But let's keep the risk in perspective. Your defendant has been sentenced, so any pressure from him should be over."

"For now. The crime syndicates never completely go away, or if they do, another one pops up. Criminal law is a lot different from corporate." She put her hands on her hips. "Let's say you're right, and we don't have to worry about the likes of Chet again. What about Bethany? If she's behind even a fraction of these incidents, as you're so convinced, how are we going to stop her? Short of catching her in the act? What if Bethany's next stunt puts Iris in danger? I'd never forgive myself."

The air between them was heavy, spiked with the silent part of her declaration.

I'll never forgive you.

James's eyes narrowed and he leaned forward but remained standing at the counter. "Don't you think I'd do anything to have prevented those things from happening? I haven't risked losing a new job by working here, from your house, for kicks. I would never live with myself if anything happened to you or Iris. Our daughter is my top priority."

The heat in her gut turned sour as she recognized how harsh she'd been. James was feeling the pressure of the past weeks, just like her. She forced herself to take a few breaths before she replied.

"I know you haven't caused any of this. I don't blame you for Bethany, although—"

"If it is her, I brought her into your and Iris's life." His eyes blazed with anger and frustration, matching hers. But what she wasn't feeling yet saw in his gaze was the one thing she'd feared since she'd let him into her life again, let him become such a loving father to Iris.

Regret. James definitely regretted all that had befallen them since he'd arrived in Blue Larkspur. Her logical mind tried to reason and tell her that his regret had nothing to do with her, personally. With their relationship. Relationships were something she'd avoided, never wanted. Nothing serious, anyway. The wounds of her father's betrayal to her family ran deep. As she looked at James her heart wept with how much he'd come to mean to her, because anything besides coming together to raise Iris was too scary, too risky for her. She wasn't willing to do what committing to James would require. Trusting him with her heart, no holds barred.

You're co-parents, bottom line.

"It's been a long few weeks, James. Today was killer. I think we both need to sleep on this and regroup in the morning."

"And what then, Rachel? Spit it out." His expression was thunderous, and she got it—she wanted to scream her frustration out and would have, if it wouldn't wake their precious child.

"There's nothing for me to say. Nothing at all."

Chapter Twenty-One

When James woke, there was no brew strong enough to shake off the uneasy night he'd spent on the sofa. The cameras and what they represented had upset everything he'd been so certain about only a day earlier. That his presence alone kept Iris and Rachel safe. The white-water fiasco should have alerted him that there was more than one bad guy in Blue Larkspur, more than a single entity that wanted either Rachel, as DA, or him, as her partner, under their thumb. The police chief informed them that it appeared as though Bethany was behind what could have been a lethal rafting trip. James experienced no satisfaction at having been right about Bethany and her capabilities. It didn't erase all the other threats aimed at Rachel, from multiple sources.

He tossed a bagel into the toaster, *Rachel's* toaster, scrambled up the eggs he'd been making for them both each morning of his stay. He'd thought about not doing it this morning, to make the break cleaner, but Rachel was Iris's mom. He owed her this much.

She's more than your baby's mother.

His stomach twisted, and that unfamiliar ache deep in his chest cranked back up. It wasn't his heart; he knew he was in decent cardio shape, or had been before coming to Blue Larkspur and all it had dumped on him. Images of crashing into Rachel on the courthouse steps, running from the restaurant that first night out together, meeting Iris. Seeing his child for the first time, those eyes looking at him, the immediate connection. He hadn't needed the DNA test but did it for his daughter's benefit. He wanted her to always know that she was part of him.

And still would be—just on a different basis than living with her and her mother afforded him. He did a quick mental calculation. He could sell his swanky condo downtown and find a house closer to this neighborhood. Iris could spend time between his and Rachel's place; many children did so. His stomach twisted again. It wasn't ideal. He'd missed out on having a father since his dad had died when he was still only six years old. The last thing he wanted was for Iris to not have her dad with her 24/7.

"Morning." Rachel's voice was a hollow version of itself, and no amount of makeup could erase the dark circles under her beautiful eyes. His resolve to leave wavered. His mind screamed at him to beg her to let him stay.

No. She'd made it clear it was time to move on.

"Hey. Your eggs and half a bagel are ready."

"Thanks, but you don't have to do this. Make me food." She moved robotically, filling her coffee mug.

"You mean you don't want me to."

"That's probably best, isn't it?" She sighed, ran her fingers through her messy hair. "James. This isn't about you. I don't want you to leave here thinking that. We're good together, as Iris's parents. I'm not willing to risk that all because we're good in bed together."

"Good in bed…we're on different pages here, Rachel. Yes, we're very compatible in many ways, but there's more. I know you know there is." That's what angered him the most. Rachel was willfully turning her back on the possibility of not only a future together, but an incredible one at that.

"You've known about my father, what his misdeeds did to our family, from the beginning. I've been conditioned from a young age to have a healthy mistrust of men. Not what you want to hear, but I can't change who I am. It's unfair of you to expect me to be able to take a chance on lo—" She stopped herself, shook her head. "A chance on anything permanent. Other than being here for Iris."

"I never saw you as a coward, Rachel." He held back his temper, but only from years of courtroom experience. Some things cut too deep to express in words, anyway.

"So you agree we need to keep our lives separate." Her expression was as flat as her statement. Her gaze caught on the table, the neat stack of computer equipment, his suitcase. Packed.

"We need space, I'll grant you that. I'll get back to you within a few days. I'm looking for a place near here, so that we can share custody as easily as possible."

"That sounds good." She sipped her coffee, didn't so much as glance up from her phone. When he heard the front door unlock a full hour before the usual time, Rachel finally spoke. "I have to be in court earlier than usual today. I asked Emily to show up now. Theo's put all of his assets on me and my family. Bethany will be caught the moment she makes her next move. You're free to go, James."

Their gazes met, and he fought against the powerful urge to walk around the counter, pull her into his arms and break down her solid ice wall of defensiveness with his kiss.

She's Iris's mother. Period. He'd done nothing to help them in the end. He'd only brought more danger with him. If Bethany was around, and his gut told him she was, it was best for him to draw her away from all things Rachel and Iris.

"Okay, then. I'll text you when I have a place near here to move into."

"Sounds good." Iris's cry pierced the room, via the baby monitor. He put his bags down, ready to go to his baby. But Emily walked into the kitchen and smiled.

"I'll go get her. You two get ready."

"Right." James grabbed his things and headed for the front door. Only after he'd thrown his stuff into his car and backed out of the driveway did he rub on his chest, trying to unfurl the tight ball under his rib cage.

If his cardiac health was good, what was this pain in his heart?

Can it be love?

THE NEXT WEEK, Rachel fell back into the routine she'd had before James, before being attacked and stalked. Well, almost. Emily's constant presence combined with her mother's frequent visits gave her the reassurance that everything really was okay. Back to normal. Parson had been sent to jail, no further "Bethany" incidents had happened, and Rachel had her evenings to herself again once Iris was asleep.

There were no more long nights in front of her laptop, searching for clues as to who'd want to harm her. No late-night coffee talk…or any other activity.

Her cheeks heated as she pulled into her driveway, grateful the grueling workweek was behind her. It had been the longest she'd had yet as DA. Not that she could put her finger on what exactly had been so rough. Her caseload had never changed, so it wasn't that. She'd been able to be home for dinner each night, giving her maximum time with her baby girl.

You miss James.

Yes, so what? She missed having someone, another adult, to talk to after Emily and Isa left. It wasn't as if James was gone…forever. He was Iris's dad, and no matter how she'd begun to doubt their ability to maintain anything but the most professional of relationships, she believed he'd be back for Iris.

Her heart pounded in her ears and she gulped, fighting back the onslaught of an emotion she'd thought long buried. The driving force behind her frantic adolescence, always needing to be the best at the law, to right her father's wrongs.

Sorrow. The old frenemy snaked around her heart and began to peel back the layers of her defenses, which weren't many. Not since she'd allowed James and how he'd cared for her, for Iris to invade her fortifications. Sinking to the cold kitchen floor, she rested her head on her knees and let the tears flow. A good, solid boohoo was just what she needed.

If she acknowledged her grief at the breakdown of their non-relationship, it would have to stop hurting, wouldn't it?

Chapter Twenty-Two

"I told you, Jake, she's not going to be that kind of co-parent. She's already let me bond with Iris, and I don't anticipate any problems going forward." James spoke to his brother as he sipped his first coffee of the weekend. Clad in a black T-shirt and sweatpants, he was glad it was Saturday, his day to regroup. And grateful that his entire family knew all about Iris. They couldn't wait to meet her, either, but James wanted to do this on Rachel's timeline.

"Right. So tell me, why aren't you still living there, again?"

"We've figured out that the harassment and threats were most likely related to a recent case she's prosecuted. Not to Bethany."

"You don't sound so certain, bro."

"I'm not, frankly. I do think Bethany's behind at least several of the incidents, and I've no doubt she somehow followed me here. There's only been one sighting of her in Denver since I moved to Blue Larkspur, and that was to visit her mother. Probably to get more cash for living expenses so that she can stay off the grid." Theo had texted him the information in the middle of the night.

"At least with me out of Rachel's place, I feel I've directed her future actions toward me, not at Rachel and Iris."

"Do you think there's any way she knows there's more between you and Rachel or that Iris is your daughter?" Jake's voice strummed with the same frustration that churned in James's gut. He'd do anything at this point to know Bethany wasn't around, wasn't about to strike again.

"Who said there's anything between me and Rachel besides being Iris's parents?" Playing coy wasn't his favorite thing.

"Bro, I know you. You're a good man, and you'd stay with anyone who needed guarding. It's what made you such a great Boy Scout. You have integrity, which I'd like to think I imparted to you."

"Still modest, aren't you?" He had to tease his older brother even in the midst of his own misery. Jake was the one who'd taken his senior-sibling responsibilities seriously after their father died. James had zero doubt that his work ethic and sense of honor were direct results of Jake's efforts.

"You know it."

They jokingly sparred for the next several minutes, catching each other up on life, until a doorbell sounded.

"Sorry, Jake, I've got to go. Someone's at the door."

"Hopefully it's Rachel. She's come to tell you she can't live without you."

"Ah…" Words lodged in his throat. Dang it, but Jake knew him too well. Yes, he *did* hope it was Rachel ringing his bell. "I'll keep you posted."

"Sure you will." Jake's chuckle was the last he heard as he disconnected and tapped into his doorbell app. The new condo had the same kind of security that Gideon had installed for Rachel. But like any security, it was limited by its hardware, and his camera didn't show anyone standing either in the front lobby or his condo door. He quickly dialed reception, which operated 24/7.

"This is James Kiriakis, condo 473. My doorbell just rang, but I don't see anyone at either door. Did one of you happen to go ring the bell?"

"No, sir, but we'll get on it and call you back if we come up with anything."

He disconnected and walked to his door, needing to see for himself if someone stood out of camera range. After validating the corridor was clear via the peephole, he slowly opened the door and peered up and down the hallway.

And saw the huge vase filled with dead flowers, a dozen withered roses, on the accent table diagonal to his entrance, just out of view of his security camera. Bile fueled his souring stomach, and he fought nausea as he forced himself to walk the few steps to the desperate object.

A single sealed envelope rested against the vase, which he noted held no water. Why would it? Dead plants didn't need hydration. He snatched the creamy white enclosure and ripped it open, pulled out a folded-up sheet of computer paper.

No more games. This isn't a warning or for attention. You know it's me. I hope you said a proper good-bye to the two nuisances in your life.
See you soon, lover.
Bethany

He crushed the paper in his hand, the sharp bite of its edge slicing into his dry palm. He knew he'd been right all along, but the validation did nothing to soothe him.

No, nothing would make him able to rest and breathe and live again. Not until he stopped Bethany.

He ran back the few feet to his foyer, grabbed his car keys and bolted back out the door, dialing Rachel as he fled. He had to make it back to Rachel's ASAP, before Bethany did. Before…

Before she wasn't here anymore.

No!

Rachel didn't pick up and he didn't want to waste time leaving a message. He placed a call to 9-1-1, alerted them that the DA was in peril, then called Theo. The last call also went to voice mail, but this time he left a message.

"Theo, it's James. Bethany's going after Rachel and I need you to send police now. Please." He threw his phone on the seat and shifted into gear, roared out of the condo's parking garage. As he sped through town toward Rachel and Iris, the sickening swirl of bile in his stomach warred with a newfound reality that he should have seen weeks ago. Over a year ago, when he met Rachel.

He was racing toward his home—his family. The only woman for him.

But was love enough to keep Bethany's unstable actions away from Rachel and Iris?

IT WAS TOO EASY, in the end. All the weeks living in her car, going hungry because she needed the gas money more, paid off. Because now she knew Rachel's schedule better than the stupid woman knew herself. She knew the exact times the babysitter showed up and when she left. The times the kid needed to eat and nap.

She knew that Rachel hadn't been sleeping this past week. Right after she realized the cameras had been found, Bethany wanted to run inside Rachel's house without a plan, just make the biggest, scariest mess she knew how to. But James had held her back, because he'd given her hope. He hadn't been completely charmed by Rachel and her evil ways. If he had, he wouldn't have left. By Bethany's count, James had been away from Rachel and the kid for eight nights. Which made her think maybe the kid wasn't his, after all. Rachel probably tried to convince James that it was his kid.

Bethany had seen him leave his Blue Larkspur condo only once, after visiting the kid before Rachel got home. Yesterday, James walked up the driveway pushing a baby stroller and took the kid back into the house, right before Bethany could get down from the tree she'd climbed up to sit in, in the wooded grove across the street.

Bethany was mad at herself for missing the chance to talk to him one-on-one. It would have been perfect to "run" into him on the sidewalk, in a different part of the neighborhood. He wouldn't have been able to move or alert the cops, not with her standing right next to that witch's squalling brat. But she'd arrived late, as she'd had to go buy some supplies for her ultimate plan. The endgame for Rachel Colton. Maybe the kid, too. Bethany wasn't one to want to deliberately hurt a kid. It wasn't the brat's fault that her mother was such a jerk. Bethany understood this more than anyone else. Hadn't her own mother betrayed her, hurt her, made fun of her time and time again? Bethany had struggled in school. Her guidance counselor told her it was okay, it was because she was dyslexic. And something about her brain just being different. But her mother had another term for it. "You're stupid, Bethany. Stupid and ugly. Learn to not expect much out of life."

No, no, no. No going back to the hateful memories. She'd gotten free of that, only used her mother as she needed to these days. Bethany was her own woman.

Laughter welled in her throat and she made sure she was wedged in the V of the tree branches, balanced with her two legs astride a thick bough as she slapped both hands over her mouth. This was happening more and more. The giggles. It was because she was anticipating the joy James would feel when he realized she'd taken care of everything for them.

James was too naive to realize how he'd been manipulated by Rachel and the kid. It made her angry to think about it. It would have been a lot easier for them both if James had stopped fighting his attraction for her and just admitted she was the only one for him sooner.

"Oh, James. You silly boy. You'll have it all figured out soon enough." And if he didn't, she'd fill him in.

But first, it was adios to Blue Larkspur's district attorney.

RACHEL'S PHONE WOKE her early Saturday morning, before Iris's wake-up babble. She grappled for the device, but her fingers shoved it off the nightstand, and the sound of it hitting the floor was immediately followed by Iris's cry for her mama. She rubbed her eyes, peered at the clock. A full hour before they usually rose on a Saturday, but her little girl had heard movement and wanted up and at 'em.

She scrambled into her pajama bottoms, having slept in an old 5K race T-shirt, and made a quick pit stop in the bathroom to splash water on her face and brush her teeth before going into the nursery.

Iris's eyes were wide and full of the wonder of a new day as she looked up from all fours on her crib mattress.

"Good thing we lowered your mattress last week, huh?" Rachel had done it out of precaution when Iris began trying to pull herself up on the crib bars. It wouldn't be much longer before the baby would pull to standing.

"Come here, precious." She cuddled the wide-awake infant to her chest, breathed in her unique scent. Already the baby-fresh fragrance had faded from Iris's scalp. Rachel's heart twinged. Everyone from Isa to Emily to her siblings told her that the time raising a child would go fast, but she'd not believed it when she and Iris had yet another sleepless night due to colic or teething. Yet Iris was almost eight months old. Where had the time gone?

James.

"Yeah, your daddy has certainly taken up our time, hasn't he?" She giggled and cooed with Iris as she changed her diaper and put the girl into a pale green romper. James. She missed him, and not just because he was such a great parenting partner. Their long talks, the fact that they both enjoyed geeking out over the most minute legal details, had all come to light as they'd pored over her cases, past and present. James had been the first to conclude that if she was being pursued by one of the bad guys she'd prosecuted, it was Parson. And he'd been right.

But he'd never let go of his belief that Bethany was behind some of the mishaps that had befallen her. And Parson had confessed to several things, from the brick to the white-water rafting incident, but not to any kind of surveillance or threatening packages. He'd remarked that his higher-ups were more direct than sending a box in the mail. The brick through her window was a perfect example.

Yet there hadn't been anything suspicious, other than the spy cameras James discovered, since they'd returned from their rafting trip.

James. She missed him so much. What a fool she'd been. These past days had given her time to think, contemplate, measure what mattered most to her. It wasn't her career, or even her family, as much as she loved both. It was the child in her arms and the man who'd fathered her. The man who'd accepted Rachel for who she was and didn't try to mold her to fit his idea of who she should be.

Did she still have trust issues? Of course. She accepted that she might always wrestle with the demons of her past at different times in her life. Who didn't? But none of it was worth missing out on a life with the one man who understood her without judgment and cared for her the most.

Another tug at her heart, this one soaked with regret. James said he'd reach out to her when he was ready, but did she have to wait for his call?

It was time to tell James her truth. How he'd captured her heart.

"What do you say we surprise your daddy with a visit?" She tucked Iris onto her hip and went back into her room to grab her phone. She'd go slowly, not scare James off with an outright proclamation of love. But she'd tell him, nonetheless. He deserved to—

A strange woman stood in her room, in front of the open sliding doors.

Rachel stopped midstride and stared at the woman standing in her bedroom, holding the meat cleaver from the kitchen block in her raised hand. Her features matched the photos James had shown her of Bethany, but this woman's face was drawn, her normally bright brown eyes dull, sunken. A stained, faded navy hoodie covered her dingy white T-shirt and battered jeans. When her glance reached Bethany's feet, her stomach flipped. The woman wore sturdy hiking boots, meant for adventure. Judging by the bag at her feet, spilling over with heavy rope and—was that a pair of bolt cutters?—other paraphernalia, it wasn't going to be a fun kind of trip.

"Ma ma!" Iris wriggled and Rachel tightened her arms around her baby. Her heart. Her life.

"Hello, Rachel." Bethany's monotone was creepier than her appearance. "I'm Bethany. The woman James loves."

"Why don't you put the knife down, Bethany?"

"Rule number one, Rachel Colton? Don't even think you can tell me what to do, or it's the end for both you and your kid." She made a stabbing motion with the cleaver. Her eyes were vacant, and while Bethany's gaze targeted Rachel and Iris, Rachel sensed the woman didn't really see them. All she saw was what she thought stood between her and a life with James.

James had been right. Bethany was not only still stalking him, and Rachel, but was in Blue Larkspur. In her home.

Threatening her baby.

Chapter Twenty-Three

Fear grabbed Rachel by the throat and dug in, triggering a whole-body reaction that included shaking, dizziness and panic. It was as if she was in a long, dark tunnel with Bethany blocking any possible light at the end. As if there was no way she could save Iris.

"Move. Now." Bethany waved the weapon at her, and Rachel instinctively clutched Iris to her as tightly as possible while her mind screamed *Run! Run! Run!*

"Where do you want us to go?"

"Shut up and listen to me or you're both dead. D-E-A-D, get it, Little Miss District Attorney?"

If she thought Parson's sneering threat at the end of his case had been scary, it was child's play compared to the sheer hatred that dripped off this woman's every word. Rachel was the focus of Bethany's rage, 100 percent. And by proxy, Iris was in the lost soul's crosshairs, too.

"I know you want James. He's yours, Bethany. He doesn't live here anymore." Rachel knew enough to realize she had to appease Bethany no matter what, even with lies. Whatever the woman would believe, whatever it took to disarm her.

"James is already mine, Rachel. He's always been mine. That's not a question." She cocked her head. The movement reminded Rachel of a marionette. "Don't make me tell you to move again."

"Fine, but I'm not walking my child anywhere near you. If you want me in the kitchen, you go there first. You seem to know the layout of my house."

Keep them talking. Theo's voice came back to her, from when he'd gone over what Rachel needed to do if she ever found herself in a hostage situation. It was part of her DA indoctrination and security training.

"I told you to be quiet. That goes double for the brat." But Bethany was backing up, through the door, and motioned for her to follow, to keep moving forward.

Rachel assessed her options as she walked toward the kitchen, Iris in her arms. She had no weapon with which to fight Bethany or that gleaming meat cleaver. Panic choked at her throat and she fought back against the sensation that she was walking to her own execution.

No. Not with her daughter pressed against her heart.

"Let me put the baby in her crib, Bethany. She doesn't need to see any of this."

"She'll see whatever I want her to." Bethany walked backward, and Rachel realized the woman did, in fact, know her home as well as anyone who'd spent time here. Shivers of revulsion wracked her, made her teeth chatter.

"D-d-did you put those cameras in my house, Bethany?"

"Yeah, I sure did." For as frightened as Rachel felt, all that emanated from Bethany was a sarcastic cockiness. Bethany thought she'd figured things out, finally had her quarry in her sights. "And guess what, Rachel? You didn't find them all, you stupid—" She ran into the corner of the heavy granite countertop with her hip and winced. "Damn this granite, this overblown house."

"Please, Bethany. Let's go outside and talk about this. We can leave Iris in the house. You and I will talk in the backyard. No witnesses, just us." If she could get Bethany outside, there was a good chance one of the officers was already outside and would have a clearer shot of Bethany than through one of her windows. Which, she realized, with a sick sink of her stomach, were all closed up, blinds and curtains drawn to keep Bethany from seeing inside.

The four walls of the great room seemed to move, and it wasn't fun like at an amusement park's haunted house. More like her worst nightmare turned into a true-life horror scene.

Save Iris.

The single thought pinged about her mind, echoed by heartbeats so fierce she was certain Bethany heard them. She struggled to keep her breathing even, to not betray her terror. Bethany's expression changed so rapidly over the course of a few seconds—from rage to anger to humor—that it was a struggle to keep up.

Breathe.

Rachel wasn't certain where it was coming from, but instinct told her to project as calm of a demeanor as possible. To show zero fear, no amount of concern over Bethany's potentially life-threatening demands. But as she watched the kitchen's overhead lighting glint off the cleaver that Bethany held in an almost loving manner, there was no denying that her time on this earth was limited. Perhaps extremely, as in whenever Bethany decided to lunge at her.

No. She shoved the image from her stressed mind and focused instead on doing what she did best. Drawing out the witness's true nature.

Make her talk.

"STAY BACK FROM the house, James." Theo's voice thundered over the hands-free system in James's car. He'd returned James's call when there was still five minutes left in his drive to Rachel's.

"Only if your units are already there." But he knew that didn't matter, either. No way was he going to leave Rachel to face Bethany on her own. "I'm hoping Bethany didn't get there yet."

"Chances of that are nil, James. I have to deal with reality. If it is Bethany, if she left those flowers for you with the message, she had at least a—what?—five-minute lead?"

"Yes." He cursed himself. "I should have never moved out last week."

"Nothing you could have done would stop someone during a psychotic break from acting on their troubled thoughts."

"We both know that's BS."

"Listen to me, son. My cruisers are seven minutes out, and I'm three. Do not, I repeat, do not go in that house on your own."

James glanced at the clock on his dashboard and saw that his ETA was, at most, only thirty seconds ahead of Theo. "Hopefully by then she'll have called me back."

But his phone remained silent after Theo disconnected, the only sound in the car besides the engine his ragged gasps for air.

"DON'T MOVE! I'M not telling you again." Bethany sidled over to the counter where the knife block sat and reached with her empty hand for another knife. Rachel wanted to look around for a make-shift weapon but couldn't afford for Bethany to think she was anything but helpless, and Bethany's gaze never left hers. If the woman didn't expect her to try to make a run for it, all the better.

It was becoming more clear with each passing second and the lack of anyone showing up—how could they, when no one knew Bethany was here?—that Rachel was going to have to do the unthinkable.

Fight back against a woman who held two lethal weapons aimed at her. All while keeping Iris safe.

"Can we talk this out?"

"Shut up!" Bethany screamed at the same moment the front door, visible to Rachel over Bethany's shoulder, opened. James walked in and headed straight for Rachel and Iris, but stopped short when he saw the knives.

"No, don't!" She tried to warn him about Bethany, but it was too late. He was already too far into the house. James stood behind Bethany by no more than six feet. Bethany could turn and shove those knives into him.

No. Stay focused. Save Iris.

"What are you doing here? Or have you come to help me get rid of the only thing between us?" Bethany switched to a cloyingly sweet tone that was scarier than her angry persona, looking at him over her shoulder while keeping both knives pointed at Rachel and Iris. In the close confines of the kitchen, there was no more than six inches from the end of the blades to her arms that held Iris.

"I've come to talk to you." James acted as if he came upon a murderous scene on a regular basis. There was no sign of the concern he'd expressed to Rachel about his sense that Bethany still stalked him. *This must be how he appears in court.*

She hoped that like his case record, James would win over Bethany and put an end to this terror.

"So you got my message." She smiled at James as if he were a pet.

"The flowers you left me? Yes. Bethany, please." He held his hands up in the universal gesture of appeasement. "Put the knives down. It isn't worth it."

"Not until I finish what I started. It has to be perfect, James. Just you and me. Only us. Stand over there or I'll cut them both."

"No!" The sob wrenched from Rachel, from a place deep inside, where her mother's soul lay.

"Rachel." James's eyes were intent and in the split second before Bethany looked at him again, he gave a quick nod toward the living room, mouthing the word "sofa." She nodded back when Bethany turned to him.

"Stop talking to her!"

"Leave them alone, Bethany. This is between you and me. Let Rachel and Iris go."

"Why do you care so much about her and her brat? Don't you see she's just using you to help with the kid? No one loves you like I do, James."

"I know that now, Bethany. Let's talk about it like adults." He took a step closer. Rachel sucked in her breath, afraid that Bethany would lunge forward at any moment. She had to get Iris to safety. But the knives—she or James might survive an injury from either weapon, but her child's tender flesh wouldn't.

"Stop it right now!" Bethany turned toward James, and Rachel took the first opening she'd had to secure Iris's safety. She darted from the kitchen into the living room, the sofa her target. If she could just get Iris away from—

"Don't move another inch or you're both dead!" Bethany's voice boomed through the air. "James, stay right where you are or I'll throw these knives. Remember how good I was when we threw axes in Bear's Tavern in Denver, James?"

"Wait, Rachel." James's tone stilled her, anchored her, drove the deepest fear into her heart. She placed Iris on the deep seat, far from the edge, giving the baby the protection of the sofa's back.

"Raise your arms!" Bethany shrieked the order, spittle flying from her mouth. Even Bethany's expression and posture were completely different than the photos James had shown her. The once-beautiful woman was a seething ball of anger and frustration. Two emotions that drove the worst of crimes.

"I'll do whatever you say. Please leave our baby be. She's innocent."

Bethany's head tilted so roughly she appeared like a doll ready to break apart. "What do you mean, 'our baby'?"

Rachel's mistake turned her stomach into a twisted ball of concertina wire as her raised arms shook.

"It's not important right now, Bethany. What matters is that you and I have the conversation we need to have. Quietly. Here, at the table." James motioned to the large dining table where they'd spent so many hours.

Would she ever have that kind of time with him again? Staring down two deadly blades held by a most unreliable criminal, the answer was clear.

These were her last moments alive. But she wasn't going to let Bethany hurt Iris.

"Stop talking! I'm not listening to you anymore. You've been seduced by the demoness! You believe her bastard child is yours!"

"Bethany, calm—"

"Noooo!" As she screamed, she threw one, then both knives at Rachel.

Rachel acted the second she saw Bethany's wrists twist, her fingers releasing their grip on the weapons. She did what any mother in the same situation would do.

Rachel covered her baby with her body, prepared to take the blades.

Chapter Twenty-Four

"No!" James dove toward Bethany, aiming to tackle her at her knees. But before he made contact, a single gunshot sounded and Bethany collapsed on the floor. Landing on all fours, he immediately scrambled and ran to the sofa. To all that mattered. Footsteps sounded all around him, and he was dimly aware of several uniformed officers charging the scene, but all he needed was right in front of him.

"Da!" Iris reached pudgy arms and he grasped her to him, inhaled her baby scent. He was a split second ahead of Rachel, who was on her knees next to the sofa where she'd pushed herself up from covering the baby. Blood dripped down the side of Rachel's face.

"Rachel, it's okay. I've got her." He used his free hand to urge her to sit all the way back on her bottom as he peered at the injury. "You're hurt."

Her eyes, wide with the adrenaline he knew matched his own, fixed on him and they shared a moment of soul communication, as intimate as when he'd moved inside her. When they'd made Iris.

"I am?" She must have seen where he stared and reached up her hands to her face, then traced the wetness. "Oh my goodness! It has to be a surface scratch. It doesn't hurt."

James wasn't so sure. "EMT!" He bellowed the request as he cupped Iris's tiny ears. "Front room!"

"Clear!" An officer shouted from the back of the house.

"Clear!" Another holstered a weapon near the front door.

"Are you both okay?" Theo stood beside them, his weapon facing the floor. EMTs burst into the house, and Theo pointed the first two toward the kitchen, to where Bethany lay moaning. She'd taken a bullet to her leg from what James could tell, and appeared fully conscious.

"I'm…fine?" Rachel looked at the blood on her hands, still dazed.

"Over here." Theo directed the next available EMT over to Rachel and stepped aside to allow the first responder room.

"We're good." James knew he'd never let Iris go again. Ever.

"Come over here." Theo holstered his gun and motioned for two other men to come forward. James recognized Caleb, Rachel's oldest sibling, but not the other man. He wore his dark blond hair in a longish, shaggy style. His hair and blue eyes were darker shades than Rachel's, but the Colton resemblance was unmistakable. It had to be one of her other brothers.

"Caleb. James Kiriakis." He nodded to Caleb, and held out his hand to the other man, who stared at it for a full heartbeat before meeting it with a firm grip.

"Dominic Colton." James's gut felt the invisible yet

tangible punch Rachel's FBI agent brother threw him. He'd heard all about Dominic when Rachel told him she'd been afraid her brothers would want to beat him up when they found out he was Iris's father. Dominic's eyes blazed with fierce protection.

"Dom!" Rachel tried to stand, but the EMT attending her kept her seated. "What are you doing here? Caleb, how did you two know to come now?"

"There's a thing called a cell phone, sister." Dominic walked over and placed a quick kiss on Rachel's cheek.

Caleb nodded. "We heard the request for backup go out, and Mom texted us at the same time, saying Theo was headed here."

All eyes turned to the Blue Larkspur Chief of Police.

Theo shrugged. "Isa and I were playing cards at her place. I made her stay put and promised I'd give her any update ASAP. So if you'll all excuse me..." He nodded, held up his phone, walked out of the living room.

"Wait, what was he doing at Mom's again?" Dominic had lines between his eyebrows that James recognized. He and his siblings had been very protective of his mother after their dad passed. Unlike Isa, though, Helen hadn't waited twenty years to find a new love.

"Stop it. Mom's entitled to her own life. And what are you doing in Blue Larkspur anyway, Dom? I thought your work kept your head low to the ground." Rachel spoke as the EMT applied butterfly bandages to a long but superficial cut that ran the length of her hairline from her forehead to her temple. James recalled that she'd mentioned Dom worked undercover in Denver. But her brother wasn't his concern right now. His gaze followed the EMTs working on Rachel's injury. Fear sliced through him as he processed the reality that she'd been spared more serious injury, even her life, by ducking in time. She'd saved Iris.

"I don't have much time. Caleb picked me up at the airport. I'm due to go back undercover but I don't have to, Rachel. I can stay here if you need me."

"Don't be ridiculous. Other than this stupid cut, I'm fine. And listen, all of you. James didn't know about Iris, that he had a daughter, until I told him which was very recently. So no ganging up on him. Got it?" Rachel's irritation normally would make James smile, but he hadn't gotten over how close he'd come to losing her. Losing Iris. All that mattered to him.

"I hear you, sis. So tell me, James, how is it that my sister and niece's lives have been threatened by your stalker?" Dominic's unforgiving gaze was back on him, and James shifted Iris to his other arm. The baby's face brightened at the sight of her uncles and Caleb held up his arms. James handed his daughter over, needing his full attention available for the justifiable inquisition.

"I messed up."

"No, YOU DIDN'T. I did, so did Theo, frankly." Rachel had heard enough. She batted away the EMT's hands and walked to James's side. Wrapping her arms around his waist, she rested the uninjured side of her head on his shoulder. As they stood together, Bethany was wheeled out on a stretcher. The EMTs weren't in the same hurry they'd been when they arrived, and Rachel overheard Theo tell Isa that Bethany had a superficial injury.

"No offense, sis, but you need to rest." Caleb's brow

lifted in that comical way that made her giggle. His humorous expression belied the concern in his eyes.

"I'm fine. You've hurt me worse when we were kids and beating up on each other. Listen, none of us believed James, that Bethany was behind all the awful things that kept happening." She ran down the litany of offenses, ending with being held hostage by knifepoint as she embraced their baby daughter. "One incident, a brick through my window, followed by a sabotaged raft ride, is attributable to my most recent case. That criminal is behind bars and the syndicate who carried out his order has been given fair warning about messing with this DA."

"So everything else was due to his former girlfriend?" A stab of annoyance pierced through Rachel's relief, but James answered first.

"Yes. This was all on me."

Dominic's lips formed a tight line and he turned away to speak to Caleb in quiet tones.

"Hey." Rachel tugged on James's collar, and he was powerless to resist her. A surge of relief layered in recognition and another stronger emotion compelled him to wrap her as tightly as possible to him, burying his face in her hair. "You handled my brothers well. I give you credit."

"My God, Rachel. Your brothers love you. They have a right to know it's my fault. I thought you, that you and Iris—" His throat constricted and his eyes burned with the terror that he'd fought since seeing the roses from Bethany.

"We're okay. Theo saved us all."

"No, *you* saved you and Iris. That was brilliant, putting her on the sofa."

She pushed back enough to look at him straight-on. "No, we were brilliant, James. We did it together. You gave the perfect distraction and had already communicated to me, without one word, may I add, to run into the living room. *We* saved our baby, James."

He wasn't about to argue with the most beautiful woman in his world, today or ever. Knowing her brothers looked on with disapproval mattered little to nothing, not when the love of his life looked at him with the same amount of love that pumped through his veins for her.

"I love you, Rachel. I love you as my partner, my soulmate, as Iris's mother. Forever."

Tears filled her eyes, changing the cornflower blue to bright aquamarine. She blinked. "I love you, too. Do you think we have a chance to be a real family?"

"Yes." He couldn't hold back any longer. He kissed her with abandon, stamping what he'd been unable to articulate until now on her very responsive lips. It didn't matter that they had an audience comprised of some very hard-to-please brothers, or that the Colton family protector and police chief looked on. All that mattered was that his family was safe, and Rachel was in his arms.

Chapter Twenty-Five

"It's nice to have you all here together." Isa spoke to Rachel as they set out the food for the next Sunday Colton dinner, just days after Bethany's arrest. A combination of catered and potluck covered the expansive quartz-topped island in Isa's updated kitchen.

"Well, not all of us." Half of her siblings weren't there, but like her mother, Rachel was thrilled to be enjoying a Sunday that didn't have the ever-present threat of Parson or Bethany hanging over it. Warm gratitude spread under her breastbone each time she glanced up to see James and know that this wasn't temporary— they were going to go for it.

"Why don't you go over to him? I can finish up here." Isa nodded toward where James stood, Iris in his arms, conversing with Caleb, Gideon and Theo. Dominic was out on the patio with Aubrey and Jasper, the ranch co-owners taking a rare afternoon off together. Ezra, even though he lived with Isa, wasn't home as the Army had sent him TDY, away on temporary duty, for the weekend.

"No, Mom. Not yet. You can't do this all by yourself."

"Actually, I can." Isa grinned. "So you and James have decided to be a couple, for real?"

Her floral-printed blouse, one she thought perfect for the spring afternoon, suddenly felt like her heaviest down jacket. She blew out a quick breath, shrugged. "We've decided to commit to one another and to our family, yes."

"Relax." Isa touched her cheek with her finger. "Stop blushing, for heaven's sake. I'm not asking about your bedroom activity."

"Mom!"

Isa laughed. "I'm just teasing and you know it."

"You seem a lot happier these days, Mom." She suspected it was about more than Rachel's trauma-drama being resolved.

"I am. You've made me open my mind, Rachel. Remember our talk about letting love in again? You were right."

"You're the one who told me to open my heart."

"Was I?" Isa laughed. "Then, I guess I'm taking my own advice." Her gaze searched the room, looked through the windows to where Theo stood on the patio.

"I'm happy for you, Mom." She didn't want to push it, to go so far as to say she knew her Mom had a boyfriend—Theo. Besides, *boyfriend* seemed too casual. Isa and Theo both did not do anything in their lives casually.

"You can't blame me for feeling protective toward you and my sole grandchild." Isa fell back on one of her master skills—hanging the subject. "At first I was concerned that you both were reacting to the traumatic events of the last month, especially last week. I'm relieved beyond measure that nothing lasting happened to you or Iris. To any of you."

"Me, too." She'd not spoken to her mother about the

specifics of having two knives thrown at her by Bethany, of seeing the woman taken out by Theo in her home. "Theo saved the day. That's for sure." Rachel was so grateful for Theo, for what he'd done for their family. He'd saved Iris's, and James's, and her own life.

"Well, as much as it's true he fired the deciding shot, it's been explained to me that you and James worked together as the perfect team to save your daughter. I can't ask for more."

"Thanks, Mom."

"And that woman—Bethany—let's keep her in our prayers that she gets the help she needs." Isa shook her head. "She's got a long road ahead of her."

"She does." Rachel didn't want to go into details with her mother, not today. But she, too, was at peace with what happened to Bethany. The woman was in a psychiatric facility for evaluation. If she was deemed mentally competent, she'd stand trial.

"No way would I ever allow Isa's daughter or granddaughter to get hurt." A deep baritone sounded to her right. "Isa would never forgive me. None of the Colton women would, I'm certain." Theo had walked up behind her but kept going until he stood next to Isa. He gave her mother a smile not unlike the special glances she and James shared. Rachel wondered if Theo was the man Isa had been talking about before.

"She's still going to have to pay for her crimes, Rachel. And for the record, I had to fire my weapon. No way was anyone going to harm a Colton woman, or girl, on my watch. I'm as happy as all of you to have the Bethany Austin case closed. I only wish Ronald Spence wasn't still free, but justice will be served."

"I agree with Theo." Isa's eyes twinkled only for Theo. *Of course you agree with him.* Rachel allowed a small giggle to escape her before she turned away from the buffet before the couple asked any questions. She wanted to be next to *her* family—her immediate family.

James and Iris greeted her with smiles and the resemblance between them took her breath away.

"What?" Lines appeared on the bridge of his nose, the same place Iris got them when she didn't like the taste of mashed carrots. "You look upset."

She quickly wound her arms around his waist and kissed him fully on the lips. Iris chortled and grabbed a hank of Rachel's hair.

"I'm not upset at all. More like awed—I am the luckiest woman on the planet!"

His green irises deepened to jade as their gazes locked. She leaned in for another kiss, but he held up his free hand. "Hang on a sec."

He strode over to Isa and gave her the baby. Turning to face everyone, who had gathered around the food, he held up his hands.

"Hey, Colton family." She noticed that Dominic and Caleb didn't lunge for James at his pronouncement. They were coming around to what she already knew. James was solid—a man of integrity. The best soulmate for her and father for Iris. "I was going to wait until more of you were here, but I'm learning that with twelve of you, that's not a common thing and I can't wait any longer." Without preamble he walked back to Rachel and bent down on one knee, pulled a small velvet box from his jean pocket.

"Rachel Colton, will you eternally bless me by becoming my wife?"

She couldn't see clearly through the tears, but it didn't matter what the ring looked like, or the expression on James's face. The certainty of their love was already stamped on her heart, in the depths of her soul.

"Yes. Yes, yes, yes!"

They embraced as a chorus of Colton agreement exploded around them. Rachel reiterated her confirmation with her lips, meeting his without reservation.

* * * * *

COMING SOON!

We really hope you enjoyed reading this book.
If you're looking for more romance, be sure to
head to the shops when new books are
available on

Thursday 12th May

To see which titles are coming soon, please visit

millsandboon.co.uk/nextmonth

MILLS & BOON

MILLS & BOON

THE HEART OF ROMANCE

A ROMANCE FOR EVERY READER

MODERN

Prepare to be swept off your feet by sophisticated, sexy and seductive heroes, in some of the world's most glamourous and romantic locations, where power and passion collide.

HISTORICAL

Escape with historical heroes from time gone by. Whether your passion is for wicked Regency Rakes, muscled Vikings or rugged Highlanders, await the romance of the past.

MEDICAL

Set your pulse racing with dedicated, delectable doctors in the high-pressure world of medicine, where emotions run high and passion, comfort love are the best medicine.

True Love

Celebrate true love with tender stories of heartfelt romance, from the rush of falling in love to the joy a new baby can bring, and a focus on the emotional heart of a relationship.

Desire

Indulge in secrets and scandal, intense drama and plenty of sizzling hot action with powerful and passionate heroes who have it all: wealth, status good looks…everything but the right woman.

HEROES

Experience all the excitement of a gripping thriller, with an intense romance at its heart. Resourceful, true-to-life women and strong, fearless face danger and desire - a killer combination!

To see which titles are coming soon, please visit

millsandboon.co.uk/nextmonth

LET'S TALK

Romance

For exclusive extracts, competitions
and special offers, find us online:

f facebook.com/millsandboon

🐦 @MillsandBoon

📷 @MillsandBoonUK

Get in touch on 01413 063232

For all the latest titles coming soon, visit

millsandboon.co.uk/nextmonth

MILLS & BOON
A ROMANCE FOR EVERY READER

- **FREE** delivery direct to your door

- **EXCLUSIVE** offers every month

- **SAVE** up to 25% on pre-paid subscriptions

SUBSCRIBE AND SAVE

millsandboon.co.uk/Subscribe

WANT EVEN MORE

ROMANCE?

SUBSCRIBE AND SAVE TODAY!

'Mills & Boon books, the perfect way to escape for an hour or so.'

MISS W. DYER

'Excellent service, promptly delivered and very good subscription choices.'

MISS A. PEARSON

'You get fantastic special offers and the chance to get books before they hit the shops.'

MRS V. HALL

Visit millsandboon.co.uk/Subscribe
and save on brand new books.

JOIN THE
MILLS & BOON
BOOKCLUB

* **FREE** delivery direct to your door

* **EXCLUSIVE** offers every month

* **EXCITING** rewards programme

50% OFF
YOUR FIRST
PARCEL

Join today at
Millsandboon.co.uk/Bookclub

JOIN US ON SOCIAL MEDIA!

Stay up to date with our latest releases, author
news and gossip, special offers and discounts, and
all the behind-the-scenes action
from Mills & Boon...

 millsandboon

 millsandboonuk

 millsandboon

t might just be true love...

GET YOUR ROMANCE FIX!

MILLS & BOON
— *blog* —

Get the latest romance news, exclusive author interviews, story extracts and much more!

blog.millsandboon.co.uk

MILLS & BOON
Desire

Indulge in secrets and scandal, intense drama and plenty of sizzling hot action with powerful and passionate heroes who have it all: wealth, status, good looks…everything but the right woman.

Four Desire stories published every month, find them all at:

millsandboon.co.uk

MILLS & BOON
MODERN
Power and Passion

Prepare to be swept off your feet by sophisticated, sexy and seductive heroes, in some of the world's most glamourous and romantic locations, where power and passion collide.

Eight Modern stories published every month, find them all a

millsandboon.co.uk/Modern

MILLS & BOON
MEDICAL
Pulse-Racing Passion

Set your pulse racing with dedicated, delectable doctors in the high-pressure world of medicine, where emotions run high and passion, comfort and love are the best medicine.

ight Medical stories published every month, find them all at:

millsandboon.co.uk

MILLS & BOON
True Love
Romance from the Heart

Celebrate true love with tender stories of heartfelt romance, from the rush of falling in love to the joy a new baby can bring, and a focus on the emotional heart of a relationship.

Four True Love stories published every month, find them all at:

millsandboon.co.uk/TrueLove